PRAISE FOR
# The Plot to Save Socrates

"Challenging fun." —*Entertainment Weekly*

"[A] *Da Vinci*-esque thriller." —*Daily News*

"A fun book to read." —*The Dallas Morning News*

"Levinson spins a fascinating tale…. An intriguing premise with believable characters and attention to period detail make this an outstanding choice for most science fiction collections. Highly recommended." —*Library Journal* (starred review)

"Light, engaging time travel yarn…neatly satisfies the circularity inherent in time travel, whose paradoxes Levinson links to Greek philosophy." —*Publishers Weekly*

"Intricately and intriguingly woven, lots of fun, and extremely thought-provoking." —Stanley Schmidt

"This is a dazzling performance…. History as science fiction; science fiction as history." —Barry N. Malzberg

"Paul Levinson has outdone himself: *The Plot to Save Socrates* is a philosophically rich gem full of big ideas and wonderful time travel tricks." —Robert J. Sawyer

"Proves that excellent entertainment can and ought to be intellectually respectable—a glorious example to us all." —Brian Stableford

"As happens with Kurt Vonnegut's Billy Pilgrim…the reader soon becomes unstuck in time…. Levinson presents one of the most unique books I've ever encountered. A highly recommended read." —Matt St. Amand

"Quick-to-read, entertaining treatment of the problems inherent in time travel with style and flair." —*Booklist*

"Readers are sure to enjoy his take on the paradoxes of time travel." —*BookPage*

# The Plot to Save Socrates

TOR BOOKS BY PAUL LEVINSON

# The Plot to Save Socrates

## PAUL LEVINSON

A TOM DOHERTY ASSOCIATES BOOK

NEW YORK

THE PLOT TO SAVE SOCRATES

Copyright © 2006 by Paul Levinson

Edited by David G. Hartwell

Map by Nicholas Frota, NonlinearMatters.com

A Tor Book
Published by Tom Doherty Associates, LLC
175 Fifth Avenue
New York, NY 10010

www.tor.com

Tor® is a registered trademark of Tom Doherty Associates, LLC.

Library of Congress Cataloging-in-Publication Data

Levinson, Paul.
    The plot to save Socrates / Paul Levinson.
        p. cm.
    ISBN-13: 978-0-765-31197-9
    ISBN-10: 0-765-31197-6
    1. Socrates—Fiction. 2. Time travel—Fiction. I. Title.

    PS3562.E92165 P58 2006
    813'.54—dc22

                        2005054164

First Hardcover Edition: February 2006
First Trade Paperback Edition: February 2007

Printed in the United States of America

0  9  8  7  6  5  4  3  2  1

*To Tina, who frequently plots to save me.*

MEDITERRANEAN, AD 150

ROME

PERGAMUM

ITHACA

ATHENS

SYRACUSE

ALEXANDRIA

500 miles

500          1000 km

ATHENS

PIRAEUS

ANDR

CYTHNOS          DELOS

SPARTA

Design: Nicholas Frota

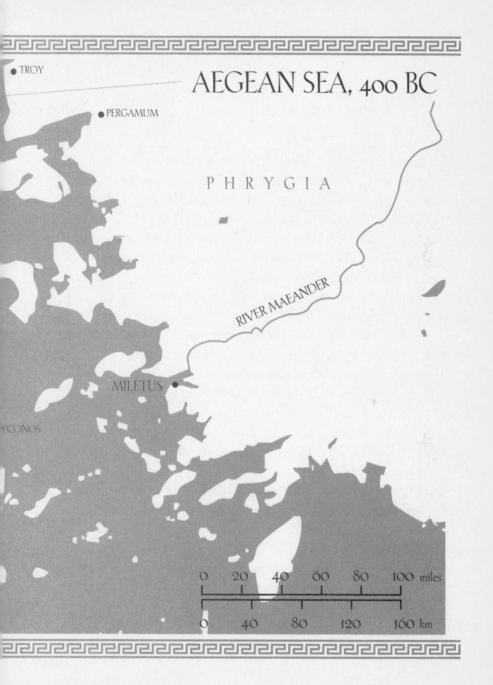

AEGEAN SEA, 400 BC

TROY

PERGAMUM

PHRYGIA

RIVER MAEANDER

MILETUS

YCONOS

0    20    40    60    80    100 miles

0    40    80    120    160 km

# ACKNOWLEDGMENTS

I thank David Hartwell and Moshe Feder for detailed and in-depth editorial suggestions, Steve Boldt for fine copyediting, Denis Wong for editorial assistance, and my agent, Chris Lotts of the Ralph Vicinanza Agency, for his helpful advice and negotiations.

Special thanks, as well, to Nicholas Frota for drawing the map on such short notice, and to David Swanser for great conversations about the *Cratylus* and about Hypatia.

Henry Magid (1917–1979), my philosophy professor at the City College of New York in 1963, first provoked my interest in Socrates and Plato, and my love for philosophy and the ancient world. I have been thinking about *The Plot to Save Socrates* in one form or another ever since.

Even in this age of the Internet, there are some things you can find only on shelves and in halls. Fordham University's Walsh Library had an early edition of Smith's 1849 *Dictionary of Greek and Roman Biography and Mythology,* and the British Museum an ancient sculpture of a Molossian hound, along with the information that Alcibiades had kept one. I thank them both.

I read many books in pursuit of *The Plot to Save Socrates.* Three were especially helpful: Charles Freeman's *Egypt, Greece, and Rome,* Tony Perrottet's *Pagan Holiday* (originally *Route 66 A.D.*), and I. F. Stone's *The Trial of Socrates.*

But my wife, Tina Vozick, and our children, Simon and Molly Vozick-Levinson, were as always my greatest resource, in conversation and inspiration.

# The Plot to Save Socrates

# CHAPTER I

*Athens, AD 2042*

She ripped the paper in half, then ripped the halves, then ripped what was left, again, into bits and pieces of history that could have been. . . .

Sierra Waters had once read that, years ago, it was thought that men made love for the thrill, while women made love for the sense of connection it gave them. Sierra had always done everything for the thrill. She had no sense of connection, except to her work. Which should have made her an ideal person for this job.

Still . . . an ideal person would have followed the plan. It was written on the only substance that could survive decades, maybe longer, without batteries, which required only the light of the sun to be read, or the moon on a good night, or a flickering flame when there was no moon. Paper. A marvelous invention. Thin and durable. And she had just torn it into pieces, opened her palm, and given it to the wind to disperse irretrievably.

*Earlier, New York City, AD 2042*

Sierra was a doctoral student at the Old School, in the heart of Manhattan. Her specialty was ancient Athens, or, more precisely, the adoption of

the Ionic phonetic alphabet by Athens around 400 BC—the sprouting of
the teeth of Cadmus, as Marshall McLuhan had put it—and its impact
on the future of the world. "A nice, tidy, manageable little topic," Thomas
O'Leary, a member of her doctoral committee, had testily commented.
But he had agreed to help her, anyway. He was accustomed to unusual
pursuits. He was an oddball, himself, an independent scholar with no
university affiliation. The Old School had a tradition of allowing one such
outside expert on its doctoral committees.

Sierra was making good progress on the dissertation—72 out of a pro-
jected 250 pages, written in under half a year's time—when Thomas called
her down to his office, just off Fifth Avenue and Eighteenth Street, on a
wet April evening. He had a copy of a slim manuscript, just a few pages in
a worn manila folder. He hefted it, as if to assess its intellectual weight. By
the expression on his face, it looked to be quite important. He slid it across
his pitted oak desk to Sierra. She had mixed feelings about this—it was no
doubt an article of some sort that Thomas had come across and deemed
relevant to her dissertation. Sierra hated the thought of having to rethink
and rewrite any of her work at this point. On the other hand, she relished
uncovering new information. It made her heart jump.

She opened the folder. She looked up at Thomas, who was carefully
regarding her, his mouth slightly pursed, a long pen of some sort dangling
from his fingers like a plastic cigarette. "It's apparently been kicking
around for a while, at least since the twenties," he said. "It surfaced recently at the Millennium Club up on Forty-ninth Street—their librarian
spotted it in an old bookcase, sandwiched between the usual stuff."

"The 2020s?" Sierra asked.

Thomas smiled. "Well, could have been the 1920s, as far as the club
goes—it was founded in the 1870s. But the librarian is sure it wasn't
there before 2023—that was the last time they did a thorough inventory
of their holdings—and the preface says something about carbon-dating
the original."

"So it's not an obvious forgery. Otherwise, you wouldn't be showing
it to me, right?"

Thomas nodded. "So far, it looks damn good."

Sierra looked back down at the document. It was ancient Greek
on the left side, English translation on the right. That was the logical

assumption—that Greek was the original, and English the translation, not the other way around. Not only because the Greek was ancient. But also because the words in front of her were apparently a fragment of a Platonic dialog, featuring his mentor, Socrates. "I've never seen this before," Sierra said.

Thomas nodded again. "Apparently neither has most of the rest of the world."

Sierra stepped out of the hot shower, slipped into her terry-cloth robe, and cuddled up with a spiced tea and the new Socratic dialog on her sofa. It had no title, no translator listed, but it read a lot like Benjamin Jowett, the great Oxford Victorian who had rendered so much of Plato into English. She had read it at least five times, already.

The first page contained a preface, signed only "Ed," which was almost certainly short for *editor,* not Edward, Edwin, or Edmond: "The following is a translation of a manuscript self-identified as written by Plato. Carbon-14 dating (enhanced mode) situates the papyrus and the ink upon it as approximately 400 CE—the date of this *manuscript*'s creation, not the date of the original writing (which, if Plato was indeed its author, would be much earlier). The manuscript was unearthed in excavations near Alexandria, Egypt, in the first decade of the 21st century."

Sierra pressed her face against the warm teacup, and her back and neck into the sofa. It wrapped around her, felt so good, so comforting, and— No, it was still on sleep mode, from last night, and Sierra didn't want to feel quite so relaxed right now. She ran her hand on the side and flicked the "read" control. The contours subtly adjusted. She felt energized, strong. She turned the page.

PERSONS OF THE DIALOGUE: Socrates; Andros, a visitor
SCENE: The Prison of Socrates

SOCRATES: What time is it?
ANDROS: The dawn broke a little while ago.
SOC.: I must have been dozing. I did not see you enter.
ANDR.: You were indeed dozing when I arrived.

SOC.: You have come to take me to my destiny? I am more than willing. But I thought I would be allowed another day or two.

ANDR.: I am here to take you to your destiny. If indeed you are willing.

SOC.: I just said that I was. I may criticize the state, but I do not presume to place myself above it.

ANDR.: The destiny I am here to offer you may be different from the one you suppose.

SOC.: Different? I would never accept a life that prevented me from praising good and denouncing evil. And placing myself beyond the state would put me in just such a compromised position.

ANDR.: Yet you would accept death, and via hands you know are unjust.

SOC.: Ah, so you are indeed here to try to persuade me against death. This is the destiny you wish me to avoid?

ANDR.: Yes.

SOC.: You are not the first suitor to make that proposition.

ANDR.: I know.

SOC.: Such a proposition obviously has much to commend it.

ANDR.: Yes.

SOC.: But I would tell you what I tell all such noble souls: attractive as such a proposition is to me, I cannot accept it. For such would entail my commission of an evil at least as great as that of those who wish to end my life. It would say that I was lying when previously I maintained that criticism of the state, to be taken seriously, required an ultimate acceptance of the authority of the state, flawed as it may be. My fleeing now, evading this authority, would make all of that a lie.

ANDR.: Suppose I were to tell you that you could leave this prison, and live, without flouting the authority of the state?

SOC.: I would say you are dreaming, and you are wrong to tempt an old man with an impossible dream. How could I possibly leave here and not show contempt for the decision of the state that I must die here?

ANDR.: What if your body did die here, but you did not?

SOC.: You mean my soul would live, but my material essence would die? There are those who claim that the two—soul and body—are inseparable. And when one dies, so must the other. Do you deny that?

ANDR.: I mean to say, your material essence and your soul would be saved, and would live. And another material essence of you would die here, absent any spirit.

SOC.: How could that be? Are you suggesting my soul will inhabit another body?

ANDR.: No. I am saying both bodies—the one with your soul, the other without—would be yours.

SOC.: As far as I know, my material body is unique—there is but one of me, not two.

ANDR.: Have you ever seen twins?

SOC.: Yes. They do seem to have the same physical body at birth, I grant you. Are you telling me that there is a twin of me, whom I do not know of? Even so, by this age—my age—we would likely not look exactly the same. The world wears our bodies in different ways.

ANDR.: No, as far as I know, your mother did not bear you and a twin. But are you seeing where this may lead?

SOC.: No, I am not. For even if I had a twin, and even if he were willing to trade places with me here at this late hour and die in my stead, when the ship from Delos arrives, it would not be right for me to allow that to happen. It would be an unspeakable act of cowardice for me, an act of evil upon the body and soul of my brother. That would be far worse than the evil of my simply escaping.

ANDR.: Yes, it certainly would be. But what if it were only his body that was left in your place? And what if he were not truly your brother—not born of your mother? And what if he were not truly alive—just a perfect copy of your body, in every way but one? What if it had no soul? It would then not be truly intelligent, not fully alive.

SOC.: Leaving aside, for a moment, the impossibility of what you are proposing, where would you take me?

ANDR.: Somewhere close to Ithaca and Syracuse.

SOC.: But those places are not close to one another. How can a third place—your destination—be close to both?

ANDR.: In my world, they are close.

SOC.: Yet you are in my world, where Ithaca and Syracuse are not close.

ANDR.: Yes.

SOC.: In what manner is your world different from mine, that Ithaca and Syracuse are close in yours?

ANDR.: My world is the future.

SOC.: Are you saying your city is more advanced in the crafts of transport than this one, and you possess there a new means of conveyance, some swift ship, which permits more rapid travel between Ithaca and Syracuse, and that is why you contend that they are close?

ANDR.: There are new means of transport in my world, but they are not the most profound reason why I say the two cities are close.

SOC.: Cities? Ithaca is an island, not a city.

ANDR.: Yes, in this world. Your world. Your time.

SOC.: Your time is different from mine? Different from this time? And that is what you meant when you said your world is the future?

ANDR.: Yes.

SOC.: You claim to have traveled here from the future? Forgive me. I appreciate your visit at this very late hour. But only a god or a liar would make such a claim. And my fellow Athenians who have sentenced me would be happy to tell you what I think of the gods.

ANDR.: I assure you, I am neither god nor liar.

SOC.: Traveling from one age to another cannot be the same as traveling from one place to another, in the same time. I think the two—time and space—are very different.

ANDR.: That is true.

SOC.: I do not understand how such travel across time could be possible.

ANDR.: Could we return to that question later and consider now how I might help you, were such travel possible?

SOC.: You wish to proceed on the basis of an impossible premise? I suppose such a conversation is preferable to thinking about the hemlock.

ANDR.: My point, precisely.

SOC.: Is your world, then, the same as this world, except that your world is in the future?

ANDR.: I would say so, generally, yes.

SOC.: Then, if that is true, you would know that I have indeed died—that I will die, in the next few days. For that, truly, is what I intend to do.

ANDR.: We know, in my world, that a body identified as Socrates indeed died after consuming hemlock. I am here to convince you that that body need not be yours.

SOC.: So far, although I can only be grateful for your ingenuity and good intentions, I cannot say that I am persuaded.

ANDR.: May I continue my attempt?

SOC.: If you wish.

ANDR.: Let us look again, then, at the nature of souls and life, and examine, if you will, the nature of copies. Do you agree that a statue could be made of you, of such precise resemblance that it could be mistaken for you when viewed at a distance?

SOC.: Yes, I have seen such statues of others. When painted with colors of proper hue, they can quite easily be mistaken for the human being whose image they embody, especially when viewed in dim lighting, in twilight or predawn hours, or, as you say, at a distance.

ANDR.: Good. Do you think it possible, then, that such a statue could be made of someone—of you—but comprised not of stone but of living material?

SOC.: Yes, I have on occasion seen fine work of that sort constructed not of stone but of wood. Is that what you mean?

ANDR.: The replica I have in mind for you would be comprised of something closer to wood than stone, yes.

SOC.: But no one, on close examination of a wooden replica of me, could possibly mistake it for me, or my body. Wood is material that is no longer alive; my body is still alive. I suppose there would be more similarity between wood—material, once alive, from a tree—and my body, once dead, and no longer alive.

ANDR.: Yes.

SOC.: But, nonetheless, surely no one could confuse a wooden replica of me, however well rendered, with my dead body?

ANDR.: No—no one could confuse those two. But in the case of wood, could you imagine a branch, pulled from a tree, that was still in part alive?

SOC.: Yes. It could be placed in water and might live for a time. Or, depending upon the tree, its branch could be placed in soil, where it might take root, and eventually give rise to a new tree.

ANDR.: Exactly. Now, do you suppose it possible for flesh to exist in that same relationship to your body, as a branch newly pulled from a tree?

SOC.: Flesh taken from a living body is to that living body as a branch pulled from a tree is to the tree?

ANDR.: Yes.

SOC.: But the branch would be mistaken by no one for the tree. Nor would flesh be confused with an entire body, dead or alive.

ANDR.: True. But just as that branch, properly planted, and if it were from the right kind of tree, could yield an entire tree, would you grant that flesh, taken from a body and properly treated, could be grown into an entire body?

SOC.: You mean, inserting a severed arm into some special soil, such that an entire body would come forth? I have never heard of such a thing, outside of stories of the gods, and you already know my opinion of gods and men and their stories.

ANDR.: Are you acquainted with the story of Cadmus, who raised soldiers from the teeth of dragons sown in the soil?

SOC.: Yes. It is at best a useful myth.

ANDR.: Suppose I were to tell you that one way in which my future world is different from this one is that we can make some of those mythic tales come true?

SOC.: You can raise soldiers from the teeth of dragons?

ANDR.: No, but we can raise dragons from the teeth of dragons, if the teeth have been preserved in the right way. We call them dinosaurs—'terrible lizards.' We can sometimes take something from the teeth—their essence—and insert it in a very special kind of soil—

Sierra sighed. That was where the fragment ended. She looked again at the preface—

Her outer doorbell sang. Damnit. Who could that be, this time of night? She looked at her watch—12:17 A.M. / 4 April 2042. She touched another device on her couch and flicked on her guest display, on the far wall. Jesus—she'd forgotten completely about Max— No, actually, she had not forgotten. He wasn't due back in New York until tomorrow evening—

The bell sang again. She cursed, put down the dialog, and buzzed him in.

He was up the stairs of her brownstone, and at her door, on the second floor, in seconds. She turned from the screen and walked to the old-fashioned peephole in her door. She peered through it, just for good measure. She had to admit, Max looked good.

She opened the door.

He walked in grinning, a present of some sort in one hand, a bottle of wine in the other.

"I thought you were coming back tomorrow," Sierra said.

"I got an upgrade to an HST," Max said, still smiling. "Long story, short flight—forty-five minutes in the air!"

"I didn't know they had hypersonic service from Iceland." Sierra realized that her voice sounded a little icy, too.

Max seemed undaunted. "Well, that's part of the long story. A friend of a friend at the conference I was attending said I could get a free upgrade—part of some promotion Iceland is doing—if I took an overnight flight tonight. Except, of course, with that quick jump into the atmosphere and back, I was here in New York well before I left Reykjavík. Incredible timing—I thought I'd surprise you!"

Sierra nodded. "Bad timing, for me."

"Am I interrupting something?" Max asked, finally getting it.

"Yeah, but not what you think."

Max managed another smile. "Oh, I'm sure I know what I'm interrupting—the dissertation, right? Look, I'm sorry. I know how hard you're working on it—"

Sierra looked at him. She felt a little bad, now. He did look appealing, standing there with wine and a gift. "All right, come on in, but not for long."

They walked to the kitchen table. Max put his package and bottle down. He reached for her.

Sierra had forgotten that she was wearing only a robe, and partially open, at that. Make that two things she had forgotten tonight—no, she had not forgotten about Max's arrival, he had come home a day sooner than expected. But she didn't realize she had forgotten about the open robe until Max put his arm around her, on the inside of the robe. The crook of his arm brushed against the underside of her breast. His hand moved slowly down the small of her back. She knew this would be a little bit longer than "not for long" . . .


She brought him up-to-date on the whole bizarre evening, in interludes of conversation over several hours.

"The Millennium Club?" Max said with something between admiration and awe. "I'm still in touch with one of the profs on my doctoral committee—he took me there to lunch last year. They have holdings in Greek and Latin to rival Harvard's." Max was an assistant professor of analogic studies at Fordham University himself and, by virtue of that expertise, had more than a passing knowledge of the ancient world and its modes of communication. "You know, I never bought that Socrates just allowed himself to die, when Crito was giving him a way to escape."

"I've always felt the same way," Sierra said, playing absently with Max's long hair. "Why not opt to live and continue your critique, your philosophy? But, you know, time travel and cloning—that's what the 'visitor' was hawking—no way they could have been available in Socrates' time, outside of science fiction."

"Time travel's a tall order in any time," Max said, "no doubt about that. But if it's ever worked out in some future time, then people would be able to get back to our time, Socrates' time, any time, probably just as easily—the arrival time would likely make no difference, once the technology became available."

Sierra considered. "Good point. . . . They've been working for years on some kind of artificial wormhole in California, haven't they?"

"Yeah—based on some equations that Kip Thorne worked out decades ago. But as far I know, it's all just theoretical."

"Better than nothing." Sierra kissed his neck. "Okay. But what about cloning?"

"Growing a twin of Socrates?" Max shrugged. "Who knows. . . . Socrates talks a little about perfect copies in the *Cratylus*. A bit reminiscent of your dialog. But I do know that the ancients had a lot more knowledge than we give them credit for. So much was lost when the library at Alexandria was burned—and it happened more than once. So, granted that they didn't have lasers, or electron or even analog microscopes. But they understood farming. They understood deliberate breeding to improve crops and livestock. So, who knows what they knew—maybe they knew how to put a swatch of human cells into some kind of medium, where it could grow into a clone. Anyway . . . even if they didn't know squat about cloning, if this 'Andros' was really from the future, he could have brought back lightweight equipment with him—hey, we already have that, today."

Sierra moved down and kissed Max, full on the lips. He had a way of making the surely impossible seem less so. At times like this she understood just why she had let him in, in the middle of the night.


She was in Thomas's office the next morning. "The librarians in ancient Alexandria make no reference to this, or anything like it. No other reference to anyone named Andros, either," Thomas said, studying his copy of the fragment, while Sierra did the same with hers.

"Jowett says the Alexandrian lists are unreliable," she replied.

"Yeah, but he was saying they included shams and spoofs, not that they overlooked Platonic dialogs that were real."

"Unreliable is unreliable. Lies of commission, lies of omission, just plain mistakes—they all add up to the same thing."

Thomas nodded slightly.

"The 'Ed' is really more key than the Alexandrians, isn't he?" Sierra continued. "We have only his word for it—or hers—about the carbon dating. The translation looks accurate enough, but we have only Ed's word about the original Greek words, as well."

"You found fault with some of the translation?"

"No big deal, but here, and here, for instance." Sierra pointed to two places in the manuscript. "*Comprised* is a little overkill, pseudo-intellectual. *Composed* would have been fine."

Thomas chuckled approvingly. "The translator is definitely a 'he.'"

"You know him?"

Thomas nodded.

"That's why you have confidence that it's not a forgery?" Sierra asked.

"I saw the original. I helped with the translation. *Comprised*, if I remember correctly, was mine."

Thomas prepared roasted green tea. Sierra sipped, enjoying the aroma as much as the flavor.

"The original manuscript was breathtaking," Thomas continued. "I was amazed it could survive so long, and in such good condition."

"How'd they manage that?" Sierra asked.

"Those Alexandrians were the cream of humanity, at that time. What a mix they were—Greek culture, by way of Macedonia, situated in Egypt, under Roman rule by then. They had literacy rates exceeding anything until our nineteenth century. They had the basis of motion pictures, in persistence-of-vision toys. They had gadgets that ran on steam. Heron of Alexandria invented them both. And they apparently had ways of preserving documents in airless containers. They survived oxidation, but not the human stupidity that torched their great library. But this one got away."

"Okay, so the manuscript is real, at least regarding the creation of this copy in 400 CE. But how do we know that the person who made that copy was just copying and not really creating the fragment—and the larger story, whatever that may have been—from scratch? Let's face it, even if we knew for a fact that Plato wrote it, that doesn't mean the story is true. It could just be another of Plato's fictions—another tale of Atlantis, right?"

"Yes," Thomas allowed. "All of those points are well taken."

"Why did you ask me to look at this fragment now?" Sierra knew it wasn't necessary to voice the end of the sentence—"now, when I'm moving so well on my dissertation"—because Thomas of all people understood that.

"I wanted you to think about this," he replied unhelpfully.

"Yes, but why now?"

"I'm going away, for a few days."

She looked at him. His tone concerned her.

"I have an aneurysm near my heart—it's likely no big deal. But I had a bypass and some digital reconstruction around the area, so the operation could be a little tricky. There's a new hospital in Wilmington, Delaware, where they specialize in this."

"How long . . . will you be gone?"

"Just the weekend, probably. So why don't you take that time to think about the fragment, decide if you'd like to get any more involved in it. . . . I have complete confidence that you'll be able to get back to your dissertation and finish it with distinction, if you decide to take a little breather on it, first."

She glanced fitfully at some of her notes for her dissertation that evening. "Phoenician alphabet comes to Greece around 900 BCE . . . Greek alphabet written from right to left, like Semitic text, 900–600 BCE . . . after 600 BCE, Greeks write left to right, top to bottom . . . 403 BCE, Ionic version of Greek alphabet used by Athenians . . . spurt in literacy . . . approximately 400 BCE, Socrates denounces the written word, according to Plato's account in the *Phaedrus* . . . 399 BCE, Socrates drinks the hemlock . . ."

She focused on the last four entries, underlining them, circling them, in her mind. Those had always been the most intriguing sections of her dissertation. The Ionic alphabet comes to Athens, revolutionizes literacy there, aggravates Socrates but not Plato—at least, not enough to stop Plato from writing—and Socrates dies shortly after. Oh, yeah, at the hands of the newly restored Athenian democracy, perhaps energized, solidified, by the written word. So Plato winds up hating democracy, because it killed his beloved mentor, Socrates—or, actually, because Socrates allowed the death sentence to be carried out, refused Crito's good offer of escape. And Plato, lover of the written word, eventually crafts his masterpiece antidemocratic manifesto, *The Republic,* inspiration for everything from the totalitarian societies of the twentieth century to the Islamic "republics" and the Far Eastern cybercities of the twenty-first—government by the wisest, or at least those who deemed themselves the most wise. . . .

Yeah, that had always been the most fascinating part of her doctoral work, anyway, and now this damned untitled fragment with a new look at the final hours of Socrates. . . . Even if Thomas was right about its 400 CE authenticity, it was likely no more than some very early science fiction, myth-writing, anyway. . . . But, damnit, that was almost as fascinating, in its own right.

She called Max. "How about we go away to my parents' place for the weekend? Bounce some ideas around?"

Max was available.

Then she called Thomas. But all possible numbers only yielded all possible voice mails. She didn't leave a message. That wasn't why she'd called. She just wanted to wish him well, tell him how much he meant to her. She knew he would never have drawn her into this fragment had his operation in Wilmington been assured of success.


Her parents had a little place on Sea Street, in Quivett Neck, near the town of Dennis, on Cape Cod Bay. But they were wintering on the Black Sea in NeoRome, formerly Romania. They had the time. Her father had been chief of detectives, NYPD, and had taken an early retirement. Her mother was a professor of mathematics at Harvard, on sabbatical.

Sierra and Max arrived just in time to see a purple sunset over the stippled gray-blue bay.

"So, did Socrates ever see anything as beautiful?" Max said softly. He ran his hand through Sierra's long, dark hair.

"Probably," she replied. "Piraeus has western views over water. . . . Certainly Plato did. He traveled as far as Egypt, after the death of Socrates, and spent lots of time in Sicily. He had to have seen at least a few suns swallowed by the sea."

"You almost expect to see the steam rise."

"Yeah." Sierra turned to Max, stroked his face, then turned back to the smoldering sunset, which had a slice of orange floating in it now. "Do you think he took Andros up on the offer?" she asked.

"In reality or in the story?"

"At this point, I'll settle for the story."

"Well, Socrates' rejection of Crito's escape plan seems pretty deep-rooted," Max said. " 'Suffering is a better response to evil than committing another evil'—didn't Socrates say something like that? And he thought running away was an evil."

"According to Plato, that's what Socrates thought."

"It all goes back to Plato, doesn't it," Max said. "Any other reliable contemporary accounts of Socrates' death? I know Aristophanes has a Socrates character in *The Clouds* and some of his other comedies, but that's a far cry from Socrates' death."

"Xenophon has a less dramatic, still mostly compatible recounting of the trial and death," Sierra said. "What Plato also has going is that no one subsequent to him, close to that time, contradicted his account. We're talking Aristotle, Plato's student, who disagreed with his mentor about lots of other things. Aristotle said nothing about the trial, one way or the other, but says a lot about Socrates, and likely would have mentioned, somewhere, any reliable accounts of the trial that contradicted Plato's. And, for that matter, there's Alexander the Great, who was Aristotle's student."

"Would it help if you had a look at the rest of the manuscript?"

Sierra nodded.

"You think he's holding out on you?"

Sierra considered. "Much as I admire him, I wouldn't rule that out completely." She thought more about Thomas. Why would he give her just a piece of a manuscript, if he had more? Didn't make sense. But, for that matter, none of this quite did.


By the end of the weekend, she had made a decision. Actually, she had already mostly made it when she had decided to come up to Cape Cod, with Max, to make the decision. Nothing like the sky and sea and shore of the Cape—the north shore, the bay shore, at least, for her—to help confirm the cosmic importance of things.

And this fragment and its implications were cosmic—at minimum, a lot more profound, if any part of the fragment was true, than anything she would be doing in her doctoral dissertation.

She called Thomas when she got back to her apartment on Sunday evening. She doubted he would be in—he hadn't been clear about exactly when he would be returning from Wilmington. There was no live voice, anywhere. She got the number of the hospital in Wilmington and tried that. No way Thomas would be annoyed to hear from her.

"Professor Thomas O'Leary?" the computer repeated the name Sierra had provided. "I'm sorry, but we have no patient under that name in our hospital."

"Perhaps he already checked out?"

"I'll check," the computer told her. "No, sorry, we have had no patient under that name for the past ten years. Should I check further back?"

"No . . ." Sierra opted instead for a human operator. About twenty minutes later, a Ms. Dobbins called her back. She sounded more like a computer than the computer voice, but Sierra had no choice but to take her word for her humanity. "Sorry," Ms. Dobbins confirmed the computer's report, "I can verify that we have had no patient under the name of Professor Thomas O'Leary, Professor Tom O'Leary, and both names without the professor, here at the hospital for the past ten years."


So Thomas had lied to her about going to the hospital—or, at very least, the hospital in Wilmington. Maybe he was at another hospital. Maybe he was in Wilmington, but not in a hospital—what attractions did Wilmington have, other than its new hospital, its old theater district, and its superhub train station?

Maybe Thomas was neither in Wilmington nor in a hospital anywhere. Why would he lie to her?

What else had he lied about?

The obvious thing was the manuscript. But why would he get her going on that only to put its veracity in doubt by telling her an easily discoverable—self-revealing, in fact—lie about something else, such as going to a hospital in Wilmington, Delaware?

Perhaps something had happened to him, along the way. But she would have heard, had it been anything bad—it would have made some sort of news.

She pressed her head back into the sofa, and this time she didn't contest the sleep settings. She felt herself nodding off and realized she was about as uncomfortable as she had ever felt in her life. Nothing like committing yourself to something, only to have it cut out from under you a few hours later.

She awoke the next morning, repeated her rounds of calls to Wilmington, the Old School, any place Thomas might have been. She got the same result. No sign of Thomas O'Leary, anywhere. She toyed with reporting him to Missing Persons. No, the most likely explanation was still that he had lied to her, and there was no point in bringing in the police about that.

She looked again at the manuscript, as she fixed her first cup of tea. Where had Thomas said this thing, or his copy of it, had recently been residing, brought there by whomever?

The Millennium Club was on Forty-ninth Street, east of Fifth Avenue. These clubs were famous for being extraordinarily protective of their members—AN OASIS OF CIVILITY IN AN AGE OF OMNI-ACCESSIBILITY, one of them advertised on a new banner unfurled outside its entrance. This, of course, had drawn a round or two of media attention. Not the Millennium Club, but Sierra doubted that she, as a nonmember, would be given much more than the time of day there.

She considered. . . . Hadn't Max said something about the Millennium Club a couple of days ago, when he had shown up at her door a day early? Yeah, one of his profs had taken him to lunch there—that meant the professor was almost certainly a member. She called Max, told him about Thomas and her predicament. One of the other things she liked about Max was that he always accepted her phone calls. A rarity in this world of allergies to omni-access.

"Goldshine? Sure, I'll give him a call right now and see what I can find out for you."

Her own phone rang a few minutes later. "Sierra Waters?" a jovial voice inquired. "I'm Samuel Goldshine. Maxwell Marcus said you'd like to talk to me about the Millennium Club?"

"Yes—"

"The best dissertation I read that decade. He's a smart fellow."

"Yes—"

"You free for lunch today, at the Millennium Club, one P.M.?"

"Yes."

---

"The food wasn't always so good here," Goldshine told Sierra, smacking his lips after tasting the blueberry-cherry soufflé. "The club finally relented and hired a new chef about six months ago—I've heard nothing but compliments. Part of his secret is he's unafraid of using new genbrids. This blueberry-cherry is actually a single fruit, as you probably know."

Sierra nodded, savoring her raw cloysters, also a new species.

"Anyway, about your manuscript fragment. As Thomas O'Leary probably told you, the club was founded in 1879. So, hell, Mark Twain could have smuggled it into the library—he was a member, you know."

Sierra washed down a tangy cloyster with ice-cold ale. "That's why it would be great if we could speak with the librarian, Mr.—"

"Charles, yes. His first name is Cyril. I checked before you arrived, and I couldn't get a firm answer as to whether he'll be in today. Something about a sister, ill, in Baltimore— Ah, Franklin, this is Ms. Waters, Thomas O'Leary's student."

A well-dressed man, about fifty, had approached their table. He bowed, slightly but graciously, in Sierra's direction. "I have definite word on Mr. Charles's whereabouts," he said to Goldshine.

"Oh, good," Goldshine replied.

"Well, I'm afraid it is not very good, for your purposes today, Professor. Mr. Charles is expected to be in Philadelphia, with a sick sister, for the rest of the day."

"Philadelphia? I thought it was Baltimore."

"Philadelphia is what I was just told, sir."

"Okay, well, thank you, Franklin."

Franklin bowed again, slightly, to Sierra and Goldshine and excused himself.

Goldshine looked after Franklin, then back at Sierra. "Well, bad luck, but I can certainly show you the general place—including the part of the library where Mr. O'Leary says the fragment was found."


The library was actually a series of libraries, elegantly appointed, as the Victorians said, on the third and fourth floors. The armchairs were burgundy, plush, and inviting. Maple tables of varying dimensions were overflowing with various newspapers, magazines, journals, some of which looked as if they could have been on the tables since 1879. And the books on the shelves were phenomenal, to Sierra's eyes . . . an autumn rainbow of rust, brown, green, and red bindings that put her small collection of Appleton editions of Darwin and Spencer that she had at home to shame.

But the nook of the library that held Plato and his progeny was the prize. Sierra recalled an old engraving she had come across as a child. It featured a man on a ladder against a library wall of shelves marked METAPHYSIK, his nose in the pages of an open book held in one hand, a second book in his other hand, a third between his knees, a fourth between his elbow and waist . . . too many books, too little body.

Sierra felt that way now, although the only things she was clutching were her hands.

"Can I be of assistance?" a deep voice inquired, with a trace of a British accent. It was not Goldshine's.

Sierra turned. A short, stocky, bald man smiled first at her, then Goldshine.

The professor gave no indication of knowing the man. "Well, yes . . . Ms. Waters, a student of Thomas O'Leary—a club member—was wondering about a partial manuscript that apparently Mr. Charles located here."

The man scrunched his face. "What sort of manuscript would that be?"

"Oh, yes, sorry, it was a piece of a Platonic dialog, apparently unknown until now, and . . . look, well, I know it sounds crazy—"

"The dialog with Socrates and Andros, taking place, presumably, right after Crito has taken his leave—"

"Yes!" Sierra burst out. "I mean, you know it?"

"Of course I do. Mr. Charles indeed discovered it. We know it wasn't here during the last cleaning, that would have been nineteen years ago, in 2023. Mr. Charles knew just what to do with it—he took it out for a proper scientific appraisal, which confirmed the authenticity of the ink, from the late Alexandrian era, about four hundred AD, if memory serves. . . . Oh, my apologies, talking about memory, I forgot to introduce myself! I spend so much time in the back stacks that I forget how to behave among people. I'm Mr. Bertram. A Millennium librarian, like Mr. Charles."

"Professor Samuel Goldshine, member since 2026." Goldshine extended his hand. "A pleasure."

Mr. Bertram took the hand, shook it briefly.

"Do you know anything more about the fragment?" Sierra pressed. "How it got to be here, who else knows about it other than you, Mr. Charles, Thomas O'Leary?"

"Oh, well, any member could know about it, of course," Bertram answered. "We don't keep any of our holdings secret from the members."

"Do you know who else Mr. Charles or you talked to about this, in addition to Mr. O'Leary?" Sierra tried a slightly different tack.

But this drew disapproving looks from both Bertram and Goldshine. "Those who serve the club would never reveal such details," Goldshine advised. "Why, at the beginning of the twenty-first century, the club even stood up to a federal subpoena once and refused to divulge its members' reading habits!" he concluded proudly.

"I can show you the other piece," Bertram offered. "That is, I can show it to Professor Goldshine, and if he doesn't mind your reading over his shoulder . . ."

"Yes, thank you—," Sierra said.

"That would be grand, thank you," Goldshine said at the same time.

"Do you know if Mr. O'Leary knows about—," Sierra began, but stopped as soon as she saw the beginning of the return of the stern looks. "Thank you," she simply said again, to both men. "This means a lot to me."


She sat next to Goldshine at a small, cherry maple desk. A green banker's light provided warm illumination. Sierra reckoned it was the real thing, not a repro, likely from the 1920s.

Bertram returned a few minutes later with a folder. He handed it to Goldshine, smiled slightly at him, then her, and left.

Goldshine opened it. There were two groups of papers, each clipped together. Goldshine picked up the first, looked through it briefly, then handed it to Sierra.

It was the same fragment that Thomas had provided. Sierra picked up the second. "Okay if I read this?"

"By all means," Goldshine said, and busied himself with the first.

Sierra turned to the second. It was smaller than the first and apparently did not begin where the first left off.

SOC.: The time is not sufficient. Even if I were inclined to agree with your proposition, which I am not, the ship from Delos with the priest of Apollo will be here in a day or two, after which I am bound to follow the wishes of the Athenians. And, surely, one or two days is not enough to grow a full-bodied likeness of a man.

ANDR.: That is true, Socrates. Even with the special craft the people of my time and place possess—the life-growing craft I have described to you—one day would not be enough to grow a man. But believe me, O Socrates, there exists a yet deeper craft, which makes that one day, any given amount of time, irrelevant for our purposes.

SOC.: What is this deeper craft?

ANDR.: It is part of the craft through which I have arrived here, from a future world, a future time.

SOC.: Ah, the godly craft, the unknown craft, which you have yet to explain to me. Are you saying that this craft gives you the power, as it is claimed for some gods, to make time stand still for some events, but move forward for others?

ANDR.: Yes, that is similar to what I am saying. But in my world, such power is reality, not myth.

SOC.: But you are in my world now, are you not?

ANDR.: True. But by virtue of my being here, you are in my world, too, are you not, Socrates?

SOC.: Yes, I would agree. If indeed you come from another world. But, then, tell me, how in your world, or in the connection between your world and mine, could time stop in such a way as to allow a man to grow seventy years in a day?

ANDR.: I will try. Let us say that, by the process of branching we were talking about earlier, a part of you could be moved to the future and placed in a soil such that the branch could grow into a complete, living likeness of you. Now, whether that growth took one day or seventy years would not matter, as long as our two worlds remained connected, and as long as your part of the connection, your world, the place and time in which we are conversing, at this moment, was this very time.

SOC.: You are saying you could return to your world and time, and then return here, at this very time, before you left, and there would be two entities of you this instant in this room?

ANDR.: Yes, that would be possible. Though I would try not to do that.

SOC.: And you could return with a living replica of me, which took even seventy years to grow, as long as at the conclusion of that seventy years, the path to this time and place, from that future world to this room, shortly after the break of this dawn, in which you and I now converse at this very moment, remained open?

ANDR.: Yes, that is what I am suggesting.

SOC.: And, if that were truly possible, all you would need to complete your plan would be a branch, as we have been describing it, of me.

ANDR.: Yes.

SOC.: I could never allow that.

ANDR.: What if I told you the branch had already been taken?

Sierra realized her hands were shaking. This fragment of the dialog ended with Andros' words. Who the hell was he?

She glanced at Goldshine, still engrossed in the first, longer fragment. She tried to calm herself. Reading this dialog in public was not a good idea, if she didn't want everyone to know how it was affecting her. Maybe that didn't matter.

She looked around. No sign of Bertram. She needed to have a copy of this, but she doubted the club's rules would allow it. Maybe she could prevail upon Goldshine to request a copy?

She couldn't chance his saying no. She reached, quietly, for her palm phone. She placed it in her palm, set the rapid photo function, then moved her palm quickly over the pages in front of her. She'd study this on the screen back in her apartment. *Thank you, Thomas,* she thought, *by dragging me into this, you've turned me into a goddamn spy.* But she couldn't say she really regretted it now, either. No, not at all.


She thanked Goldshine, profusely and truly, and walked home, down Fifth Avenue, with her thoughts. Goldshine had seemed more amused than thrilled by the fragments, in the end. Well, he probably didn't believe they were real, even if carbon-14 said they had been copied in 400 CE. Time travel and cloning in the ancient world were a lot harder to believe than an error or fudging of carbon-14 dating in the present. Time travel was hard to believe in any world. . . .

Goldshine had said he'd return the fragments to Mr. Bertram. "And come to my lecture next week—'The Vulgate and the Vulgar.' "

She had looked for Mr. Bertram. But he had receded into the stacks. She would have loved to question him further about what he knew about the fragments. He seemed like something of a fragment from another time and place himself.

The stone lions on the steps of the New York Public Library on Forty-second Street looked especially stoic today, as if they had the lost Library of Alexandria on their minds. Somehow that Library of Alexandria, burned by the Christians, burned by the Muslims, reputed to have a copy of every manuscript at the time, was a keystone in all of this. The preface to the first fragment had said it was discovered in excavations near Alexandria in the first decade of the twenty-first century. What excavations? Exactly when?

She thought about what Thomas had said about the Alexandrians in Egypt. A magnificent culture, one of the three Hellenistic pieces of the sprawling empire Alexander the Great had left on his untimely death at thirty-three . . . Alexander the Great, who died in 323 BCE, a year before his mentor, Aristotle. Aristotle, student of Plato, student of Socrates . . .

But the scholars of Alexandria were by and large not great philosophers. They were mathematicians, astronomers, like Ptolemy, whose calculations of the moon's orbit would have been good enough to land a rocket there. They were tinkerers, like Heron of Alexandria, who invented the toy steam engines and persistence-of-vision devices Thomas had mentioned. Heron had invented lots of other things—automatic doors, coin-operated machines. . . . Had he tinkered with a time machine, too?

Not likely, from what Sierra understood of physics. Steam engines and motion pictures and automatic doors operated on Newtonian principles. Time machines, if they were real, would likely operate on a physics that made current quantum gravitics look like child's play.

She reached her brownstone, on Eleventh Street, between University Place and Fifth Avenue. For a second, she thought she saw Thomas sitting on her front stoop. He looked terrible, somehow twenty years older than a few days ago. The operation hadn't gone well. . . . What had they done to him down in Wilmington, or wherever he was?

But as she approached, she realized the old man on her staircase was just a derelict staring at his photophone.


She entered her apartment and checked her screen. Good, the second fragment, photographed with her palm phone, was there, as expected. She was a researcher, she assured herself, not really a spy, and that surely took precedence—the pursuit of truth—over any conventions of the club. Yet she still felt a little bad.

She showered and put on something more comfortable. She had dressed up for her lunch at the Millennium. She returned to her screen and printed out a copy of the second fragment. Not because she was afraid of losing what was on her screen—her grandparents had told her that, in the early days of the computer, people were often afraid of that and printed out documents as a way of saving them. But Sierra printed out the second fragment because it seemed more connected that way, more a part of the first piece of the manuscript that Thomas had given her.

Security in numbers. Two fragments made each seem more legitimate, more real. But that feeling, she knew, was still mostly illusion. Two people, buttressing each other's story, made neither story more likely, unless at least one of the people was already known to be trustworthy. What if both were liars? The two pieces of the dialog she held in front of her, each with Greek on one side, English on the other, could well just both be fragments of the same lie. She shook her head, beginning to feel as if she were having a Socratic dialog with herself.

She looked back at her screen and requested information on "excavations," "Alexandria," "2001–2010." Hmmm . . . the search yielded stories about a couple of apparently minor activities in 2008 and 2009. Nothing about a new Platonic manuscript. Well, Thomas had given no indication about how well the "discovery" had been reported or publicized at that time.

She searched "Andros." Nothing other than that it was the name of an island near Athens, which she already knew. People in the ancient world were often called by the place of their birth. But the Andros of her dialog presumably came from the future. . . .

She put in another request, "Alexandria," "inventions." Heron of Alexandria dominated the eight hundred hits . . . Also known as Hero . . . Date of birth and life uncertain—estimates ranged from 150 BC to AD 250 . . . Most common date, AD 75 . . . Invented the "aeolipile"—ah, yes, the toy steam engine . . . His manuscript, *Heron's Formula*, lost for years. Fragment recovered in 1894, complete copy in 1896 . . . He wrote in Greek . . .

She searched on Socrates, Plato, Aristotle, Benjamin Jowett, 1817–1893. . . . She came upon Jowett's quote "The way to get things done is not to mind who gets the credit for doing them." She wasn't sure she agreed.

She read the *Crito* anew. No hint of Andros—man or island—anywhere. Just the angst, everywhere, of Socrates' refusal to escape. She looked at the *Apology* and *Cratylus,* too.

It was evening when she finally turned away from the screen and thought about eating. In a feat of perfect timing, that was just when the screen beeped—she had set it to alert her about any news stories that mentioned Thomas O'Leary.

She clicked and read the brief report in the *Athenian Global Village:* ". . . three men missing in a boating accident in the Aegean . . ." Two of the names meant nothing to her.

But the third was "Thomas O'Leary, a scholar from New York . . ."

She searched frantically for more information about Thomas and the accident. She searched on his name, his picture, the titles of his books . . .

She got nothing more about the accident.

But in her fast scanning of the photos, something caught her eye. She looked more carefully, expanded it to full screen, maximum resolution. She enhanced the part she wanted to see more of. It was a grainy, sepia-tone photo, on a page, appropriately enough, with an old-fashioned Web address, and a stat box that said it hadn't been visited in twelve years.

She rubbed her eyes and looked again.

No doubt about it, unless Thomas had an ancestor who looked exactly like him. There, standing in front of the Millennium Club with two other gentlemen, was Thomas, looking just as he had the last time she'd seen him.

No real problem in that, she'd seen photos of Thomas taken more than twenty years ago, and he looked pretty much the same as now. He had one of those faces, she had recently heard him remark, that looked fifty when he was thirty and fifty when he was seventy.

Except this photo, hanging nicely on a page about Victorian New York City, was captioned "a new literary club, 1883, a few years after its founding."

CHAPTER 2

*Alexandria, AD 150*

He was known as Heron of Alexandria. And by other names.

Tonight he walked by the sea, alone. He often preferred his own company, because that allowed him maximum pursuit of his ideas. On the other hand, implementation of plans usually required more than their progenitor.

The night was nearly moonless. He could hear more of the water than he could see. He closed his eyes and attended to the waves. They slapped against the boats in the harbor, like skilled hands upon some soft, supple instrument. He knew none was the boat he was waiting for.

In the darkness he could perceive not only water but time more clearly. He reflected: time was really the complete opposite of space, which flourished in the light. In the night, space was foreclosed, usually to just a few steps around you. The arena was left to time. . . . No matter how much he had of it, he never had enough. Where was she?

Footsteps on the stone behind him brought him back to the present. He turned. It was Jonah, walking quickly. The lights of the great university winked behind him.

"Sorry to disturb your contemplations," Jonah said.

"I would not have told you my whereabouts had I not wanted to be disturbed under any circumstances," Heron replied. The question, of course, was whether the circumstances Jonah would be conveying would rise to the requisite significance. But Heron thought that his chief assistant had a pretty good record on that account.

"A woman wishes to see you, at the university."

Heron's left eyebrow arched.

"I cannot confirm she is the one you have been awaiting," Jonah continued. "She speaks Greek, but says she is from the North, not the East. She looks . . . different. I do not believe she comes from either place."


The Museion—the House of the Muses—glowed with oil lamps and late-night thoughts. Heron and Jonah proceeded to its shining wing, the Great Library, which held a copy of every book on earth, some seven hundred thousand, at last count. Rooms contained readers and voices—not necessarily debating but reading out loud. It reminded Jonah of the Sabbath prayer sessions in the synagogues of the Delta quarter of the city.

They passed Ptolemy in the hall, pacing with a scroll, muttering about some astronomical equation. They knew better than to interrupt him with a greeting.

They turned into a corridor. "I heard your breeze pipes this afternoon," one of a group of students said to Heron admiringly. "It was truly the breath of Pan!"

"Thank you," Heron replied.

Jonah looked at his mentor inquiringly.

"A windmill connected to an organ," Heron explained, as they walked on. "I finished it just this morning."

They reached a room. Jonah pushed aside the curtain.

"Heron of Alexandria," Jonah announced, and extended his arm to Heron, then to the woman seated at the small table.

She stood and smiled, politely. "Ampharete. I won't insult your intelligence by pretending that is my real name, or telling you where I come from, because none of that matters."

Heron nodded and noted her long curly brown hair. "You are not from the East—at least, not from the distant East, as I had been told."

"The East was just a route of travel, not my origin. The enormous distance of my origin, however, is true."

"You speak Greek well," Heron said, "though I cannot identify your accent. You told Jonah you are Northern?"

"I was near Hadrian's Wall, just last year."

"It will be the limit of Roman territory, certainly in the north, despite my admiration for our emperor, Antoninus Pius, and his predictions, would you agree?"

Ampharete just smiled. "Might we go someplace else to converse? Much as I love this magnificent library, I do not feel completely at ease here—too many wise people walking about."

"Wisdom makes you uneasy?"

Ampharete kept her smile. "When combined with prying eyes, yes."

Heron looked at Jonah, who nodded slowly. "I think I know a good place," Jonah said.

They walked along the coast. Jonah pointed to an eating establishment. "Not as adventurous as some of the facilities in Canopus, to the east, but it is quiet and the food is good. Are you hungry?"

Ampharete nodded. "Yes, I am starving. Thank you for thinking of that."

They were seated with a good view of the sea. Ampharete ordered date wine and lamb. Heron, gazing out at the sea, distracted, ordered just wine. Jonah took it all in and ordered nothing.

"Let us speak of Plato, and the picture he paints of people and their inability to rule themselves," Ampharete began.

This drew Heron's attention from the sea. "Mobs often make stupid decisions, on the basis of emotion rather than reason. Do you think Plato is wrong?"

"Plato's view that only the most wise should rule can justify any tyrant or group of tyrants who happen to be in power."

The wine arrived. "Your lamb will be here soon," their server, a Nubian, advised Ampharete.

"Thank you." She sipped the wine. "Strong," she said, and sipped more.

"Plato performs a very important, continuing service in human affairs," Heron continued. He picked up his wine cup, brought it to his lips, and drank, deeply. "If any ruler—tyrant or mass of people—should do anything too brutal, too bizarre, then any party, aggrieved by this, could point to Plato's work and say, look, this action goes against some absolute principle of ethics, some ideal law of human conduct. It is therefore not rule by the wisest."

Jonah smiled slightly, aware that his mentor was mainly indulging his penchant for playing the Sophist, and arguing the other side of a point he in fact agreed with.

"In any case," Heron said to Ampharete, "even if I agree entirely with you, what would you have me do about it?"

She sipped again, put down her cup, and reached into her garment, already parted slightly at her right breast. She produced a document and handed it to Heron.

"Nice skin," Jonah observed, looking at the parchment, but thinking it also applied to the part of Ampharete that he could see.

Heron examined the document, emptied his wine cup, looked at the document again. He ran his fingertip under each line, in precise and steady motions, until he reached the end. "Interesting—not part of the Platonic canon. Is this a gift?"

"Yes," Ampharete responded.

Heron passed the parchment to Jonah. "Please make a copy of this, at your earliest convenience." Heron turned to Ampharete. "Let us assume, to start, that Plato did not write this. It would likely have been known before now, if he had. But if not Plato, who?"

Ampharete sipped some more, then returned Heron's gaze. "Perhaps it was you."


The lamb arrived, sliced in little pieces, on a thin skewer. Ampharete thanked the Nubian, took a piece of meat, smiled, all without breaking contact with Heron's eyes.

"You flatter me," he said carefully. "This is a fine fable."

"Part of what I would like to know is whether it is a fable or true."

Now she glanced at the manuscript. She took another piece of lamb, closed her eyes. "The food is delicious."

Jonah nodded, accepting the compliment.

"The dialog speaks of Syracuse and Ithaca being close in the visitor's world," Heron said. "Socrates says they are not very near each other in his. Last time I looked at a map, Syracuse was still in Sicily, and Ithaca one of the Ionian islands, presumably the home of Odysseus. Not very close at all."

Jonah shifted uncomfortably.

"My point—," Ampharete began. "What—"

Jonah's body was across hers. He pulled her off her seat, onto the hard floor. "Apologies," Jonah said, embarrassed.

"Aegyptian," Heron said, rattled. He pointed to the door, through which a blur of a person had just exited. Heron helped Ampharete and Jonah to their feet, then gestured to the wall behind Ampharete. A gleaming ivory knife handle still quivered there. "Some of them deeply resent the Museum, and its usurpation of their culture," Heron said. "But why was he aiming at you?"

Ampharete smoothed her garment and shook her head. "I do not know. This is a violent world." She smiled a tremulous thanks at Jonah and surveyed what was left of her meal on the table. Most of it was on the floor. "So much for the savory lamb."

"So much for the safety of this eatery," Heron said dyspeptically, and looked at Jonah.

Heron's assistant managed an apologetic smile. "It seems this fabulous tale of Socrates attracts a murderous interest."


They walked back in the direction of the Museum. "I have access to quarters in the library more private than you saw before," Heron told Ampharete. "I would invite you and advise you to stay the night—you will be totally safe there."

"That would be very welcome. Thank you," she responded.

They approached the library from a different direction. They entered through a passageway camouflaged to look like an elaborate garden. "It is a combination of living plants and mirrors," Heron whispered. "One of my favorite designs. It works even better in the day, or in full moonlight."

The marbled hallway was white and devoid of people. Rows upon rows of pigeonholes lined the walls, each with a roll of papyrus, and a written label attached to its outer edge. Ampharete peered at the labels, flickering in the light of the oil lamps. "I wish I had time to read some of this," she said wistfully.

"It is thought by many that the golden age is behind us," Heron remarked, "that it ended with the exodus of scholars in the reign of Ptolemy the Seventh, some two hundred years after the death of Alexander. Some people think *this* is the golden age—we are in it, at this moment, more than one hundred and fifty years into the empire of Augustus. Both groups are wrong. The golden age is ahead."

Ampharete nodded.

Jonah opened a door and beckoned Ampharete to enter.

The room within was spacious, with a hearth in the center, and several adjoining rooms. "These are my private quarters," Heron said. "I often spend the night here. The library treats me well. Please, make yourself comfortable."

Ampharete sat on a bench, against a wall, which was quite comfortable indeed. Jonah stood by the outer door, casting glances down the hall. Heron busied himself in one of the other rooms.

He emerged with wine and bread. "The grain is very good," he said to Ampharete. "I find it more satisfying than the lamb."

He bid her to join him at a table near the hearth.

"It looks as if we are alone," Jonah said to and about the hallway, and sat with the two at the table.

"You are right, this is very tasty," Ampharete said about the bread. Heron poured the wine.

"Still abstaining?" Heron asked Jonah.

Jonah shook his head no. "Your example persuaded me."

Heron poured a cup for him. "That, and you are less worried about attacks in this place than in that place by the sea. And you are not concerned about your dietary restrictions."

Jonah acknowledged the accuracy of his mentor's analysis.

"Do you notice anything different about Ampharete's manuscript," Heron inquired of his student, "other than its incredible content?"

Jonah looked at the walls of the room, on which were also pigeonholes with protruding scrolls of papyrus. Ampharete followed his gaze and noticed not only the scrolls, but various devices, lodged here and there. She was unsure of the function of most of them.

"This manuscript is parchment, not papyrus," Jonah replied. "*Charta pergamena,* as the Romans call it."

"Good. And what does that tell you?"

"It was likely not created here, at the library, but at Pergamum," Jonah answered. "But, of course, the original might well have been created here, and this one might be but a copy."

Heron nodded and turned to Ampharete. "Perhaps you would be good enough to help us understand this manuscript—starting with, just where did you acquire it?"

Ampharete's mouth was filled with bread. She chewed, and drank wine to wash it down.

Heron took advantage of the silence. "Or did you perhaps write it yourself?"

Jonah poured himself another cup of wine, sat back, and smiled in anticipation of a conversation he knew he would enjoy witnessing.

Ampharete swallowed her wine, licked her lips. "So, in your schema, the bearer of a document is the same as its creator?" she asked Heron.

"When it is a document I have never laid eyes on before, the bearer being the creator is always a distinct possibility. . . . But, leaving aside the question of who wrote this, for the moment, I am still very interested in where you obtained it."

"Athens, the Academy. But it was in a group of seemingly unrelated documents, not close to Plato's other works."

"Ah, yes, mother Athens. A good many of our books come from the library at the Lyceum. They were brought here with the intent of making copies, and then returning the originals, but I am afraid that in many cases, that has not happened." Heron looked disapprovingly at his student.

"That has been going on for hundreds of years," Jonah observed, unfazed.

"And now you bring us another document from Athens," Heron resumed his questioning of Ampharete. "Why did you seek me out about it?"

"One of the other books in the unrelated pile was of your authorship," she replied.

"Oh?"

"Your *Pneumatica*."

"Ah, yes, one of my favorites—the power of thin air."

"Do you believe in travel through time?" she asked Heron.

"Why do you ask? Because that is what our friend Andros is apparently talking to Socrates about in your document?"

She nodded. "And I find the subject fascinating."

Heron closed his eyes, as if to see time more clearly. "I do not think travel across space and travel across time are the same thing, at all. I agree with Socrates about this. I think space and time are very different. I do not believe time is just another dimension—a fourth dimension—like height, width, and depth."

Jonah sharpened his attention.

"Go on," Ampharete prompted. "Please."

Heron's eyes remained closed. "I am not even completely sure that time exists, in a physical sense. It may be a kind of Platonic form, but unlike the objective, real forms, time may be a form that we rational beings create, or perhaps help create, with our minds."

Ampharete focused on Heron's face. She wished she could see not only through his eyelids but into his soul. "Yes?"

"And if, by some miracle of invention, we could travel through time, that could create paradoxes which would make Zeno of Elea's look like one of my automated little puppet shows, would it not?" Heron's eyes danced beneath his lids, as if he were following such a puppet show. His lips curved slightly in unconscious merriment. "If I, today, had finished constructing a device, in this room, which allowed you to travel even a day into the past, and you used it to travel into the past to kill or otherwise distract me from completing the device, how would you have been able to travel in the first place into the past, with no device then constructed?" Now he opened his eyes and looked at her.

"I would have to be exceedingly careful not to kill you or otherwise prevent you from finishing your work," she said. "I have no doubt Jonah would protect you, in any case." She smiled at Jonah, who returned it.

"Your care—and Jonah's—might not be sufficient. Suppose a man on a camel stopped, for a few moments, to admire your shape as you strode through Alexandria yesterday. He resumes his travel, at which point I have walked in front of him. His camel, frightened, kicks me in the head. I am hurt and unable to finish my work on the device which brought you back to yesterday."

Ampharete smiled, full luminosity. "Thank you, on both accounts."

Heron looked puzzled. "The first is for my compliment. The second?"

"Is for demonstrating how much serious thought you have already given to time travel," Ampharete replied. "I doubt that many others, if any, in Alexandria ad Aegyptum have done so."

Ampharete, drained from her day's journey and the evening's events, accepted Heron's invitation to sleep in one of the bedrooms adjoining the main room.

Heron and Jonah examined the manuscript. Jonah began to read aloud from a part in the middle:

ANDR.: Think of the good you could do, if you lived but another ten years, even another year.

SOC.: As I said to Crito, I would do more harm than good, if those extra years, or year, were to come to me illegitimately.

ANDR.: Must a life always be a prisoner to the circumstances which brought it to be? Cannot a child born of an illegitimate union do good in life?

SOC.: Yes, but that is a different circumstance than the one you are proposing to me.

ANDR.: In what way, Socrates?

SOC.: A child born of an illegitimate union had no decision, no part to play, in the process that brought that child to be. I, on the other hand, am fully aware of my circumstances, and, moreover, would be not only aware but an active participant in the escape you are proposing.

ANDR.: Suppose I were to take you with me, against your will. Would that remove your compliance in the circumstances of your escape, and the moral consequences you draw from it?

"It is standard Socratic chatter," Heron interrupted. "Anyone could be its author."

"You find this unexceptional?"

"In form and style, yes. In content, in the story it purports to tell . . . yes, I certainly think it bears more scrutiny. . . . It does resemble Plato's handiwork."

"You now think Plato wrote this?" Jonah asked.

Heron shrugged. "The simplest explanations, the ones that require the least number of components, are usually the best. That is the way mechanical objects work, too. That is an important principle. Plato is the accepted author of all of the other Socratic dialogs. So, before we explore the likelihood that this dialog had another author, we must first examine the question, why would we think that Plato is not the author?"

"Because it is not part of the traditional Platonic collection, as you said before," Jonah replied.

"Perhaps Plato thought this dialog did not merit preservation."

"So you think this is a tale of unreal events and places, like Plato's Atlantis?"

"I would not be so sure that the Atlantis is an account of something unreal," Heron replied. "As for this Andros story, there are more reasons than untruth to want a story unpreserved, unknown to posterity."

"Sometimes we might want that silent fate for a story precisely because of the opposite. . . . Is that what you are saying? Because it conveys a dangerous truth that the author would rather not be known?"

"This is complicated," Heron said, looking at the mosaic on the floor and then the manuscript on the table.

"Is it possible she is right"—Jonah gestured to the door behind which their visitor slept—"and you yourself wrote this sometime in the future?"

Heron laughed, a little. "I guess that is something I will have to find out."

"Does it bear something unique of your stamp, the way you organize words, the way you think?" Jonah picked up the manuscript and un-scrolled it further.

"Do you see that here?" Heron took the manuscript from Jonah.

"I am not sure."

Heron offered his student lodging, too, but Jonah had important er-rands to run, at the home of his parents, early the next morning.

"Should I take this?" he inquired about the manuscript.

"You are not likely to do any copying tonight," Heron replied. "But I think I have enough strength to give it another reading."

Jonah nodded his leave.

Heron returned to the manuscript.

One part, in particular, interested him. It actually appeared several times in the dialog, in slightly different words, but all saying the same thing.

Heron looked at one of those sections.

soc.: It will make no difference, to the present or the future of the world, if I die here or escape with you.

Socrates first said that right after Andros' offer—or threat—to re-move Socrates from the prison, against his will.

Heron needed to think about that. He wanted to ponder its meaning before he discussed it with anyone, including his trusted student.

Jonah finished his tasks earlier than expected the next morning and pro-ceeded, quickly, to the library. There were just a few readers in the spa-cious main hall. They bent over labeled cupboards, their backs to Jonah. The pale pastels of their garments blended seamlessly with the tiles on the walls.

Jonah entered Heron's special quarters, quietly, in case Ampharete was still asleep. Heron was an early riser.

But there was no sign of Heron, either near the hearth or in his bed-room. So he was already gone.

Jonah looked under the table, in case his mentor had left a note that had fallen off, but the floor was empty as well.

Jonah considered his next move. He could not be sure that Ampharete was in her room, either. He could go to her door and listen . . . for what? Her snoring? A woman as graceful as she certainly could not snore. . . . Maybe he would hear rustling? Something about his listening at her door, even for good reasons, felt distasteful to him. He had no wish to invade her privacy . . . at least, not without her participation.

In the end, he decided, unhappily, that a sharp rap on her door was his best course of action. He applied his hand to the task.

No response from the bedroom.

He tried again.

Still no response.

She must have left the premises, too.

He opened the door, just to confirm. . . .

Ampharete looked beautiful in bed, half-uncovered, completely asleep, ringlets of rich, brown hair on her neck and shoulders.

Jonah withdrew, fast, and closed the door. He knew he would not be able to long resist what he saw. Her image was still all he could see. . . . It drew him. . . . She was intoxicating. . . .

He sat, awkwardly, at the table, and tried to recover his thoughts. Ampharete was still here, Heron was not, that was good—or, what was good was that Ampharete was here.

He saw the ringlets of hair, on her soft skin, again. . . . She must have been a sound sleeper—

Now he did hear rustling in her room.

Her door opened.

She poked her head out. "Jonah . . ."


He fixed a breakfast of bread, honey, dates, and water mixed with a splash of wine for Ampharete. Heron's kitchen was well stocked, and Jonah had always been told to help himself to its provisions.

"Do you, per chance, have another copy of the manuscript?" Jonah asked.

"You did not make a copy of it?"

"I left the manuscript with Heron last night, and he apparently took it with him."

"You have the impression Heron will be gone for a while?"

"I do not know."

"I wish I had heard him leave," Ampharete reflected. "But I was exhausted last night. I was in the arms of Morpheus as soon as I reclined."

Jonah wished those arms were his. He felt blood flowing in his cheeks. "You do not seem as disturbed as I might have thought about Heron's absence. You traveled all this distance to see him. . . ."

Ampharete smiled. "His leaving tells me something useful."

"What would that be?"

"Obviously, something about my presence, the manuscript I carried, provoked his departure."

"To where, do you think?"

Ampharete finished the last of her morning wine before she answered. "I would think there is a good chance he went back to Athens."

"He visited Athens several years ago."

"I meant much further back than that."

Jonah regarded her. "You think that, despite what he told you, he indeed has a time-traveling device, and he used it to go back to Athens at the time of the death of Socrates?"

"I think that is a possibility, yes."

"If he were able to travel to the past, in any kind of measured way, then he could use that same device to return to the present. And he would have returned right after he left."

"That assumes many things," Ampharete said darkly.

"You think he died in the past? Who are you? What is the source of your knowledge?"

"I am someone with no certain knowledge of anything."

Jonah turned his face away. "We shall see."


Ampharete saw more works of Aristotle than she knew existed, in the next few days, as well as works by his student Theophrastus—some 240 texts addressing everything from ethics to physics. She also saw many works by Heron, but nothing of the man.

Jonah said she could stay in Heron's quarters as long as she liked. She accepted his offer. No one bothered her there, just the specters that had accompanied her to Alexandria in the first place.

But she knew Jonah did not trust her. How could he? Certainly he knew much of what his mentor was doing. He therefore had to have some big inkling of why she was so interested in Heron, why she had come to Alexandria. She had in fact done little to disguise it.

She also knew that Jonah was unhappy that she did not have another copy of the manuscript. "I know where to obtain others," she finally decided to tell Jonah, on the fourth evening of her visit, as they walked along the shore.

"Where?"

"Suppose I told you no place in this world right now."

"You mean, someplace in the past? Are we talking about that again? Where, Socratic/Platonic Athens?"

"Yes, possibly. But not only there."

"Where else?"

"Not only then," she said.

"You mean the future."

Ampharete stared out at the Pharos Lighthouse, the Seventh Wonder of the World. It was the only one that performed an actual task. It was apt that Heron the inventor made his home here. . . . But she agreed with Heron and Jonah that the Library of Alexandria and its myriad combs of honeyed knowledge was a greater wonder still.

She returned her attention to Jonah. "If the story in the dialog is true, then there is no reason it might not have been written in the future and carried back here."

Jonah looked out at the sea. "Who are you? Where do you come from? I have asked you this more than once, and you have never given an answer."

Ampharete followed his gaze to the sea. "Out there. That is where I come from."

"I know you are not talking about Rome, or Gaul, or even the ruins of Carthage. I doubt you are speaking even of Atlantis."

Ampharete laughed. "Which is more absurd? That someone could be from Atlantis, or from the future?"

"Atlantis would be less so—it invokes no paradox."

Ampharete studied him. A cold, sharp breeze snapped through his black hair.

"Are you from Atlantis, then?" he asked her.

"Both. I am from both." And she reached for him and kissed him on the cheek. Jonah, surprised for a second, reciprocated and pulled her close. He rested his hand on her waist and kissed her face again.

She pulled away, after a moment.

"I know," Jonah said, breathless, "not here."

She shook her head and turned back to the sea.

She could feel his hot, dark eyes on the nape of her neck.

"I must leave here now," she said. "I have stayed too long already."


They met early the next morning in Heron's room.

Ampharete was ready to leave.

"I want to go with you to Athens," Jonah said. "But I am loath to leave Alexandria in Heron's absence."

"I had a mentor once, too, whom I may have loved as dearly as you do Heron," Ampharete told Jonah. "He encouraged me. He . . ."

"What happened to your mentor?"

"Perhaps the same as with Heron," she said slowly. "I do think there is a chance I might locate Heron, in my travels . . . but the future is always opaque."

Jonah smiled, ruefully. "Even for those who ply the currents of time?"

"Especially so."

"Were you . . . blown off course at some point in your journey?"

"You might say that, yes."

"Do you think you might reach some place you did not intend when you leave Alexandria?"

"Yes, that is a real possibility."

Jonah closed his eyes, and rubbed them. "I would like to accompany you. Would that be possible?"

"I would value your . . . companionship," Ampharete said carefully.

"I understand."

Ampharete sighed. "I first need to inquire about getting a boat."

———————

Ampharete had a fair supply of Roman currency tucked away in her garments. She booked passage for two on an old galley, the *Lux,* with drab sails and long oars. It was scheduled to head northwest in Mare Nostrum. "Better to travel as anonymously as possible," she told Jonah. They looked back at Alexandria as the *Lux* left the harbor. The sun hung low and the city gleamed.

The captain was a wiry Phoenician named Melqat. "The Romans own the sea, yet they leave the captaining to their conquered," Ampharete advised Jonah.

"In the case of the Phoenicians, that is commendable," Jonah said. "They know the seas better than anyone."

They came upon Melqat as they strolled the ship, after a quiet dinner of provisions Jonah had taken, in haste, from Heron's quarters at the library. Melqat was looking at the stars.

"Greetings," he said to them, in a polyglot but passable Greek.

"What do you forecast of the sailing to Athens?" Ampharete inquired.

"Eurus is kind tonight. I expect an easy trip to Piraeus."

The easterly wind was not only steady but warm. Ampharete and Jonah stayed up most of the night, observing the stars, talking about the food and drink in Piraeus, and how long they should pursue the pleasure of the Athenian port before proceeding to the Academy and its library.

But the weather turned worse the next morning. By afternoon, the *Lux* was being whipped around like a puppet in Heron's steam show. "What happened to Eurus?" Ampharete called out to Melqat, as he and his mates worked to secure the lighter cargo.

"It seems Poseidon had other ideas," the Phoenician replied.

By evening, they were in a full-fledged gale. The sails were brought down, the oars came in. "We are not going anywhere in that," Melqat informed Jonah and Ampharete.

"Is the ship safe?" Jonah asked.

"Oh, the *Lux* has seen much fouler than this," Melqat assured them.

But Ampharete was not assured. "Our ship may be safe," she said to Jonah after Melqat had walked on, "but our itinerary could be blown to bits."

Jonah nodded and clutched his midsection. "Not to mention what I ate this morning."

"We have medicine for that." She reached into her robe and gave Jonah a small capsule. "Swallow this."

Jonah looked dubious. "What about you?"

"I have never been bothered by the sea."

A big swell convinced him. Jonah put the capsule in his mouth and gulped it down.


The temperature remained high, the wind strong and wet. Ampharete was sure it was blowing in the wrong direction. She and Jonah found a place that wasn't soaked. They drank wine and discussed places—real, imagined, and in between—places that Ampharete said would be real, someday. "Imagine a world that ran on the mechanical principles Heron has discovered, with machines that themselves were commanded by mathematical equations. That is my world," she said.

"Archimedes of Syracuse said, give me a lever big enough, and I can move the world."

"Yes."

"That is wondrous, but it is also cold." Jonah shivered a little.

"I am surprised to hear you say that. I would think, as a student of Heron—"

"There is much more to my mentor than mathematics and mechanical gadgets. For him, those are paths to the cosmic soul."

Ampharete nodded. "Our mathematical machines house and convey libraries bigger than Alexandria's, available to anyone in the world who wants them—any writing or image or sound in them, anytime. This, we hope, has made those holdings indestructible. Some say we help preserve and extend the soul of the cosmos, in that way."

"If you are so happy with your world, why are you so eager to change it by undoing the death of Socrates?"

Ampharete regarded Jonah.

"I am sorry," he said quickly. "I sometimes get cross when I have too much wine."

"Is that the only reason?"

Jonah peered up at the sky. "The storm is obscuring the stars . . . there is much in the way of my knowing you."

"I have told you far more about myself and what I am doing here than I had intended."

Jonah breathed in the wet, salty air. "I believe you." He opened the blanket that he had wrapped around him. "We can continue this in the morning. In the meantime, you are welcome to stay next to me in this blanket for the night, in case the sea turns cold."

Ampharete accepted and soon fell asleep. She moaned and shuddered, and Jonah was as powerless to stop it, as he was the wind.


The sea had turned not only cold but black and brooding by morning. Melqat confirmed Ampharete's misgivings. "We are south of Crete, and the winds are hustling us along in a southeast direction towards Africa, as you no doubt have noticed. My oarsmen cannot counteract that."

Ampharete nodded understanding.

"The shipmaster explained to you the terms of your passage?" Melqat asked.

Ampharete nodded again. "Yes, no refunds. But money is not the issue—"

"I know what you want. We will do the best we can. But our arrival in Piraeus may take an extra week or more than expected. Longer if we have to stop in Africa for provisions."

Ampharete thanked him.

"Does the delay matter?" Jonah asked, after Melqat had left.

Ampharete looked up at thick, gray clouds that buffered the sky. "You think the heavens are unclear?"

"I know. The heavens are nothing compared to the future."


The *Lux* narrowly avoided the sands of northern Africa. "But we are badly off course," Melqat explained, the next day. "I expect we will make first port in Sicily. After that . . . I am not sure. We might well get better prices for our cargo in Rome than in Athens. I am sorry, but, money moves the world."

"An interesting definition of Archimedes' lever," Jonah said, almost below his breath, as Melqat nodded and left.

Ampharete decided to confide in Jonah, at least somewhat more. "There is a device in Athens, near the Lyceum, that journeys through time. I suspect that is where Heron might have traveled."

"Will not the device be there regardless of when you arrive? . . . Are you are afraid Heron has taken it?"

"I am not sure who has taken it. All I know is that it will no longer be there sometime late tomorrow evening." She shook her head. "I should not have stayed so long in Alexandria, but your library was irresistible. . . . I wanted to arrive near the Lyceum shortly before the device was taken by Heron or whomever. If I had arrived too early, and my presence in the city became known, that might have scared away the interloper. . . . But that might have changed history, too. . . . I did not want that to happen."

"What are our choices? There are always choices. But I know of no ship or other device that can get us to Athens any faster—do you?"

"No. Not in this age."

"What else, then? Should we return to Alexandria? Seek our fortunes in Rome? Does either have a special connection to time? Heron never mentioned that they did."

Ampharete shook her head and took his hand. "Not that I know of. But there are two other places on this earth where there may reside such devices."


Melqat knew of both places. "Phoenicians have been sailing to them, on and off, for centuries. My own brother has been to Britannia several times."

Jonah nodded. "There are detailed accounts in the library about some of the voyages to the other place."

"It is all a question of time and money," Melqat continued. "If you are willing to wait until we complete this present voyage, to everyone's satisfaction, you can then have a conversation with the shipmaster. He is empowered to charter the *Lux* to you, outright, for sufficient compensation. He is an authorized agent of the merchants who own this ship. He pays me. He would likely agree to a voyage to Britannia. But, for a voyage to the other place, he would need something more—the *Lux,* after all, might not return from such a long voyage. We know, alas, of several voyages across the great sea that did not return. And, truthfully, I would need something more for such a voyage, as well—much as I love, personally, sailing to the ends of the earth." Melqat's eyes twinkled—more from the enticement of a long voyage than the money, Ampharete thought, but she could not be sure.

"The money is no problem," she said. "But I will need to think about the time."

"You mean, how long are you willing to wait for the *Lux* to be available for charter, or how long might it take to reach the other place, compared to Britannia? The longer voyage could take several months, according to the logs I have read."

"I am concerned about all possible sources of delay," Ampharete replied.

"You might try to charter another ship," Jonah suggested to Ampharete, later. "Surely the *Lux* is not the only one available for such voyages."

"I would not trust any captain other than a Phoenician." Ampharete looked at the sky and the sea. The storm had washed them crystal clear. Everything glinted in the sunlight, free for now of its gray captivity. "It is beautiful. If only our journey could be restored as fast as the sun." She sighed. "I suppose we could look for another ship in Sicily, captained by a Phoenician, and avoid waiting until the *Lux* discharges all of its cargo, passengers, and obligations."

"Melqat does seem a very capable captain," Jonah allowed.

"Yes, he is a good gubernator of the sea."

"How crucial is it that you reach the new destination, whichever it is, at a particular time? Is it . . . like Athens?"

"I am not sure. I have only seen one of them, in Britannia, in this time period."

"You did not arrive at Athens when you came to this time . . . our time . . . in the first place?"

"No."

"Of course not—you arrived in Britannia," Jonah said. "You mentioned Hadrian's Wall."

Ampharete nodded.

"So why do you not just return to that place . . . your time location in Britannia? Surely that trip is easier than—"

"No. The time device is gone in Britannia—it was set to be self-returning . . . do you understand?"

Jonah slowly nodded. "It went back to the place—the time—from which you departed, in Britannia in the future? As would a door that closes after opening, or a bird that returns to its nest? One of my mentor's greatest passions are devices that operate of their own accord, like living things."

"Yes."

"But why? Would it not make more sense for the device to stay—"

"And leave the device in a place where unknowing people might discover it? You see, near Athens, there is an excellent hiding place. But not in Britannia now. The hiding place there is very vulnerable to discovery. To danger. Ironically, very populated areas—like Athens today—can make excellent hiding places. Who cares about another closed door? But in emptier areas, new devices can stick out like wounded thumbs. Of course, in places with no population at all, hiding is not necessary."

"I think I understand," Jonah said. "And the place to the west, across the vast sea?"

"That place is so thinly populated, at present, and with people so primitive, and so unconnected to the rest of the world, that the device should be safe there. It is hard to imagine that any discovery of the device there, if it happened, could do any long-range harm. But I cannot even be sure any devices will be there."

Jonah considered. "Some think Simon Bar Kochba—one of my people who led a brave but unsuccessful rebellion against Rome—may have sailed there. I dismissed it as just another Atlantis tale. But now . . ."

"Your mentor may know more than he has told you."


"The breezes beyond will be cooler," Melqat said to Ampharete, as the *Lux* neared the western coast of Sicily. "You will require heavier garments for that voyage, whether to Britannia or the west, regardless of who captains you."

She regarded him. "I do not like waiting."

Melqat smiled. "I can appreciate that emotion."

She returned the smile. "I have an idea. What if I chartered another ship, to complete the *Lux*'s voyage back to Athens? It would take far less time to transfer cargo and passengers than for the round-trip from here to Athens—far less time for me to wait."

"You want the *Lux* that badly?"

She retained her smile. "I have grown comfortable with it, and her captain."

"And what about Heron's devoted student?"

Ampharete raised a questioning eyebrow.

"I was just wondering how comfortable *he* was with the *Lux*'s captain," Melqat said.

"Let that be my concern."

Melqat nodded. "I have docking preparations to oversee. Would you consider dining with me tonight, without the boy?"

Ampharete kept her smile. "Dinner? Certainly."


Jonah and Ampharete looked on as the first of the cargo was transferred from the *Lux* to the *Hermes*. The receiving ship was lighter, curvier, swifter, than the *Lux,* but less reliable for long voyages.

Ampharete leaned her arm over the side of the *Lux* and exhaled slowly. "Melqat says it may take a few days to acquire the needed replacements for the crew, and then the *Lux* will be on its way." Not every oarsman on the *Lux* had agreed to join the voyage west, despite Ampharete's promise of extra payment, up front.

"Fortunate that you brought along those gold coins," Jonah said. "I do not think I have ever seen a gold so clear and so pure."

"They were made by a different process."

"I understand. . . . One aspect of all of this which still makes no sense to me is why you did not take your time device directly back to the time of Socrates. Were you afraid you would be unable to find passage, back then, from Britannia to Athens? If so, then why did you not travel to Athens in your own time—you told me the city endures in your era—and then journey backward in time from that place?"

"There are many aspects of this that make no sense, to anyone."

"I know, but I am interested, in particular, in that one aspect that makes no sense," Jonah insisted.

"You want to know what exactly am I doing here, in this time, your time, when my concern is Socrates?"

"Yes."

"We have a description of a time traveler's encounter with Socrates—if the story in the dialog is true—which would mean that travel to that time is possible."

"Yes," Jonah said again.

"But I cannot seem to do it. I tried it. But there is something about this time, the reign of Antoninus Pius in Rome, that seems to block our attempts to journey further back in time."

"Why? What could that be?"

"I do not know. Some future historians think of his reign as the height of the Roman Empire—the time when it best achieved its deepest ideals. . . . Perhaps the time vehicles in some future age were purposely calibrated to come to this time, and no further back, and I happened to use one of those. . . . I am not unhappy to have met you in this time and place, however."

Jonah turned away from her and looked out at the sea.

She decided to pursue this part of the conversation no further. "I still need to learn what your mentor, Heron, has to do with this."

Jonah looked farther out into the sea. "Perhaps I will see my mentor when the *Hermes* reaches Athens, and I will learn the answer." He turned his sad, brown eyes to Ampharete. "But how can I convey the answer to you? I wish I could accompany you on the rest of the *Lux*'s voyage, but my place is with my mentor, if not in Alexandria, then Athens. That is still the most likely place to find him, even if, as you say, the time device is gone."

Ampharete nodded.

"We likely will never see each other again," Jonah continued. "The *Lux* and the *Hermes* will be traveling in opposite directions. Although . . ." He did not complete the thought.

"Yes," Ampharete completed it for him, "in the future, all roads meet."

CHAPTER 3

*New York City, AD 1889*

"Good morning, Mr. Charles."

"Good morning, Mr. O'Leary."

The two men shook hands in front of the Millennium Club. They were about to enter for lunch.

"Have you seen the latest in the papers about President Harrison?" Charles asked. "Every week, every day, we are paying the price for how that rascal came to win the election. An outrage!"

"Chauncey Depew should have accepted the Republican nomination," O'Leary said. "He would have won handily."

Charles scowled. "This Harrison business is the worst thing that could happen to the American political process. On the hundredth anniversary of the Constitution, no less. It shows the bankruptcy of the electoral college."

O'Leary smiled, sourly. "I agree completely about the electoral college. But I wouldn't bet that this is the *worst* that will happen. . . . Shall we have lunch?"

———

"I must say, the food here has much improved since the new chef arrived," Charles said, as the two put pearl-handled forks to their lunch. "This kidney pie is quite good."

O'Leary nodded and sipped his claret. "So, shall we get down to business?"

"By all means." Charles took another mouthful of pie.

O'Leary opened his portfolio and extracted a slim manuscript, all in Greek. "Do you expect Mr. Jowett might be amenable to translating this?"

Charles took the manuscript, looked at it, then at O'Leary. "You know, you look younger every time I see you."

"Why thank you. And you, as well. For me, it's no doubt the time I am able to spend by the sea."

Charles looked back at the manuscript. "Mr. Jowett is no youngster, you understand. I can't be sure he'll have the stamina, the concentration, or even the inclination."

O'Leary sipped more wine.

"But I do find this story as intriguing as the first time you showed it to me," Charles said. "About Mr. Jowett, I would guess his response would be governed, more than anything, by whether he thinks the account is true or apocryphal."


Thomas O'Leary walked southeast to Grand Central Depot after lunch.

Benjamin Jowett was in Oxford, England, Thomas knew. The ever-accommodating Mr. Cyril Charles had promised to send Jowett a letter about the manuscript, but his response could take weeks or longer to arrive.

Even though Thomas had all the time in the world in one sense, he was nonetheless impatient by temperament. Sitting around and waiting did not suit him.

Thomas boarded a Hudson River train to Riverdale. William Henry Appleton, also a member of the Millennium Club and the great American publisher of Charles Darwin, Herbert Spencer, and other notables, had a splendid summer residence up on a hill overlooking the river and had given Thomas a standing invitation to come by anytime he "found himself in the neighborhood." Thomas had tried to reach Appleton via the telephone recently installed in the club, but the publisher apparently had yet to install one in his summer home, so Thomas decided to find himself in Appleton's lush green neighborhood. Thomas had already told him about the manuscript.

The June afternoon was especially fine, and Thomas relished the walk up the long, winding hill.

Appleton's man Geoffreys brought Thomas into the study. The publisher was poring over some correspondence, but seemed not the least put out by the interruption.

"I'm sorry for just barging in like this—," Thomas began.

"Nonsense! Between the books that I publish and the letters I must read and write, I'm always in the market for some plain, old-fashioned conversation." Appleton brandished a stack of papers. "All of this is from your voluble namesake, Thomas Huxley!"

Thomas O'Leary smiled. "You have a wonderful spot here. The elms are magnificent, and I've never seen such a clear view of the Palisades."

"Thank you," Appleton replied, beaming. "The grounds are indeed superb. This house itself "—he gestured to several of the walls—"needs renovation and expansion. Shall we stroll outside?"


"I suppose you've come to talk to me about that new Platonic manuscript you have uncovered," Appleton said, as they walked by a tall stand of oaks.

Thomas nodded.

"It all depends upon whether it's real or a fake, now, doesn't it? Which is to say, that would determine whether or not I would be willing to publish it—in English translation, of course, by Jowett if we could get him, and with a suitable preface by yourself—and, of course, if it were real, I would almost certainly decide to publish it. But I'm sure you know that, already."

"What if I told you there was a way that we—or someone in whom we have complete confidence—could go back to ancient Athens and actually verify the account, firsthand, as an eyewitness?"

Appleton's eyes lit up for an instant. Then he laughed, heartily.

Thomas smiled, just a bit. "I assure you, I am not joking."

"If you are not joking, I would conclude that the very corroborating action you are proposing is itself a work of fiction, and I would recommend its publication as a dime novel, to a suitable house, which D. Appleton and Company most assuredly is not." William Henry Appleton, the son of Daniel, who had founded the company, was still smiling, though not as much as when he had been sure Thomas was joking.

"You are one hundred percent certain, then, that time travel is impossible?" Thomas asked.

"Yes." Appleton furrowed his brows. "Though perhaps ninety-nine and ninety-nine hundredth's percent would be more accurate. . . . I admit I am leery of pronouncing anything absolutely impossible these days, given that Auguste Comte once said that knowing the chemical composition of stars was impossible, shortly before the science of spectroscopy was discovered."

Thomas nodded. "Precisely. I once heard someone describe that ironclad attitude as 'never dogmatism.'"

Appleton grunted appreciation. "But time travel is a different matter."

"Is it? Are the years of our past more difficult to touch than the stars of our sky? We certainly have much more information about the past than we do about the universe beyond our planet."

"I suspect the mechanisms of travel are very different—and difficult—for time," Appleton said. "They would require more than the bump on the head received by Mr. Twain's Yankee!"

"Did you enjoy that novel?"

"Yes, I did. A very clever fantasy."

"You published Lewis Carroll," Thomas said. "Appleton and Company is no stranger to fantasy."

"That was my son's idea—I wasn't in favor of it. And we knew it was fantasy when we published it. . . . Are you proposing that we publish this dialog as fiction? The Royal College of Science did publish a delightful tale about locomotion through time just last year."

Thomas smiled. "'The Chronic Argonauts' by H. G. Wells. I expect we will be seeing a lot more from him. . . . But, look, as for my dialog, I am just hoping you will publish it, whatever its label."

Appleton nodded. "Nonetheless . . . we need to know whether the events it describes have any elements of truth, whether the manuscript itself is genuine or a forgery, before we can contemplate any kind of publication. . . . How did you come to get ahold of it in the first place? Most of the Platonic inventory came to Europe when the Turks sacked Constantinople, and Byzantine scholars fled to the West, isn't that so?"

"Yes," Thomas replied. "This Andros manuscript came to me a different way . . . which, I am afraid to say, may have entailed some travel through time, somewhere along the way."

Appleton shook his head, grunted again. "All right, I'll admit that I am a little interested—just getting a jump on Houghton in Boston would be sweet. They turned this project down, right?"

"Laughed me right out of the office."

"Well, believe you me, I would love to be the one who had the last laugh on this, at Houghton's expense and shortsightedness especially. . . . All right, then, will you stay for dinner? Fill me in, if you will, on this time travel business? Even as a form of fiction, it may have its appeals."


Dinner was succulent venison and plum. "The family is all off on vacation, on Cape Cod," Appleton said. "I'm on vacation up here on Wave Hill, from our Bond Street offices, and the family's all on vacation from me! What a life, Thomas!"

Thomas nodded compassionately. He was actually glad Appleton's family had temporarily deserted him for New England. Otherwise, he and Appleton might not have been able to have this crucial conversation. Thomas had found himself in this Riverdale neighborhood on a lucky day, indeed.

The butler excused himself, and Thomas resumed his explication— such as it was—of time travel.

"You see, I, personally, have no idea how the devices actually work. All I know is that they obviously do work, because I have used them, to get from here to the future, and to the past. I am pretty sure they were invented in the far future—though, as incredible as it sounds, I also have some reason to believe they may also have originated in the past."

"Originated in the past, or perhaps just arrived there?" Appleton asked.

"Well, that is indeed the question. . . . Are you familiar with an Alexandrian mathematician and inventor who went by the name of Heron?"

Appleton shook his head no.

"Not surprising—most of his work has been lost. But, apparently, he was a very prolific inventor—a Samuel Morse and Alexander Graham Bell and Thomas Edison all rolled into one, even a Leonardo da Vinci of sorts. He invented all kinds of things—water organs, gas organs, automated doors—years, millennia, ahead of everyone else! And the really peculiar thing about him is, no one is really sure exactly when he lived. Estimates pop up all over, from 200 BC to nearly 300 AD—"

"Not that remarkable in itself—after all, we know so little about those golden ages," Appleton said wistfully. "But you think this fellow Heron was hopping around in time and had something to do with that absconding of Socrates? Assuming the fantastic events in your dialog are somehow true?" Appleton shook his head in disbelief.

"Yes, I think Heron may indeed be a part of it."

Appleton wiped his mouth with a lacy napkin. The butler reappeared. "Coffee for me," he said, and looked at Thomas.

"The same, thank you," Thomas said.

The butler receded.

"So what, precisely, would you like from me at this point," Appleton asked Thomas, "other than an expression of possible interest in publishing the manuscript, which I am afraid is all I am willing to give you on that matter now?"

Thomas grew icy serious. "I intend to be traveling—through time. I want you to bear witness to what I have just told you and be prepared to perhaps publish something about that, as well, should I not be able to return."

"You do have a flair for the dramatic, Thomas."

The butler came with the coffee. The two men sipped.

"And if you, and the manuscript, turn out to be a fraud, you are prepared for me to bear witness to that, too?" Appleton asked. "Speaking, of course, only hypothetically."

Thomas looked at Appleton. "Yes."

"Do you intend to do this . . . traveling . . . all on your own? Would more people make it more dangerous?"

"Yes, but it's dangerous enough with just one, dangerous in many ways. I do have at least one . . . colleague . . . in mind."

"May I inquire who?"

"She is a student of mine . . . in another . . . time. She is bright and very poised."

Appleton sipped some more. "When would you initiate your trip?"

"If you agree to lend your support, very soon."

Appleton scratched his head. "I probably asked you this already, and you probably answered, but why, exactly, have you now approached *me* with this proposition?"

"You are the American publisher of Charles Darwin, the most important thinker of our century. You have a powerful sense both of what is right to publish, and how to make a profit from it. This escape of Socrates would fit right in with your inventory."

Appleton smiled. "If it really happened, it would easily exceed in importance anything else in my inventory." Appleton closed his eyes and grew even more serious than Thomas. "May I have until tomorrow evening to provide a response?"


The next morning, Appleton put aside his voluminous correspondence with Huxley, as well as a provocative manuscript by the German Ernst Haeckel, and picked up the small sheaf Thomas O'Leary had left with him. Appleton considered. The formal rules of the Millennium Club prohibited any business from being enacted on its premises, but some of his best acquisitions had come from connections made at the club.

The question regarding this bizarre dialog was whether it would be such an acquisition. As everyone in publishing knew, the woodwork was crawling with Platonic forgeries, some quite old—such as the *Epistles*, which, as Mr. Jowett had rightly noted, was constructed of passages plagiarized from Plato.

Well, there was no doubt, at least, that the dialog in front of Appleton had not been plagiarized from anything known of Plato. Not from anyone else, either, as far as Appleton could tell. It evoked a lot of Socrates, but Appleton had never come across anything even remotely resembling the core of this strange story.

Appleton applied himself to the pages. His Greek was actually a bit better than he let on.

SOC.: Have you considered the effect of drama, the theatrical reenactment, on human affairs?

ANDR.: I have, Socrates. But likely not in the way you would consider it.

SOC.: I consider such retellings to be disfiguring of the truth. Certainly they are not as legitimate as the conversation you and I are now conducting, in which all points of view can be expressed.

ANDR.: Does theater deliberately distort the truth?

SOC.: Yes, and it does so much in the same way as writing. The drama, written histories, are not just mirrors of what actually occurred. Rather, they choose from the life story, the truth of life, the points or examples they wish us to see and leave the others in darkness.

ANDR.: But are dramas and written accounts nonetheless not still worthy because of the truths that they do convey? Do not the comedies of your friend Aristophanes have barbs of value, in as much as some of the barbs hit the truth, or close to it, even as others may miss it?

SOC.: Yes, I suppose that is so. But would you also not agree that a lie that is close to the truth can do more harm than a lie that is so obviously incorrect that no one could mistake it for truth?

ANDR.: Yes, I would agree.

SOC.: So would that not be another problem with the proposition for escape you are offering me? You are trying to substitute a happy ending, dramatically satisfying, for the truth of my death?

ANDR.: No, I would not agree, Socrates. For three reasons.

SOC.: What are the three reasons?

ANDR.: First, who is to say what the truth actually is or was meant to be in this matter. Perhaps you were supposed to evade death, all along, and your dying is the result of some other tampering with the living flow of history. Second, I am not at all sure that escaping would be more dramatically satisfying—better for the story—than your dying. Self-sacrifice on behalf of a greater good has great dramatic appeal. That is in part why, in the plan I am proposing, your double would also die of the hemlock here, even as you escape. Third, if the choice were simply between dying now, and living, would not the living be, obviously and irrefutably, closer to a life story than death? Does not the distorting eye of drama inevitably follow death—indeed, excel in death—with life unable to continue to tell its own story?

SOC.: Those are indeed good reasons, Andros, and you present them well. I could offer arguments against each of them, but they would not sweep aside the essential grains of truth that your reasons possess. Still, your plan is futile.

ANDR.: Why? Are you saying that, even though you are perhaps persuaded by my arguments, you are nonetheless not going to follow their logical conclusions? That does not sound like the Socrates I know!

SOC.: Perhaps, then, you do not really know me as well as you suppose.

ANDR.: I know you from—

SOC.: Dramas, written accounts, forms less than life, yes. It does not matter. It will make no difference, to the present or future of the world, if I die here or escape with you.

ANDR.: Why not?

SOC.: You do not know the real, deepest reason I have agreed to die here.

ANDR.: The reasons you have given me—and Crito—are not true?

SOC.: They are true. But there is a deeper truth, below—

Appleton's reading was interrupted by a knock at the door. His man poked his head and his hand in. "Telegram from England, Mr. Appleton—"

"Haven't I told you about Coleridge, Geoffreys? How a knock on his door shattered his concentration, his vision, and so all he was able to produce of his beautiful dream was the glistening fragment 'Kubla Khan'?"

"Yes, you certainly have, sir. But you said you wanted to know the instant a reply arrived."

"True."

"And your door was already partially open."

"True, as well."

"And you were reading not writing, sir."

"Yes."

"And I don't believe you are in an opium trance—Coleridge was in such a state when the knock on the door broke his spell, is that not so?"

"All right, all right—let me have the telegram."

Geoffreys walked in and placed the telegram on Appleton's desk. "And would you care for some tea, sir?"

"Yes, thank you."

"Very good, sir." Geoffreys inclined his head, slightly, and left.

Appleton scooped up the telegram. It was from B. Jowett, Oxford. Appleton had sent him a telegram early in the morning New York time, almost noon in England. Appleton's query was lengthy and costly, but he figured the pursuit of truth and profit deserved no less.

"Unable to undertake the project you describe," Jowett's reply read. "Health failing. Aristotle taxing. Authenticity uncertain."

Appleton drummed his fingers on the table, read the telegram several times.

Geoffreys appeared with the tea.

"Never mind that," Appleton snapped. "I'm taking the train into the city."


"I thought I might find you here," Appleton said genially. He shook hands with Thomas, who was lingering over a bourbon at the Millennium Club's bar. "Should we retire to the library and a bit more privacy?"

Thomas nodded and took his bourbon.

"Anything for you, sir?" the bartender asked Appleton.

"No thanks, Franklin. Not at the moment."

Appleton and Thomas made their way to a quiet, out-of-the-way table. "Here's something you may find of interest." Appleton handed the telegram to Thomas. He looked at it, nodded, and returned it.

"Not surprising," Thomas said a bit wearily.

"In what way?"

"I'm referring to Jowett's skepticism, of course. Easy to be skeptical, when you do not have the evidence at hand."

"You mean the manuscript?"

Thomas nodded. "I don't suppose you telegraphed him that."

"No, but I did cable a few choice excerpts."

Thomas raised an eyebrow.

Appleton smiled. "If all I cared about was money, I could certainly make more in a carriage or haberdashery business. . . . But, Thomas, I actually find Jowett's response quite heartening."

Thomas raised an eyebrow further.

"A scholar such as Jowett does not use words casually," Appleton explained. "His health is not good, he is busy with a new Aristotle translation, and yet he is able to say, even in these circumstances, that the authenticity of your Platonic dialog is 'uncertain'—he just as easily could have said the dialog was rubbish!"

"You may have a point. What excerpts, exactly, did you cable him?"

"About half a page from the beginning, when Andros first appears, and then several from the middle, when he talks with Socrates about drama."

"Hmmm . . ."

"Frankly, Thomas, I am surprised you are not happier about Jowett's response—I do find it encouraging. What's the matter—"

Thomas batted the question away. "I agree, it could be encouraging. You are probably right about that. It's just . . . something else."

Appleton scrunched his face, a telegram of attentiveness. "Yes?"

"One of my colleagues—the young woman I was telling you about—seems to have gone missing. She did not appear when and where she was expected. You have no idea how . . . difficult, destructive that could be."

"To the girl?"

"To everyone."

Appleton absorbed that. "Of course," he said, after a few long moments. "If someone could travel in time—and, mind you, that is still a pretty big 'if' in my book—but if someone who was traveling in time went missing in time . . . that could well knock some little thing out of kilter, like the horse that lost its footing in the Roman cavalry, causing that rider to fall, losing that battle . . . causing the Empire to fall."

"Yes."

Appleton nodded—to himself, to Thomas, to unseen people that he imagined might be traveling through time, right by him, at this very instant. . . . "I should very much like to see the machinery—is that the right word?—for this time travel, if it exists. Is that possible?"

"It is not very far."

Thomas led and Appleton followed up a narrow, spiraling ladder—set, appropriately enough, against Jowett's and other translations of Plato, Aristotle, and the Greeks. Appleton noticed Xenophon's *Memorabilia* and Libanius' *Apology of Socrates.*

"He was a Byzantine," Thomas called down, as Appleton examined the Libanius. "That dates from about 350 AD—minor work, nothing there that we don't have in Plato and Xenophon."

Appleton nodded and returned the volume to the shelf. "I was just picturing a slim edition of your new dialog here."

Thomas smiled to himself. "A nice picture." He pushed on a trapdoor that opened upward. He entered and Appleton followed.

"Just like my neighbor's attic—," Appleton started to say, then stopped. "No, this resembles no attic I have ever visited."

The large room, lit with multiple skylights, contained a sleek, metallic chair in the center. Appleton approached. "Why do I feel like a moth to a flame? . . . May I?" He put his hand near the chair.

"Yes, please do. Touching will do it no harm."

Appleton touched it. "Not cool, like metal. Almost warm, like wood."

"It is some kind of composite—neither metal nor wood."

"Gutta-percha? Some kind of rubber, perhaps?"

"Perhaps."

Appleton ran his palm over the chair, then whirled around to Thomas. "I still do not believe this time travel business—I surely do not understand it. How can someone be missing? How can someone be late, traveling in time? A late time traveler—isn't that an oxymoron? Let's say your friend was delayed in the past or the future—could she not just set her machine, this chair, to return to this time, her appointed time, in any case?"

"Yes, assuming she was still—"

"Ah, yes, I see—assuming she was still alive! Sorry—I know you are discomforted by this. I didn't mean to be so blunt."

"That's all right," Thomas said. "Death is not the only reason some-one might be missing in time. She might have just decided not to re-turn."

"Yes, I see. So, someone not keeping a scheduled rendezvous means either they were deceased—because an ill or injured traveler could re-cover and keep the appointment—or made a decision to go it alone, to diverge from the schedule."

Appleton stepped away from the chair and looked back at it, around it, as if to see it in fuller context. He looked at Thomas. "How does it work?"

"A good question. Do you mean, how does it work in terms of how one would use a camera to take a photograph—what the photographer needs to know? Or, how does it work in terms of what principles and techniques were necessary for its construction—what did the inventor of the camera need to know?"

Appleton smiled. "I'll start with the average Kodak photographer—have you gotten your hands on one of those little boxes yet? They're quite something."

Thomas nodded. "Well, you see that little panel on the side of the chair? Go ahead, you can sit in it. I'll show you how it works."

Appleton approached the chair, then hesitated.

"Not to worry," Thomas said. "I won't actually send you back in time—I'll just show you how it would work."

Appleton nodded and sat in the chair. "Quite comfortable."

"Yes, it is. Now, if you drape your arm over the right side of the chair . . . that's right. . . . There, you feel the panel?"

"Yes."

"The touch of your palm should open it—yes, there it is."

"Can anyone's palm open it?"

"Yes. As far as I know. The outer part of the panel, I believe, is just there to keep the inner part safe from stray animals, inadvertent dam-age, what have you. . . . The locking feature is part of the inner panel."

Appleton ran his fingers over it. "Feels like the keys of a typewriter. We have several in the office—the secretaries love them."

"Good comparison."

"What happens when you press these keys?"

"Absolutely nothing, unless you know the correct sequence."

"Ah, I see. And what would happen if I did?"

"Several things. First, the chair would sprout a transparent bubble—as clear as glass, strong as Bessemer steel, even less combustible."

"Like a diamond crystal?"

Thomas nodded.

"What next?" Appleton asked. "How would I . . . guide it, to where I wanted to go?"

"A voice would speak to you."

Appleton laughed.

"I am serious," Thomas said. "As if through a gramophone, a voice—already recorded—would inquire of your destination."

"And I just tell it where, and this chair will take me there?"

"When, not where. If you leave from just off of Fifth Avenue, that is where you would arrive."

"I see. But . . . suppose I were to ask this chair to whisk me to the past before there was a Fifth Avenue, before there was even a city here?"

"That could be a problem."

"But, that aside, all I have to do, once I have engaged the voice by entering the required sequence, is say when in the past I want to go, and the chair will take me?"

"You could also typewrite the destination with the keys, if you did not wish to speak. And the chair could take you to the future, too. But, yes, that is the way it is supposed to work—in principle, at least."

Appleton caught the qualification. "Sometimes this chair doesn't work . . . the way you expect."

Thomas nodded.

Appleton placed his fingers on the keys and exhaled slowly. He started to vacate the chair, then reversed himself and leaned back into it. He started to speak—

"No," Thomas cut him off. "It wouldn't be wise for me to give you the sequence at this point."

Appleton nodded, reluctantly. "You're right, I'm sure. . . . You didn't invent this, did you?"

"No. I . . . happened on to it."

"Where? Here? In the club?" Appleton said in disbelief.

"Why do you think they call it the Millennium Club?"

Appleton laughed a little. "We are a full decade and another century away from the new millennium. I always did think the name was a bit . . . premature."

"Yes."

"You say you do not come from this time. Do you come from the time when this chair was invented?"

"No, I believe this chair was invented neither in my time nor your time, but in a time farther in the future."

Appleton took that in, leaned back in the chair once more, then stood. "I would like to believe you, Thomas. But I do not want that to cloud my judgment. We could settle this now, if you could show me indisputable proof."

Thomas smiled thinly. "I am going to leave in that chair, in a few moments. I always like someone to witness my departures . . . in case I do not return. I was waiting, actually, for another club member, Mr. Cyril Charles, to serve today in that capacity. But you arrived. If you would be good enough, after I depart, to convey my apologies to Mr. Charles, I would be in your debt."

Appleton nodded his acceptance of the task.

"But it might not be safe to be in the same room with a chair that is departing—or arriving," Thomas continued. "We're playing with powerful forces of nature here. . . . Might I suggest that you walk back down the spiral stairs, wait precisely a minute, and then come back up to the room? I'll leave the door unlocked for you. You'll confirm my successful departure when you see that the chair and I are no longer here."

*Right*, Appleton thought, *either a successful departure through time or you're some kind of damned clever magician.*

But a few moments later Appleton carefully backed his way down the narrow, spiraling ladder. When he reached the bottom, he straightened his vest, took a deep breath, and started to count. He thought he heard a soft, penetrating pop, like a bottle of wine uncorked, but he couldn't be sure. He reached sixty, took another deep breath, and climbed back up. The trapdoor was indeed still unlocked. Appleton entered the room.

It was indeed devoid of Thomas and the chair, but otherwise exactly as Appleton had just seen it. He walked to where the chair had been, got down on his hands and knees, and scrutinized the floor. As far as he could see, there was not the slightest indication that the chair had just been there. He ran his hand over the floor. Not even a difference in dust, though that was likely because the entire room was immaculate. He pulled out his magnifying glass. Fine print occasionally drove him to use it. His competitors had no regard for aging eyesight. He used it now to inspect the floor. Nothing unusual under this magnification, either. Perhaps a stronger lens would show more.

Appleton rose and looked around the room. He felt the way he did when he picked up a great manuscript for the first time. A Spencer, a Darwin, a Draper . . . He felt the swirl of the cosmos in this room. . . . He felt in touch with significance.

Which proved nothing, of course. Yet that was his feeling, and it was irresistible.

He straightened his vest, again, then climbed down the spiral stairs a second time. He looked at his pocket watch and marveled at how much had happened in the short time he had been in the club today. He put the watch back in his vest and walked back to the bar for that drink, after all—

Ah! And there was Cyril Charles, sitting at a table in the rear of the bar, with another, much younger man. Appleton approached the table—not sure, however, just what he would tell Mr. Charles, with this other man at the table. Maybe nothing. The man was well dressed. No, Appleton realized it was just that his clothes were brand-new. Appleton smiled, Charles nodded, and—

Appleton, focusing on Charles, bumped into another member, at large in the bar.

"Oh, excuse me," Appleton said.

"Sorry, excuse me," a familiar voice said.

Appleton turned. "My God—Thomas—"

"Apologies for my clumsiness," Thomas O'Leary responded. "Would you join us?" His hand swept to Charles and his young companion.

Appleton sat with the three men at the table. Though he had not yet even ordered his single-malt Scotch, he was practically in a stupor—he had just seen Thomas in that room upstairs, not ten minutes ago. Was there another exit that Thomas had not revealed? And how had Thomas managed to spirit that chair out of the room? "How—"

The bartender appeared with drinks. Clarets for Thomas and Mr. Charles, and a deep amber wine of some kind for the young man with the new clothes. "The usual, Mr. Appleton?" the bartender inquired.

"Uh, yes," Appleton managed.

"Very good, sir." The bartender turned away.

"You look a bit flummoxed," Charles said to Appleton. "Is everything all right?"

Thomas smiled brightly at Appleton.

The young man sniffed his drink and nodded.

"Why, yes, of course," Appleton said. There could be an explanation for this in the time travel, he realized, if time travel was indeed what was going on. "William Henry Appleton." He smiled and extended his hand to the young man. "What's that you're drinking?"

"Oh, sorry, boorish of me," Charles said. "Should have introduced you. He is Greek, speaks little English, I'm afraid."

"That is date wine he is drinking," Thomas added, still all smiles. "The bar here is extraordinarily well stocked."

Appleton's thoughts raced. One thing he understood: he needed to be exceedingly cautious about what he said. If some kind of time-travel business was afoot here, and he put his foot in his mouth, said the wrong thing—

"His name is Jonah Alexander," Thomas continued. "He will be visiting for the summer at the university. He arrived just this morning."

"New York University?" Appleton asked, because he knew it was safe to say. He knew Thomas was affiliated with that handsome terra-cotta building on Washington Square and Waverly.

Thomas nodded and looked at Appleton with a twinkle, or something special, in his eyes. *He knows that I know he teaches at New York University,* Appleton realized, *which means he knows that I am proceeding carefully with this conversation. . . . That must be good.*

The bartender returned with Appleton's drink. Appleton thanked him and stole a look at Jonah Alexander. He appeared to be about twenty-five years of age. Appleton could not decide if he was a graduate student or a young professor. Appleton also wondered about his name, which seemed as much Hebrew as Greek.

Appleton mustered his best Greek, smiled at Jonah, and said he was happy to meet him.

Jonah returned the smile. Then he said something Appleton could not understand.

"He speaks an older dialect," Thomas advised.

"Maybe we should confine ourselves to English," Charles harrumphed.

Thomas nodded and said something to Jonah in Greek not fully comprehensible to Appleton.

Jonah regarded Appleton. "Yes," he said in English, in a thick accent. He extended his hand and the publisher shook it.

"He is here to help with the new Socratic manuscript," Thomas said, and looked intently at Appleton. "I am glad we had the chance to talk about that, yesterday."

*I will not tell him that I already told him about the telegram from Jowett,* Appleton decided about Thomas at that moment. *Whatever is happening here, Thomas is either pretending very hard that the two of us did not meet in this bar, under an hour ago, or this Thomas—wherever he has come from in his travels in time—in fact did not meet me here, and take me upstairs, and introduce me to the mysteries of that chair.* In either case, Appleton saw no overriding necessity to ask Thomas how he could possibly have forgotten about the telegram.

"Yes," Appleton said. "It seems like a fascinating project. . . . I took the liberty of contacting Benjamin Jowett about it early this morning— I trust that was not too bold of me—"

"Not at all," Thomas said enthusiastically.

"Beat me to the punch," Charles said, a bit less so.

"Mr. Charles was going to put the manuscript in the post to Mr. Jowett," Thomas explained. "I have several more copies."

"Oh, well, please do so," Appleton said to Charles. "I just cabled a few excerpts to the Jowler, and I received a response—here it is." Appleton produced the telegram—the second time for him; whether likewise for Thomas, he could not tell.

Thomas looked it over, then at Jonah. Thomas spoke to Jonah in his strange-sounding Greek. Jonah responded, at some length, in the same dialect.

"It's still mostly Greek to me," Charles said, barely smiling.

"I can translate," Thomas offered. "He said no one other than Socrates and Andros themselves can know with certainty if the events in the dialog really happened. Unless someone else actually witnessed the events. But people closer to the events—in time—might have a better way of judging than people far removed from the events."

"And he is an expert in Socrates and the Golden Age of Athens?" asked Appleton. He looked at Jonah and smiled apologetically. He felt uncomfortable referring to people in the third person when they were in his presence, even if they spoke little English.

Thomas translated to Jonah.

"No. Later," Jonah said, in English.

"His specialty is Hellenistic culture, about 150 AD," Thomas added.

"I see . . . ," Appleton responded. He had a wild idea that perhaps Jonah's specialty was a very special kind of specialty indeed, a specialty that came of sitting in a chair that carried him from AD 150 to the present, but Appleton was getting to the point where he could no longer tell if he was reasoning well or imagining well. He confined himself to asking, "And was this manuscript known in Jonah Alexander's time—the time he studies, I mean—and lost thereafter?"

Thomas replied without asking Jonah. "Yes, perhaps so. That is what we are hoping Mr. Alexander will help us to determine."

Thomas and Jonah excused themselves a few minutes later. "He is tired from his trip," Thomas explained. He turned to Jonah. "An afternoon nap might do him good."

Jonah apparently understood enough of that to respond. "The air"—he touched his chest—"no good."

*Well, certainly not as good as by the balmy Mediterranean, 1,750 years ago, or anytime,* Appleton thought. "You have accommodations?" he asked Jonah and Thomas.

Thomas nodded. "He is staying with me, on the university's mews, for the time being." He extended his hand to Charles and Appleton and smiled warmly. "Thank you, for everything, both of you. We shall be in touch."

Appleton watched the two leave. "Shall we have a light lunch, Mr. Charles?"

Charles smiled. "Must it be light?"

The two walked their drinks into the dining room.

"So, when did you first meet Jonah Alexander?" Appleton asked, when the two were seated.

"Oh, couldn't have been more than ten or fifteen minutes before you appeared. The two were already at the table. They seemed surprised to see me—odd, because Thomas and I had made an appointment yesterday to meet here today. But . . . Thomas has not quite been himself recently. Likely because of that manuscript. Would you agree?"

Appleton's thoughts sped along a slightly different but connected path. First, if Thomas and the young man were at the bar down here at precisely the same time as Appleton had been with Thomas upstairs with the chair, that confirmed that some kind of impossible process had to be involved, which could just as easily be time travel as any other marvel that overthrew the laws of nature. Only an archangel could be in more than one place at the same time—and the last time Appleton had looked, neither Thomas nor anyone else in Appleton's acquaintance qualified.

But one way Thomas could be in two places at once was if there were two Thomases, from different points in time. . . . Now, then, Appleton knew he had been upstairs with one Thomas—Somber Thomas—and the chair. But if Appleton's crazy idea that Jonah was a visitor from the past was correct, then that meant Jonah had to have arrived in the chair prior to Appleton's and Somber Thomas's presence. Had he arrived in the chair that Thomas and Appleton had found in the room? But then, how did Happy Thomas—the Thomas who had just left with Jonah—arrive here? Had he just walked in the front door of the club and risked bumping into Somber Thomas, right in front of the doorman? Or had he taken a journey through time, too, after his visit to Wave Hill yesterday? . . . If so, where was *his* chair? Well, there was certainly space upstairs for more than one. . . . In any case, Happy Thomas and Jonah had to have come down the winding ladder before Somber Thomas and Appleton had gone up, if they had indeed arrived here in that room. . . . The club had plenty of out-of-the-way corners where they might have relaxed, prior to making their way to the bar.

Appleton realized with a start that Charles was looking at him. "It is a very complicated matter, this manuscript," Appleton replied. "What do you make of it?"

"The death of Socrates is one of the most important events in history," Charles said. "Every schoolboy knows about it. But it happened so long ago, we really know very little about it. Thomas's manuscript certainly could shed a whole new light on that tragedy." Charles shook his head, slowly. "But I don't know. The story it tells is so incredible—travel from the future to the past! Can that possibly be?"

Appleton considered what to say next. Did Mr. Charles perhaps know about the chair upstairs, and was he testing him? Or was he as he seemed, as ignorant as Appleton had been about the chair, until this last hour, and the proof that the presence of the two Thomases now seemed to provide? "You say you and Thomas had an appointment to meet here today," Appleton said. "May I ask if you and he had set an agenda? I don't mean to pry, but it may help us understand."

Charles nodded. "To talk about the manuscript. . . . And, oh, yes, Thomas mentioned something about showing me some piece of equipment."

Appleton sighed and decided. Thomas had not sworn him to secrecy. He would be betraying no confidence. In fact, to the contrary, Thomas had told him that he wanted Appleton to bear witness . . . and Thomas had said he had intended to show the room with the chair to Mr. Charles today. "Shall we delay our lunch, for a bit?" Appleton asked. "There is something I should very much like to show you."


Appleton climbed the ladder, with Mr. Charles behind him. Appleton pushed on the trapdoor and was relieved to find that it still opened. An oversight on Thomas's part, an error in a hasty calibration, or part of his plan?

Appleton was less happy that there was nothing in the room except daylight from the sky portals. He would have loved to have shown and explained the sleek chair to Charles. He would have loved to have seen and sat in it again.

But Mr. Charles was impressed with the room, nonetheless. "Quite an attic. The Club has no end to surprising places."

Appleton nodded. "This may be the attic to Attica."

"You think this is where Thomas discovered the manuscript?"

"In a manner of speaking, yes." But there was little point in being coy, at this juncture. "This may be where Thomas traveled back to ancient Athens to retrieve the manuscript, or—"

"What?" Charles looked around the room.

Appleton started to talk about the chair.

"Come now," Charles interrupted. "Even if that were possible, how on earth would Thomas, anyone, be able to get from here to Athens in the time of Pericles and Plato? Surely there were no sea vessels here capable of such an expedition—our city was inhabited by savage red men, back then. No mere canoe could have made such a voyage!"

"I have no good answer," Appleton admitted.

"But do tell me more about this chair."

Appleton told Mr. Charles everything that he knew about the room and the chair.

"Hmmm," Charles considered. "So you did not actually see Thomas leave, disappear, in that chair."

"No, but then how do I account for my seeing him up here, and then downstairs in the bar—with you and Jonah—immediately after? And you say the two were with you in the bar while I was up here with Thomas."

Charles considered. "I have no good answer to that, either. Perhaps Thomas has a twin."

Appleton chuckled, drily. "You mean like what the Andros character was saying about Socrates in the dialog?"

"I'm not necessarily saying someone created a twin of Thomas. Maybe Thomas has been a twin all along. . . . Look, that is certainly less preposterous than traveling through time!"

"That is true. But then we still have the problem of the manuscript—how it came to be, how Thomas got it in his possession—"

"I'll tell you what I think," Charles said quietly, so as to not let anyone hidden in the woodwork overhear the insult he was about to utter. "I think Mr. O'Leary is our writer. Mind you, I don't know what he hopes to gain by doing this. Or, perhaps he did discover it somewhere, or someone gave it to him—they are digging up all kinds of things out of Egypt, these days. I'm willing to grant him that. Have you heard about the recovery of Aristotle's treatise on the Athenian constitution? But whatever the explanation, I rather doubt that your traveling chair is—"

Appleton held up his hand, then pointed to the center of the room. "See that?"

Charles squinted. "It may be just be an odd cloud over the sun."

"I don't think so," Appleton said, staring. He was looking at air, through air, he realized, but something seemed to be *in* the air, coalescing from the air, like a swelling crystal of clear ice in a pool of transparent water.

"I think we best leave," he said to Charles shakily.

"Why?" Charles said, eyes fixed on the center of the room. "I am beginning to see something now, too."

"I want to stay as much as you, but Thomas told me it may not be safe— Look, let's just go down the ladder—we can wait there, listen for sounds of anyone walking around, and then come back up and see just who they are."


The two men huddled, ears cocked upward, at the foot of the spiral steps.

"I can't hear a thing," Charles complained.

"Nor I. But let's not talk."

"How do we know we are even safe down here," Charles whispered loudly. "If that mysterious force is dangerous, maybe it goes through walls."

Appleton glared at him. *Now he believes it.*

The two waited.

Charles started to talk— "Wait," he said excitedly. "Did you hear that?"

Appleton nodded. The sound was muffled. It reminded him of a freight train's echo, after it had hurtled by his home on the Hudson in the quiet night. Different from the wine bottle uncorking, but that chair had been leaving, and this one was presumably arriving.

And then the echo was gone.

The two men stood still, breathing heavily.

"Should we climb up and investigate?" Charles asked, this time in a genuine whisper.

"No harm in waiting a little longer. I saw no other exit, when I was up there with Thomas."

"You have the patience of a saint!"

"Comes from being a publisher."

Charles rolled his eyes.

But Appleton knew that, clever retorts aside, he could not be 100 percent sure that there was indeed no other mode of egress from the attic, as he had realized before. After all, he had not even known that there *was* an attic at the top of these stairs, before today. "You may be right," he said to Charles. "Let's proceed."

They started up the winding ladder.

They heard footsteps above as they reached the ceiling.

Appleton signaled that they should back down the steps. "Whoever it is," he said quietly, "we'll get a better look, and from firmer ground, when we're off of these stairs."

They reached the bottom and looked back up.

The door opened.

Appleton's eyes widened in involuntary admiration of the legs and backside that came into view.

Mr. Charles gasped. "Young ladies are not allowed in the Club unaccompanied."

# CHAPTER 4

*New York City, AD 2042*

"There's got to be a rational explanation," Max said, sipping white tea at Sierra's teak table in the kitchen.

A cup of tea was on the table for Sierra, too, but she was pacing. "He told me he was in Wilmington, he's vanished in the Aegean, his picture was apparently taken more than a century and a half ago—the only thing rational I can get out of that is he flat out lied to me, and likely more than once. The only thing I know for sure about him now is he's been missing since the weekend—or, at least, out of touch with me."

"Okay, he lied. Professors lie to students all the time—the recommendation was sent out last week, I'd love to let you in my course but the dean won't let me, I like students who ask difficult questions. . . . So he lied to you about Delaware. Maybe he likes his privacy. That's not what you're really upset about."

"I'm worried about him. What the hell's he doing in the Aegean? What the hell is someone with his face doing in the past?"

"Searching for Socrates?"

"If you're joking, I'm not in the mood."

Max put down his tea, stood up slowly, and opened his arms. "Come over here," he said softly.

Sierra shook her head, paced a moment more, then came to Max. He wrapped his arms around her, stroked her hair, kissed her gently on the forehead. "Let's try to start with what we know. We can leave the impossible, the paradoxical, till later. That photo on the Web isn't going anywhere."

Sierra nodded. "Okay."

They both sat at the table. Sierra tried her tea. "This is good—thank you."

"That tearoom on the corner is great," Max replied. "All right, look, I did a little research—before you called about Thomas."

"Yeah?"

"And I came across an old book by I. F. Stone—*The Trial of Socrates*—do you know it?"

Sierra shook her head no.

"Well, it doesn't say anything about Andros or a visitor from the future who tried to rescue Socrates, but it puts Socrates and his death sentence in an interesting light. According to Stone—who taught himself to read the original Greek—Socrates hated democracy almost as much as Plato did."

"Hmmm . . . the usual rendition is Socrates had it in for all kinds of governments, and Plato had the real animus for democracy," Sierra reflected. "Karl Popper considers Plato the godfather of all the totalitarian monsters of the twentieth century—a bit tough on Plato, I always thought. Stalin and Hitler had plenty to draw upon without Plato."

"Well, Stone agrees with Popper. He just thinks Plato got a lot of that from Socrates. He also thinks that kind of hatred would give Socrates another reason not to want to escape. Not because Socrates doesn't want to put himself above the Athenian government, but because he wants the Athenian government—the democratic government—to look especially bad, to all of posterity, by killing him."

"When was Stone's book published?" Sierra asked.

"Nineteen eighty-eight."

"Any chance he's still alive? We've got plenty of people walking around in their hundred and teens these days, with the gentherapy—"

"Stone died in 1989. He was already in his eighties when he wrote the book."

Sierra shook her head glumly and drank more tea. "Andros is saying there would be a clone of Socrates to take his place and die. In that scenario, the Athenian democracy would still have the death of Socrates as a blot on their record. But Socrates seems to be rejecting this incredible escape offer, anyway. So he must be rejecting it for another reason."

Max nodded. "All right, one more thing, then. And this may be the best or it may be nothing."

"Okay."

"I was able to get into the British Open University Online Holdings—you know, they're very restrictive, been that way ever since the pirates hijacked their system in the twenties. But I, ah, know some people with clearance at my school—one of the perks of being faculty, not student."

"And what did you find on the OU-OH?"

"I got to do an extensive search on Benjamin Jowett. The OU-OH has a listing of all of Jowett's papers and writings. Most are at Oxford. A few are at the British Museum. What do you make of this?"

Max gave Sierra a single sheet, a printout of part of the museum's Jowett holdings. These were dated 1889. One near the top had been circled by Max.

Sierra read it, aloud. " 'Rec'd from C. Charles, NYC, twenty-seventh July, Platonic dialogue, likely apocryphal.' "

"It's probably just that—another apocryphal dialog—Jowett no doubt received tons of those, some even written by his Victorian friends. Still—"

"No, this may be more."

"What makes you think that?" Max asked.

"Cyril Charles is the librarian at the Millennium Club who gave the fragment to Thomas. I tried to see him there today."

"Charles is a common enough last name. That part is probably just coincidence."

Sierra looked at him.

Max smiled. "On the other hand, there may be one *C* too many in that 'C. Charles' for just coincidence."


Max accompanied Sierra to the airport the next morning.

"You sure you want to do this?" she asked.

Max shrugged. "I have no classes or appointments today. If we stay in London any longer, I can get someone to cover. . . . This is more important . . . you're more important."

She squeezed his hand.

They walked over to the HST desk. The hypersonic flight would get them to London in an hour and a half.

"Another promotion special?" she asked.

"Frequent-flier miles. My rich brother earned them on his moon flight and gave them to me as a birthday present."

They were on the plane a half hour later. Sierra promptly conked out on Max's shoulder. Neither had gotten much sleep the night before, but Sierra had also had an exhausting day.

Max checked on his palm phone for any additional news about the missing boat in the Aegean. He and Sierra had been checking just about every hour.

No further news. Just that same initial report in the *Athenian Global Village* that Sierra had come across last night.

She shifted her head and moaned in her sleep.


*London, AD 2042*

"The British Museum, Great Russell Street," Max instructed the cabbie. The hydrogen car zipped out of Blair, the new HST annex. "I love these London cabs," Max said, "especially the way they make turns."

They pulled up to the museum thirty minutes later. "Almost as long to get from Blair to the museum as across the Atlantic," the cabbie commented in a singsong subcontinental accent.

They walked up the wide flight of stairs. "You think they'll let us in to see the Jowett papers?" Sierra asked. "I know, now's a nice time to ask."

Max smiled. "The Web page says they honor all university faculty IDs. I could have called them to confirm, but I might have been told yes, incorrectly, or no, incorrectly. We're better off being here and seeing for ourselves."

They entered the museum. A rippling holographic arrow pointed them to the library. Fortunately, just about everyone else seemed to be headed to the recently confirmed Ikhnaton mummy.

They passed the Ancient Greece section. They resisted the Elgin Marbles, but Sierra couldn't help peeking into an elegant little room that contained a carving of Socrates, a Roman copy of a Greek original dating from about 380 BC, some twenty years after Socrates had consumed the hemlock. The plaque called it "famously unattractive." Next to Socrates was a sleek statue of a fierce Molossian hound—Alcibiades, one of Socrates' most famous students, had kept one as a guard dog, the plaque advised.

"Doesn't look that bad to me," Max said about the Socrates.

"Probably looked nothing like him in any case," Sierra replied.

They left the room and approached the reference table. Max introduced himself, showed his ID, and explained his need.

"I'll check for you, sir." A redheaded woman, about twenty-five, walked off to a glass-enclosed room. In the revival of 2010s style that was currently sweeping London, one complete cheek of her backside was visible in the see-through jeans she was wearing.

Max grinned. "England swings."

Sierra shook her head.

The redhead returned, all apologies. "I'm terribly sorry, sir, but we don't have the Jowett papers now. They're on loan."

"On loan? But I checked your Web page just this morning, and—"

"I know, sir. We get complaints like that all the time. I'm afraid we're a bit behind in updating the page. I can chase the manager for you if—"

"No, not necessary." Max took a breath. "Do your records say where the papers are now—where they were loaned?"

"I can check on that for you, sir." She walked again to the glass-enclosed room.

Max was upset, but he enjoyed the second showing.

The redhead came back, with a big smile this time. "The Jowett papers are on loan to the Parthenon Library," she said brightly.

"I don't believe it." Max nearly cursed. Sierra did curse. "In Athens?" Max asked.

The redhead gave Sierra a look, then smiled at Max. "Oh, no. Course not. They're right down the street."

"The Parthenon Library?" Max asked.

She nodded. "It's part of the Parthenon Club."

Max thought. "Do you know if they let in the public, or professors visiting from America?"

"I doubt it, sir. The club is very restricted. Shall I ring ahead for you, just to be sure?"

"No thanks. If you could just give me their address, we'll walk over and check."


The two walked out into a cloudburst.

"It's refreshing," Max said. But the two went for cover under a green canopy on the sidewalk in front of the museum.

"These goddamn prehistoric clubs are going to drive me crazy," Sierra said. "What do you suggest we do?"

Max considered, then spoke to his palm phone. "Samuel Goldshine." Sierra looked at him.

"It's a worth a shot," Max said. . . . "Sam . . . Maxwell Marcus here." Max smiled and nodded. "Well, Sierra Waters and I are in London, right in front of the British Museum. . . . Yes, she very much appreciated your help yesterday, she had a wonderful time. . . . But, strange as it may sound, we now need to get into the Parthenon Club here in London, and I thought . . . Yes? Spectacular! That's just what I was hoping. . . . Okay, I really appreciate that. I'll wait to hear from you."

Max finished the call and looked at Sierra. "Many of these clubs have reciprocal arrangements with clubs in other cities. I remembered Sam told me that, when he took me to the Millennium. He said there were at least half a dozen just in London. We lucked out with the Parthenon."

"He's going to see if he can get us in as his guests?"

"Yes."

"Sweet man," Sierra said.

The phone hummed. "Sam? . . . Yes? Thank you! Much appreciated! . . . Sure, I'll tell her. Thank you. Thanks again!"

Max put the phone in his pocket and looked at Sierra. "He says the doorman at Parthenon will be expecting us. Should we wait out the downpour? Oh, and he said to tell you that he'll be having lunch at the Millennium Club later, and he'll see if Mr. Charles is in today, and he'll also try to find out anything more he can for you about the manuscript. I think he likes you."

They hurried in the rain along Southampton Row to the Parthenon.


The doorman was indeed expecting them.

"He looks even older than those hundred-and-teenagers you were talking about," Max whispered in Sierra's ear.

But the doorman not only welcomed them, but escorted them up a steep flight of stairs and across a mahogany-furnished room to the librarian's office. "Mr. Gleason should be back here in a moment," the doorman informed them.

And Mr. Gleason, argyle vest and tweed trousers, was indeed in front of them in a moment.

Max explained the purpose of their visit.

"I believe someone else is looking at them," Gleason said about the Jowett papers.

Max's mouth hung open.

"It's not quite the coincidence you might suppose," Gleason explained, in a lilting Irish accent. "He has been looking at those papers for several days now. Indeed, we borrowed the papers from the British Museum at his request."

"Can you tell us where he is now?" Sierra asked, as casually as possible. But she turned around and tried to make out who was seated in the large, dimly lit room.

"I'm sorry," Gleason replied. "I have no doubt told you too much about him already. I can tell you, however, that he is not in this room, which our members use only for casual readings of newspapers, periodicals, and such."

"Any chance at all you could tell us his name?" Max gave it one more try.

Gleason shook his head no. "Sorry. I wish I could be of more help."

"All right, thanks then, we appreciate your taking the time to talk to us." Max took Sierra's arm and turned to walk away. "Oh, one more thing." He turned back to Gleason. "Do you suppose we might, ah, avail ourselves of the club's dining facilities for lunch? We've come all the way from America, and we're famished."

"You'll have to ask the dining manager, Mr. Forbish, but I am sure the club would be able to accommodate you, on a pay-as-you-go basis, as special guests."

"Thank you," Max replied.

"Mr. Forbish is on the second floor."

Max and Sierra smiled and left the desk.

"So your plan is . . . ?" Sierra asked, as they walked toward the staircase.

"Not to leave this place until we find that man with Jowett's papers."


They had prawn à la Pericles for lunch. "Well, what do you expect," Max said. "We're in the Parthenon."

"It's good," Sierra said.

Two well-dressed gentlemen walked by and looked at their prawns, approvingly.

"The food is much better, since the new cook," one commented to the other, "wouldn't you agree?"

Sierra shook her head to Max. "We've got to come up with a better strategy. Whoever it is who's reading Jowett's papers could be walking by us right now, and we'd never know it."

"I know it," Max said doggedly. "I could try really pressuring Gleason in the library, but I don't think that would work."

The two continued eating and scheming. "I guess our best bet is going back down to the library," Max said, "making ourselves as inconspicuous as possible, and hanging out until Jowett's devotee returns the papers."

"Gleason strikes me as someone who would see us trying to be inconspicuous and confront us about it. Maybe we would be better off finding a comfortable place to loiter outside and see if anyone coming out of the club looks familiar."

"You're hoping for who, Thomas?"

Sierra shrugged. "The thought occurred to me. It would at least explain his absence."

Max ate the last of his prawns and sipped his sparkling plumcot water. He looked off into the distance, thinking.

"You seem to have an admirer over there," Max said, gesturing with his head to the back of the dining area, behind Sierra. "He couldn't be that interested in the prawns, not to mention they've already been eaten."

"Would it be too obvious if I turned around and looked at him?"

"No need to. He seems to be coming right this way."

"Ms. Waters? Is that you? Pardon me for barging in!"

Sierra turned to see a man in a starched white shirt and extravagant suit. He looked about seventy. But definitely not Thomas.

She smiled her best. "Do we know each other? Have we met? You do look familiar," she lied, to draw him out. Obviously, if he knew her name, he was more than a randy Brit.

He smiled. "Well, I can say *I* have met *you*. *You* have not *yet* met *me*, but you will, again."

No, not really British. His accent was American, almost New York-ish, but not quite that either.

"Why, was I sleeping?" she asked impishly.

He laughed. "I'm William Henry Appleton."

Neither Sierra nor Max immediately recognized the name. But it seemed, to both of them, that they should.

"Ah, the ephemerality of reputation," Appleton said. "There was a time when two young scholars such as you would have known the name Appleton instantly!"

"You were looking at the Jowett papers?" Max asked.

Appleton nodded. "Mr. Gleason downstairs was good enough to tell me of your interest."

"You published Charles Darwin and Thomas Huxley in the nineteenth century—or your great-great- or whatever grandfather did—I have some of your books," Sierra said, happy to have finally recognized the name, but astonished. Her stomach felt as if her prawns had sprouted wings there and become butterflies.

Appleton bowed slightly. "I am afraid to say, I am indeed the Appleton who did the deed."

Max was on his feet and pulled out a chair. "Please, would you join us?"

"You see," Appleton said conspiratorially, after he had seated himself and acceded to a cup of tea, "I must be exceedingly careful what I say to you, lest I unleash the hounds of paradox upon us."

"You met me in the past," Sierra repeated what he had already told her. Appleton nodded.

"Then, wouldn't it be safer—less likely to invoke paradox—if you weren't talking to us at all now?" Sierra asked.

"Yes, I am sure it would. But I have no choice—that is, if I want to be of help in this whole matter."

"How is that?" Sierra asked.

"You told me about this meeting, now, when we conversed in the past. Indeed, you *requested* that I meet you here today, because that was the final stimulus that started you on your journey—but I'd really prefer not talking about that part of our past conversation—the part that was about this meeting. It is a little *too* circular and therefore too dangerous—if you get my drift." He drew small circles in the air with his index finger.

Max shifted uncomfortably in his seat.

"Oh, you needn't be concerned about your presence here, Dr. Marcus. Ms. Waters mentioned that you were—would be—here for this conversation."

"Thanks," Max said a bit sourly. "But that wasn't really what I was most concerned about. Can you tell us about the Jowett papers you were looking at?"

"Oh, by all means. I was comparing Jowett's copy of the manuscript with the one I brought along with me. You of course have seen part of it, as well."

"The part I've seen was supposedly unearthed in Alexandria in the early part of our—twenty-first—century," Sierra said. "You're claiming you've come here from . . . ?"

"From the year 1889."

Max looked at Sierra, to make sure she recalled that was the date from the page of the Jowett log.

"So the copy of the manuscript in your possession cannot be the copy I have seen, assuming its account of where it was discovered is true," Sierra said.

"Well, that would not be impossible by any means. That is to say, I know, for a fact, that I have come here from 1889, with a manuscript in hand, and it is nonetheless quite possible that you saw a fragment of the same dialog—another copy of it—that was buried in Alexandria until the beginning of this, your, century. But, it could well have been one of my copies, rerouted through my future and your past, you see."

Sierra sighed.

Max spoke. "Can we see your—or Jowett's—manuscript?"

"I don't think that would be advisable. It is too soon."

"That's ridiculous!" Sierra exclaimed in sheer frustration.

Max's palm phone beeped. He had set it to check for further news about Thomas. He shook his head. "Nothing more," he said to Sierra, "just a reprint of the same story, now in the *EU Mercury*."

Appleton's eyes were on Max's hand. "Is that a *carte de visite?*"

Max half-laughed. "Yeah, in a way, it is. A calling card, circa mid-twenty-first century."

Sierra softened, a little. "I'm sorry to be cross-examining you, Mr. Appleton. Can you tell us what you wanted to talk to me about—what it was that my future self asked you to brief me about, to prime me for, when she, I, talked to you in the past?"

Max nodded encouragement. Even if this guy was a complete nut, it couldn't hurt to hear what he had to say.

Appleton sipped his tea. "Quite good. But, honestly, not as robust as what I am used to."

"It's all in the water," Max said.

Appleton nodded. "I would like to talk to you," he said to Sierra and Max, but mainly to her, "about whether you think the story in the dialog—that is, as much as you have been able to read of it—is true."

"Do you?" Sierra asked.

"Well, how am I here?" Appleton answered with a question.

"And from that I'm supposed to conclude . . . ?" Sierra asked.

"That time travel is possible. And if that is true, then that makes the dialog believable."

"We don't know for a fact that you time-traveled," Max pointed out.

"Or even that you are really William Henry Appleton—or *the* William Henry Appleton."

"I could show you pictures."

"DNA facial reconstruction," Max countered.

Appleton looked confused.

"It would work like this," Max continued. "You're not Appleton; you want us to think you're Appleton; you get DNA from one of his descendants and grow a new Appleton-like face from it."

"What is DNA?"

"It's . . . it's the way in which characteristics are inherited in evolution," Sierra answered.

Appleton struggled to understand. "The vehicles of Darwin's natural selection, that allow organic traits which survive, which are naturally selected, to move from parents to offspring?"

"Yes, that's it." Sierra nodded. "These . . . vehicles determine what we look like—what our faces look like, basically. So, Max was saying that, for all we know, you could be someone other than William Henry Appleton, who obtained his DNA—the vehicles that determine what we look like—and you used them to make your face look like Appleton's. We know how to do that, in our world."

Appleton looked at Max. "I would say that's preposterous, but I have recently learned to be more judicious in use of that word. Would the process you describe work for underlying bone structure?"

"No," Max admitted. "But you might have had a bone structure similar to Appleton's in the first place."

Appleton considered. "Fair enough. . . . Let us try a different tack, then. Have you no other evidence of time travel, other than my audacious claim?"

"The photo of Thomas," Sierra said quietly to Max. "In front of the Millennium Club in the 1880s."

Appleton heard it perfectly and smiled with pleasure. "Precisely. And the Millennium's much nicer than the Parthenon," he whispered, "wouldn't you agree?"

"How well do you know Thomas O'Leary?" Sierra asked.

"He was the one who first drew me into this, I can tell you that."

"His modus operandi," Max muttered.

Sierra ignored it. This time, Appleton either did not hear or pretended as much.

"How, exactly, did you get here?" Sierra asked him.

"I traveled forward at the Millennium Club in New York—I arrived there a few weeks ago. Then I flew here—air flight is magnificent!—and waited for you to arrive."

"You came here to meet us because I asked you to," Sierra said.

Appleton nodded.

"But that request was made in my future, and it was intended to get me to that place—that time—to make the request. When exactly did that request originate, in the first place?" Sierra asked.

"I don't know. You'll have to ask yourself."

Sierra scoffed.

"I apologize for seeming to make light of that aspect," Appleton said. "It's a snake swallowing its tail, a mirror pointed at a mirror . . . that's why it's better not to talk of that."

"What else do you . . . did I . . . want me to do?" Sierra asked. "You mentioned starting on my 'journey.' "

"You are actually already embarked upon a journey, if you think upon it. You wanted me to encourage you to continue that journey, so you could help save Socrates!"

Sierra scoffed again, louder. "What makes you think I want to do that? I don't particularly feel that way now."

"No? Why, then, are you here?"

"I'm here because of Thomas," Sierra said hotly. "If I want to save anyone, it would be him."

"You don't care about Socrates?"

"I didn't say I don't care about him. Obviously, I'm interested in him, and what happened to him. Any person with a working brain would be. Hell, the only death that received more attention than his in history is Jesus Christ's. But that doesn't mean I'm obsessed with saving Socrates!"

"You don't care that he died, what that meant to freedom of speech?" Appleton pressed.

"Yes, I care, I just said I did. And, yes, I believe in freedom of speech."

"Then wouldn't you want to stop that Athenian jury of five hundred from sentencing Socrates to death? He was sentenced because they said his speech was corrupting the morals of minors. They were not talking about lewd activity—they were talking about plain politics!"

"Let's say Socrates wanted to die?" Max spoke up. "Suppose he wanted to die because he wanted to discredit the Athenian democracy. Would you deny him his right to die?"

"Yes, I would. And all the more reason if somehow, in his tortuous reasoning, he thought his death would make Athens, the birthplace of democracy, look bad."

"You don't seem to have much regard for Socrates, yourself," Sierra said.

"I never said I did. Only that his rescue would be worthy."

"God, I feel like we're in a Platonic dialog right now, right here," Max said.

Appleton just smiled.

"Did you write that dialog?" Sierra asked him.

"I am very flattered. But I assure you, I did not."

"How can you be sure of that, given what you know about time travel?" Sierra pressed. "Perhaps you will write the dialog in your future."

Appleton nodded acknowledgment. "Yes, I would have to admit that I cannot rule out anything in my future entirely. All right, then, I'll amend my previous statement to, I feel certain, indeed in my very bones, that I am not the author of that dialog."

"Why don't *you* go back to 399 BC and save Socrates?" Max said impatiently. "For all we know, you already did."

"I assure you, I am not Andros."

"You just admitted you couldn't give us any assurances," Max said.

Appleton nodded. "Yes, but Andros is described in more detail in a part of the dialog I believe you have not seen. That description is clearly not me."

"Is it me?" Sierra's voice quavered.

"That is not clear. Though the name Andros certainly suggests the masculine."

"Will you show it to us?" Sierra asked. "I mean, at least that part that describes Andros?"

Appleton considered. "Yes, I will." He signaled the waiter. "Put this on my account, please. Thank you." He turned to Sierra and Max. "I found, when I arrived in New York in your time, that my lifetime membership at the Millennium was still valid, after all of these years—more than one hundred and fifty years, in fact, plus I no doubt already expired back then." Appleton rolled his eyes. "It's absurd, I know, but there you have it and here I am. That's what I call support for the membership! And, of course, we have always had reciprocal arrangements here with the Parthenon."

The three made their way, in edgy silence, down to Gleason at the librarian's desk.

But the desk was empty. "Unpersoned," Max noted the obvious.

"Hmm," Appleton grunted. "I'm sure he'll be back in a minute."

But the desk was still unpersoned ten minutes later.

"What is it with these club librarians?" Sierra complained. "The Millennium was missing their librarian yesterday, as well."

"Really? Not my experience with either club, at all," Appleton said.

The three shuffled their feet and juggled their anxieties for another few minutes.

"All right," Appleton finally said, frowning. "Perhaps there is another way of getting at this. Would you care to follow me?"

He started walking before he received a response. Sierra and Max looked at each other . . . and followed.

They reached the other end of the room, and a door with a gleaming new keypad. Appleton seemed familiar with it. He ran his fingers over the keys and opened the door. "I believe it's not just the keys but my palm signature, as it was explained to me."

They walked down a long flight of stairs. Lights invoked by their presence flickered into a soft, soothing glow.

Two sleek chairs came into view, in the center of the otherwise unfurnished room.

Appleton introduced the visitors to the chairs. "Those can provide another way that you can obtain the dialog, perhaps even more."

Max and Sierra approached the chairs. "These don't look like reading chairs," Sierra said.

"Well, I suppose you could sit and read in them, but—"

"Sierra is referring to chairs we have, in this century, in which you sit back, and a screen emerges from an arm, and you can read any book you like," Max explained.

"Ah, no, these would not be that kind of chair."

"So, you took a chair like that from 1889 in New York City and arrived in our time in New York, 2042, then boarded a plane here to London with the reservation Thomas left for you. . . . But you have not actually . . . traveled in either of *these* two chairs," Sierra reiterated for her own understanding, after Appleton had told them what he knew about the chairs.

"Yes, that is correct," Appleton said, still not happy with having to explain all of this to Sierra and Max. But with Gleason absent, and Appleton's primary charge to get Sierra on her way, he had no choice.

"And where, exactly, do these chairs—all of the chairs—come from?" Max asked. "Who put them in the Parthenon and the Millennium clubs?"

"I honestly do not know."

"But you believe these chairs can only go back in time, not forward from here?" Max asked.

"Yes. Thomas sketched that part of this out to me. And some of this I figured out myself, and it was not quite as Thomas had said. Perhaps there are different levels of control, dependent upon the traveler's possession of different codes. In my experience, once you sit in the chair and initiate its activity, you are provided with a menu of choices—they are recited to you. None of the destinations are beyond this, your, time."

"What's the earliest?" Max asked. "The time of Pericles, Plato, and Socrates?"

"No, that is one of the frustrating aspects. The earliest time that I seem to have access to is 150 AD."

"So, assuming we also have access to that time in these chairs, how would that give us a look at the dialog?" Sierra asked. She realized the answer a split second later. "Because 150 AD is much closer to 399 BC and the death of Socrates than we are now."

Paul Levinson

"Exactly," Appleton said. "And I was thinking, if you could arrange a visit to the legendary Library of Alexandria—reputed to have a copy of every manuscript ever written and disseminated in the ancient world—well, that library might well have a copy of our dialog. But such a journey would be very hazardous—I assume any journey would be, that far back in history."

"But the journey would tell us something, even if the library did not have a copy of the dialog," Sierra mused.

"If the chairs move us in time, but not place, how would we get from London in 150 AD to Alexandria?" Max inquired.

"It was Londinium, then," Appleton replied. "Roman, of course. The Romans obviously traveled regularly to and from London, then, so there shouldn't be too much of a problem. And Rome to Alexandria would be easy in just about any century."

"I see you've given this some thought," Sierra said.

"Well, yes, I was thinking of undertaking the trip myself. Would you care to join me?" Appleton asked Sierra. "There are only two chairs, as you can see," he said to Max apologetically.

"I thought you said it didn't make sense for you to travel back to that time," Sierra said.

"I said I wasn't Andros. And we're not talking about precisely that time, anyway."

Max swiveled around and lifted himself into one of the chairs. "It does feel comfortable, I'll give it that."

Appleton looked at him, understood his intentions. "It won't work without the code."

"I'll put it to you this way," Max responded. "If Sierra goes back at all—if these contraptions do work—I'm not letting her go back with you."

"Max—," Sierra began.

"Gratifying to see the age of chivalry yet survives," Appleton said drily. "But there is no record of you appearing anywhere in the past, so, you see, you cannot—"

"I'm not getting out of this chair," Max insisted. "What are you going to do, get club security or Mr. Gleason down here to help you?"

Appleton considered.

"Look," Max said to Sierra. "If you want to walk away from this, that's fine. But if you're thinking of accepting Mr. Appleton's invitation, let me come along with you. I'm a bit more agile."

"That's not the point," Appleton said.

"Are you concerned that Max's going back could cause one of those snakes to swallow its tail?" Sierra asked.

Max joined her in drilling Appleton with their eyes.

No one moved or said anything further.

"All right, then, go," Appleton said very reluctantly.

"I'm still not sure *I'm* going," Sierra said. "Where, exactly, will we end up when we've traveled through time? . . . This is crazy."

"Presumably right here, in a structure that existed in 150 AD," Appleton said. "There should be provisions for you there—clothing, money."

"How do you know that?" Sierra asked.

"The people who built these chairs, whoever they are, provided receiving vestibules at the destinations. I was told there was one in 150 AD in New York—well camouflaged, presumably, from the red men back then. There must have been something similar in London."

Sierra thought. She slowly nodded and sat herself in the second chair. "What about your classes at Fordham tomorrow?" she asked Max.

He grinned. "When we make the return trip, we'll just come back today, or earlier. Isn't that how it works, Mr. Appleton?"

The publisher nodded.

"What is it in your part of the dialog that makes you sure you're not Andros?" Sierra asked him. "Can you at least tell us that? You're getting what you wanted from this—I'm going ahead with the journey."

"Andros is younger."

Sierra sighed, closed her eyes. "Maybe we'll also be able to find out more about Thomas," she said to herself.

Appleton gave them the codes.

Clear bubbles emerged, two crystal cocoons.

Appleton hurried up the stairs and closed the door.

"Mr. Appleton." Gleason's voice surprised him from behind. "We have an unexpected visitor. He is . . . availing himself of the facilities at the moment. I asked him to meet us here."

"Who—?" Appleton began.

Jonah Alexander strode up and nodded. He looked around. "Where is she?" he asked in Greek.

"On her way, to your time," Appleton replied, in English.

"I thought you were going with her," Gleason said.

"Her companion insisted otherwise. He took the other chair. She would not have left, without him."


*Londinium, AD 150*

It was just a heartbeat, an eyeblink, and the bubbles receded.

Sierra and Max looked at each other. They knew immediately that they had traveled to a different place. The air was sweeter, richer—earthy and intoxicating.

Their eyes did not take too long to adjust to the new lighting. It was almost the same as in the basement of the Parthenon Club. But this was daylight.

That was the only thing similar. The structure that surrounded them was considerably smaller than the spacious Parthenon basement, and it seemed to be made of sandstone. Clusters of thick, little translucent windows were on all four walls.

"The Romans built this?" Sierra asked, still seated.

"I'm no expert, but I'd say it's more likely someone built this to look like it was Roman, probably even more from the outside." Max glanced around the enclosure and gestured to what looked like a small hearth, made of gray stone, against a far wall. Something seemed to be glimmering inside it. "That's definitely not Roman," he said, and walked over to investigate.

Sierra joined him.

The glimmer came from a screen. It said, in English, "Our records indicate that there are two of you, English is your primary language, and you are in no need of further assistance. Please confirm by pressing the lower left corner of the screen, twice. Confirmation must be received within sixty seconds."

"Or what?" Sierra asked the screen.

A clock with a ticking second hand appeared.

"I don't think it's voice-enabled," Max observed. "Whoever wrote this likely didn't want to be overheard."

"Nice of Mr. Appleton to assume we wouldn't need any assistance."

"He likely didn't program this. Who knows what screens he was shown on his travels."

The second hand passed the 4.

"We're not even sure we're in 150 AD," Sierra said.

"The only other choice was 1889. I suppose we could be in some primitive dwelling somewhere then—hell, we could still be someplace in the twenty-first century. There's no way we'll be able to tell for sure from this vantage point." Max looked around and suppressed a shiver, even though it was not very cold. He pointed to the hand on the screen. It was rounding 8. "Twenty seconds to go. Your call."

Sierra was breathing heavily. "I—"

They heard a noise outside. "Was that a horse?" she asked.

"Not sure."

Sierra cursed, then leaned in and pressed the lower left corner of the screen, twice.

Four things happened:

- The two chairs made some sort of sound.
- The message on the screen changed. It read, "You can return here anytime. Your presence will be recognized, and return conveyance will be provided." Then those words vanished, and the screen was blank.
- Two big stones in the hearth parted, revealing a cache of clothing within.
- And some kind of projection device, inside the hearth, cast a light on the right-hand wall. The outlines of a door, worked out of the sandstone, became visible.

"I take it that's our exit," Max said.

"We're probably supposed to put some of that on, first." Sierra pointed to the clothing.

They were nondescript one-piece garments. "Togas," Max said, trying to make sense out of his. "I guess these can go over what we're wearing?"

"I don't think whether they fit over our clothes is the issue. We probably should be more concerned about what the Romans would say if they got a glimpse of these colors and fabrics." Sierra undressed. She could feel Max's eyes on her body, as she reached for a toga. She smiled at him. "Your turn."

Max exchanged his clothes for a toga. "It looks like one size fits all."

Sierra nodded. "I hate to leave those chairs. Probably that's why they cleared their throats before—to let us know they're available for the return trip right now if we want it."

"Let's hope they're here when we return. The screen said conveyance would be provided."

"Yeah," Sierra said, not very reassured. She took his hand.

"Appleton said something about money." Max looked around.

"I thought I felt something sliding around in here. I mean, in the togas." Sierra ran her hand through her garment. "Wait. Here." She produced a fistful of high-denomination coins. "And here." She fished through more folds. Max did the same with his. Both togas had literal silver and gold linings.

"Appleton, or whoever's running this, is well connected through the ages," Max observed.

Sierra nodded and sighed. "Is your Latin okay?"

"*Satis.* Anyway, I recall reading that they're already speaking some sort of slang here at the peripheries of the Empire. So if our accents sound strange, we can just tell them we come from the other end, from Egypt, and we're talking southern jive."

Sierra shook her head. They collected their twenty-first-century clothes and put them between the two stones in the hearth.

"I think we'll have to risk wearing our shoes," Max said, glancing at his autumn-leaf bucklers. "We won't get very far barefoot."

Sierra agreed. "Mine look a little like sandals, anyway."

The two headed through the door.

Max emerged first. Sierra followed, but held on to the door. "Should I let it close? It feels like it's going to swing tight shut."

Max looked at her and the door.

"We could be locked out," she said.

Max examined the outside of the door, and the stonework around it.

He pointed to a small, quartzite slab. "This could be some sort of scanning device." He put his hand against it. Something clicked and clacked in the door. "It could have received our palm prints from the chairs."

"Yeah. But no guarantee it will work once the door has slammed shut behind us."

"No guarantee about anything," Max said.

Sierra let the door close. She placed her hand on the translucent slab. Nothing happened. The door remained closed.

Max cursed. "Let me try." He placed his hand on the slab and got the same result. He pounded on the door until his fist hurt.

Sierra, pacing to and fro, muttering, put her hand on the slab again. The door clicked and clacked—and cracked open. "Yes!" She breathed in and out, clapped Max on the shoulder, and opened the door. She stuck her head inside. "Oh, no!"

Max put his head next to hers. The chairs were gone.

"I saw Appleton hustle up those stairs right before our chairs took off," Max said, thinking out loud. "Maybe it's unsafe to be close to the chairs when they're revving up for travel. Our two chairs waited until we were outside, locked us out, and left."

"Why'd they leave?"

"I don't know. Appleton called them back to 2042, they returned there or to some other time, automatically. . . . Who knows." Max shrugged, shook his head angrily, and kicked the door, which Sierra and he were still holding open.

"What do we do now?" Sierra asked. "Maybe holding this door open is preventing them from returning."

Max considered, then took his hands off the door. "The screen said the chairs or whatever would be here for our return."

"Lot of damn faith to place in a glimmering screen." Sierra looked at Max, the sky, and then let the door go, too.

It closed quickly.

Max's hand reflexively shot out to the slab. It clicked and clacked, and the door cracked open, again. "At least we know that this door mechanism works. We can go back inside and see if we can summon the chairs. Or we can see what Londinium holds."

Sierra was undecided. "All right," she said at last. "Let's at least try to verify that we are in 150 AD. We can always rush back here if the Romans don't like our Latin."

Sierra and Max walked up a small incline. She looked beyond. "Reminds me of Vermont."

Max joined her gaze. "Yeah, or New York east of Jamestown." He turned and took one last look back at where they had been. "Not much more than a pile of rubble, half-buried in the ground, from this angle. Good camouflage."

Sierra squinted at the sky. The sun was buffeted with clouds, but the gray and white were bright. "Hard to tell precisely with those clouds, but I'd say it's midafternoon."

Max nodded. "Or right after lunch. Those chairs were certainly precise."

"So, we have, what, five or six hours to sundown?"

"Yeah." Max looked around. "I'd say the Thames is that way, south. Let's hope we don't have to wait too long to test our Latin."

*"Tamesis fluvius."*

They trudged down toward the river, on light reddish soil.

"Can a ship really sail from here to the Mediterranean?" Sierra wondered.

"Look at those wharves," Max responded. "And the size of those boats. This is a major river port. I don't know if they run ships from here to Rome on a regular basis, but it can certainly be done."

They saw two men ahead—tall, reddish brown hair like the color of the soil, in their midtwenties like Sierra and Max. "Celts, I guess," Max said.

Their mellifluous speech, incomprehensible to Sierra and Max, confirmed it. The Celts approached the two visitors, singing at Max, looking at Sierra. The pleasure in their eyes when they regarded Sierra was perfectly clear.

Max was glad to see they were unarmed. "Max," he said, and put his palm to his chest.

"Maximus!" one said, and laughed. "Hail, Caesar," the other said in Latin, and laughed, too.

Max smiled and summoned his best Augustan delivery. "Can you take us to Rome?" He reached in his toga and pulled out a silver coin for each Celt.

The two stopped laughing and looked intently at Max and Sierra. "They're probably deciding whether to kill us and take the rest of our money," Sierra whispered in Max's ear. "But this is the height of Roman domination of Britain, if I remember correctly, so we may be okay."

The Celt who'd said "Maximus" nodded. "Follow us," he said, in Latin.

Many more people, Romans and Celts, soldiers and tradesmen, women and children, were mingling by the river. Grain, cloths, pottery, copper, and iron all seemed to be doing brisk business.

"It's the parade of London, all right," Max remarked, "but there's not much else recognizable." He looked around and across the river. "I guess that could be the Southwark promenade."

"Without the digital inlay," Sierra agreed.

Their guides studied them. "Germania?" one of them asked Max.

Now Max laughed a little and nodded. "I can understand why you'd think that," he replied, in English.

"We will introduce you to a shipmaster," the Celt said, in Latin.

"Thank you," Max replied, the same way.

The two Celts walked away.

Sierra looked discouraged. "You've got a lot of confidence in people."

Max grinned and patted his toga. "I have a lot of money, so do you. If those two silver pieces bear no benefits, we can try someone else."

"You're getting more eloquent by the minute."

"Yeah, England is good for my diction, in any century— Ah, here we go. That was fast."

The two Celts returned with a third man, about ten years older, who also appeared to be Celtic.

"You're really sure you want to do this?" Sierra asked Max quickly and quietly.

Max nodded. "It's not our money. Let's see what it can buy us. We can always back out at the last minute and forfeit our deposit or whatever."

"*Magister navis,*" the more talkative Celt introduced the shipmaster. Then he left with the younger man.

The shipmaster smiled. "I understand the two of you would like passage to Rome." His Latin was excellent—crisp and precise.

"Yes," Sierra replied. "Or possibly Alexandria, or Athens."

"Makes no difference. It will cost you the same—ten of those silver coins, for each of you, for a total of twenty."

Sierra and Max looked at each other. They could tell from the shipmaster's demeanor that they were likely being overcharged. "Agreed," Max replied.

"Good," the shipmaster said. "And your timing is good, as well. I can have you on a ship that leaves tomorrow morning. . . . Rome seems a popular destination—I guess that is not surprising. Yours is the second passage from here that I have booked in as many days."


Allectus, the shipmaster, was from Britannia Superior—the northern part of the island. He invited Sierra and Max to an early dinner at his "modest villa," about a thirty-minute walk, northwest. They supped on suckling pig and imported wine. "Better than Falernian," Allectus proudly announced.

"Bacchus' own." Sierra knew the name. Neither she nor Max had ever tasted Falernian wine, ancient and fabled for its taste, but they agreed that Allectus' offering was delicious. The three drank copiously and talked into the night.

Allectus told them of his recent travels up north, to Hadrian's Wall and beyond. "Vallum Antonini is the new boundary, pressed right up against Caledonia."

Sierra and Max did their best to discover who had departed in one of Allectus' ships to Rome, just yesterday. "He was older than me, and he seemed to be Greek, but his accent was very odd, so I cannot be sure," Allectus told them.

"Can you tell us his name?" Sierra asked.

"I cannot," Allectus replied firmly. "You would not want me to reveal your name if a beautiful woman plied me with wine and asked me."

Sierra smiled fetchingly. "You do not know my name."

"True." Allectus turned to Max. "I know yours is Maximus, and you paid for the booking, so that is all I need to know." Allectus lifted a jar of wine, caressed its slender neck, and poured some into a bowl. He touched its neck again and looked at Sierra. "This amphora reminds me of you. You have a neck at least as nice, and I would wager you taste even better. Perhaps I should call you Amphora."

Sierra laughed, sipped, and tried to press her advantage. "What did this man—your passenger—look like?"

"Back to him again? Not as good as you, not as good as him"—he pointed to Max, who nodded thank-you—"not even as good as me. He was older, but not old. What more can I say?"

"He spoke Greek to you?" Max asked.

"No, no. I said he seemed to be Greek—he spoke Latin."

"What made you think he seemed Greek?" Max asked.

"I am not sure—perhaps his accent. There was something strange about him. But I should say no more—let us talk of something else. Let us talk of wine and beauty." Allectus turned to Sierra.

She spoke to Max in English. "If I had a damn palm phone with me, I could show him Thomas's picture."

Max nodded, dubiously. "That would take quite a phone—did Thomas invent one with a cross-temporal connection?"

"No. I have his picture in my phone. Your picture, too."

Allectus' eyes were wide with interest. "What language are you speaking?"

"A kind of German," Max told him, in Latin.

"Ah, yes."

"Have you ever heard that language before?" Sierra tried again.

"No. But coming out of your mouth, I know I will never forget it." Allectus turned to Max. "Forgive me for being so blunt—it is the wine."

Max smiled graciously. "Nothing to forgive. Her beauty is enchanting." And he wanted the shipmaster to keep talking.

But the wine had another effect, and the three were soon sound asleep.

Max woke the next morning and breathed in the cool, sweet air of the portico. Sierra was still sleeping beside him, half-wrapped and cuddled in coarse but comfortable sheets. He resisted his impulse and settled for just a quick, soft kiss on her lips.

She opened her eyes. "Where's Allectus?" she said groggily.

"I don't know. Inside, I assume."

The two rose and walked inside.

A short, thin man, whom they had not seen before, quickly approached them, with a pouch and a small scroll.

Max took the pouch. He put his forefinger in and looked up, dismayed. "He's apparently refunded our fare. It feels like it's all here." Max counted the coins. "Yeah, all twenty are here."

Sierra opened the scroll and read, " 'I am sorry, but I drank too much and I talked too much last night. I am returning the payment you provided for your voyage. I wish you well.' "

They thanked the short man, declined his offer of bread and watered wine.

They ran down to the river. They had no idea what Allectus' ship—the *Vesta*—looked like. But they asked a variety of people who seemed as if they might be knowledgeable, and eventually they heard that the *Vesta* was about to depart, nearly an hour earlier than originally expected. "The captain said the currents were favorable," several onlookers confirmed and explained.

Max pulled a silver coin from his toga. He gestured with the coin to the closest onlooker, a boy about twelve. "Can you take us to the *Vesta*, right now?"

The boy snatched the coin and nodded vigorously. "Yes. Follow me."

The boy ran, and Sierra and Max followed. The *Vesta* was docked about half a mile downriver. "Look," Sierra said to Max, and pointed. Allectus was on the shore, talking to a group of Celts and Roman soldiers.

"That is the *Vesta*," the boy said.

"Thank you," Max replied.

The boy left, running again.

Sierra and Max approached Allectus. He caught sight of them. "He doesn't seem very pleased to see us," Sierra observed.

Allectus turned from his group and greeted Sierra and Max with a deep frown. "You—," he began.

But a second group of Roman soldiers arrived and commanded everyone's attention. "Go," Allectus told Sierra and Max. "It is not safe—"

The second group of soldiers suddenly drew swords on the first group. Completely surprised, the first group fell quickly.

The Celts did a little better. Several of them came over to Allectus, to protect him. Allectus said something in Celtic. One of the Celts handed Max a weapon.

The attacking Romans were upon them. Two Celts shielded Sierra. The Romans lunged—

Sierra saw Max. Three Romans were on top of him, slashing. "Max!" She saw him go down in rivulets of blood.

She turned to get Allectus. She felt a fist in her stomach, then something smashed her jaw, and she was unconscious.

*Near the Coast of Gaul, AD 150*

Sierra became aware of salty air, a warm hand on her forehead, and her stomach pressing against her throat. She opened her eyes and saw Allectus.

"You are awake," he said, relieved and concerned. "I am afraid the sea does not agree with you."

"I actually love the sea," she said, in English. Then she caught herself and translated. "Someone hit me in my stomach . . ."

"You also received a blow to the head. You have been unconscious for nearly a day and a night."

She raised herself, shakily, on an elbow, for a moment.

"You need more rest," Allectus said. "You were lucky to escape. As was I. Fortunately a large group of my people were nearby. They know how to fight Romans." His lips twisted. "Although I am not even certain our attackers were Romans, though they were dressed like them. But something about them—"

It all came back to Sierra now, like jagged glass in her soul.

"Max!"

"I am sorry." Allectus took her hand. "Your friend perished. He fought bravely."

"No!" Sierra cried, and threw aside the hand. She knew Allectus was lying about the last part. She had seen Max slaughtered before he had had a chance to even raise his blade.

"You will be safe here—"

"I want to go back—"

"You need to rest now," Allectus repeated. "It is too dangerous now for . . . visitors in Londinium. I do not believe the attackers were seeking me. . . ."

Sierra closed her eyes and tried to understand.

"We will be stopping briefly at various ports along the way," Allectus continued, "but our destination now will be Athens, not Rome. I want to stay as far away as possible now from Romans, until I learn more about what happened in Londinium."

Sierra said nothing.

"I do not know your name," Allectus concluded. "I will call you Ampharete, until you tell me otherwise."

CHAPTER 5

*Phrygia (Later, Asia Minor), 404 BC*

Alcibiades woke up suddenly. He sighed, started to fall back asleep, then heard the sound again. He had been sleeping, naked, half on top of a Persian woman, also naked and sound asleep on her stomach. He had met her just this afternoon—or was it already yesterday afternoon? He could not recall exactly when they had met or her name.

He moved himself carefully—not to avoid waking her, because, with the amount of wine she had consumed, it might well take a thunderclap in her ear to wake her. He moved slowly off her back and over onto his own because he did not want to make any noise that might let any possible intruder know he was here and awake.

Alcibiades now quickly and quietly got to his feet and looked around.

A figure stepped forward from a far corner.

Alcibiades looked for where he had left his knife—alas, it was on the other side of the unconscious Persian beauty. He looked at her flowing hair and cursed. He had gotten up on the wrong side of their bed.

"There is no need for weapons, I assure you, not now," the figure said, in a peculiar yet comprehensible Greek. He stepped closer.

"Why? My situation is hopeless?" Alcibiades looked around the room.

"No. Just the opposite—I'm here to save you."

"From whom?"

"I will explain later. For now, you must ready yourself."


Alcibiades dressed.

The figure looked at the prone form. "She has attractive lines."

Alcibiades smirked. "Are you a Pythagorean?"

"In a manner of speaking, perhaps yes."

The two walked into an adjoining room and took seats at an empty table.

"Are you hungry?" Alcibiades asked.

"I could eat. Thank you. But we must be quick."

Alcibiades rose, opened the door to a different room, and summoned a slave.

"You enjoy the Phrygian hospitality?" the visitor inquired.

"Are you still thinking about that lovely line in the next room, or the food and drink to come?"

"Both."

"Well, then, I should say that I do very much enjoy the hospitality, but I loathe being in this Persian land. I intend to return to Athens very shortly."

"That is precisely why your life is in danger tonight."

"Oh? You have yet to tell me from whom."

"I am not sure," the figure answered. "History says the Spartans are behind this. You have some enemies in Athens, too, as you know. But those specifics really do not matter. Your beloved mentor, Socrates, will be sentenced to death by his own people—your people, those same Athenian people—in five years. Were I not here, you would meet your death tonight. In a sense, you still will—except, I have a plan that will also enable you to live."

Alcibiades laughed, shook his head, snorted.

The slave returned with fruit, bread, knives, and wine.

Alcibiades dismissed him.

The visitor took wine.

Alcibiades took a knife, as if to cut a fruit, then swiftly moved around the table and put the knife to his visitor's neck. He held him close with his elbow and other arm.

Alcibiades was lean and about forty-five years of age. The visitor was at least twenty years older and softer.

The visitor was at a disadvantage. "I am at your mercy."

"I am afraid my supply is all but depleted. Let us start again: Who are you? What are you doing here?"

"I told you: I came to save you."

"And how do I know you did not come to kill me?"

"I could have killed you in your sleep and availed myself of your Persian hospitality."

Alcibiades laughed again, brought the knife closer to his visitor's neck, then relaxed his grip a bit. "Well, it is certainly true enough that you might have tried. . . . But you still have not told me who you are. Is coming to save me the only reason you ventured into this slave farm?"

"That is what you consider Phrygia?"

"Why, do you have a higher opinion of this land? I am here only until more Athenians come to their senses, but I suppose that is akin to hoping that asses can discuss philosophy."

"Phrygia has a proud past, and a prouder future. One day, one of the greatest conquerors in the world will cut the Gordian knot in this land and go on to subdue much of Asia. It might interest you to know that this conqueror's mentor's mentor's mentor is none other than your Socrates."

Alcibiades' face flushed. He exhaled. He let go of his visitor. "I will admit that you tease my interest. Let us speak of Socrates. I will let you keep breathing—for a little longer. I have a weakness for mentors and madmen."


The slave refilled their wine.

"Tell me more about this student of Socrates' who, you claim, will mentor a student, who in turn will mentor your world conqueror."

"He is not you, if that is what you are wondering, Alcibiades."

Alcibiades made a derisive sound. "You speak with the assurance of a prophet—I do not believe in them."

"You may, before the evening is over."

Alcibiades grunted. "I know that student of Socrates could not be me—I know better than to waste my time with students, who are likely to wound your heart, in due time."

"As you wounded Socrates'?"

Alcibiades grew thoughtful. "I doubt it. I do not know if anyone could."

"Did he wound yours?"

Alcibiades shook his head. "No. . . . I did spend an uneventful, frustrating night with him under the same cover, but that is not the same as piercing your heart. . . . But tell me, who is this seminal student? I would like to see how impressive are your powers of imagination."

"Imagination has no part in this. I come from the future, as you will soon see in plain evidence."

"I will look forward to that evidence. But, in either case, whether of fanciful poetry or future history, who is the student? Is it Xenophon? He is young enough to attract a brilliant student, now unknown, but I doubt he has the depth to truly inspire anyone."

"Not Xenophon. You are correct."

"Who?"

"Plato."

Alcibiades' eyes narrowed. "Plato? Yes, he has the intelligence and the depth. But he is a brooder, a pessimist. He takes no joy in the flesh. . . . Zeus help us if the world is to be ruled by someone he engenders with his tutelage!"

"Once removed," the visitor corrected.

Alcibiades nodded. "And Plato survives the death of Socrates, of which you spoke earlier?"

"Yes."

"Let us talk, then, about death—my death."

"Good. I wanted to recall your attention to that event, and how we can subvert it."

Alcibiades looked at a small hole on a near wall, covered by a mat. "It is still dark outside, but dawn will be here in an hour. Where are the assassins you speak of?"

"They will be here soon."

"So why do we not just wake up anyone who is sleeping, carry out anyone who cannot be woken, and let the assassins find an empty dwelling?"

"If they do not kill you tonight, they will keep looking for you until they do."

Alcibiades cleared his throat. "And your plan?"

"We leave everything in this house, just as it is. Except, exactly in your place, where I found you in bed, we place a replica of you, not really alive, but seeming to be. He is murdered in your place."

"And everyone else?"

"Our knowledge is that only you were murdered here tonight."

Alcibiades considered. "I cannot say I care about her deeply, or even at all. I met her just this past afternoon. But I do not feel good saddling Queen Esther with some half-alive demon, who will be slaughtered right on top of her, as she sleeps, probably dreaming of me inside her."

"Queen Esther, the wife of Xerxes?"

"I am joking about her name, of course. I cannot recall her name."

"In my day, Esther is thought to be a myth, created by the Jews."

Alcibiades laughed, sourly. "So the man who spins tales about the future is intolerant of tales about the past? Well, I never had the pleasure of knowing the real Queen Esther personally—a little before my time— but from what I understand, she truly existed."

The visitor took that in, closed his eyes. "I sometimes wish I could be just a tourist in my travels. There is so much to learn, and enjoy, here, and at other times. But matters of life and death, it seems, take precedence."

"Who are you?" Alcibiades demanded.

The visitor opened his eyes. "As I told you, I am from the future. But not just the near future. I am from the far future, and I travel, and I live, at some length, during certain times. And I do what I can."

Alcibiades shook his head, disbelieving, but perhaps not as much as before. "Why are you so eager to save my life?"

"I think you can be of help in my greater plan, to save your mentor, Socrates. He has said, more than once, that you are his most beloved student. He would listen to you—"

Alcibiades started to object.

"—but there is not time to discuss this now," the visitor said tersely. "Your killers will be upon you, soon."


Part of the visitor's plan was already in place. Two of his men were standing guard outside the dwelling, with what the visitor claimed was a replica of Alcibiades, wrapped in cloth, and strapped to a wheeled, upright contraption. Each man was lightly armored and carried a long spear and a short sword.

"Your guards have been very patient, waiting here all of this time," Alcibiades remarked.

"They are well trained."

Alcibiades began to talk to the men.

The visitor interrupted, "They speak no Greek."

Alcibiades nodded, then approached the living shroud. "May I? I have an urge, in my vanity, to look at myself."

"Of course. You would see him very soon, in any case."

Alcibiades was surprised to find his hand was trembling. He unwrapped the top of the cloth—and gasped. He was looking at himself, sleeping, breathing.

"Is he drugged? If I woke him, could we talk?"

"No," the visitor said. "He has no mind, no soul. He inhales and exhales, in the way that any living creature breathes, and he looks like you, in a sense he *is* you, but he is just the shell of you. He has never really lived."

"How . . . ?"

"A tiny piece of your skin was taken from you, without your knowledge—probably as you slept with one of your lovers—some time ago. And, from that, we were able to grow . . . this."

"And you propose to bring him into my room and place him on top of—"

One of the men said something in a language unknown to Alcibiades and gestured to the right with his spear.

The visitor looked in that direction, as did Alcibiades.

"Your killers are very near," the visitor said. "We may have to change our plan."

Alcibiades squinted into the dark, strained every bit of his hearing. "What does your soldier think is out there? I cannot see or hear a thing."

"His hearing is a lot more acute than yours or mine. It is enhanced by . . . let me just assure you that their hearing is to ours as the strength of Hercules is to yours."

Alcibiades was not entirely convinced. "How are my killers approaching?"

"They came most of the way on horses, I believe. They have likely dismounted now and are approaching on foot."

"How many?"

"Likely six or seven."

Alcibiades looked at the two armed men.

"I assure you, as well, that these men will be more than adequate to the task," the visitor said.

"I have a sword inside, I can help."

The visitor shook his head. "No, no, please. I implore you. If you get killed, all of this will have been wasted effort. You need not establish or demonstrate your courage here—it is already well known throughout the Aegean—"

"My reputation is not my concern. My honor demands that I defend myself with my weapon, and not stand idly by while others risk their lives for me." He spun away from the visitor and went back inside.

The visitor quickly followed and signaled the two others to join him.

The two guards brought the shrouded figure indoors. Alcibiades glanced at it again and shook his head, incredulous—

There was a noise outside that everyone inside heard.

The two men picked up their long spears.

There was another noise.

The two men opened the door and charged through it, making deep, guttural sounds.

Alcibiades went for his sword.

He was back at the door, armed, a moment later.

Screams and cries and thuds all banged on the door.

Alcibiades rushed forward—

The visitor restrained him, with a strong arm on his shoulder.

Alcibiades shrugged it off, violently, and went through the door.

Eight Spartans, wounded in at least three times as many places, lay dead on the ground outside.

The visitor's two men looked at Alcibiades and nodded. There was not a scratch on either of them.


The guards dug shallow graves and buried the bodies.

Alcibiades shook his head, slowly. "Spartans. I was once a friend of Sparta."

"They may have been mercenaries," the visitor replied. "We do not know who hired them, or who gave the order. Perhaps your old friend and fellow student Critias."

Alcibiades bared his teeth. "I do hate him—he has become a traitor to Athens."

The visitor nodded. "Let us go inside, again. But not for long."

Alcibiades looked at the horizon, and the imminent dawn. "What do we do with your plan now? Is there still a need—"

"Yes. The future says nothing about the exact number of the assassins, and who died, other than you. Only that the woman in your bed survived."

"Precise assassins."

"Well, one version says although you were surprised in your bed, you leaped out of it, grabbed your sword, and fought bravely, nakedly, to the end."

Alcibiades nodded. "That's certainly what I would have done. Your plan had my replica dying like a paralyzed dormouse."

The visitor gestured sympathetically. "There is only so much one can do with a half-living being."

Alcibiades shook his head and walked inside.

The visitor followed, along with the two guards and their spears.

There was a noise in the far room, where Alcibiades had been sleeping.

The guards pointed their spears.

The door opened.

"Ah, the dreaming beauty walks," Alcibiades said.

She smiled. "Alcibiades."

"You do not look the least bit tired," he said.

"I was not really sleeping." She smoothed the silk she was now wearing.

The visitor finally spoke. "What . . . are you doing here?"

Alcibiades looked at him. The visitor's mouth was open in surprise.

"Likely the same thing as you, Heron," she replied. "You look older."

The visitor said something in the language Alcibiades did not understand. The guards lowered their spears.

"You two know each other," Alcibiades observed, looking back and forth, with growing interest, at each of them.

"Her name is Ampharete," Heron said. "At least, that is what she told me."

Alcibiades smiled at her. "You are a very sweet vessel."

"How did you manage to get back here?" Heron demanded of Ampharete.

She began to answer—

"I am as eager to learn about all of this as you," Alcibiades interrupted, telling Heron. "Maybe more so. But I may have an even keener interest in saving my life. You say there may be more killers on their way. Much as I have faith in the prowess of your two men . . ."

Heron regarded Alcibiades. "You are right, of course. Let us finish our work here, and then we can retire for a few hours to a safer place, about twenty minutes by foot from here."

Heron turned to his two guards and spoke again in the language incomprehensible to Alcibiades. The former student of Socrates glanced at Ampharete while Heron was speaking and noted that she apparently understood what was being said, or was feigning understanding pretty well.

The guards lifted the shroud and carried it into the bedroom. Everyone followed. They unwrapped the breathing but utterly insensate body. One guard supplied it with a bloodied sword, no doubt from the assassins so wonderfully slaughtered outside, Alcibiades figured. After the sword was placed in the body's hand, the two guards rent the body with spear and sword thrusts. The body shortly stopped breathing.

Alcibiades watched with a strange fascination. He turned to Ampharete. "Are you going to disrobe now, stretch out on your stomach, and lie still, to complete the foretold scene?"

"Not really necessary," Heron answered. "I will tell the slaves that you died valiantly defending this woman, and yourself, and that your last blows were struck on these vile assassins to enable her escape."

"Where are the slaves now?" Alcibiades looked toward the back of the house.

"Hiding in the back there, no doubt. Whatever they may have seen or think they saw outside, they will believe my story when they find your replica's body. And they will spread the word."

"You are quite the exacting dramatist," Alcibiades said, with an equal mixture of distaste and admiration.

The group was ready to leave as the sun arrived in full. "The slaves are ready to bear witness to your brave death," Heron told Alcibiades. "They will remain here in the dwelling."

Alcibiades nodded. "I have no right to take the slaves with me, in any event. They belong to the friend of the friend who owns this house."

"Good."

"But I do not like to see anyone's possessions ill-treated," Alcibiades continued. "Are you sure the slaves will not be held liable for my 'murder'?"

"The weapons are not slave weapons," Heron replied. "And it is plausible that, although your defense was heroic, it was swiftly extinguished and woke no one. The slaves will not be blamed for anything."

Alcibiades accepted the reasoning.

Ampharete joined them.

Alcibiades looked at her, smiled, then looked at the upright, wheeled contraption. "An interesting device."

"I invented it," Heron said.

"Oh? I was thinking our Ampharete might enjoy being carried in it. Why walk when you can ride?"

"That is where your sleeping double was carried?" she asked.

"Yes," Alcibiades replied.

Ampharete wrinkled her nose. "I would rather walk. I have already sampled you asleep."

Alcibiades laughed.

"Let us start moving then," Heron said. "We will walk to our first stop, rest, as I mentioned, and then head south towards the river. Eventually we will take a boat to Athens, and then—"

"I am not very popular there, at the moment, as you know," Alcibiades said.

Heron nodded. "I do not intend for you to be staying there, at this time, very long."

They all started walking, one guard a little in front and the other a few feet in back of the party.

After a few minutes, Heron moved close to Ampharete. Alcibiades walked with the lead guard.

"What exactly were you trying to do with him back there?" Heron asked Ampharete.

"I told you—same as you, save him."

"By slumbering in his arms? How did you expect to save him in your unconsciousness? Dream his defense?"

"I was not sleeping."

"You looked sound asleep to me."

"That was the idea. I heard you enter. I heard you tell Alcibiades you found my form attractive—"

"I accept that you were awake. But what would you have done had I been one of the killers?"

"I would have grabbed a sword and thrust it through your neck."

Heron regarded Ampharete. "You seem more . . . aggressive than when we last met, in Alexandria."

Ampharete's face tightened. "I had reason to be aggressive then, too. I tried to conceal it."

"You would have jumped out of Alcibiades' bed totally naked and attacked me?"

"Presumably my nakedness would have been a distraction."

Heron smiled, despite himself, and shook his head. "I guess I will have to accept that point, as well. But what would you have done if you had successfully staved off the killers? For that matter, how exactly *did* you manage to get here? Last time I saw you, you were also sound asleep, in my quarters in Alexandria, about five hundred and fifty years from now," Heron mused. "That was nearly ten years ago, in my life. . . . Were you faking then, too?"

"I believe I was sleeping."

"You sleep a lot—or pretend to. . . . How many years has it been for you, since Alexandria?"

"About two. . . . You ask a lot of questions. Let me ask you one: How did *you* get back here, seeing as how you were in that same room in Alexandria five hundred and fifty years from now?"

Now Heron's smile grew a little grim. "Obviously, we both have access to the chairs."

"Yes, but until this current trip to the last days of Alcibiades, I could only go as far back as your time, in Alexandria."

Now Heron's smile left completely. He looked away and silently worked his jaw.

"You are more than just a . . . traveler in the chair," Ampharete said.

Heron spoke in a whisper, "It is very dangerous to talk about this."

"No doubt you have been to the future, far beyond the Library of Alexandria," Ampharete continued anyway. "Do you come from there?"

"Yes."

"You are not really Heron of Alexandria?"

"I am more really Heron than the original. He lived around 150 BC, invented very little. Most of what the world attributes to Heron is mine, brought back from the future. I have seeded the ancient world with many devices, some of which even your world has yet to discover."

"And you set this . . . Socratic dialog in motion?" Ampharete asked.

"Only in the sense that I invented the time chairs. And so, in a technical sense, I made it possible."

"It was not your idea to save Socrates?"

"Oh, no."

"Whose idea was it, then?" Ampharete asked.

"I do not know. I was, am, attempting to enable what is in the dialog to be true. I have been working at this, constantly, since you first brought the manuscript to me in Alexandria. But I do not know who wrote it. And I do not know if the person who wrote it was the person who came up with the plan to rescue Socrates."

Ampharete shook her head. "It occurred to me that you could be Andros—both of you do come from the future."

"I may be, for all I know. I have not encountered Socrates, yet." Heron pondered. "The dialog gives very little description of Andros. It does say Andros is much younger than Socrates."

She gave Heron an appraising look. "You are now not much younger than Socrates, that is true."

Heron said nothing.

"But you gave a good performance of Andros to Alcibiades in the house," Ampharete said. "Do you know Thomas O'Leary?"

"I do not."

"He is older than you—perhaps as old as Socrates." Ampharete described Sierra Waters's—her—mentor.

"No," Heron said. "I do not know him."

Ampharete exhaled. . . . "Let us talk about something else—about how we both managed to get back here. As I said, the time stream, or whatever it is, seemed blocked any time before 150 AD."

"It was. I unblocked it. There was no way I could unblock it for me alone. Either it is open or shut. I opened it, to come back and rescue Alcibiades—as both a rehearsal for Socrates and also to get Alcibiades' help with Socrates—I hoped that no one else came through. Obviously, you did."

"Why do you care so much about rescuing Socrates? Just for the satisfaction of bringing that dialog to life? I suppose I can understand that. . . . You are an inventor. The dialog is a script, a recipe, and you seek the pleasure of having it realized."

"It is not only that," Heron responded. "Socrates did not deserve to die. He may have wanted to die, he may have goaded the Athenian democracy into the horrendous deed to shame them forever, but that does not mean it was right. The world would have been better off had Socrates lived."

"Are you sure?"

"How many minds have we had like his in all of history? One thing I know: intelligence of that kind is rare. The human species needs every bit of it we can get. And the same is true of democracy—I would like to remove that stain from Athens."

"But the plan in the dialog would save Socrates and let his empty double die, just as you arranged for Alcibiades. How would that remove the black mark placed on democracy by the death of Socrates?"

Heron smiled wearily, defiantly. "I plan to change that part of the plan—"

Alcibiades joined them. "Is that our haven, ahead?" He pointed. "I hope so. I am sorely in need of a few hours' sleep."

Heron walked up to the front guard, who loped swiftly, quietly, to the house.

"It should be vacant," Heron called back to Alcibiades and Ampharete. "My guard will confirm that."

The guard soon returned and beckoned them to follow.


The house was smaller than the one in which Alcibiades and Ampharete had been resting. This one had just a hearth, a kitchen, an open courtyard on the first floor, and two bedrooms on the second floor. Alcibiades' face crinkled in appreciation. "It is good to see the Greek style, this far east."

Heron nodded. "You can sleep upstairs. We dare not stay here more than a few hours."

"Yes." Alcibiades looked at Ampharete.

She approached him, stroked his face, and kissed him on the lips.

He pulled her close to him, and extended the kiss.

Then he turned and walked upstairs.

The two guards took up posts outside.

Ampharete and Heron sat at a small table in the kitchen.

"I wanted to ask you about Jonah—," Ampharete began.

"In a moment." Heron stood and looked around the kitchen. "I believe there is some good wine here. . . . Ah, yes." He opened a cupboard and pulled out two jugs, and a big shallow bowl. He brought them to the table and poured a little wine—a thick sludge—and a lot of water into the bowl. "I will taste it, to make sure it was not poisoned." He sipped, and sipped again. "Good." He closed his eyes. He waited a few seconds, then opened his eyes, and sipped again. "Good," he said again, and passed the bowl to Ampharete. "At least we know there is nothing in the wine that can kill us quickly."

She sipped. "It is good. It feels good to relax." She passed the bowl back to Heron.

He sipped. "So you want to know—"

They heard shouts and thuds outside.

One of their guards came crashing through the doorway, backward. He shoved his sword into the groin of one of his attackers. Three other attackers were upon him. Two other attackers came through the door and went for Heron and Ampharete. All of these attackers were oddly clad.

Heron, unarmed, seized a wine jug and smashed one of his attackers in the face. The attacker was momentarily stunned. "Get the knives in the cupboard," he screamed to Ampharete, who was already headed in that direction.

Heron upended the table and shoved it in the path of the second attacker.

Their guard, wounded and bloodied, dispatched the last of his three attackers and lunged at the one Heron had stunned with the wine jug. The guard thrust his knife into the attacker's exposed neck and cut till he severed the jugular.

Heron and Ampharete set upon the other attacker with their knives. Their guard, finished with the first attacker, turned to help.

The door burst open again with five more attackers.

The guard said something to Heron and rushed toward the attackers. He killed two, but received a mortal wound through the eye from a third.

Alcibiades came running down the stairs, naked except for the sword in his hand.

Two of the new attackers were now upon Ampharete. They threw her to the floor. She dodged a sword thrust.

Heron tackled the fifth attacker.

Alcibiades uttered a primal cry. He jumped on both of Ampharete's attackers. His sword went quickly and deeply into each of them. One managed before he died to cut Alcibiades' leg. Alcibiades rose, limping, to Heron's aid.

The inventor was fighting a desperate, losing battle. His knife was no match for the attacker's brawn, let alone his weapon. Alcibiades kicked Heron's attacker in the head and shoved his sword up through the attacker's mouth. He helped Heron regain his feet, steadying his own wobbly leg, as well.

"Please," Heron rasped. "Save yourself." He reached into the sweat-soaked woolen cloth in which he was wrapped and produced a thin, damp scroll. "These are instructions. They will tell you what you must do when you return to Athens—how to skip ahead briefly to the time of your mentor's death, and how you can help prevent that."

Ampharete, pale, sweaty, also a little shaky on her feet, came over to them. Alcibiades put the table upright, positioned it so as to not be visible from outside the door, and sat Ampharete and Heron down. He collected two swords from the attackers and put one in Heron's and one in Ampharete's hands.

"Good," Heron said. "Now go, please, if you can." He put the scroll in Alcibiades' hand.

"I am not going anywhere." Alcibiades put the scroll on the table. "Except outside to look around."

He picked up the long spear from the fallen guard and walked slowly to the doorway. He crouched down, to the side, and listened. Then he moved his head to the edge and looked beyond.

He came back to the table. "It seems safe now, at least for the moment. They are all dead out there—eight of those strangely outfitted men, and your other brave guard."

Heron sighed. Ampharete moaned and put her head on the table.

Alcibiades touched her shoulder. She moaned again. Her eyes were shut.

"She must have hit her head hard on the floor," Heron said.

Alcibiades gently lifted one of her eyelids. "She is semiconscious. I have seen men in this condition before. She should be better with a few hours' rest." He kissed her on the forehead.

"You need to move," Heron insisted.

Alcibiades considered. "We can give her a ride on that wheeled contraption. You and Ampharete are more important to the success of your plan than I am."

"You are wrong," Heron replied, but offered no further argument.

Alcibiades poured wine on his wound. He wrapped it in a piece of garment Heron provided, then dressed himself, as best he could, with the armor from the slain guard inside. He put the scroll with the instructions near his chest.

He looked at one of the dead attackers. "I have never seen garb such as that. And they fight better than Spartans, almost as good as your guards. Are they from the future?"

"Either that, or they were trained and dressed by someone from the future," Heron replied.

"I did not know there were that many chairs," Ampharete said groggily, dreamily. She picked her head up from the table.

Alcibiades looked at her and smiled. She smiled back, then closed her eyes and put her head back down.

"What does she mean about chairs?" Alcibiades asked Heron.

"That is the way we travel to and from the future."

"I do not understand any of that. But . . . let us start walking, so we can have a chance of at least living into the future, the usual way. How far are we now from the boat to Athens that you mentioned?"

"About three hours by foot to the river—perhaps longer, in our condition. It is a tributary of the Maeander, which will take us to Miletus. From there we can take another boat to Piraeus and Athens."

"Can you walk to the river?" Alcibiades asked.

"Yes. I am exhausted but not hurt. What about your wound?"

"Not as bad as it might have been."

The two men carefully placed Ampharete in the upright cart and fastened her snugly, so she would not slip out.

Alcibiades looked again at the bodies. "Should we risk the time to bury them? At least your guards?"

"No."

The two walked as fast as they could on the path, Heron taking charge of Ampharete, Alcibiades of the long spear. Ampharete occasionally muttered a phrase, or a name, none known to Alcibiades. "Max . . . Mr. Appleton . . . Thomas . . ."

"Those are names from the future," Heron said.

". . . Melqat . . . ," Ampharete mumbled.

"Well, that one at least I can recognize," Alcibiades said. "It sounds Phoenician."

"Yes, it does," Heron said. "But I do not know him."

"Tell me more about Socrates—or how I fit in your plans for him. He and I are not on the best of terms these days."

"That does not matter. I am hoping you will be able to convince Socrates by your example."

"You mean, the fact that I survived?"

"The fact you both died and survived. Socrates will think you died tonight. When he learns of your death, he will grieve. Despite what you think, he still loves you. When you come to see him in his prison, right before he is about to drink the hemlock that the Athenian court of five hundred citizens so ignobly prescribed, your very presence will be the best argument in favor of his following the course of escape."

"No one else among his students tried to save him?"

"His old friend Crito came to talk to him—he had a ship chartered and an escape route all mapped out—but to no avail."

"Crito is a sincere man, but no genius."

Heron nodded.

"What about Plato?" Alcibiades asked. "You told me—"

"As far as we know, Plato left Athens after the sentence was pronounced, before it was carried out. Plato inspired people with his words. As for his personal bravery . . ."

"I understand. And this will happen five years from now, you say?"

"Yes."

"Explain the chairs to me. How do they work? Where are they located?"

"The second question is much easier to answer than the first. The chairs we hope to travel to, now, are situated in a small dwelling, similar to the one we just left, about midway on the road between Piraeus and Athens. There are also chairs in other locations and times, in cities that have not yet come to be, in places you never heard of."

Alcibiades took this in. "And your answer to my first question?"

Heron considered. "Are you familiar with the work of Heraclitus? . . . Yes, of course, you are—Socrates spoke of him."

Alcibiades nodded. "He was born not very far from here—in Ephesus, a little north of Miletus—and flourished about sixty years ago. 'Heraclitus the obscure,' I have heard him called. Not because few know of him, but because many find his thinking almost impossible to comprehend."

"I consider him one of the greatest thinkers in all of human history," Heron said.

Alcibiades smiled. "That is high praise indeed, given your unique vantage point in history."

"Heraclitus recognized that you can never step into the same river, exactly the same river, twice, because new water is always flowing. And yet we are right in thinking there is a reality to the river Maeander, a reality which endures, and makes the river Maeander distinct from any other river, such as the river Caÿster. So the river always changes, yet stays the same, has continuity—both are true."

"Yes, that is a profound, if vexing, observation."

"And what is true of rivers, of all existence, is also true of time itself, because time is part of existence," Heron continued. "I, and others throughout history, have recognized that essential point. And if that is so, then travel from one time to another should be possible, even easy, since, even though time always moves, it also stays the same—stands still, is the same time."

"A tempting comparison, but not without flaws. A river stays the same, if I understand Heraclitus, because its path through the earth stays roughly the same, even as the water always changes. But time stays the same—if indeed it does—for precisely the opposite reason. Last year—the equivalent of the water—stays the same, regardless of the path that time takes in the future. Is that not so? You are able to come back here, whether from ten or a hundred years in the future, because this time has remained stable?"

"Not entirely—"

"Still, you are here. . . . If I believe your account, I guess your presence now demonstrates that time travel is possible, whatever the theory behind it." Alcibiades considered. "But how did you make such travel *physically* possible? Heraclitus, unlike Parmenides, was a great believer in the reality of the physical world."

Heron nodded, vigorously. "Yes, yes, I am an inventor more than a philosopher—constructing devices that actually work has always been the love of my life."

"Then . . . you invented a chair that embodies this . . . Heraclitian principle?"

"Many tried, throughout history, and did not succeed. They grasped the essential idea, but lacked the proper equipment. Just like the moving picture device which I created—will create—in Alexandria will not be anything more than a toy until, nearly two thousand years later, the machinery existed to make it a vehicle of popular theater." Heron sighed. "It is difficult to discuss events across time without being confusing. . . . But I can tell you that, in my distant time, machinery finally existed that allowed me to construct a special chair that drew upon the nature of time and space, of minutes and tributaries. . . . I was able to manipulate that intertwined fabric and poke passages right through it. The chair invokes forces that do that, and this allows anyone sitting in the chair to travel through time."

Alcibiades considered. "I still am not sure I completely understand. . . . But . . . you were moved to invent this—to utilize the craftwork at hand, in your future time, to take advantage of the Heraclitian principle—because of this manuscript that you speak of?"

"No. I invented the chairs before I ever knew of the manuscript. I traveled back to Alexandria, to many other places, and lived there, for short or long periods of time, and learned what I could, contributed what I dared to their cultures, left roots for the future. But I am here now, with you, in this time and this place, because of the manuscript, yes."

"Why? Surely there are other great men in history worth saving. Why now? Why Socrates?"

Heron nodded. "I can appreciate why you would ask such a question. But you cannot understand, from where you stand, here in this time, how much attraction this time has to all who have come after. This time, your time, is extraordinary in human history."

"Not because of me, I assume."

"No . . . because of—"

"Socrates," Alcibiades completed Heron's sentence.

"Yes, but more than Socrates. There was a flowering of the mind in this time that set all subsequent human history on its course. Not only philosophy. The serious study of history, mathematics, nature . . . the practice of drama, music, the arts—"

"Socrates is distrustful of the arts."

"Yes, but his name has come to be associated with this time, and all it contained . . . perhaps because of the way he died. The world has never fully recovered from the death of Socrates. Every tutored person knows about it."

"I suppose I can understand that," Alcibiades said. "And who wrote the manuscript? Was it Plato?"

"No one knows, with certainty. There are theories . . ."

"So you are risking your lives on the words of someone whose identity is unknown to you? Believe me, I am not complaining in the slightest that you saved my life, but—"

Ampharete stirred. "Where are we?" she asked hoarsely.

"Nearing the small boat that will take us to Miletus, then to Athens," Heron replied.

Alcibiades put his hand on her forehead. "How are you feeling?"

"Thirsty."

Alcibiades lifted her head and gave her water. "You look better. Most of the color has returned to your face."

"I am feeling better. How is your leg?"

"Fine. I have been cut much worse than this."

"I think I can walk now," Ampharete said.

"Good timing." Alcibiades smiled. "We will soon be on the sea, where you can recline and take your ease."


The three approached the small ship on the river tributary a little later. Ampharete not only had her color but her legs back.

Two men stood guard and started talking to Heron when the party arrived.

"What is that language?" Alcibiades asked Ampharete.

She started to answer, then hesitated.

"It is Latin," Heron replied. "A language spoken on the mainland north of Sicily."

"Near Roma?" Alcibiades asked. "I have heard it mentioned but never spoken."

"Yes, Roma," Heron replied.

"Will speakers of this language be important in . . . the future?"

"Yes, very much so."

"Is their world the one in which you constructed the chairs?"

"No," Heron replied. "Most of their world was gone a long time, by then."

One of the guards took the wheeled contraption to the ship. Heron followed, to complete arrangements for the voyage.

The other guard stayed near Alcibiades and Ampharete. He kept watch at a respectful distance.

"He is not only here to protect us, but to prevent us from leaving Heron and his plans," Alcibiades muttered.

"You would fight ten of them if they tried to prevent your going with Heron, would you not?" Ampharete countered.

Alcibiades grunted his acknowledgment. "He told me strange stories about traveling across time in special chairs. Are they true?"

"I do not know what he told you, but, yes, I came to this time in a special chair."

"Tricksters in time," Alcibiades said, with a slight smile. Then his eyes narrowed. "You are weeping." He reached out to her face.

She turned away and rubbed her eyes. "I am sorry."

"I know," Alcibiades said gently. "This has been very trying."

She shook her head. "I lost someone, earlier." She swiveled around and took his hand. Then she kissed him on the mouth, suddenly, passionately. . . . "Was that a trick?"

"You would know better than I."

"You are a very intelligent man."

Alcibiades smiled ruefully. "My mentor, Socrates, used to say I was his most intelligent student."

"I think my mentor, Thomas O'Leary, is the smartest man I ever knew. . . . Though I could be wrong. . . . Sometimes murkiness of motives can be mistaken for intelligence."

"Did you make that up, or did Thomas?"

"I am pretty sure I just did."

"What is unclear about your mentor?" Alcibiades asked.

"Why he drew me into this."

"You do not know? You did not ask him? You do not strike me as shy about extracting information."

"He was already gone when I started to pursue this."

"He travels through time, too?"

"Perhaps—I think so. All I know is he disappeared on a boat in the Aegean, in my time."

"Is he the one who—"

"No," Ampharete replied. "I was speaking of someone who was . . . murdered before my very eyes." Her eyes welled again with tears. "I have not spoken to anyone else of this. I have kept it hidden in me. But what happened tonight . . ."

"I understand." Alcibiades stroked her shoulder. "We will be traveling in the Aegean soon." He looked off a long distance, in space and time. . . . He turned back to Ampharete. "You and Heron are similar in more ways than one—you both devote your lives to a plan whose creator you do not know."

He pulled her close and kissed her again. "But perhaps that is true of all of us, in every time."


The trip to Miletus was unexceptional. This time, all the passengers—other than the guards—did get some genuine sleep. They debarked and boarded a larger boat across the Aegean Sea to Piraeus, the port of Athens.

Heron resumed his sleep; Alcibiades and Ampharete their conversation.

"Do you know where in this sea your Thomas vanished?" Alcibiades looked west in the moonlight.

Ampharete shook her head. "The announcement I heard was brief. More than enough to alarm me. Too little for much else."

"Hermes was taunting you."

"That is as good a way as any to describe the manner in which most information is conveyed to the public, in my time."

"Socrates would say the public deserves to be misinformed, that the very notion of usefully informing the masses is an oxymoron."

"Why is that?"

"Because he thinks the people are incapable of truly knowing," Alcibiades replied. "Therefore it is pointless to inform them. Attempts to do so can lead to harm."

"No one can know anything?"

"Well, Socrates thinks philosophers, at least, can know many things . . . and so should always strive for knowledge."

"Sounds like Plato," Ampharete said.

"Ah, Plato again? I understand from our friend Heron that Plato has had quite an impact upon your future. Yet, from what little I know of him, it is a borrowed impact—he received that thought about the fundamental impossibility of educating most people directly from Socrates. I was there when Socrates said it."

"And what did *you* think of it?"

"I am not sure," Alcibiades replied. "People are stupid. There is no doubt about that. But there can be an odd glory in the average person, in the aggregate of humanity, even so."

They passed by Icaria, Mykonos, Delos. Alcibiades called out each of their names to Ampharete. Heron awoke to make navigational observations and adjustments. He conversed in Latin with his guards, scribbled some notes to himself, then returned to sleep.

Ampharete stared at the islands and the sea. The moon was bright enough to give them definition.

"Still wondering if Thomas is out there, somewhere in the future?" Alcibiades asked.

"Yes, but I was also thinking, this is likely the closest I will ever get to Homer."

Alcibiades smiled wistfully. "That is Cythnos ahead, Andros to the north, and Athens—"

"Andros?"

"Yes, the north part of the island is nearly parallel with Athens. Surely it is known in your time, though perhaps by a different name?"

"No, we know it by that name."

"But that island has some special significance to you?"

"It is the name of the visitor from the future, in the dialog you and Heron were speaking of, who proposes the escape to Socrates."

Alcibiades turned his head and looked north. "Perhaps your visitor comes from there. We could investigate."

Ampharete looked in its direction. . . . "No," she finally said to Alcibiades, "I think our safest course now is to return to Athens and the chairs."

"You are concerned about my safety?"

"Yes, but not only that. You have been set free from your fate in Phrygia. History—the history I know—says nothing about what happened to you after that night, because on that night you died. The less we diverge from that history, the better. There is no point in courting divergence with an expedition to the island."

Alcibiades considered. "Are we not risking much more with my return to Athens? People know me in Athens."

"Very true. But Heron no doubt has a plan for that." She looked in the direction of Heron's sleeping form.

They reached Piraeus in pastel dawn light. The sky and the sea were a single milky shell.


*Athens, 404 BC*

Heron directed their landing, to what he reckoned was a "reasonably safe place—very few of them, hereabouts, these days."

Alcibiades looked around, grimly. Ampharete excused herself for a few minutes.

"Spartans and other agents of the Thirty are everywhere," Heron said to Alcibiades. "We need to be very careful."

"I hate them," Alcibiades said, from the depths of his being. "The mass of people—I feel both ways about them—I love them and hate them. But the Thirty are stupidity enthroned. That is far more danger-ous than democratic stupidity."

"It may interest you to know that both the people and the Thirty mirror your feelings about them, exactly. The people of Athens are not sure about you. The Thirty *are* sure—that is why they want you killed."

Alcibiades nodded.

"But, if it is any comfort, the Thirty will not last much longer. Democracy with all of its warts will soon be back here—and you will live to see that, perhaps even go on to play a role in that, now that we have saved you."

"Are you not concerned that my presence in Athens, after my re-ported death, can distort history?"

Heron regarded him. "You have been talking with Ampharete. With all of her intelligence, she is nonetheless a novice in time traveling. There are ways you can influence history without being known."

"The complexities of this time travel are supremely fascinating," Al-cibiades mused, "worthy of Zeno and his paradoxes. You have apparently saved me from my Spartan executioners. Although some may think I died last evening, in fact I did not die. And, given my predilection for causing trouble, that presumably means I *will* play some role in our ongoing his-tory. But if that is the case, and you come from the future, then how did you ever come to know that I died in the first place—how did you get the idea to come back and rescue a man who in fact had not been killed?"

Heron smiled, thinly. "One solution to this paradox, of course, is that even though we rescued you, other killers will soon dispatch you, before you have a chance to play your new role. But I will do my utmost to see that we are not extricated so easily from the jaws of this paradox."

"I am in your debt," Alcibiades said, tartly but truly.

"These paradoxes, by the way, are far more profound than Zeno's. You can walk, unhindered, from one place to another, even though there is always a half of a half of your distance left, because when those halves get very small, they no longer matter in the real world. In other words, the mere real act of walking punctures Zeno's paradox. With time travel, probably any activity—certainly any real transgression across time—forces the paradoxes into existence. To sit in that chair, to use it—you feel as if your arms are resting on the very oars of the universe."

Alcibiades considered, for a long few moments. He sighed. "Here is a more practical question: You arrived from the future in one of your chairs?"

"Yes."

"And the guards? Two fought bravely and died. We have two more with us now. That makes four who arrived in their chairs?"

"No, the guards come from this time. I trained them at a secret school in Sicily."

"You trained them?"

"Yes, over a period of time. And I had help from a few more experts that I brought back here—or a little before now—from various times in the future."

"You—"

"But it is better that we do not talk about that—I would not want you to go searching for that school."

Alcibiades nodded. "Let us return, then, to the question of the chairs. There is one chair, your chair, that is waiting, presumably, in a house not far from here. Ampharete presumably came in another chair. How, with those two chairs, can the three of us expect to go forward in time five years? Can two people sit in one chair?"

"No. Only one living being can travel in a chair."

"How then—"

Ampharete appeared, as if on cue.

"An excellent question," Heron replied softly, "the answer to which has yet to be determined."


The three walked forward, a guard in front and a guard to the rear, near what was left of one of the long walls that had protected the road from Piraeus to Athens, until the Spartans destroyed them.

"This will all be rebuilt and bustling in decades and centuries to come," Heron remarked. "The path will be teeming with people and commerce."

"And in millennia to come this will all be bright as daylight." Ampharete pointed to the last of the dark in the sky. "We will have lights that exceed the stars and the moon."

"How?" Alcibiades asked.

"By harnessing the power of lightning," Ampharete replied.

"Babylon electrified," Heron said.

Ampharete thought she recognized the reference. Her grandfather had had an old nineteenth-century book, bound in green cloth and lettered gold with something like that title, on his shelves. That perhaps was where she had first discovered her love for those old books and their bindings. And somewhere along the way in this strange journey, she had somehow come to know one of their editors, Mr. Appleton. . . . Which was more crazy—that she had met the editor, or had just heard the title spoken by an inventor who had been dead for two millennia? Both occurrences were insane, beyond any semblance of reason. . . . And yet here she was, looking at the ancient Athenian sky, and it seemed as any dawn.

"Did those speakers of Latin discover that power?" Alcibiades asked.

"Not that I know of," Heron replied. "I have helped them, brought them to the edge of their future, with some techniques, based on nature, that I brought to the past from my time. I did that with the power of heated water—steam. But I have not yet tried electricity."

"Did the citizens of Rome change the world with your steam?" Alcibiades asked.

"No, that was not my plan."

"Then why—?"

"I believe that in order for discoveries and new principles of knowledge to be well implemented, they have to be first introduced to people long before," Heron explained. "In that way, generations upon generations have time to become gradually accustomed to the new device. People accept a new invention because they already expect it, even though they may not be aware of that. Two and a half millennia from now, the world is finally becoming comfortable with ideas that were generated right now, in your time, not only by me, but by others who were born in this time— Ah, here we are. There is our house, with the chairs inside."

The guards entered the house first, took about five minutes, exited, and pronounced it safe.

"Are you sure?" Alcibiades pressed Heron, after he had translated. "We were surprised on the other side of the Aegean. We never discussed who that second group of killers were—they were obviously far more effective than the first. Are you certain they will not surprise us here again?"

"There are no guarantees," Heron replied. "But would you not agree we only increase our vulnerability by standing here and talking? If the house is being watched, word may have gone out, already, that we have arrived."

Alcibiades acknowledged the point.

Ampharete spoke up, uncomfortably. "There is something else. The guard told Heron that there are only two chairs in the house."

Alcibiades lifted a questioning eyebrow toward Heron.

"True. You have to be in one of those chairs," Heron said to Alcibiades.

"I will stay back," Ampharete said.

"I prefer you come with me," Alcibiades said. "Heron can protect himself back here far more easily than you."

"That is not the point," Ampharete said. "Heron knows more about the workings of the chairs and the pitfalls of time travel than I do. If something goes wrong five years from now, you will be better served with him beside you."

Alcibiades smiled. "I would still prefer your company."

Heron whispered to the guards.

Alcibiades braced, expecting the guards to try to take him by force into the house.

"No—" Ampharete reacted to something else.

One of the guards suddenly drew his sword and turned on his companion.

Only the other guard's swift reflexes saved him.

The two grappled with blades and fists.

"One of them is a traitor," Heron shouted.

"Yes. But which one?" Alcibiades shouted in return. He drew his weapon. "I will kill them both, to be sure."

"No." Heron grabbed Alcibiades' arm. "They are lethal fighters. You could be killed."

"He is right." Ampharete took Alcibiades' other arm. "We should go inside. If the traitor wins, you can surprise him in the dwelling with your knife."

Alcibiades looked at the battling guards. He stood his ground. "I have never seen men fight like this. Where did you say they received their training?" he asked Heron.

"What did you say to them?" Ampharete demanded of the inventor.

He ignored her and spoke to Alcibiades. "As I told you, they were trained with methods of the future. . . . Please. Let us leave this field to them. Do not jeopardize all that we accomplished in the past day."

Alcibiades thought for another second, then went, reluctantly, with Ampharete and Heron. He thought that the good guard had a fifty-fifty chance of besting the bad one, whichever each one was, whatever good and bad meant in this situation. But Ampharete was right that he could stand by the door inside and gain the advantage. He certainly had no intention of leaving in any chair before this situation with the guards was resolved. "What if the traitor triumphs?" Alcibiades asked Heron, anyway, to gauge his reaction, as they entered the house.

"Two of us, at least, will be long gone from here," Heron replied.


Two chairs stood mute sentry by the hearth inside.

Heron talked to Alcibiades. "The essential result is that you go forward in time now. May I suggest that you sit in the chair? It will take you away, and then Ampharete and I can discuss which of us will follow."

Ampharete slowly nodded her agreement.

Alcibiades did not. "Why is my going the essential outcome?" he demanded. "This is my home, in time as well as place. I can live here five years far more easily than either of you."

"True," Heron replied. "But your living here now, after we rescued you from death, could have unforeseen consequences. In the current time sequence, as history has reported it, you were murdered last night, as you know. My plan is to have you appear immediately before the death of Socrates, to help convince him to accept an offer to escape, an offer far better than Crito's. If Socrates believes that you were not really killed last night—if he learns in the days or weeks or months ahead that you live—then that would deprive your sudden appearance in his prison five years from now of its major impact. You would just be another beloved disciple pleading with him to escape."

Alcibiades looked at the chairs, then the door, and did not move. "You said I perhaps had a role to play here, in the restored democracy."

"Yes," Heron replied, "after you play your role in saving Socrates."

Alcibiades considered, said nothing.

"Let me be more clear," Heron continued. "Socrates aside, it is not advisable for you to be here for the next five years. No one has done any analysis about how your presence here—how the smile you give a pretty woman in the marketplace, how the coin you put in a beggar's hand, how the slightest inflection of your behavior—can infect and distort history."

"Have you devoted such thought to your plan to rescue Socrates?" Alcibiades replied. "If he utters a word to anyone after the death you say he will encounter, will not that distort history, too?"

"I am afraid we cannot afford any further luxury of discussion," Heron said. "If you will not get in the chair voluntarily, I am prepared to exercise force—"

Alcibiades laughed in Heron's face.

Ampharete started to speak—

The two guards burst in, very much intact, in concert, and with weapons in hand.

Alcibiades coolly stepped between Ampharete and the guards, his own weapon in hand.

Heron walked to one of the chairs and sat. He barked orders to the guards, incomprehensible to Alcibiades.

"He told them to take you to the other chair and be careful not to hurt you," Ampharete translated. "And now we know what he said to them outside: feign a fight to throw us off guard."

The guards approached, carefully.

Ampharete withdrew a small knife from her robe.

"Stay behind me," Alcibiades said. "If they are afraid to hurt me, I am your shield."

The guards moved suddenly and tackled Alcibiades.

Ampharete was half-pinned. But her hand with the knife was free. The neck of one of the guards was within reach. She stabbed, repeatedly.

The other guard cursed in Latin and drove the tip of his weapon toward Ampharete's face.

Alcibiades intercepted it. The point sliced Ampharete's shoulder. Alcibiades sank his own short sword into the guard, before he could do more damage.

"Are you hurt?" Alcibiades asked Ampharete.

She shook her head no.

He looked at her shoulder. "I disagree. You have to take that other chair."

"No," Ampharete replied. "Heron is right about that."

"You would not survive back here, alone," Alcibiades said. "Especially with that wound. I assume you have better medicine in your future."

"I would not need to stay here too long. I have . . . friends in the future. They will come back with another chair."

"To trade places with you? I doubt that." Alcibiades shook his head. "And another guard is likely to come through that door sooner than one of your friends in a chair."

Ampharete sighed, looked at the chairs.

Alcibiades looked at Heron in the chair. The bubble was already in place, and the whole chair seemed to shimmer slightly. "Is he already . . . underway?" Alcibiades asked.

"No, that is the 'ready-to-leave' state."

"Why is he waiting?"

"It is not safe for us to be so close to the chairs when they make their departures and arrivals. He will not move until you are in the other chair."

"Or away from here? Is that true, too?"

"I guess so. But maybe the best solution is neither of us goes. I could stay here with you and—"

"It is not safe for you here even with me," Alcibiades said. "I might not be able to protect you—I have barely managed, even now." He took her hand. "You will be safer in the future, the far far future, your time. . . . Go there now, if you can, if the chair permits it." He put his arm around her and moved her, so she was in front of him and his back was to Heron. He leaned down, picked up Ampharete's knife, and gave it to her. "He will not expect you to have this knife. Use it to make your escape in the future, if need be. Acquaint yourself with Heron's plan. Then return to the time of the death of Socrates. I will be there. . . . If I understand these processes of time travel correctly, it will not seem like a very long time for you. And I will be nurtured here by the knowledge that you will at least be safer than you are here, with these dogs from Hades on the loose." He looked at the dead guards. His lips curled.

Ampharete kissed Alcibiades, tearfully. She pulled a thin scroll from inside her garment, placed it in his hand, and walked reluctantly to the vacant chair.

He watched as the bubble emerged, and the chair shimmered.

Then he walked out into the new Athenian morning. He glanced at the sky and heard a sound like wine quickly filling an empty vessel. He could not tell whether the sound came from the house or his heart.

CHAPTER 6

ANDR.: Are you aware of what happens to the body when hemlock is consumed?

SOC.: It kills the body. I know this, as do you. It is the reason we are having this conversation. We perhaps differ on what hemlock, or any poison, does to the soul. I believe, though I admit I am not certain of this, that the soul can survive any agent of physical death.

ANDR.: I would like to consider with you what hemlock does to the physical body.

SOC.: What purpose would there be in such a consideration?

ANDR.: You are aware, I assume, that the death brought on by hemlock is a very painful and lengthy one? Three days of convulsions. Your body riddled with agony. Your face so contorted that your closest students would not recognize you, long before you reached the point of death.

SOC.: Yes, I am aware of that.

ANDR.: And it does not disturb you? Forgive me for parading such details before your eyes, Socrates. I do not wish to be cruel, to cause you pain, now—except that I wish to help you avoid much greater, unnecessary pain, later.

SOC.: I do not welcome pain. Having decided to accept the wrong decision of the untutored masses, I did not wish to see that decision rendered in a way that would bring me such pain. And neither did I, nor do I now, welcome death. But I accept it, for the reasons I have explained. And if it comes wrapped in undue pain, and the only way I could escape that pain was to escape the death, then, alas, I must accept the pain, too, though I would imagine no one is unhappier about that than I.

ANDR.: You would be surprised how many people will be unhappy about your death, Socrates. People who will not be persuaded by your reasoning. People who, like Crito before me this past night, will walk the rest of their days with wounded hearts and angry souls. Angry at the Athenians for putting you to death. With fury and contempt for those whose decision you say you must respect and want to be respected. Schoolboys, young men who pride themselves on their mastery of ethics, old men sitting under trees, all will join in this condemnation.

SOC.: No doubt the young men will be more severe in this condemnation than the old. You look to be less than half my age.

ANDR.: Does that mean I have less than half your wisdom?

SOC.: No. But it may mean you love life a bit more than I, and for very different reasons.

ANDR.: You disagree, then, with Heraclitus, and his view that old and young are the same?

SOC.: The "Weeping Philosopher"? His short bursts are provocative, but they lack sustained reasoning.

ANDR.: Could a judgment or an insight be true, even if did not benefit from detailed reasoning or the support of evidence?

SOC.: Yes, I suppose someone not versed in philosophy could make a true statement.

ANDR.: Are you familiar with the observation of Heraclitus that a river both changes all the time and remains the same?

SOC.: Yes, and I doubt any amount of reason or evidence could either prove or refute it. Does it have some logical connection to our consideration of hemlock, or to our different ages?

ANDR.: Heraclitus' observation about rivers, applied to time, is the basis of the knowledge that made my visit to you possible, and which I promised earlier I would explain to you.

soc.: I would be interested in learning more about such knowledge.

andr.: If we accept that time is like a river, and we see some merit in Heraclitus' claim that a river both changes and stays the same, then perhaps time changes and remains the same, as well. Far in the future, people discovered how to build devices that exploited this property of time, which allowed them to travel between future and past, past and future, as if they were the same—

*Athens, 404 BC*

Alcibiades put down the manuscript and scratched his scalp. These words were similar to the conversation Heron and he had had about travel through time, in their hurried journey to the river Maeander. Was Heron somehow Andros, despite his being older than half of Socrates' age? Alcibiades also wondered about the words of his mentor—they at once seemed like Socrates and did not. But Alcibiades could not tell why. To read rather than hear his mentor's voice was strange.

Alcibiades had been in Athens for a month since his presumed death. He had stayed away from everyone he knew, most importantly Socrates. The events of that night and the next day had been so incredible that they seemed a dream. He was grateful that Ampharete had given him a copy of this manuscript, for these weighty words on the thin scroll were his only proof that his recollections were real.

But Alcibiades would have known that anyway, he realized, even with no proof in his hands. No dream, no recollection of a dream, could have left so searing an impression.

No—he took what he had heard and learned that evening and day, what he saw anew every time he read this manuscript, very seriously. Especially about time travel.

He had returned to this unremarkable house halfway between Piraeus and Athens—unremarkable on the outside, extraordinary beyond comprehension on the inside—several times. He had always taken great care to make sure no one else was around. But he also knew that carefully hidden eyes could elude even the greatest care.

Now he rose and walked to the doorway and looked outside, as far and acutely as he could. It was a little past sundown, and the sky was weak. Nothing had much clarity or color. He was hungry and started to leave—

He heard something—no, he sensed it—behind him, back in the house. He turned around. The air almost seemed to be spinning inside itself, like a little current going in reverse against the bigger current around it. He looked more intently. The effect was becoming more pronounced. It was just above where the chairs had been.

Safety . . . Ampharete had mentioned something in those last moments, which he had recited over and over like a precious poem, about dangers in departures and arrivals. Heron had also written about them in the scroll he had put in his hand in Phrygia. Alcibiades walked outside the house.

Now he listened as carefully as he had been looking. . . . He thought he heard something, inside. Not a wet, whoosh sound, but an aftermath of a clack, what was left of a seabird's cry after the bird had flown almost out of sight.

He listened for more. He put his ear closer to the house. . . . He heard steps.

He walked inside, hand on the hilt of his weapon.

A young, dark-haired man smiled at him. "My name is Jonah. I have news of the future."

"How do I know it is not death you seek to convey to me?" Alcibiades kept his hand on his sword. But it relaxed, a little. He could see that the young man carried no visible weapon. Nor did he seem especially strong. But who knew what techniques of injury the future had invented.

"I wish only to talk," Jonah said.

Alcibiades realized Jonah had the same odd accent as Heron. That was no proof of good intentions, but it made Alcibiades feel a little more comfortable, nonetheless. He regarded the young man. "You come from the time of Heron?"

Jonah nodded. "From the great city of Alexandria, yes. And recently from places much further away. . . . I know this is the city of Athens. Does Socrates still live?" Jonah took a step towards Alcibiades.

"Stay where you are." Alcibiades gripped his sword.

Jonah stopped. "I wish only to talk to you."

Alcibiades looked around the room. He stared at the chair in which Jonah presumably had arrived. It was a temptation. But where would Alcibiades take it? To the night of Socrates' death, as Heron had wanted? Alcibiades knew that he needed more knowledge before he traveled to that event, unescorted. . . . This young man could be a source. . . . But this place did not seem safe now. Who knew who else might arrive out of the empty air in those chairs. . . . Alcibiades finally nodded to Jonah. "Not here," he said, and gestured to the doorway.

Jonah walked through first. Alcibiades followed, hand still on the hilt of the sword.


The two entered a drab, drafty inn for dinner. Alcibiades did not trust Jonah enough to take him to any of the secret places in which Alcibiades had been living and hiding.

"I have cut my beard and arranged my hair in a way that I am not likely to be recognized," Alcibiades said. "And the value of this poor food is that no one I know is likely to be here. I am sorry that you have to be subjected to it."

Jonah bit into a dark, tough bread. "I have tasted far worse in the future. Much of the food in that world tastes like it was made of cloth or straw."

Alcibiades shook his head, then smiled crookedly. "On the other hand, the women are extraordinary. Would you agree?"

"Yes."

Alcibiades looked at him. "You know her," he stated quietly.

"Yes."

"Did she ask you to come back to Athens and talk to me? I had assumed you were here on Heron's instructions."

Jonah swallowed his bread and sipped some soup. "I do not know if she would want me to tell you this. I am not even sure she knows that I know this."

"Yes?"

"She will die, sometime in the future."

"Everyone will die."

"No, I mean, she will be murdered, horribly. She will be beaten by a group of religious fanatics, and her flesh—"

Alcibiades held up his hand. "Enough."

"I am sorry." Jonah ate more bread.

"When will this happen?"

"About two and a half centuries after the time of my origin, in my city, near my magnificent, helpless library. . . ." Jonah's voice thickened.

"I will not let that happen."

"It has already happened . . . already will happen . . . the whole world of the future beyond the time of her murder knows that she was brutally killed. The most intelligent, beautiful woman of her time. The daughter of the last chief librarian of Alexandria."

"Was Ampharete really his daughter?"

"No. She says she originally lived more then two millennia from now."

Alcibiades considered. "Was Ampharete her name . . . when she was killed?"

"No. She was called Hypatia."

"Then how do you know with such conviction that the two were the same person?"

Jonah put down his bread. "I was there, several months before the murder. I saw her. Ampharete . . . rearranged her face, but she did not change her voice, or her . . . manner. Ampharete and Hypatia who was murdered are the same person. And so is Sierra Waters, which is her original name."

Alcibiades clenched his fist in anger. His voice rose. "You were there? You knew that Ampharete was this Hypatia?" Alcibiades realized he was shouting. Fortunately, the only other patron of the inn, an old man with unkempt gray hair, had passed out on his table. "And you did nothing?" Alcibiades managed to keep this a little less loud, though his emotion was scalding.

"I was there months before the murder. I did not know then that she was going to be murdered. I left to go to the future, as my mentor had instructed. When I found out about her death, I tried to get back there, to save her."

"And?"

"And the passage through time was blocked."

"By whom?" Alcibiades asked, though he thought perhaps he knew.

"Heron is the likely one," Jonah said, in a strangled voice.

"You picked a fine mentor," Alcibiades said venomously.

"He picked *me*—but he is no longer my mentor, now."

Alcibiades tried to calm himself. He partially succeeded. He took a deep breath. "What are his motives? Why is he so dedicated to saving Socrates? I truthfully am skeptical of anyone so devoted to such a self-less goal."

Jonah shook his head sadly. "He is an inventor. To him, the possibility of perfecting history is like perfecting one of his wondrous devices. He will continue to tinker, to do whatever is necessary, to make the process work. Nothing else is of consequence to him now."

Alcibiades decided that he trusted Jonah enough to offer him shelter in one of his many hideouts. Besides, the only way Alcibiades could be sure that Jonah did not follow him to his dwelling tonight was to kill him, and Alcibiades neither distrusted nor disliked Jonah nearly enough to do that.

Alcibiades did not attempt to seduce Jonah, though he found him attractive enough and was reasonably sure Jonah would have been receptive. Alcibiades' situation was already complicated—he did not want to risk adding sexuality to the mix. Or perhaps he was just getting old. . . .

The two began strategic temporal planning in the morning.

"We have one chair now available to us here," Alcibiades said, "as a result of your journey. But we cannot take it to save Ampharete from destruction, because the way to the year in which that happened is blocked."

"Yes," Jonah replied.

"But presumably you or I could take it to five years from now, to help prevent the death of Socrates."

"You would be a better person to undertake that journey than I."

Alcibiades did not contest the point. "Do you know if Ampharete was . . . will be . . . there? Or had she already been . . . killed?"

"I do not know if she was there with Socrates, but I am sure that Hypatia was killed afterwards. . . . When I saw Ampharete as Hypatia, she

154

looked a little older. Still beautiful as the early afternoon, even with her face remade, but older."

"If there is a chance that Ampharete will be there with Socrates, then that could be our moment—perhaps our only opportunity—to save her. Save two birds of passage with one magical net."


Alcibiades and Jonah paced the small room.

"What was the outcome of Andros' proposal to Socrates?" Alcibiades asked. "Do you know?"

"The dialog says Socrates said no. But—"

"I know. I meant, do you have any firsthand knowledge, or even reports from anyone who actually was there in the prison, about what happened? Dialogs and the events they describe are not always the same."

"Heron believes Socrates might have gone with Andros in the end," Jonah answered. "This might be more of a hope, a plan, on Heron's part, than actual reality. I am not sure."

"You were not there on that night."

"No, I was not. That is why I do not know if Ampharete was there."

"Does anyone else share Heron's . . . impression of success?" Alcibiades asked.

"Thomas also conveyed it to me."

"Ah, yes, the mysterious man. Ampharete thinks very highly of him."

"Ampharete was his student. Her assessment of his capacity may have been shaped by that perspective."

"You do not share her view?"

"I do not know him well enough to make a reliable judgment," Jonah replied.

"How did you come to meet him? Where did it happen?"

Jonah sighed. "Ampharete came to Alexandria the first time, as Ampharete. . . . I first met her then. She showed Heron the Andros manuscript, and he went off to Athens to seek the truth. Ampharete and I followed, but our ship was blown in the wrong direction, far to the west. Ampharete convinced Melqat, its captain—he was a coarse man but a fine seaman—to take her across a great ocean, further west. I sailed east, to Athens, where I found Heron. But he was a different man."

"In what way?"

"He was older, less pleased by contemplation, more driven by his goals. He told me more than five years of his life had passed since he and I had last been in contact, even though it had been less than five weeks for me. He asked if I would be willing to sail across the great ocean to the west. He told me it would take a year. He wanted to know exactly what Ampharete had seen and accomplished. He wanted me to help put her on the path."

"The path?"

Jonah nodded, said nothing. Then: "Yes, the path that would lead her to you, in Phrygia."

Alcibiades sped through conflicting emotions.

"Heron was my mentor," Jonah proceeded. "I agreed to his request. He chartered a boat for the voyage. But he did not accompany me."

"I assume you found chairs at the end of that voyage?"

"Yes, and more. A river that was salty even far upstream of its mouth. Cliffs so sheer and sharp of edge, they looked as if they had been cut by a master builder. There were barbarians living in the forests who resembled people from the Far East, yet I had traveled almost due west."

Alcibiades reflected. "Pythagoras of Samos argued that the earth is a sphere. Anaximander of Miletus placed his map of the earth on a cylinder. Perhaps what you found in the west shows this was a wise choice." Alcibiades' thoughts swirled . . . from Pythagoras and music to Miletus and Ampharete . . .

"Eratosthenes, closer to my time, offered measurements for the circumference of the earth, which he believed to be round," Jonah said. "By the time of Thomas O'Leary, everyone was sure this was true—people had actually left this planet and looked back at it from the sky."

Alcibiades walked to the door, opened it, and squinted at the late morning. "You have left the earth, to walk through the zodiac?"

"Not I. But the people of the future, of Thomas O'Leary's age."

"I suspect that age would be incomprehensible to me. But you have yet to tell how you came to meet Thomas O'Leary."

"Heron described him to me. Heron wanted me to make sure that Ampharete took the right journey. That required my befriending Thomas, in the year that his people called 1889. Heron told me where to find the chair at the end of the ocean. He told me how to use it, to arrive in the time of Thomas."

Alcibiades shook his head slowly at the immensity of what he was being told.

Jonah continued, "I suspect you might well find yourself at home with much of the logic, even the knowledge, of that age. Much of it arose from this time."

Alcibiades regarded Jonah. "Your former mentor said the same."

"The main difference in the ages resides in the devices, the manner in which the knowledge is applied in the real, physical world. This was already clear when I became Heron's student."

Alcibiades gaped at the sky. "Which do you suppose is stranger, to walk upon the sky, or talk to me now?"

"Our conversation," Jonah replied without hesitation, "my presence in your world. Travel across any distance, even to the sky, is just an extension of what we already do. Birds travel to the sky every day. But travel from one time to another is something very contrary to nature. It threatens to make a mockery of all existence."

"I think you are right," Alcibiades replied. "Should we forget about Socrates, then, and live our lives as if none of this time travel had already occurred? No, I do not believe I could ever do that."

"It is too late to forget about Socrates. Too many feet have been set into motion."

"We might make things worse, by being there, and unwittingly contributing to an unfortunate outcome," Alcibiades mused.

"By not being there we might also contribute to a bad result, and we would have no way of refining and possibly improving our actions. If we were absent, all we would be was absent, with no room for corrections."

"And how do you propose the two of us get there, with just one chair?"

"I propose that I take the chair," Jonah said. "I have served my purpose here with you now—I have told you what I wanted to convey, what you needed to know about Ampharete and the peril that awaits her. There is nothing more I can do here. You, on the other hand, may yet have some further role to play, back here, on the road to the death or the rescue of Socrates—despite what Heron told you."

Alcibiades looked at the sky again. "I think you are right about that, too," he said eventually.


The two walked quickly back to the house that contained the chair.

"You must stay outside," Jonah said, "or go outside before I use the chair."

Alcibiades nodded. "I know. I will stay outside."

Jonah started to say something—

Alcibiades hugged him. It was a strange, hybrid hug, born in the mixture Alcibiades felt of sharing the same helpless fate with Jonah, of feeling connected to him, but also suspicious of someone he hardly knew, and angry that Jonah had somehow manipulated Ampharete, and therefore Alcibiades, too.

Suspicion chose his words. "Can I trust you?" Alcibiades asked hoarsely, dangerously.

"Yes," Jonah answered firmly, "though you know I cannot prove it."

Alcibiades shook his head, but loosened his grip. "Will I see you again?"

Jonah smiled slightly, enigmatically. "Yes, though in circumstances you now cannot even imagine, and I dare not tell you more. . . . Except . . . choose your paths very carefully, at every step in this process."

Alcibiades sighed, smiled, let go of Jonah completely. "I do not believe in the gods, but may Hermes guide you, in any case."


Alcibiades changed his manner of living, slightly, in the months ahead. He risked contacting several close friends, whom he thought he could trust. His trust was well placed. He worked with them to bring down the hated Thirty.

He got the news one day near dusk, by a fruit stand in the marketplace. "Critias and Charmides are slain," his friend whispered, "democracy is restored in Athens!"

"If that is true, there is no need to whisper."

His friend laughed, then spat on the ground. "The despots are dead!" he shouted. Then he whispered again to Alcibiades. "Those two sent those Spartan killers after you. I do not know about the other assassins you mentioned. But at least those two tyrants are gone."

"The cousin and uncle of Plato," Alcibiades muttered.

"Who is Plato?"

"Just stay alive," Alcibiades responded, "and if my information is right, you will soon know a lot about Plato."

His friend nodded and left.

Alcibiades bit into a sweet fig and examined the fading sky. So, he had succeeded in ridding Athens of the Thirty, and restoring democracy—the very democracy, if he could believe Heron and Ampharete and Jonah, that would in several years sentence his mentor Socrates to death.

Hard to believe, but Alcibiades was beginning to believe it.

Yet he had much to consider. Should he try to seek the leaders of Socrates' enemies and kill them, those in the democracy who would rally the forces against his mentor? That was his instinct—stop the murderers in democratic guise right now. Crush them like worms in their tracks.

But if he did that, would other enemies come forth to destroy Socrates, to insure that he met his appointed fate, whatever the efforts of Alcibiades or anyone else? But what was the truly intended fate of Socrates—of Alcibiades, of any human being—and who or what intended it? In a world in which travel through time could reverse death, fate seemed deprived of its power.

And if Alcibiades did crush those demagogues who would draw forth the enmity against Socrates, he might be removing the very reason Ampharete had come back here in the first place, the very reason Heron had saved him—to help rescue Socrates, to convince him to accept Andros' offer, after Socrates had been convicted and sentenced to death. If there was no trial, there would be none of that . . . no one to save Alcibiades from that first wave of killers.

It seemed he had no choice but to let events take their course—if not their natural course, the course that perhaps he had helped set into motion. He had always agreed with Pythagoras on the supremacy and independence of the human soul. But it seemed that the free soul met its match in the labyrinth of time travel.

---

The air was saltier than usual today, about six months after Jonah the traveler had taken his leave. Alcibiades breathed in deeply while he walked toward the marketplace in Athens. It was not a good idea, he knew, to be in so public a place in full daylight—even with the Thirty gone. He recalled his conversations with Heron, never far from his thoughts. Alcibiades was a dead man, as far as history knew. The dead were obliged to tread lightly in the sunlit world.

But Alcibiades wanted to be outdoors today, among people. He would try to stay anonymous in the crowd. The challenge excited him.

He closed his eyes as he walked and enjoyed the air even more. He felt as if he were on the sea, or breathing in the scent of Aphrodite and Ampharete.

He arrived at the marketplace—the agora of Athens. As always, the place was filled with people of all shapes and sizes. Alcibiades smiled. He always felt good here. Fortunately, no one looked familiar.

He had a craving for figs, which he satisfied at a little stall. He bought four. He walked off, a little to the side. He leaned against a wall and bit into the sticky fruit. He explored the sweet pulp with his tongue, teased it with his teeth, then consumed the fig whole. He did this four times, with his eyes closed and the tangy air in his nostrils. He thought of her each time.

Alcibiades opened his eyes and started walking out of the market, to one of his secret places on the road.

He spotted a pair of men in the distance. They were young men, not much older than boys.

Alcibiades squinted. When he was sure who they were, he turned around, so he could decide what to do without being seen.

One of those men was Plato.

Alcibiades' thoughts spun like foam in a sea squall. Plato—responsible for what the world would know of Socrates, according to Alcibiades' informants from the future. Accounts by Xenophon and Aristophanes would survive, but none of the others that Alcibiades knew. And that horse fancier and that playwright would be minor contributors to the world's knowledge of Socrates. It would all be Plato, the sycophant.

Alcibiades could stop that, end that, right now. He could kill Plato, and most of his damnable dialogs would never be written.

He heard the hounds of paradox baying in some corner of his brain. Without Plato as Socrates' Homer, who would know about Socrates in the future? Who would care enough about him to want to do anything to stop his death? Would Xenophon and Aristophanes be enough?

Would any of that be enough to get Heron on his way to that bed in the night in Phrygia?

Of course, there was another way of depriving Plato of the last word about Socrates. If Socrates lived, then Plato's accounts would play a different role. Maybe Alcibiades could even prevail upon Socrates to commit some of his thoughts to writing. His mentor was not illiterate, after all, though Alcibiades had heard him say many times that he detested writing, that it brought no good to the world.

As for Plato, murder was not the only way to control him. Indeed, it was a clumsy way, even with no paradoxes of time. There were better methods, which might even be able to turn this boy into an ally.

Alcibiades stepped into the shadows, so Plato could not see him. Plato and his friend passed by, oblivious to the near death that stared at them from just a few feet away. Alcibiades shuddered and marveled again at the shackles of time travel. Did he have any choice about anything at all now, or was he ineluctably funneled, touched and woven by Ampharete and Heron, into the prison that held Socrates?

His one consolation, when he thought of Ampharete and Heron and Jonah, was that none of them seemed to have free choice in this.


Alcibiades put the months that followed to use. If he was to be at Socrates' side at the time of his greatest need, he might as well fortify his hand. He could not rely on that mysterious Andros, any more than he could rely on the unseen Thomas, or even Jonah. Even if some force of the universe, partly of human creation, had obligated him to save Socrates, Alcibiades would depend on himself and what he could bring to that prison. And then he would save Ampharete.

He quietly began recruiting a small but deadly cohort. A slim majority of five hundred had sentenced Socrates to death, according to Jonah, but far fewer would be guarding him. A dozen men, well armed and instructed, could carry Socrates to safety, regardless of what he wanted.

There were many, Alcibiades knew, who remained disaffected from the restored Athenian democracy—a mob that ruled, even though it was preferable to the haughty Thirty. From those disaffected, Alcibiades—once a general, always an inspiring leader—raised his small, loyal cadre.

Of the house that contained the chair, Alcibiades saw less and less. The mechanics as well as the paradox of time travel receded, its headache muted, as he focused on the practical matters at hand.

Until, one day, he saw Ampharete walking in the agora.

"I hesitated to smile at you," he said, after they had clasped hands and set forth toward Piraeus. "I was afraid that perhaps we had not yet met, that you were a younger version of yourself." He felt surprisingly awkward. It was this time travel.

"Do I look younger than the last time?" she asked.

"You only look beautiful."

Ampharete smiled. "Take me someplace private, and I will show you how well I remember our first meeting."

They stopped well before Piraeus, at an outcropping of stone, surrounded by soft, green grass. Alcibiades took her down by the sea. He had been here before, decades earlier. The sand looked as if it had been trodden only by wind and water since.

He scooped her up in his arms, so she sat against his palms, and her legs wrapped around his waist. He saw the sky against the sea, the keen blue on blue, then he closed his eyes to that and everything except Ampharete.

"You were gone a long time," he said hoarsely, later, as they lay spent, content, like shells in the ebb tide.

"It was not as long for me," Ampharete murmured.

Alcibiades rolled onto his back and looked up at the uncluttered blue. "This time travel tests the very limits of my comprehension."

Ampharete put her head on his chest.

"I met your friend Jonah," Alcibiades said.

She lifted her head. "How is he?"

"You are in his deepest heart."

"I am glad he is well."

"Is he in yours?"

"I care for him."

Alcibiades ran his hand through her hair.

"Did you meet anyone else of interest back here while I was away?" Ampharete asked.

"I saw Plato."

"Does he love you?"

Alcibiades laughed. "I doubt he loves anyone." He stopped laughing. "We did not speak. I merely watched him. . . . I almost killed him."

Ampharete sat up and looked into Alcibiades' eyes. "You must not do that—ever."

Alcibiades pulled her close to him, turned her face to him, and kissed her forehead. "Jonah told me that you will be put to death sometime in the future, in the throes of this Roman Empire, in a city called Alexandria, named after the student of the student of Plato. I would gladly kill him to prevent that."

She touched his chest. "Where will you be . . . in this future, where I am killed?"

"He did not say."

Ampharete brushed her lips on Alcibiades' chest, cupped his face in her hand. "Everything is different, because of you. The moment you were saved, the instant we stopped those murderers in Phrygia, everything changed. We may not have seen it, at first. But every breath that you have taken since then has made the air just a little bit different . . . every person who has seen you, even for an instant, is different. Before we saved you, history—your future, my past—was what it was. Now, nothing is certain, and everything is possible."

"You are not disturbed by what Jonah told me?"

"I am saying that something, anything, you might do in an hour, a year from now, could change that . . . and without your killing anyone."

"Yet you and Heron saved me, knowing that it would unhinge history. Heron did it because he wanted my help with Socrates. Presumably he thought that benefit was worth the risk. And you . . . ?"

"I came back to Phrygia in search of Thomas. Jonah had told me that you were a key."

Alcibiades nodded. "He told you this in your land across the ocean?"

"Yes. And I know Jonah was doing his mentor's bidding. . . . You were an experiment for Heron. I am somehow part of that. You and I are still an experiment for him."

"And if he is not happy with the results? He would kill us? Do you suppose a later version of Heron was somehow responsible for that second attack? That he sent back that second group of soldiers from the future to correct what his first guards had done . . . and erase something I will do tomorrow, next year, or when Socrates is in prison?"

"Possibly," Ampharete replied. "But Heron did a good job of almost being slaughtered by that second group. It did not feel to me that he was acting."

"Would his earlier self be in position to know that—know that his later self had sent back a second group of assassins to undo what his earlier self was trying to accomplish?"

"No . . . ," Ampharete conceded. "But his later self would have to have instructed those second assassins not to kill the earlier Heron. . . . It all happened very fast, but it did not seem to me as if those assassins were in any way shielding Heron."

"I suppose that is so. Yet Heron survived." Alcibiades exhaled slowly. "It seems to me that this time travel can falsify anything, everything—nothing is real, nothing is reliable, in a world in which the causes of things can be pulled up like turnips and tossed away."

The two were together for three days. Alcibiades woke on the fourth morning and found Ampharete pacing in the inner courtyard of their hiding place. A Molossian puppy was asleep in a corner.

Ampharete smiled at Alcibiades. "I bought him for you in the agora this morning."

"I used to have one."

"I know." She reached into her pocket and withdrew a wafer-thin device. "And this I brought from my own time to help me translate my language into yours, and your language into mine, so I could converse more effectively here. It would work just as well for you."

She placed the wafer into Alcibiades' hand. "See? You press this little picture and say a word, in your language. The device will say the word, in my language."

Alcibiades pressed the picture. He said, *"Polis."* The device spoke up: "City."

"And it works in reverse," Ampharete said. "To go from my language to your language, you just press this other little picture, here, and say a word in my language." She pressed the picture and said, "Skill." The device responded, *"Techne."* She pressed the device again. "And look at this—when you become proficient in a new language, you can use this part to learn how to speak in regional tongues."

"You mean the way Greek is spoken slightly differently in cities far away?"

"Yes. So if someone comes back here and speaks a strange version of my language, you may be able to comprehend it."

Alcibiades looked at the device, then placed it against his chest. "Thank you. I will be very careful with these gifts." He caressed her face. "Do not go."

"I do not want to."

"But that is what you are planning. That is why you gave me these gifts."

Ampharete was silent.

Alcibiades sighed.

Ampharete spoke. "I want us to forget about Socrates, forget about Heron, forget about everyone—but they will not forget about *us.* Whoever sent that second group of killers on the other side of the Aegean can find us here. I do not want you to have cheated death, only to have death take you after all."

"I will not let that happen—"

"You cannot stop it. You can stop killers, but you cannot stop the cosmos from sending more killers. The only way forward for us now is to proceed with Heron's plan—or whoever's plan it really is." Ampharete grasped his hand. "We will meet on the night of Socrates' presumed suicide—"

"No—"

"Listen to me. You have already changed history, are changing history, by being here—that is dangerous enough. We cannot let emotions rule us!"

"Emotions have nothing to do with this."

Ampharete started to reply and stopped.

"Logic is my guide in this," Alcibiades said. "The chariots of our lives are running out of control—I suspect it cannot be otherwise when the roads they traverse are made equally of minutes and centuries. We can be sure of almost nothing in that quickness. But we can know ourselves, and if we stay close, we can know each other. We at least can rely on that."

Ampharete shook her head and strode out of the dwelling.

Alcibiades was not sure if she knew how to get to the chair from this place—

Ampharete burst back into the room. Her face was slick with tears. She flung her arms around Alcibiades and kissed his lips, repeatedly.

"I will stay," she finally said. *For now,* she thought shakily.


One day, Alcibiades realized it had been exactly one year; it was the anniversary of his "death." It was a cold day. Ugly rain was in the sky.

Ampharete was napping. Alcibiades looked at her and thought, *You are the brightest thing in the world today.*

He fed the hound, told him to stay, and trudged to the house with the chair. He felt drawn to it on this strange anniversary, really the birthday of his rescued life. The dwelling looked even more desolate than usual. Good, that was its best protection from intruders.

But as he approached the door, he sensed activity within.

He held back, quivering, waiting for the noise to stop. Someone was coming in the chair. Jonah, Heron, who?

He heard nothing. Only the throbbing in his ears.

That was helpful. No noise was good. It meant he could enter.

He opened the door.

Someone was in the chair.

Socrates—

CHAPTER 7

*New York City, AD 2042*

Thomas O'Leary walked up to William Henry Appleton in front of the Millennium Club in Manhattan. It was the middle of the twenty-first century, and it was pouring ice-cold April rain.

Thomas shook the water off of his partially wrecked, spider-strand umbrella.

Appleton chuckled. "One thing we'll never learn, regardless of how far we progress, is how to construct a workable umbrella. . . . Isn't that right, Thomas?"

Thomas grumbled agreement and pushed open the door.

Mr. Bertram, one of the Club's librarians, was just leaving through the vestibule. "Are you gentlemen here for lunch?" he inquired pleasantly.

"Why, yes, we are," Appleton replied with equal cheer.

Bertram nodded and spoke softly, "It's especially good today. . . . Don't tell anyone I told you this, but I've noticed the members are enjoying the food much more since we signed on that new chef!"

"I love all the food of this era!" Appleton exulted.

Bertram trained a gimlet eye on Appleton, but decided to give him the benefit of the doubt. "Well, yes, I suppose you could say this is a new era for the Millennium's cuisine."

Thomas smiled briefly and nodded. Bertram took his leave.

The two men climbed the carpeted staircase to the elegant Victorian dining room.


"You're especially serious today, Thomas," Appleton observed, as he scooped out a juicy piece of new multismo melon. He put it into his mouth and savored the flavor. "Extraordinary!"

"The lines are converging," Thomas responded.

"You mean in 399 BC?"

"Yes."

"Then they have already converged, and what has happened has happened," Appleton said.

Thomas waved the point away. "Spare me. I'm not in the mood for that today. What has happened has already happened, true, but if it is to bring something new into the world, something of which we are not aware, then in our existence it has not yet really happened. Or, it has happened in a way that makes no impact, in which case we have wasted our time, and that is not a very happy prospect to contemplate, either."

"The wheels are moving back there—they already have moved back there—and there is nothing we can now do to change that. This is the point I was making. There are no chairs upstairs. Jonah says that Heron—"

Thomas scowled.

"I know you don't care for him," Appleton continued. "But this could not have happened without him. You had the ideas. He had the gadgets."

"That's true enough about the equipment. You're probably too generous to me regarding the ideas."

"Oh?"

"I can truthfully say I don't really know who really came up with these ideas, this plan, in the first place—except it wasn't me."

"It has to be Andros."

Thomas sighed. "We're all embroiderers of a plan whose creator we do not know. I have been woven into this, and I have woven. I've spent . . ." Thomas paused and shook his head. "I've woven others into this, including Sierra, including you—"

"I'm quite pleased to have been so woven, I assure you."

Thomas winced, then smiled a little. "We have to be closer to the event. We can't just sit here."

"What do you propose? We have no means of transport to the past. No chairs in residence upstairs."

"None here, no."

"None in London, either," Appleton said.

"Right. That leaves us Athens."

Appleton put down his spoon. "We can't go to Athens—you've said so yourself, many times—we have to avoid that vanished boat, at all costs. And this is precisely the time the boat went missing, isn't it? Miss Waters thinks you're in Wilmington—you told her this morning you were going there. But she'll soon find out you went to Athens instead, when she reads in that electrical newspaper that your boat disappeared in the Aegean. You don't want that to happen—you don't want to be in that boat. So now you propose going to that very part of the world?"

"We'll fly by fast plane," Thomas responded. "We'll go to the place between Athens and Piraeus that I told you about—it's still there—and take the chairs. No boats. No disappearances at sea."

"There has to be another way, that does not take us so close—"

"There is no other way. There are no other chairs. We can't just sit and talk and wait. I can't just throw her to the wolves of time—I'm responsible, one hundred percent, for her being in ancient Athens right now."

Appleton shook his head. "It still beggars the brain to think of one person in two places at the same time. She's here in New York City, right, and a somewhat older self is back there in the golden age of Greece . . . Whilst a slightly younger version of *myself* is in the Parthenon Club in London right now."

"Yes."

"Are you sure?"

"About Sierra being in 399 BC Athens?"

"No, I know you're not sure about that," Appleton said. "How could you be? But you have reason enough to think that she likely is there."

"Yes, I do."

"I meant, are you sure about flying to Athens now?"

"Yes," Thomas replied.

"Should I call for the check, then?"

"No, we can wait for the after-lunch macaroons. We're not in that kind of a rush. Besides, the chairs should take us back to 399 BC, or close to that year, regardless of whether we arrive in Athens today or tomorrow."

Appleton looked out the window of the hypersonic transport. There wasn't much to see, but he loved it anyway.

Thomas pored over the dialog. There was a lot to see, and he loved and hated it.

Appleton, with some effort, moved his eyes from the blur outside and regarded Thomas and the dialog.

"Heron cannot be Andros, because of their ages," Appleton said.

Thomas nodded.

"What about a younger Heron?" Appleton asked.

"We know from multiple sources that Heron invented the chairs when he was fifty-two, in the future. Heron at that age or older would have had to recruit the younger Heron. That creates a pretty nasty paradox—young Heron gets a visit from older Heron, or his representative, about a device young Heron must later invent? Risky. If young Heron later invents the chairs because of information his older self gave him, where did that information come from in the first place?"

"I see the problem," Appleton said. "Still . . . okay, let's consider some less paradoxical candidates. Maxwell Marcus is accomplished in ancient culture and modern science."

"He is. But his ancient Greek couldn't possibly be good enough to carry on that level of conversation with Socrates."

"And Jonah?"

"Just the reverse. His Greek would likely be comprehensible to Socrates, even with their different dialects, if Jonah spoke slowly and clearly, but he couldn't possibly have such ease with our science."

"He's a very bright boy," Appleton countered. "He has spent a lot of time with Heron, and with us here as well, and seems to know more about the chairs and their operation than anyone other than Heron. . . . Still, I agree that Andros seems to have a depth of wisdom, an ease of advanced knowledge, that is beyond Jonah or anyone of his age. . . . All right, let's look at this question a different way, then. Let's say we knew, for an absolute fact, that Andros was *not* Heron, Maxwell, or Jonah. Who, then, do you think Andros might be? Someone we don't know from Adam, or someone—"

The landing announcement came on, in six soothing renditions.

*Athens, AD 2042*

The HST clicked in tightly and smoothly, like a paper clip to a magnet, on the landing strip at Athens Realport. "The old airport was blown up two times, earlier in this century," Thomas told Appleton. "They finally built this out here, on the sea, and it stuck. Much more defensible than anything on land."

"Who blew it up?"

"Terrorists. They were like locusts back then."

Appleton grimaced.

"You had them in your day, too," Thomas continued. "Just not as well organized." *William McKinley will be president and assassinated by an anarchist, a few years after Cleveland finishes his second term*, Thomas recalled. *Just two years after your own death.* He was glad Appleton could not see his near future.

They took an amphicab over sea and land to the house with the chairs, halfway between Piraeus and Athens. The house had been many things over the millennia, most recently a brothel. Now it was a medium-priced restaurant. The chairs, when they were present, were against the walls of a private room in the back.

Thomas and Appleton entered. Their eyes took a few moments to adjust to the loss of sunlight.

A lone man was sitting at the bar, his back to the entrance. He turned and offered greetings. "Good to see you," he said to Thomas. He nodded at Appleton and sipped from a short, thick glass, which he raised. "The ouzo is delicious—would you care for some?" He spoke English in a slight Greek and unidentifiable accent that sounded mostly peculiar but also a bit familiar to Appleton.

Appleton squinted at him. "Have we perhaps had the pleasure of meeting before?"

The man at the bar squinted back. "I don't believe so."

Thomas grunted. "William Henry Appleton, meet Heron of Alexandria and many other places."

The three sipped ouzo at a table. "We have the place to ourselves," Heron said. "I paid the owner well."

"He knows about the chairs?" Appleton asked.

"He knows there is something in the back which is mine, and which he should pay no attention to, other than to make sure no one else pays attention to it. He probably thinks I'm a dealer in drugs. He is happy to take my money."

Thomas smiled, sourly. "We are in a way, aren't we? Your chairs are a psychedelic to history—dilating this, contracting that, except they change not only the perception but the reality."

"What is *psychedelic*?" Appleton asked.

Thomas explained.

"Yes, I can see the resemblance," Appleton said. "And this time travel also can kill us, just as surely as too many doses of drugs." He talked about the three men vanishing in a boat in the Aegean. "And, with the three of us here, we now have fulfilled the requisite number."

"Let me assure you," Heron said, "I, at least, have no intention of traveling anywhere away from here by boat."

"I assumed as much," Appleton replied. "Nonetheless, these time trips have a habit of taking us to places we did not intend, and by unexpected means. . . . And we're much closer now to three men in a boat in the Aegean than ever before, aren't we?"

"Where—when—were you intending to go from here?" Thomas asked Heron.

He smiled. "Well, that is the prime question, isn't it? . . . You know when . . . to the fateful night, just after Crito left Socrates."

Thomas sighed. "The dialog says Andros is half Socrates' age, and I thought that exempted you. Perhaps I was wrong. Maybe the dialog lied, or the age of Andros got trampled in some copying, and you are Andros, after all."

"Oh, no, I am certain I am not," Heron replied. "Indeed, I have had similar doubts about the dialog and the age it gives to Andros and was thinking *you* are the most likely to be that visitor from the future."

Thomas scoffed.

The two stared at each other.

"Fruitless debate, if I may," Appleton finally broke the vacuum. "Why not just travel back, not to talk to Socrates or do anything back there, but just observe. That would tell us who Andros was, once and for all, would it not?"

"I have traveled back to that night, many times," Heron said.

"And what did you see?" Appleton asked.

"Nothing. Nothing useful. Athenians in front of the prison—no one with a sign that says 'Andros.' I cannot just burst into the prison and start asking questions—"

"No, no, of course not," Appleton said. "And the next morning?"

"No indication that Socrates escaped. But that tells us nothing. If the plan in the dialog was successfully executed, no one would have known that Socrates *had* escaped."

"Yes, I see . . . ," Appleton said.

Thomas shifted uneasily in his seat and drained the last of his ouzo.

"Would you care for more?" Heron inquired.

Thomas shook his head. "So you plan to travel back to that evening now, again."

"Yes."

"And you're leaving the rescue of Socrates entirely in the hands of Andros, whom you profess not to know. Even though you both come from the future."

"The future's a big place," Heron replied. "I do not know who Andros is. But I'm not going to quite leave everything up to him—or her."

"You think Andros is a she?" Appleton asked. "Sierra Waters?"

"Sierra Waters is many people," Heron replied. "She is Ampharete, she is . . . but, no, I do not think she is Andros. Beyond that, I am just saying that I do not know who he—or she—really is. Socrates certainly does not say anything in the dialog—nor does Andros— to make us think Andros is a woman. But Andros could have been a woman disguised as a man. I simply do not know. I have had well-paid spies in Athens, for months prior to and after the recorded death of Socrates. No one has come across or heard of anyone with the name Andros."

"It is easy enough to change a name," Appleton said.

"Of course," Heron said. "That is part of the problem."

"What help are you going to offer Andros?" Thomas asked.

Heron finished off his own ouzo, smacked his lips, and looked at Appleton, who was finishing his. "Are we all done with this marvelous anisette concoction, then?"

Appleton nodded.

"Good." Heron stood. "Then let us adjourn to the private room, and I will show you what I have done."


The door of the private room snapped open to Heron's palm.

Appleton gasped. He was still caught off guard by the everyday miracles of this time, a century and a half after his own.

What he saw inside, on one of the three chairs against the wall, was beyond gasping.

"That must be Socrates," Appleton managed. "He looks nothing like his pictures."

"Not Socrates," Heron corrected. "The clone of Socrates. You see—"

"I know. Thomas explained."

Thomas was frowning. "You claim not to be in touch with Andros, yet you are going back to 399 BC with this sleeping double of Socrates. What then? Socrates' jailors will find *two* of his dead bodies, riven by hemlock, after the living man escapes? One produced by Andros and one by you?"

"You're not an engineer, Thomas, that is your problem," Heron responded. "Redundancy. The very word is one of complaint in the mouths of sophists and philosophers: to be redundant is to talk too much, to make the same point unnecessarily more than once. But real life is different. Are not our very bodies redundant—two lungs, two eyes, two ears? Yes, I do not know if Andros really has access to a clone of Socrates. But why take chances? If my Socrates makes a crowd of three, I'll just kill him and bury him where no one will find him. A simple matter."

Appleton shuddered.

Heron turned to him. "Come now. Surely Thomas explained this, if he explained anything to you at all. That sleeping fool is not really alive. He certainly has no soul, never had one. He is just a collection of living parts that adds up to a mindless double of Socrates."

"That's true enough," Thomas acceded. "But what about the collections of living parts that do add up to complete, sensate human beings? Who else do you expect in the prison of Socrates?"

"Ampharete is the one I'm most certain of," Heron replied.

"With Maxwell Marcus?" Appleton asked.

"Lost somewhere in the past, I am afraid," Heron replied. "He is off my radar."

Appleton looked troubled.

"It's a location device—," Thomas began.

"I am concerned about the man, not the technology," Appleton almost snapped. "I am sorry."

"Lots of people disappear in the past, and then resurface," Heron offered, with just a trace of consolation. "It's big place, too, after all." And he laughed.

Appleton said nothing.

"What about Jonah?" Thomas asked.

Heron shook his head sadly. "I am afraid I can no longer rely upon him—he has ideas of his own—"

"A point in his favor," Thomas muttered almost under his breath. "Where in time is he?" Thomas inquired more audibly.

Heron ignored all of it, in any case. "I am afraid he hates me now—he holds me responsible for . . ."

Thomas's eyes narrowed. "The death of Sierra?"

Heron began. "I—"

Appleton grabbed Heron's shoulder. "What are you saying? You expect that young lady to die in the prison of Socrates tonight? That's unacceptable and dishonorable!"

Heron carefully removed the hand and regarded the Victorian. "Not tonight. Not in Athens, in any millennium."

"When, then?" Appleton demanded.

"In Alexandria, in 415 AD. Her name was Hypatia, then—"

"Hypatia!" Appleton's mouth twisted in anger. He struggled for control. "A brilliant mathematician, a philosopher . . . I know what happened to her," he said a bit more levelly. "I know the story. Kingsley and others have told it. One of the worst moments in history—she was stripped naked, hacked to death with oyster shells, her body burned. . . ."

"You do not understand—," Heron began.

"I understand *this*. If there is any chance in the cosmos that she is Hypatia, then I do not blame the Alexandrian boy in the slightest for hating you." Appleton looked at Thomas, who had turned away from the conversation. "You have no opinion? She was your student, for God's sake—you brought her into this."

"It is everyone's fault, not just Thomas's," Heron said. "She did not—"

Appleton exploded. He cursed and moved quickly. He jumped into one of the chairs and quickly tapped in all of the departure signals. He mumbled to himself, "I assume these chairs work the same as the ones in London and New York." The bubble came up and shimmered its imminent exit in time—

Heron pulled Thomas into the outside room.


The two returned, quiet and shaken, into the private room a few minutes later.

"My God . . . ," Thomas said.

Only one of the three chairs was against the wall. It was empty.

"The Socrates chair was programmed to travel along with the first chair that went back," Heron said. "I could hardly have depended on the unconscious clone to drive it."

Thomas sighed heavily.

"Why on earth did you bring that Victorian buffoon here with you in the first place?" Heron demanded.

"I don't trust you," Thomas replied evenly. "I was grateful for his help. . . . And he's no buffoon. He's just . . . well, Victorian. He feels strongly about honor."

Heron made a derisive sound.

"I know," Thomas said. "You're the exception. You feel strongly about nothing, no one, other than yourself and your machines."

Heron turned on him, lip curled. "You don't know what I feel," he said, his voice bitterly cold. "I love history. I love humanity. I want to improve the hand fate has dealt us—resist it, remake it—not just numbly accept it. In my time there are terrible things wrong with this world. Far worse than anything you have seen."

Thomas balled his hand into a fist, half raised it, shook it . . . then paced away and back to Heron. "You and I fighting each other won't help anything at this point. . . . Were the chairs set for 399 BC?"

"The general vicinity."

"What the hell does that mean?"

"There's fine-tuning that I do, when I want the chairs to arrive on a very precise date. Doesn't always work even when I do that. As you know."

"And you hadn't yet done that when Appleton took off in the chair?"

"That's right."

"Great." Thomas shook his head. "And here's another problem: we now seem to be short a backup Socrates double."

"That's no problem."

"No?"

"There are plenty more where that one came from," Heron explained.

"You got a whole factory of them somewhere?"

"Redundancy, I told you. Let's just say I have more than enough, ready and waiting. They're easy enough to grow." Heron pulled a phone out of his pocket and spoke quickly in a high-pitched version of English that Thomas found hard to comprehend. "Right. As soon as possible," Heron concluded. He put the phone back in his pocket. "We should have another double here in under an hour."

"You ordered that from where? The future, your original time, where they speak that falsetto English?"

"I requested the clone from this time. We have several, not very far from here, by small, private, fast plane."

"Glad to hear it," Thomas said, with more than a touch of sarcasm. "Where did you get the DNA, by the way?"

"From Socrates, of course, when he was asleep, before he was put on trial. That part was simple."

Thomas nodded. "We still have a problem with the one chair—a little crowded for you, me, and the new clone."

Heron looked at the lone chair. "Yes, that is something I will need to think about. Clones are easier to make than these chairs."


The clone arrived sooner than expected. Two men gently nestled the sleeping body against the wall near the chair and left without a word.

Heron and Thomas hadn't said much to each other either in the interim. Both had retired to palm phones and ruminations.

Now Heron stirred. "I've made a decision about the chair and the clone."

"Oh? When did this become just your decision?"

"The clone and the chair are mine, why shouldn't the decision be?"

"What have you decided?"

"The clone goes back in the chair," Heron replied. "We don't want Andros to make his proposal to Socrates on that night in 399 BC with no Socrates double to back it up. If that happened, and Socrates decided in the end to accept the offer, all subsequent history would be shaken."

"Who other than Andros back then will know what to do with the clone? You're placing a lot on Sierra's shoulders."

"There is Alcibiades," Heron responded.

Thomas considered. "Have you heard anything about him since you snatched him from his Phrygian death?"

"He is right where I want him to be right now, and so far behaving just as he should."

"Everyone is your puppet in this," Thomas said grimly.

Heron regarded him. "It cannot be otherwise with time travel. One loose end is all it takes to unravel eternity. You already know this."

Thomas nodded.

"I don't really understand you," Heron said with sudden heat. "I don't understand why you got involved in this in the first place. I don't understand why you are questioning me now. At least I have been honest with you about *my* motives—"

Thomas had the element of surprise, and it prevailed as he turned on Heron. He pressed his arm against Heron's throat and pushed him against the wall. He marshaled every bit of his strength, which was still considerable even at his age, at least for short durations. "I'm tempted to break your neck and put you and that living corpse on a boat, along with me, and end this thing now and forever, right now."

"It wouldn't end it." Heron struggled for breath, surprised at the older man's strength. He tried to push Thomas's arm away, with little success. "There are other people still afoot, processes already in motion, as you know," he rasped.

"I know." Thomas kept his arm as steady as he could.

"We can only make things worse, not better, by not being a part of this now. You know that, too."

Thomas growled his grudging acknowledgment.

Heron made a bit of progress with the arm. Most of his voice was back. "It's her—I understand that. You regret drawing her into this."

Thomas released Heron and stepped back. "I agree with your reasoning about sending that goddamn zombie back." He walked to the unconscious figure, clad in a robe. "Let's get him into the chair."

Heron thought for moment and decided not to avail himself of the knife he had in his pocket. He had almost reached for it when he had been pinned. He had full access to it now.

"Yes," he said. "Let's put that ghost of Socrates in his chair."


Heron took a few minutes to adjust the chair so it would arrive precisely on the evening of Crito's—and Andros'—visit to Socrates in his prison room. Thomas paced.

"It's set," Heron said, and left the chair. "We have thirty seconds to leave the room."

The two men stepped into the public part of the restaurant, which was still empty as on any late afternoon.

"More ouzo?" Heron inquired.

"I don't think so," Thomas replied. "I could use some fresh air."

"Oh, you'll be getting plenty of that, I wouldn't worry."

Two men walked through the door—the same ones who had brought the second clone. They locked onto Thomas's shoulders with an unbreakable grip. They were a lot stronger and younger than

Heron. The only one surprised by their entrance was Thomas.

"You arranged for this via palm phone when you were setting the coordinates for the chair?" Thomas asked.

Heron nodded. "Something like that. One thing I really love about this age is no one is ever really very far away."

Thomas struggled a bit, but realized he'd do best to conserve his energy. "Was this your solution to the three chairs and the four of us all along? Is that what you intended for Appleton?"

"Perhaps. I improvise. Right now, you look like far more of an unstable threat to us than he does." Heron addressed the men. He translated for Thomas: "I told them to take you to the boat."

"You're worried I'll go back to that night in the prison in 399 BC and undo your work."

"Not really. I'll be closing the time around that night, after we take Socrates. It must be sacrosanct. Otherwise, people could keep going back and reversing what we're doing. Socrates would be saved and unsaved and saved and unsaved, forever, in a never-ending loop. . . . But I don't propose to stand here and tell you every facet of my thinking, like some self-impressed villain in a grade-B movie." Heron gestured to the guards. "I'm just worried about you, in general."

The men nodded and escorted Thomas out the door. "It's beautiful out on the sea today," Heron said after Thomas. "Enjoy."

Heron poured himself another glass of ouzo and nursed it and his options.

He placed a call with his palm phone. "Yes. Make sure the story appears in the *Athenian Global Village*. It is essential that Ampharete see it and begin her journey."

Heron put the phone in his pocket and sipped more ouzo. An amazing circle, this time traveling. . . . Ampharete had drawn him into this, back in Alexandria. Now he was making sure *she* was drawn into this, with the prior help of Thomas. Heron wondered who else was helping to pull the spiral.

Thomas couldn't get a response from his escort until they were on the boat, which was waiting for them in Piraeus. He wasn't even sure what language they spoke—he hadn't recognized the language in which Heron had addressed them. It sounded ancient. Thomas hoped they were multilingual. He tried English, Latin, and Greek, modern and ancient.

"The two of you are going to die on this boat, too. You understand?" Thomas was seated in a corner of the cabin. The two figures blocked any egress.

"You are going to die," one of them finally responded, in Roman Empire Latin. "We are going to kill you, and live." He said something Thomas did not understand to the other hooded figure. The two laughed.

One of them placed his palm on the scanner near the controls. The boat came to life and was soon making its way out of the harbor.

"This is being run automatically, by itself, like a living thing, you understand?" Thomas said.

The hooded figures ignored him.

"And it will burst into flames." Thomas made waving gestures. "And all three of us will die, not just me."

"That is a good story," the second hooded figure responded. "Who told it to you?"

"I . . . it was foreseen."

"You know an oracle who can see the future?"

"You are seeing the future, right now, yourselves," Thomas said. "This is not your time, is it? This is your future, and you are breathing in it. And I have been in contact with people who have seen a little of the future beyond this moment, yes. And they told me that this boat will shatter into a thousand pieces, like the top of a volcano, and will be consumed by the waves, with three men aboard."

"Maybe we should just kill you right now and leave the boat. And then, when it is consumed, the world will think that three men were on board."

"Yes," Thomas said, "that would satisfy the prophecy. But how long do you think you would live after you left the boat—"

"We are excellent swimmers, I can assure you."

"And I can assure you that once you reached land, your patron Heron would find a way to kill you. Do you think he wants you alive, in this time? Has he told you exactly how you will return to your Rome, or wherever you want to go in your world?"

The two Romans talked quietly, swiftly, beyond Thomas's comprehension.

"I know a way to get you back to your time and your world," Thomas said.


The Romans were indeed excellent swimmers, and Thomas was nearly as good. More important, one of them had an inflatable device tucked into his garment that enabled the three to easily reach land on a nearby island, mostly devoted to tourists. The name of the island was Andros. They shortly heard from a local that a boat had blown up several miles out to sea.

"We saved your life," one of the men said to Thomas. They had divested themselves of their hoods and their robes in the water. They just looked like two Roman soldiers now, underdressed, out of central casting from more than a century of movies about Rome. "Now it is your turn to get us home."

"To Rome?" Thomas looked around the island and smiled. Its name was Andros. But he did not have time to savor the ironies of time travel. Right now he had to focus on these two soldiers.

"Rome will do," one of them said. "Our home is in the northeast."

"We will need first to travel to a different place, distant from here, to get you to Rome. But the journey will be swift—we will travel by a wondrous kind of ship that sails the sky." Thomas gestured to the air. "It should not be too difficult to get you on board. This whole . . . land . . . has been almost one empire now, something like your Empire, again, for almost thirty years." Thomas had a variety of long-established digital aliases that he used in his travels. As soon as he was able to log on to his master account, he would likely be able to arrange for phony intra–European Union IDs for the two Romans.

They caught a rusted ferry to Athens Realport. Fortunately, the ferry's digital connections were good as new. Thomas paid for the passage, arranged for the IDs as well as three tickets on the next HST to London, on the strength of his palm print. When it came to collecting money, Thomas had found that even the most dilapidated equipment managed to work, whatever the time and the place. He also paid for casual business attire for the three, at a men's clothing kiosk at the realport. They boarded the plane with no problem. Thomas plied the Romans with strong drink, and the two passed most of the short flight in laughter and light naps. Thomas stared out of the window in silence, when he could.

They landed at Blair Annex. "The Parthenon Club," Thomas told the cabbie, after the three had bundled in.

The hundred-and-teenaged doorman was at his post. "Good evening, Mr. O'Leary. Joining us for a late supper tonight?"

"Not sure, Herbert. Is Mr. Gleason in?"

"I believe he is, sir. At the library. Shall I let him know you are here?"

"Not necessary—we'll just go straight up there."

"Very good, sir. And would you sign in for your guests? After-hours policy, you know."

"Certainly." Thomas took the proffered pen and looked at the guest book. He looked at the two Romans, who smiled at him stiffly. The problem was they would not be leaving tonight—at least, not in this millennium, or the previous millennium, if the chairs were in place upstairs. . . . Well, he would just have to remember to sign them out himself and plead that they were indisposed in the men's room, if Herbert or anyone else took an undue interest. He wrote two names in the guest book. Julius Roma, Tony Roma.

Thomas nodded at Herbert, then beckoned the Romans to follow him upstairs. They approached Gleason, who was clad in his customary argyle vest and tweed pants, at the librarian's station.

"Mr. O'Leary. Good to see you." Gleason extended his hand.

"Mr. Gleason. We're here about the chairs." Thomas gave the librarian a firm handshake.

"Of course. Follow me." Gleason gave the Romans a courteous nod. He understood enough about the chairs to know that if Thomas had not introduced his two companions, there was no point in pushing it.

Thomas, for his part, was relieved by Gleason's response. Thomas knew that if fewer than three chairs were down the long flight of stairs, Gleason would have said so at this point.

The librarian led the party to the far side of the room, and the door with the sleek, new keypad. Thomas grasped the significance of the moment: Heron had designed the chairs, and their accommodations in the London and New York clubs. If he had any suspicion that Thomas had survived the destruction of the boat in the Aegean, Heron might well have changed the keypad combinations and palm-print authorizations by some remote, backdoor means, or perhaps instructed someone else—for all Thomas knew, Gleason—to do so. Of course, Thomas's entry into the room with the chairs now might well give Heron some signal that Thomas was alive. But he had no choice but to walk into the room, if he could, and use the chairs.

Thomas pressed in his entry code, with his palm against the scanner. The door opened.

"Will you be requiring any further assistance from me tonight?" Gleason asked.

"No, thank you for your help." Thomas realized he had been talking in English, which meant the Romans understood nothing. Good. "Oh, one other thing," Thomas said to Gleason. "A Mr. William Henry Appleton, an American, arrived here several days ago. Please show him every courtesy regarding the chairs."

"Very good, sir." Gleason nodded to the Romans and left.

The three walked down the stairs, into the soft, cascading lights. Four chairs came into view. Excellent, Thomas thought—more than he had expected. He seated each Roman in a chair, set the controls, and explained, in Latin.

"You will be arriving in Britannia, in Londinium, in the middle of the reign of Antoninus Pius, your time. You will find suitable clothing and money when the chairs complete their journey, which should be instantly."

"We understand. We have already used the chairs."

"Of course. You traveled from your time to this time in the chairs."

Tony Roma nodded. "You will not be coming with us?"

"No. I will be going . . . other places. We will likely never see each other again. Thank you . . . for saving my life."

Tony nodded again. "There may be others like us who will want to kill you—Heron trained many and paid us well."

"I know." Thomas pressed a code on the arm of each chair and withdrew. The clear bubbles emerged. Thomas took one more look at the ancient Romans dressed as modern Greeks in the two chairs. He walked quickly up the stairs.

*London, AD 2042*

Gleason was waiting for Thomas on the library floor. "You did not accompany your guests in the chairs?"

"No." The question and answer were not so obvious, Thomas knew. He could well have accompanied the Romans in the chairs and been gone weeks, months, years, and then arranged to return to this time and place. Gleason's question really meant that Thomas looked the way he had a few minutes earlier, which meant that he hadn't traveled anywhere, stayed awhile, and returned in a heartbeat.

"Well, I'm pleased you're still with us in the club, sir," Gleason continued. "Oh, I had a question about your Mr. Appleton?"

"Yes?"

"Our computer is not completely clear regarding cross-temporal tabs—"

"The end of the nineteenth century—pounds to dollars—prevails."

"Of course, sir. I should have known. . . . Will you be staying for the night, then?"

"I could use a little rest . . . but, no, I don't think so."

"Can we tempt you with a late supper, then?"

Thomas considered. "Could you have Mr. Forbish pack one of his sliced-duck sandwiches for me, and call me a cab—I think I'll be heading back to Blair."

"Very good, sir."

Thomas ate his sandwich and washed it down with a pretty good lager and lime, as he waited in the airport lounge for his plane to board.

It was late Monday evening in New York City now—the very time, if Thomas was figuring correctly, that Sierra was discovering via the *Athenian Global Village* on the Web that his boat had gone missing. He could stop this entire unraveling snake right now, with just a phone call

to Sierra. . . . Or would it stop? Could he really be sure of the consequences of such a call?

The problem with the phone call was that he would have no control
of the situation, no real chance to influence Sierra's actions, from so far
away, if his words were not enough. She could hang up the phone and
step onto the invisible conveyor that had drawn her irresistibly into this,
anyway—the conveyor that he had already set in motion. . . . No, seeing
her in person, sitting next to her in the same actual room, was his best
chance for changing things.

Assuming he really, truly wanted to change them. Of course, he
didn't want Sierra dying as Hypatia.

But what if Sierra was not Hypatia, after all? Did he want to risk
deleting everything else Sierra and Ampharete had accomplished?

And if she was? There had to be another way to prevent Sierra from
dying as Hypatia . . . something later on in the flow, something other
than editing Sierra out of this at the very beginning.

Staying here in London, talking to Appleton when he got here, getting him to prevent Sierra and Max from going back to Londinium that
first time was no good. Thomas sighed. He felt terrible about Max's
death. But he dared not do anything that might get in the way of Sierra's
first meeting with Heron in Alexandria, AD 150. That visit had drawn
Heron into this plan. Dangerous as he was, he was absolutely crucial to
all else that followed—

A soft but penetrating voice announced that his flight was boarding.

He walked to the entrance gate and realized again how little real
control he seemed to have over anyone's actions, including especially
his own. An odd part of him thought, *If the plane I'm boarding crashes,
never makes it to New York, well, that would be one way of resolving this.*

Thomas got little rest on the plane. He ran his fingertips over silky, up-
holstered armrests and fathomed the threads of history. He recalled the
first time he had seen Sierra, the first time they had talked. It seemed so
long ago, another lifetime . . . which it was.

His plane landed, on time and without incident. It was past midnight,
local time, Tuesday morning. Had Sierra gone to sleep? She already

knew about the missing boat. She and Max would be flying to London today. Appleton—having met with a slightly older Sierra back here a few days ago—was already there, but he would be back here in New York again in a few days. Thomas considered. Sierra, Max, Appleton . . . none of them had seen him in this period, as far as he knew. He had to be exceedingly careful and make sure no one saw him unless he wanted that to happen. An inadvertent encounter with any of the three could wreak havoc.

He walked on the new cobblestone pathway to the cabport. The cobblestones might as well have been eggshells. He couldn't afford a single misstep. . . . He stopped, abruptly, and walked in another direction.

He couldn't risk going back to his apartment just yet. The safest thing was to spend the night in an airport hotel.

*New York City, AD 2042*

The alarm clock showed him no mercy. He cursed it, even though he knew full well, barely awake, that he had been the one to set it for 6:45 A.M. He had sentenced himself to five short hours of sleep.

He grabbed breakfast in the coffee shop. He often wondered how his stomach had come to be so tolerant of food from so many different places and times. Well, right now it was only the places that were mixed in his digestion—ouzo from Athens, duck from London, and eggs over easy from New York, all in 2042.

Eggs over easy. He had the distinct feeling that they would be the only things to go over that way in the next few days.

His new palm phone rang in his shirt, as if to prove it. He had picked it up in Blair. His old one was somewhere beneath the azure waves of the Aegean.

It was Mr. Charles on the phone. "Where are you, Thomas?"

"Back in New York, not in my apartment, long story."

"Ah, just got back myself—but I was here in New York, at my nineteenth-century post. Had several meetings with you, back then, in fact—"

"Yes."

"Though I suppose you might not recall all of them—some perhaps being a bit later in your life than where you are, now. Strange business, this time travel. Appleton and I were just discussing it—"

"Back then?"

"Yes. But that's not the reason I'm calling you. There's something going on at the Club—"

"Right now?"

"Yes. We have the continuous camera surveillance in the room with the chairs, you know. And it sends notifications to my home, and yours, when anyone enters the room—I'm surprised you didn't see it—"

"I'm not home."

"Yes, yes, of course. I just got home myself."

"Someone entered the room? From the stairs or the chairs?"

"I believe the chairs."

"One person?" Thomas asked.

"Two. They apparently arrived in the middle of the night—I haven't looked back any further—then they left for a little while, and then returned to the room. But they haven't taken the chairs again."

"They're still there in the room?"

"Yes."

"Can you see who they are?"

"One is definitely Sierra Waters."

"Good . . . and the other?"

"I don't know the face. A man. But they were speaking Greek."

"How are they dressed?"

"Modern clothes."


Thomas caught a cab to the Millennium. With any luck, he'd get into Manhattan just under the morning rush hour. The timing—this tiny part of the timing, at least—was good: the Club didn't open until 9 A.M. That would give Charles and him a chance to get upstairs and see who was in the room with the chairs, with no one to trip over downstairs. He only hoped that Sierra and her companion would still be there. He had no way of keeping them there. He certainly couldn't call the police and report a break-in at the Club.

He tried to piece together Sierra's likely trajectory. If she had been across the Atlantic at any time other than the recent past—even at the end of the nineteenth century—then sailing or steaming across the ocean would have been a cumbersome option. She would have been better off first using the chairs in Athens or London, then flying to New York.

Okay. So that meant Sierra and her companion were already in New York, in the past? Possibly. But . . . Sierra and friend could conceivably also have come in the chairs from the future . . . maybe from Heron's time, whenever, exactly, that was.

Heron had blocked travel to the future in his chairs, which is why Thomas didn't usually think about that. But Heron himself had of course traveled from that future to now, as well as further back.

New York City's expressways were remarkably unblocked this morning, and Thomas was in midtown Manhattan before eight. He'd asked Charles to meet him in front of the Club. Thomas's cab pulled up. Charles was there, reliable as always.

He also had the keys.

"Anyone else around?" Thomas asked. He still was not sure if he wanted a meeting with Sierra now, but his overriding need was to see who had been captured in that spiderweb of a room.

"No one I recognized in the past ten minutes I have been here," Charles replied, "except that derelict selling algae-dogs."

"This early in the morning?"

Charles nodded. "I find them vile any time of day." He applied his keys to the door. "Our overtime guests are still upstairs. I routed their images from the room to my palm phone."

"Can I see?"

"Only Ms. Waters has been in camera range for the past ten minutes. It might take me a few moments to retrieve the earlier—"

"Let's just go in and see for ourselves."

The two men walked quickly on plush carpets, up the wide central staircase, to the series of libraries with big, burgundy armchairs and wide maple tables. Thomas saw what he always did when he was here and the place was empty: Samuel Clemens, Henry Adams, the Roosevelts Theodore and Franklin, John O'Hara, Ogden Nash, I. F. Stone, Carl Sagan, Walter Cronkite . . . Thomas had seen all of them, and many others, famous and anonymous, relaxing in these armchairs at one time or another. Other than Stone, of course, not a one of them had any knowledge of real time travel, and the little room upstairs . . . well, maybe Clemens, and, come to think of it, Thomas wouldn't put it past Nash or Sagan, either.

Thomas and Charles approached the Greeks in the bookcase. The Plato, the Xenophon—

"You've actually met some of these, shaken their hands, haven't you?" Mr. Charles asked.

"Yes."

Charles turned from the books to Thomas, then back to the books, with equal awe. "I envy you." He turned to the spiral ladder. "Shall we?"

Thomas climbed the steps, with Charles behind.

Thomas reached the top and pressed his palm against the trapdoor in the ceiling. It clicked, almost imperceptibly, and opened inward.

Thomas heard voices, speaking in Greek.

He climbed up into the room. Mr. Charles followed.

"Thomas!" Sierra cried out, delighted.

Thomas beamed and felt his heart pound. But he couldn't take his eyes off Sierra's companion, who was looking with great interest at Thomas and Charles. He was indeed dressed in contemporary clothing.

Sierra saw that Thomas noticed. "The clothes should make him less conspicuous here," she said.

The man said something to her in Greek.

"My God!" Charles exclaimed, no longer able to contain himself. "Is this Alcibiades? I thought he was younger."

CHAPTER 8

*Athens, AD 2042*

Sierra looked out into the cobalt. It was half sky, half sea, and the line between them quivered like a bruised lip. She saw tiny specks of white in the distance. They could have been the pieces of paper she had just torn, the pieces of a plan, but she knew they were only mindless birds.

She thought of Alcibiades' lips, slightly parted, peacefully asleep in their bed back in ancient Athens, nearly twenty-five hundred years ago this morning. She would kiss them again, soon. She had taken the chair here to her own original time in the future, along with Heron's instructions that she had carried with her for nearly two years. The years never mattered—she could help implement Heron's plans whenever she wanted. She had left Alcibiades a note this morning, explaining what she was doing, letting him know she would be coming back to him after she had finished executing Heron's requests. What had since changed is she had now decided, finally, that she could no longer be a cog in Heron's machine. She and Alcibiades could save Socrates on their own. And save Max, if there was some way they could, and find Thomas, too, if he was still alive.

Heron's plan called for her to travel back to the night of the dialog, to be Andros' backup, whoever he was. It called for her to seduce

Socrates if necessary. At seventy or so, he was no less open to such temptations than when he had been fifty. "He was still a stallion, the last time I saw him," Alcibiades had told her, more than once. These Greeks had a healthy lifestyle—cereal, fruit, fresh air, olive oil.

Heron's plan was clear. It told her how to set the chair with utmost precision to arrive at just the right time. "Drug him, if your other entreaties fail," Heron had said, and provided her with ample ingredients. "Call upon Crito and his friends, if need be. He never wavered in his zeal to save Socrates." And Heron had provided her with the exact details of their locations.

The double would already be in the prison. Andros would have seen to that, or Heron. Yet according to the dialog she had seen, Socrates would refuse Andros' offer in the end. It wasn't clear why. It was almost as if he wanted to die, but that didn't make much sense, either. I. F. Stone's idea—that it was to embarrass the Athenian democracy—just did not seem sufficient. To wrack your body with a convulsive, corrosive poison that turned you inside out—hard to believe that anyone, even Socrates, would do that, would allow that to be done to him, just to make a political point. Especially not when an alternative was at hand—indeed, one that would have allowed him to make that same point and survive anyway. . . . The only reason Sierra could think of was that Socrates trusted the death of his body more than the death of his double's, which he would have had difficulty understanding, however good the explanation of Andros.

So, the dialog said Socrates would turn down, had turned down, Andros' offer. And Sierra was the insurance that he would nonetheless change his mind. Heron planned on saving Socrates whether he wanted to be saved or not. The arrogance that came with travel through time. But Sierra had to admit that a part of her had come to admire it.

She regarded the sky and the sea, again. In addition to the birds, and the long-gone shreds of the paper she had torn, Thomas was out there, too. Was he long gone, also?

She had attempted to arrive a day before Thomas would vanish. But despite Heron's claims, the chair was not precise enough. Or maybe she needed a little more training. She had arrived the day after Thomas's boat had disappeared.

She had walked this shore and the docks near Athens and Piraeus all this morning and afternoon, talking to everyone she could find having anything to do with the sea. No one had seen anyone like Thomas. No one knew of three men who had chartered a boat. It was a long shore, and there were lots of out-of-the-way docks. But Sierra thought that if she walked and talked here for the rest of her life, she would find out no more. And now the *Athenian Global Village* carried the report that had been the deciding factor that had pulled her onto this path.

It was an unsigned story. It had been so all along. No one at the *Athenian Global Village* was sure who had written it. Several of the staff were on vacation. And the Greek media were in something of an uproar today because two men were suspected of having used forged IDs to fly from Athens to London the day before. She could see the writing on the wall-screen: she was unlikely to find anything more anywhere under this Grecian sun.

But nor could she just go ahead now, follow Heron's plan, and hope that it saved the people she cared about. Maybe her self-appraisal had been wrong. Maybe she did have a deeper connection to something other than her work.

She would find out now, once and for all.

She kissed the sky and the sea good-bye and headed for the bar, halfway on the road from Piraeus to Athens.


She approached the restaurant cautiously. It had been empty when she had arrived this morning. If it had stayed that way, there would be a chair waiting in the back room. She would take it back to Alcibiades.

She waited outside, from a safe distance, for a few minutes. . . . But there was no point in waiting, she realized. Sooner or later she would have to enter the bar, see if anyone was there, and if the chair was still available. It might as well be now.

She opened the door and walked inside. Rays of sunlight followed her and lit up particles of dust in the air.

The particles led to a lone man at the bar.

He looked tired, drunk, or both.

He looked at her and smiled so hard his eyes teared. He walked over to her and hugged her. He didn't seem drunk.

"I have searched the millennia for you, my dear. I have seen things, talked to people . . . and here you are, right in front of me. I guess I could have just stayed here to begin with, and not moved a second or an inch. You know, I learn something new about time travel every day."

Sierra relaxed. "Mr. Appleton."

They went into the private room in the back, on the authority of Sierra's palm. She thought it would work. There was no reason to think Heron would take the drastic step of locking her out. But she was relieved, anyway.

Two chairs were against the wall. "I know we don't have much time to talk," Appleton said. "Who knows when Heron will return—and you no doubt need to be on your way. But there are some things I need to tell you."

Sierra nodded.

Appleton cleared his throat. "When I first came to this room, I sat in one of the chairs. I knew how to command it—Thomas had shown me. It took me to the age of Socrates. I arrived a few years before his death. Ironically, the *body* of Socrates had arrived in the same place, about fifteen minutes before me. It had been seated in another chair, in this room. I don't know why it went back to the same time and place as I did—I assume Heron intended that, for whatever reasons."

"Did you command your chair to arrive at that particular time?"

"No. I just commanded it to travel. You see, I was in a fearful hurry. I . . . I think Alcibiades was more shocked by *my* appearance than the body of his mentor. But it was you I was seeking."

Sierra put a comforting hand over Appleton's, which was shaking. "Why?"

"It's not easy for me to tell you this."

She had never seen his face, or anyone else's, look so sad.

"Heron believes that you will die an awful death, under the name Hypatia, in the fifth century AD, in Alexandria."

"I know." Sierra squeezed his hand.

"Yes, I went back to tell you that, but Alcibiades told me that he already told you. . . . So my goal, now, is a little different."

"Alcibiades told me about your visit."

"You see, I've been thinking about this. I think both of you should come forward to this time. Board an airship back to New York. Live your life, enjoy your life, together. Why risk dying, needlessly?"

Sierra shook her head no, slowly. "We won't die."

"You can't be sure of that. But we *can* be sure that *Socrates* cannot survive, will not survive, even if he goes with Andros—surely you understand why. If you stay enthralled in this, you will have risked your life for nothing!"

"Have you actually seen Socrates die? The real Socrates, not a double?"

"No," Appleton said. "But I need not have seen that to know that Socrates cannot survive. Think about it: Have you seen any change, even the smallest, since you and I and your colleagues started dashing around in time? Anything?"

"If we rescue Socrates and leave his double to die, we won't see any changes until Socrates appears at some other time in history. Perhaps he'll be taken to the far future, beyond your time or mine."

Appleton considered. "True, if he is taken to a future beyond yours. But how can you be sure that is the reason, and not simply that he—despite your best efforts, despite jeopardizing your own life—will not survive?"

"We can't decide this argument by logic," Sierra said, "only by seeing what actually happens if Socrates is really rescued, and what happens afterward. Heron and Thomas seem convinced—"

"Are they?"

Sierra said nothing, then, "I suppose I don't know Heron well enough to be certain about anything regarding him."

Appleton shook his head. "If I am wrong, and you go back to New York, and live your life, then who will be hurt by that? If it is written in some book of inevitability that Socrates is to be saved, then someone else can do it, will do it, and you will be safe. You and Socrates will both live. Alcibiades, too. But if I am right, and you go back to that night—"

"I'm not going back to that night."

Appleton looked at her, hoping to be hopeful.

"I'm not going back to New York, either—not yet."

"Where are you going, then?"

"Back to Alcibiades."

"Good—"

"And we'll approach that night at the prison together."

Appleton shook his head sadly. "I fear nothing of value can come out of that attempt. And you'll be risking—"

"If anyone is going to die in the attempt to save Socrates, it will be Alcibiades, not me," Sierra said, voice raw with emotion. "He is dead already, in one universe. I want to make sure he stays alive in this one."

"Then save him! Don't let him die like your friend Maxwell—"

"That's exactly what I'm trying to do!"

"Take him to New York, then, not the prison."

"I'll never convince Alcibiades to stay away from Socrates," Sierra responded. "He's a stubborn man. He—"

Sierra and Appleton noticed a light flickering on the wall. "I believe that means someone has entered the restaurant," Appleton said. "I saw it flicker about an hour before you arrived—I opened the door of this room, just a crack, to see who was out there. It was just a delivery of wine, but—"

"You think this could be Heron?"

"I don't know. It could be—"

Sierra hugged him, impulsively. Then she let go and ran to one of the chairs. "Please, do what you can to give me a few moments, if it is Heron out there—"

Appleton walked toward her—

"Please—," she repeated.

He stopped. He struggled with emotions that were pulling him, literally, in two different ways. "Yes," he said hoarsely, after a long moment. "I'll do what I can."

"Thank you," she said, seated in the chair, leaning over the control panel. She looked up one last time at Appleton. "What will you do, after I leave, if . . . ?"

"If I can still move of my own volition? I don't know. Maybe take the sky back to New York, and then a chair to my own time and family. . . . I doubt I'll publish anything about this, or even speak of it to anyone, for now." He closed his eyes and saw the nineteenth-century Hudson, flowing in blues and greens outside his window. He missed his past. "I'm sure it will seem as if I hadn't been gone at all."

*Athens, 400 BC*

Sierra's chair reached its destination in a pounding pulse beat. The bubble retracted. She took a deep breath and walked on what she prayed was a 402 BC or thereabouts dirt floor.

She had no way to confirm the date in this house. They didn't hang calendars on refrigerators in this age. She did not know where Alcibiades was, except he was not here. She knew the location of most of his hideaways, but since she couldn't be positive of the date, she thought it didn't make sense to look for him in any of them. Who knew who else might be there right now.

The agora was the logical place to learn the date.

She found the stash of local clothing and changed.

The sun was bright and kind. The air was rich, salty, exciting—like a big margarita come to watercolor life. Jimmy Buffett, one of her favorite old-time singers, would have fit right in here.

She approached a peddler on the road. "Do you know Socrates?" she asked him. That would be a good way of homing in on the date—or, at least, the important aspect of the date for her, which was arriving after she had left Alcibiades but before the death of Socrates.

The man squinted at her. His face creased in a thousand lines. He walked past her.

*I guess I can take that for a no,* she thought—*or perhaps he didn't understand my Greek.*

She next encountered two men, who looked to be in their twenties. Their garb said they were reasonably well-off, likely of the merchant class. They smiled at her, copiously.

She returned the favor. These seemed better prospects than the peddler. "Do you know if Socrates is speaking, anywhere in the polis?"

They stopped. One looked, bemused, at Sierra. The other laughed.

"Socrates?" the bemused one responded. "If he is speaking somewhere, it is to himself. No one pays any attention to that annoying old man."

"No, why not?" Sierra asked, still smiling. Good, this at least meant Socrates was alive, and she had not arrived too late to help Alcibiades on that night before the hemlock. She regretted that she had left Alcibiades at all.

"Socrates licks the behinds of the aristocracy, everyone knows it," the one who had been laughing told her. He had stopped laughing now, but looked pleased with himself that he dared to utter such a coarse phrase to a woman he did not know.

"So Socrates is not corrupting the morals of Athenian youth?" Sierra asked. So much for the main charge that would be brought against him at his trial—though there was no way of knowing if these two specimens were representative of anyone other than themselves.

This time they both laughed. One started to ask if she would like to join them for some late-afternoon wine—

"Thank you," she interrupted him. "A very gracious offer that I would otherwise accept gladly, but I do have an appointment with someone in the agora."

He started to say something else. Sierra gave him and his friend her maximum-amplitude smile and walked briskly away toward the marketplace.


She approached Athens and glanced at the remnants of the long walls. She had noticed them when she and Alcibiades and Heron had first walked this path from Piraeus. They seemed to spring from the earth like stubborn thumbs of stone, awaiting the tender hand of someone to hold them and make them live for centuries. Konan would do that, if she remembered correctly, in 393 BC. Just as she aimed to do about Alcibiades. . . . Everything here breathed his presence. Even the architect, Hippodamus of Miletus, who had designed these walls. Miletus meant Alcibiades to her, too.

The sun was weakening as she entered the agora. The aromas and breeze upon her face were more vivid than anything she saw. But she looked anyway, everywhere. She saw no one familiar.

Looking at people, of course, invited their attention. It was unwanted by Sierra until—

"Excuse me. I could not help but notice your gaze." He was a man about the age of the duo on the road. Except he was calm and serious.

"I am sorry. I . . . was looking for someone," Sierra said.

"Who? Maybe I know him."

Sierra considered. She couldn't say Alcibiades, because he was supposed to be dead. She shook her head. "It is . . . private. But thank you for your offer." She started to walk away—

"Take a chance with me. Take a chance with the cosmos," he said. "Mention his name. Maybe I can help you."

"I . . ." She shook her head again and walked a step farther—

"I will take the chance, then. Is it Alcibiades you seek?"

She regarded the young man. He had broad shoulders.

"Are you Ampharete? He described you to me quite carefully, and you look like his description. But words and images are not the same, and the first can never do full justice to the second."

"Who are you?"

"I am Plato, one of his loyal students. I or someone like me has been watching for you in the agora for months now. Alcibiades was hoping you might return."


Sierra let Plato take her to Alcibiades. She tried to say as little as possible during the thirty-minute walk, aware that her companion was a conduit to all future history, arguably one of the most important people who had ever lived.

If he lived. If not . . . well, Sierra couldn't even begin to fathom the twisted consequences.

She hoped Plato couldn't hear her heartbeat. She struggled to keep it from drowning out her every thought.

What had Plato done at this time in the original history—the history of the world she had grown up in, before she had been drawn into this? Not much was known about him in these years.

What had Alcibiades told him? Whatever it was, Sierra thought she could rely on Alcibiades not to have told Plato anything that could compromise their situation—or the whole subsequent history of the world.

"You are quiet and thoughtful," Plato said. "In my experience, that is unusual for a woman."

Alcibiades loathed Plato—or what he would become. What had happened that would change that? "And is it in your experience that generalizations about a category or class of people or things apply, inevitably, to all members of that class?"

Young Plato smiled slightly. "Are you a philosopher, Ampharete? If so, you are the first woman philosopher of my acquaintance."

And could she really trust Plato? Perhaps he had deluded Alcibiades in some way, and Alcibiades' dislike of Plato would be justified, after all, by some kind of treachery Plato was about to pull, on her and Alcibiades. . . . "I studied philosophy," she said, "does that make me a philosopher?"

"I would say no. Philosophers have many students, and most are not themselves philosophers."

"Are you a philosopher, then? Is your friend Alcibiades?"

"You can ask him yourself. He is in that dwelling." Plato pointed to a nondescript two-story house, about a hundred feet down the road. Ampharete had not seen it before. "As for my opinion," Plato continued, "I would say Alcibiades is more a king, in training, than a philosopher. Though perhaps there is no contradiction in the two pursuits."

"And you? Would you call yourself a philosopher?"

"It is not for me to call myself anything—it is for others to decide. Socrates says that love of anything in excess—including knowledge—can lead to bad results. For if you love something that much, then you can easily come to love its mere appearance, and then you are only fooling yourself."

"How is . . . Socrates? Have you seen him, recently?" Sierra could not contain her question.

Plato looked at her with nearly a smile in his eyes, and then at the dwelling, which they were now about to enter. "He is fine. He was here, talking with Alcibiades, just last evening."

They entered the house. It looked—and felt—small, about five hundred square feet. Sierra dared not ask if Socrates might be in the house. She would find out soon enough.

She walked down the narrow hall with Plato. Whom would she be more thrilled to the core to see in the next moment—Alcibiades or Socrates? She had not even completely caught her breath or wits yet about Plato—

"Ampharete."

She had her answer.

He stroked her face with the soft part of his thumb and pulled back an inch or two to look at her. "You were away longer than you intended. I know you did not want that."

*Plato will see this,* some part of her brain thought. She didn't care . . . it didn't matter . . . everything had changed. History had changed the moment they rescued Alcibiades. Just as she had told him many times. Every word that he or anyone who knew him now spoke was writing a new page in history. So the Plato she had been reading all of her life might well be altered, had to be altered, in some small way informed and re-formed by what Plato just saw, or thought he saw, her tongue caressing Alcibiades'. . . . Good, that was a better history, a better world, if only for that. Her goal, her job now, was to make this the history that lasted, that took. The history that everyone into perpetuity would know.

She looked around.

"Plato left," Alcibiades said. "You met him in the agora?"

She nodded.

"It was almost coincidence," Alcibiades continued. "I hope you weren't too surprised. I decided to include Plato in my circle just a few months ago. I thought it was safer to have him inside, and close to me, than outside, and close to who knew what or whom."

"Your circle?"

"Yes. A small group, mostly old friends, that I have been gathering to help me with Socrates. Some good fighters, some good thinkers, some both."

"Is Socrates here?"

"No. He was here last evening."

"So . . . he knows?"

"He knows that I am alive, of course. But I have not yet told him about the trial, his death sentence, about Andros, whoever he is."

"How many years to the trial?"

"Months now, not years. Six months."

Tears welled in Sierra's eyes. "I did not want to be gone that long. Almost two years . . ."

"But you are here with me now."


They made love . . . had a simple dinner . . . made love again.

"Those chairs are hopelessly imprecise," Sierra said.

"You are still unhappy about the six months? It could have been worse. You might have arrived six months from now, or six months after that, or five years ago."

"I know."

"It is probably inevitable, given the nature of miracles," Alcibiades said. "You become accustomed to the miracle, you almost take it for granted, so you want more perfection from it. That is the way with all tools. And the chairs are only tools, miraculous tools." He pulled her closer to him, so her hair fell on his face. "This would not be possible without the chairs," he said softly. "I can have no complaints about them in that regard."

"I do not want you to go through with this. You are likely to get killed."

Alcibiades laughed. "It has been that way for a long time—I already was killed once, if memory serves."

"That is why it is especially likely that you will be killed again."

"The cosmos cleaning up after itself? Keeping things tidy?"

"It has been suggested, by poets and physicists—philosophers of nature—that you cannot escape your fate," Sierra replied. "The universe resists all attempts to alter its lines of time."

"You expect me to walk away from this? But I am not supposed to be here now, whatever I do. If you are right about the fates being vexed by attempts to change history, I am their prey now, whether I try to save Socrates or not."

"Saving Socrates would be a worse affront. He has had far more impact than . . ."

"Than me? I agree. That is precisely why I want my survival to mean more than I ran and I schemed." Alcibiades rolled over and away from Sierra.

"I do not belong here in this world, either," Sierra said gently. "You and I are two odd numbers. Perhaps, added together, away from here, we will be an even number. More pleasing to the universe."

Alcibiades smiled and turned back to her. "You are certainly pleasing to me." He kissed her. "Perhaps we should ride the chairs one hundred and fifty years into the past and steal old Pythagoras from Samos—he would have been impressed with your numerical reasoning."

"I am not saying we have to run away. I just do not want you there on that Andros evening. Maybe there are other ways of saving Socrates—perhaps we can prevent him from being put on trial altogether."

Alcibiades shook his head. "The dangers to history would be insurmountable. You know that. At this moment, a few handfuls of carefully selected men, including Plato, know that I am here. Socrates knows I have survived. At the last minute, when the death of Socrates is imminent, I will tell them more. I may tell Socrates more, sooner. But to work to try to prevent him from being brought to trial? That would require me or my intermediaries to contact, attempt to influence, many kinds of people—over whom I have very little control. I would be better off just murdering his accusers, before they have the chance to make their allegations."

"What is wrong with that?"

Alcibiades chuckled. "You have changed your mind about murder? I should count myself lucky that you care for me."

"I am trying to make sure that *you* are not the one who is murdered."

"If I killed those men, others would arise to take their place. It is a mistake to think that just certain individuals killed Socrates—no, Athens killed Socrates." Alcibiades sighed. "There are more sides of this than you may realize. I have even discovered— Wait, let me show you something."

Alcibiades rose and walked to the far side of the little bedroom. He returned with a scroll.

Sierra opened it:

SOCRATES: What time is it?

VISITOR: The dawn broke a little while ago.

SOCRATES: I must have been sleeping. I did not see you enter.

VISITOR: You were indeed asleep when I arrived.

SOCRATES: You have come to take me to my destiny? I am ready. But I thought I would be allowed another day or two.

VISITOR: I am here to take you to your destiny. If indeed you are ready.

SOCRATES: I just said that I was. I may criticize the city, but I do not presume to place myself above it.

VISITOR: The destiny I am here to offer you may be different from the one you suppose.

SOCRATES: Different? I would never accept a life that prevented me from praising good and denouncing evil. And placing myself above the city would put me in just such a compromised position.

VISITOR: Yet you accept death, and via hands you know are unjust.

SOCRATES: Ah, so you are indeed here to try to talk against death to me. This is the destiny you wish me to avoid?

VISITOR: Yes.

SOCRATES: You are not the first man to make that offer.


"It's not the same," Sierra said the obvious. "I mean, other than 'Visitor' instead of 'Andros.' . . . Socrates said 'suitor' in the original dialog. . . . But which is the original?"

"Exactly. And there indeed are many differences throughout, though most are minor," Alcibiades said. "Although I suppose it is not so minor to see 'man' instead of 'suitor'—at least that tells us that Andros is not you."

"I always knew that. I would have talked differently to Socrates in that prison."

"I am sure you would." Alcibiades stroked her back. "But that could well have been lost by the time the dialog was written."

Sierra examined the scroll. "It feels newly written—though you are more familiar with ink and papyrus than I am."

"I agree. It looks to me as if it was written in the past few months. It has a new smell."

"Who do you suppose wrote it? Did you?"

Alcibiades laughed. "A reasonable guess. But, no."

"Plato?"

"The logically preeminent choice, given what you told me about his extraordinary future. But if Plato wrote this, that would mean he has knowledge of this plot. I did not tell him about it, I assume you did not—so, who did? Heron?"

Sierra shook her head. "Heron barely talks about Plato now . . . I suppose that could be deliberate. . . . Do you think the same person wrote both versions?"

"Another good question. I am not sure. This one does seem, perhaps, as if it was written before the one that we know."

"An earlier draft?"

Alcibiades nodded. "Maybe . . . 'Visitor' is more general than 'Andros'—as if the author at first was not sure whether to reveal the visitor's name."

"Or perhaps 'Andros' was first, and the author decided to disguise it."

"Perhaps," Alcibiades allowed. "But the choice of words in the 'Visitor' version also seems a little more common, more general, than in our version. Not only 'man' instead of 'suitor,' but also 'sleep' instead of 'doze,' 'ready' instead of 'willing.' The differences are very slight. . . . But with this kind of scroll in existence, and its knowledge of the trial of Socrates, we have to tread carefully. Much as I would enjoy killing Anytus—"

"He was Socrates' harshest accuser," Sierra said. "He stirred everyone else up."

"Yes, but by killing him, we might make things worse—encourage others to crawl out from under their rocks. This scroll shows that someone else knows what is going to happen. . . . At least in our current circumstance, we know exactly when Socrates will die, so we can rescue him. If we kill Anytus, who knows what might happen instead."

Sierra put the scroll down and nodded. She knew he was right about not attempting to prevent the trial by killing people. A person killed could make just as many unpredictable ripples as a person saved. She had told him no less the last time they had been together.

They were awakened the next morning by birds, sunlight, and a messenger.

"There are strangers in the agora," he told them, his eyes averted as Alcibiades and Sierra hurriedly dressed.

"Do you know who?" Alcibiades asked.

"No."

"Wait for us outside. We will join you in a few minutes."

The messenger bowed his head slightly, and left.

"This might not be important," Alcibiades told Sierra.

"Or they could be Heron's men," she replied.

"We still need Heron to get the sleeping double into the prison—and for who knows what else." Alcibiades shuddered.

Sierra looked at him.

"The double that came back, a little before Appleton . . . I told you about him," Alcibiades explained. "It had already been invested with hemlock. . . . I could not bear to look at it, even though I knew it was beyond feeling pain. It was only there for that one morning—Appleton took it back with him. But I grieve for it—I grieve for Socrates."

Sierra took his hand.

Alcibiades pulled her hand to his lips. "I suppose I had better go and see who is in our agora."

"You cannot go. You are supposed to be dead, remember?"

"I will be careful. I will wear a hood."

"I will go," Sierra said. "I do not need a hood. No one in Athens knows me—"

They heard the hound outside. It barked savagely, then stopped.

Alcibiades grabbed his weapon. "Stay inside."

Sierra thought for a moment, then moved toward the door. She looked for a weapon—

It didn't matter.

The door flew open. One of the Roman mercenaries was on top of Alcibiades. Sierra pounced upon the mercenary and pummeled the back of his neck with her fists. Alcibiades got out from under and stabbed the mercenary in the front of his neck, swiftly and repeatedly, with his small knife.

Alcibiades stood up, breathed heavily, and looked at Sierra. He crouched by the door and peered outside.

The messenger, three of Alcibiades' guards, and just one other Roman mercenary were sprawled dead in the dirt. The hound was sliced in two.


Alcibiades and Sierra walked for twenty minutes to a new hiding place. Plato and several of Alcibiades' men were already there. They looked as if they had spent the night in the house.

Alcibiades told them what had happened. Plato looked at Sierra several times with cool, appraising eyes. The other men went outside to keep guard.

Alcibiades caught Plato's last look. "She is not responsible," he said to Plato disapprovingly.

Plato looked again at Sierra, then Alcibiades. "Is it possible your logic is clouded by your feelings?"

Alcibiades started to say something angry—

"I may have been followed," Sierra interrupted. "Saying I am responsible does not mean I wanted this."

Alcibiades took the point.

Plato, apparently choosing not to be insulted, resumed his scrutiny of Sierra. "Yes, that is what I was thinking. Who knows about the two of you?"

Sierra, not sure what exactly Plato knew, did not answer.

Alcibiades did. "The people who helped me escape my fate in Phrygia."

Plato nodded. "Perhaps they changed their minds. It may not be safe for you anywhere near Athens. The best place for you—and Ampharete—is away from here. At least for a few days, maybe longer."

"I agree," Sierra said.

"I know you do," Alcibiades snapped.

Plato watched with interest.

"I am sorry." Alcibiades softened. "I just do not believe in solving problems by running from them."

"Socrates says the same," Plato murmured deferentially. "But—"

"Surely a few days, even a few weeks, cannot make much difference." Sierra stood her ground and looked at Alcibiades. They both knew that what was at stake would not happen for six months.

"She is right," Plato said quietly.

Alcibiades smiled, despite his finding little humor in the situation. "So, you prefer a woman's counsel to Socrates'?"

Plato thought for a moment before he responded. "The advice of Socrates holds in general terms. Ampharete's pertains to this specific occasion. No general advice devised by man—even Socrates—can be expected to hold all of the time."

Alcibiades regarded him.

Sierra knew what he was thinking: Alcibiades was beginning to see what the future saw in Plato. That still did not mean, of course, that Plato could be trusted.

"We will leave, for a little while," Alcibiades finally acceded.

Plato nodded. "I and the others will escort you to Piraeus. You need not tell us where you will be sailing. That way, if one of us is a spy, your new location will not be compromised."


Plato and three other men walked ahead and out of earshot of Alcibiades and Sierra.

"How would Heron know you are here?" Alcibiades asked.

"There must be something in the chairs that sends him a signal," Sierra replied. "Sends him a . . . scent, across time, the way a hunter tracks prey."

Alcibiades struggled to make sense of that. He decided to grant the magic—after all, it was no less incredible than people traveling across time. "We do not know with any certainty that he is hunting us."

"I know of no one else who commands such mercenaries," Sierra responded. "But there could be others from Heron's time with similar resources."

Alcibiades nodded. "I still am suspicious of that second attack in Phrygia. The Romans appeared to have had Heron in harm's way, true. But he survived, nonetheless."

Sierra started to reply, but she and Alcibiades were distracted by Plato and his party, who were heatedly discussing something with two men who had appeared on the road before them.

"I do not like the looks of those two," Sierra said.

"They look like Romans dressed like Athenians," Alcibiades growled, and put his hand on the hilt of his weapon.

"At least they are just talking."

"Stay back here," Alcibiades said sharply. He hurried forward, weapon drawn.

The two Romans drew their weapons—whether because of Alcibiades, or something Plato or the other men said, or because they would have drawn them, anyway, at this point in the conversation, Sierra did not know. She did know she had no intention of hanging back and passively observing what could be Alcibiades' death—and young Plato's, too. She withdrew a knife she had acquired at the last house and ran forward.

The Romans were already upon Plato and the three men. Alcibiades reached them with shouts and sword. He thrust it into the exposed side of one of the Romans, who was wheeling around after dispatching two of Alcibiades' elite force.

The other Roman was encountering better resistance from Plato's party. The philosopher was armed, but his comrade was doing a heroic job of keeping the Roman's sword on him and not Plato.

The valiant fighter finally succumbed as Sierra arrived. Alcibiades jumped on his killer, but the Roman shrugged him off, stunned him with a knee to the groin and a fist to the solar plexus, and went for Plato. Even forewarned and forearmed, the young philosopher was at a distinct disadvantage.

The Roman threw Plato to the ground. Plato put up a feeble defense with his sword.

Sierra helped Alcibiades to his feet. He was still wobbly.

She looked at Plato. The Roman's weapon was raised high, held by both hands, about to land a killing blow.

Sierra shrieked and rushed forward, lunging with her knife.

The Roman was momentarily distracted.

Plato rolled on the ground.

The Roman's weapon missed him by an inch and plunged deep into the soil. He raised it again.

And Sierra got lucky. Her blade went clean through the Roman's left eye, straight into his brain.

He gasped and died.

Sierra felt something she had never before known. *I just saved the future,* she thought. That one lunge had safeguarded Plato and his role in human history—as far as she knew. It was a heady, astonishing moment. She looked at the sky and thought she saw the birds freeze in place against the clouds and the sun.

Alcibiades, Sierra, and Plato walked as best they could the rest of the way to Piraeus. Only Sierra was not limping.

"That mercenary was more determined to kill you than me," Alcibiades said to Plato.

"Perhaps," Plato said. "But why?"

Alcibiades shook his head. "I do not know."

Sierra said nothing. Heron would presumably be apoplectic to know his mercenary had almost killed Plato. Among the consequences for history, no Plato would mean no one of his literary genius to tell the story of Socrates. . . . Could that be what Heron wanted? She shook her head. She at least agreed with Alcibiades that, even in view of what had just happened, it still did not make sense to tell Plato much more and risk history even further.

"Sometimes when these killers get enraged, they vent their murderous attention on anyone in front of them, whether or not they are the intended target," Plato said.

"Perhaps," Alcibiades said. "But my advice to you is leave Athens, too. And, since we know that I was the target, at least earlier this morning, you would probably be safer away from me, and Ampharete, as well."

Plato considered . . . and agreed. "I could not leave right away, however. I would need to inform the others in our group of the danger. No one other than the three of us knows what happened here today."

Alcibiades nodded.

"And what do I tell our mentor? Is he in danger, too?"

Alcibiades and Sierra knew that Plato had to know that more was afoot here than they would tell him. But they stuck to their script of silence about Socrates, anyway. To utter anything aloud was to make it more vulnerable.

"Socrates is not in any immediate danger" was all that Alcibiades said.


Alcibiades and Sierra looked back at the harbor, as their hastily chartered little boat slipped into the Aegean. The day had turned chilly, and they hugged each other for comfort of many kinds.

"My history says that Plato was present in Athens during the trial of Socrates but left before he took the hemlock," Sierra remarked. "That was the start of his extensive travels, about twelve years, as far away as Egypt."

"I guess we sent him on his way, then, eventually," Alcibiades said.

Sierra pulled Alcibiades closer.

"We will not have the luxury of sailing for twelve years," he said. "We will need to get back here as soon as possible."

*Sailing to Byzantium, but only for a little while,* Sierra thought. "It is still difficult to figure Plato's role in all of this."

"I trust him a little more, now," Alcibiades said. "I cannot fathom him being in league with our adversaries, with the tip of that sword kissing his chest."

"His dance with death impressed you more than Heron's?"

"Plato seemed far less at ease with arms than Heron, despite his broad shoulders and young age."

"If Heron was trying to kill Plato back there, he is playing far more dangerously with history than secretly rescuing Socrates and leaving his double to die of hemlock." Sierra shook her head. "I am beginning to think that Heron may not be our only adversary."

"Who else?"

"I have no idea."

Alcibiades frowned. "Whoever else may be opposing us, I believe Heron has determined to stop anyone who could interfere with his plans for Socrates—including me, including Plato. But given what you have told me about the impact of Plato's future writings, I grant that killing him would leave a gaping hole in history." Alcibiades sighed. "But I also think it very unlikely that Plato was the author of that alternate dialog. Unless he is a superb actor, if Plato knew what the author of that dialog knew, he would have blurted out something during that peril on the road to Piraeus."

Sierra shivered through Alcibiades' arms. "If Plato did not write it, who did?"

Alcibiades pressed his face against her hair. He was nearly shivering himself. "The answer to that question would explain many things."

CHAPTER 9

*Athens, 399 BC*

The trial of Socrates was now just weeks away.

If the prosecution and death of Socrates could be blamed on any one man, it would be Anytus. Sierra had learned what she could about him since she and Alcibiades had returned to Athens.

A popular if ineffective general in the Peloponnesian Wars, a middle-class opponent of the hated Thirty, Anytus was something of a hero in Athens, 399 BC. Among the many reins Anytus sought to grasp in his calloused hands were those of the revived Athenian democracy. And he hated Socrates.

"Fathers frequently are angry at Socrates because he seeks to help their sons lead better lives," Alcibiades once told her. "Anytus the tanner was furious when Socrates said to him that he should not limit his son's education to horses and hides."

Sierra decided she needed to talk to Anytus, though Alcibiades was against it. She knew he would be unhappy that she was going against his wishes. She would deal with that later, after she had made this attempt. If she could deflect Anytus from his historical course, that would save Socrates without risking the life of Alcibiades.

The home of the tanner was not hard to find. "I am here to see your master," Sierra told the female who came to the door. "I apologize for not having an appointment."

The woman nodded, went back into the house, and returned a few minutes later with a middle-aged man. "I am Anytus," the man said.

"My name is Ampharete. Could we talk for a few minutes? Perhaps walk? The air is cool and appealing this morning."

"What would you wish to talk about?"

"A thorn in many of our sides," Sierra answered. "Socrates."

Sierra found Anytus not only congenial but surprisingly confident— only a man secure in his public position would be so forthcoming about his political views with a stranger. The two walked along quiet lanes, muddied from a heavy rain that had fallen the day before.

"He was close friends with some of the Thirty," Anytus said about Socrates. "When others fled this city—either in protest or to protect their lives—Socrates remained happily behind, practicing his craft on any who would listen."

"You think he is a threat to the restored democracy?"

"Yes and no. There are truthfully very few people who pay him any attention, other than his devoted students."

"Perhaps the best course of action would just be to ignore him," Sierra said. "Socrates is certainly no youngster."

Anytus shook his head. "Sophocles lived to be ninety. Gorgias of Sicily is still hale in his eighties. Socrates is only seventy. Philosophers have an unfortunate habit of living a long time . . . But I have no course of action in mind, one way or the other, about Socrates."

Sierra considered. Her information was that Anytus was already riling people up about Socrates.

"And what are *your* grievances against the incessant talker?" Anytus inquired.

"It is a matter of love more than politics." Lies that were closest to the truth were usually the most convincing.

Anytus eyed Sierra. "He has turned your young man against you?"

"Actually, it is an older man whose affections are at stake. He cares more for Socrates than—"

Anytus waved off the explanation. "You may be speaking of lust, not love, then—but I do not need to know your personal affairs, any more than you need to know mine. But it is interesting that your grievance is personal. Mine is, as well. He has turned my son against me!"

"How so? If you do not mind my asking." So now Anytus was getting to the nub of this.

Anytus sighed, stopped, looked up at the sky, and then at her figure. "You are not yet a mother, is that right?" he asked softly, sadly.

"No, not yet."

"It is not an easy thing, bringing a son into the world. There is an inevitable tension between father and son—the poets have described this. Sons should not just embrace the lives and professions of their fathers."

Sierra nodded. She agreed.

"But if someone kidnaps a son—kidnaps his mind, influences him unduly against the father—then much damage can be done. The relationship can be wounded beyond repair."

"Is that what Socrates did to your son?"

Anytus nodded, unable to speak.

Sierra regarded him. Tears were in the older man's eyes.

Anytus recovered his voice. His face was set in a strange expression, intense but calm. "Thank you. Thank you. I believe I know why you came to me today. I am not usually a superstitious man, but your coming here today was no accident. You helped me see the way. I know, now, what I must do. Thank you."

And he turned and strode quickly away.

"Wait . . ." Sierra started after him, then stopped. What had she just done? She had come here to *defuse* Anytus and had instead just set the fuse burning. . . . She swallowed, attempting to understand. Her stupid talk about love and politics had gotten Anytus to focus on his anger. Why had she said that? It had seemed right, a way of getting Anytus to feel that he and she had something in common. But the result was that, like some inescapable omen, Sierra's conversation with Anytus had had just the reverse of the effect she had wanted.

She looked after the receding figure. She could have killed Anytus, that would have been another way to stop this. Ever since Max had died before her eyes, killing seemed perversely more natural to her. But she was not a killer. And Alcibiades was right that, even with Anytus dead, someone else with an equally deep grievance against Socrates, personal or political, could foment the trial. Socrates was that kind of person. He rubbed people the wrong way, even those who loved him.

Maybe this way *was* really safer—if the trial had to happen, let it happen, let it happen in the way history and she and everyone now involved in this knew it would happen. In that way, the most reliable measures could be taken to rescue Socrates.

But that would still be no help in keeping Alcibiades safe.

She walked back slowly to the latest secret place she was sharing with Alcibiades. Like many other of such places, this had turned out to be not so secret.

She met Antisthenes on the road. He was Socrates' oldest student, now in league with Alcibiades. She had only a slight recollection of Antisthenes in her studies—he started the Cynic school of philosophy after Socrates' death, but most of his writings had been lost. He looked to be about the same age as Alcibiades. He now knew Sierra. Well, she could only hope that Antisthenes would write nothing about what was now going on. Or, if he did, that that would be among his writings that did not survive.

He was running with two other men. "Alcibiades was attacked. He was worried about you—"

"Is he safe?"

Antisthenes nodded. "Yes. He escaped with just a scratch on his arm. I am going to warn the others. Do not go back there."

"Do you know where he is now?"

"I do not. But when I see him, he will be happy to hear that you are unharmed. Where should I tell him you—"

"Tell him I will find him, and not to worry," Sierra said.

The three men resumed their run.

Sierra considered her options. Alcibiades could be in any one of half a dozen secret places she knew about. But there was only one place that only he and she knew about . . . the house with the chairs.

She approached warily. She could see no sign of Alcibiades or anyone outside or inside the house, from where she stood. She moved closer and heard nothing. She applied her palm to the inobtrusive part of the door-frame that she knew would receive her print. She had installed it on Heron's instruction. She had programmed it to admit only Alcibiades and her. This gave her some relief now—no one unauthorized could enter. But that did not mean that no one dangerous could not enter, or could not arrive on the inside via the chairs.

But the two chairs on the inside were empty, as was the room around it. She sat heavily against a wall. How long should she wait here for Alcibiades?

One of the chairs made a noise, as if in answer.

It was the chair's way of announcing another chair's imminent arrival. She had heard sounds like this before.

She walked out the door and looked at the world beyond.

But the heart of her attention was inside the house, on the cessation of sounds that would tell her the new chair's arrival was complete.

She reentered gingerly.

Andros would have to be arriving here sooner or later, for this was presumably the only showroom—that's how she thought of these places—that existed in this part of the world. Of course, Andros might well have come from this golden age of Athens to begin with . . . though Socrates in the dialog certainly appeared to be meeting Andros for the first time.

"Heron!"

The engineer laughed sourly. "You seem surprised—whom were you expecting?"

"Andros."

"Ah" was all Heron said.

"But you're not Andros, after all, are you?"

"I hope not. I'm here to stop him."

The two shifted a bit around the room.

Sierra focused on Heron's garb. It was a robe appropriate to the time, same as hers. Could there be a weapon somewhere in the folds? Of course there could. And Sierra had no idea what kinds of tiny, lethal devices Heron might have access to in his future world.

"We have to stop stirring the pot," Heron said. "We have to simplify."

"Why don't you just go back and tell your earlier self not to have invented time travel?" Sierra tried to eye the door without Heron's noticing and saw that was impossible. Didn't really matter. She couldn't outrun a bullet, a laser, likely not even a well-thrown blade.

"Time travel didn't write this dialog. Time travel didn't come to Socrates with the clone idea. One or more human beings did that."

"One of whom was Andros," Sierra said the obvious, her mind still on some way of getting out of this room.

"We seem to be contributing more to this plan to save Socrates than Andros. We still have no idea what his plan was, is, other than to save Socrates." Heron shook his head. "Maybe there was no plan, other than to get all of us involved—Jonah, you, Alcibiades, Thomas, Appleton, me—stumbling along, making up the plan as we proceeded."

Sierra considered.

Heron continued, "I feel very bad about your friend Max. Perhaps there is some way we can go back to Londinium in 150 AD and fix that. But it would be very difficult, without causing more deaths in the long run."

Sierra stared hard at Heron and wondered again if he had a weapon. "Did you kill him? Was that what you meant by 'simplifying'?"

"No. I could never—"

She bolted for the door. A tendril of liquid agony ripped her right leg and brought her to her knees. Heron did have a weapon.

"Please, it is not safe for you out there," Heron said. "Stay with me."

She got to her feet and took a wobbly step toward Heron. She wobbled sideways, backward, sideways.

"You should sit," Heron said, concerned. "Your leg is almost paralyzed now. You will not be able to walk anywhere on it."

She took another jellied step, wobbled back, sideways again, almost fell, lurched sideways . . . and hoisted herself into the chair that she had maneuvered herself next to.

"Don't do that." Heron leveled his weapon at her, but hesitated.

One of Sierra's legs was no good, but both hands were fine. She typed in a code and the bubble went up.

Heron's hand quivered. Then he went for the door.

*Of course*, Sierra thought with jagged satisfaction, and massaged her insensate leg. *You wouldn't risk damaging one of your precious chairs.*


Sierra had had no time to ponder her destination in time. Her split second permitted a decision about just the basic coordinates . . . past or future, near or far?

The past was wrong. She couldn't risk running into herself. She chose future. Near the action. One month, if her sweating fingers had typed true.

The bubble receded.

She slowly eased herself out of the chair. Her leg was still dead. She had no idea how long it would take to come back to life, if ever. Her best hope on that score was that Heron had no reason to want her permanently disabled. Heron could have aimed for her head if he had wanted her dead.

But what her leg meant for sure, right now, was that she couldn't move fast, or far. She appreciated the depth of her predicament. Heron was likely able to trace the date of her arrival, with the equipment in one of the chairs where she had just been seated.

Well, Heron was not in the room now. That at least was clear. But he could be outside, waiting for her. She could do nothing about that. The only way she could avoid Heron's weapon if he was outside right now would be for her to immediately try another skip with the chair. But that would only delay confronting the same problem.

Painfully, Sierra moved toward the door. There was certainly no point remaining in the room, a lame duck.

But where was Alcibiades most likely to be? The answer depended on this exact date. Sierra moved outside, dragging her leg.

No bullet or scorching laser hit her. Just a damp night, colder than when she had left. But Sierra breathed it in, gratefully, and did her best to leave the premises behind her. Her leg felt as if maybe it was beginning to regain a little sensation.

She hobbled down the road toward Athens. She found a fairly good stick along the way, but the going was still slow. She decided to investigate the closest of Alcibiades' secret places. It was not far and was as good a place as any to start.

Several men who looked familiar were in front of the dwelling. She tried to approach without making noise, but lost her footing and slipped in the brush. The men saw her. She regained her feet and stood her ground. There was no point in attempting to run and falling on her face.

They recognized her.

"Where is Alcibiades?" she asked. "Is he safe?"

"He is in Athens."

"Do you know what the date is?" she asked.

"It is the night of Socrates."


"It takes almost an hour, by foot, to reach the prison," one of Alcibiades' men told Sierra.

"What time is it right now?" she asked.

"The sun set a few hours ago. Would you like us to carry you to the prison?"

Sierra considered. She saw no horses. These men were likely her best bet. She nodded. "Yes. Thank you."

*Of all the nights to arrive with a bad leg, she* thought. But she realized that Heron had probably set all of his chairs to arrive tonight, regardless of what she had commanded.


The trek took longer than expected. Sierra rubbed her leg. It was beginning to feel better. "I think I can walk now," she told her escorts.

The men put her down carefully.

She walked a few feet and felt a rush of sensation. She stopped, then walked again. She nodded. "How much further is the prison?"

"Very close."

---

The prison was not what Sierra had expected. She realized she had no idea exactly what the prison of Socrates looked like, but this was little more than a house.

At least it wasn't a cave on a hilltop overlooking the acropolis, as some historians had claimed. Sierra was not sure her legs could have risen to that occasion.

Alcibiades' men suggested they all hang back and watch. Sierra's pulse was now racing far too quickly for her to do that. The men, deferential to the end, did not try to stop her. She walked toward the house.

Several other men were in front. Presumably Crito would be able to bribe or talk his way past them. Or perhaps he had done that already. Sierra did not know the exact time of any of the events that had happened or were supposed to have happened tonight.

She was sure that no one in front of the prison looked like Alcibiades. Was he already inside with Socrates?

She trembled with the thought that he might not have arrived here at all.

One of the men in front of the prison looked in her direction. She caught her breath but continued to walk forward.

"Is it possible for me to visit with the prisoner?" she asked one of the men, in her politest Greek. "I wanted to say farewell."

The man, armed with a long knife, regarded her. "Disrobe."

She thought for a second.

"Disrobe if you wish to enter," the man repeated.

She could not be certain that Alcibiades' men were where she had left them. Nor could she be sure that they would come to her aid if these prison guards tried to take advantage of her disrobing. But she had to see what was happening inside, see if Alcibiades was there. She slipped off her robe. She hoped nothing about her body would give away her mid-twenty-first-century origin. She was shaved, but she did not believe that was completely alien to this time.

"You may enter," the guard said.

She thanked him, put her robe back on, and walked inside.

The lighting was minimal—just the little moonlight that leaked in, supported by a few flickers of candles. The layout was what Sierra had seen in other Greek dwellings. A hall with several adjoining rooms. A second floor with what she assumed were bedrooms. A courtyard in the middle without roof, with entrances from the inside that were open. She could smell the night air almost as keenly inside as out. An image popped into her mind from the adventures she had seen on so many screens in her life in the future: a helicopter overhead, hovering above the open courtyard, reeling out a swaying ladder that Socrates could climb and make good his escape. Of course, for that to work, Socrates had to want to make that climb.

Something was different in the smell of this house, this prison of Socrates, if that's what it was. This place smelled . . . more intensely lived in than the other places back here in which Sierra had spent time. Well, Socrates was supposed to have lived here almost a month, waiting for that damned ship from Delos, for that hemlock—

A man emerged from one of the rooms. An elderly man—

Not Socrates.

He looked at Sierra. His eyes were teary, his face was puffy. He nodded at her, then shook his head in the most hopeless, hapless motion she had ever seen. He walked past her and out of the house.

Was this Crito?

Stunned, defeated, depleted to the core that his old friend had turned down a perfect plan for escape. But not perfect enough by Socrates' standards. Because—according to Plato—Socrates couldn't abide the label of cowardice of the soul that such an escape would have branded him with for all posterity.

"Ampharete!" Alcibiades stepped out of a room and pulled her into his arms.

She kissed and hugged him and wept.

"I thought it better that Crito did not see me," Alcibiades said softly, and brushed her face with his palm. "I let him talk to Socrates alone. I saw no point in intruding. Better to leave that aspect of the Platonic tale intact for history."

Sierra nodded. She realized that Alcibiades looked pale, uneasy.

"What is wrong?" she asked, though she knew that these circumstances were enough to short-circuit the strongest soul.

"Would you like to meet Socrates now?" Alcibiades replied.

The two walked down the hall. Sierra looked at Alcibiades for some indication of what to expect. His face said nothing, except it was too distressed to communicate anything else.

Socrates was standing at the portal of his room. He looked more mundane, less angelic, than Sierra had expected, though she realized those expectations were reflections of history and myth, not reality. He looked nothing like that stupid statue. Had she passed this man on the street—in third-millennium-AD New York or third-century-BC Athens—she would not have given him a second glance. Only Alcibiades' demeanor told her this was Socrates, which was more than enough.

Alcibiades introduced her to his erstwhile mentor. History had not indicated much about Socrates' attitude toward women, other than that he was married, but had no women students. Sierra caught the look in his eye. Socrates was a man, even on the edge of his deathbed, who enjoyed women. Interesting that history had been largely mute about that. Likely the work of Plato.

Socrates smiled at her with his eyes.

"Could you tell us, again, what you told me about the visitor?" Alcibiades was not smiling.

Socrates nodded. "I do not believe he will be coming."

"Not tonight?" Sierra asked. "He has been in contact with you?"

"Not any night."

"And why not?" Alcibiades prompted, again.

"Because I created him."

"What?" Sierra asked.

"I dislike writing, I find it abusive of the truth," Socrates said. "But I am not a perfect being. I have my vices. I have a wife. I like my wine. I have the implements of writing, and sometimes I cannot help myself, and I use them."

Sierra was speechless. "You did a good job of concealing that last vice," she finally said.

"Thank you. Shall I show you its results?"

"Yes, please do," Sierra said.

Socrates had already turned around and walked into his room. He leaned over something in the corner. He returned with a papyrus manuscript and placed it in Alcibiades' hand.

Alcibiades brought it close to his face. He sniffed. "Newly written." He began to read: " 'Socrates: "What time is it?" Visitor: "The dawn broke a little while ago." . . .' "

Sierra pressed her face into reading range. What Alcibiades was reading aloud was indeed on the papyrus.

"I am afraid I have written many of these," Socrates interrupted. "My student Plato has most of them. I am going to die very soon, so I suppose there is no gain in concealing that now."

"Many copies of this one dialog, or many dialogs?" Sierra asked.

Socrates looked at her appreciatively. "Many dialogs."

"Why did you write this one?" Alcibiades asked unhappily.

Socrates looked at him. "You have lost some of your springtime, my dearest friend. It grieves me to see that. But, to answer your question, I wrote this to see what impact it would have. To see what might happen if those words survived my death. I believe Thales called such activities 'experiments.' "

Alcibiades shook his head.

"And apparently it has already worked. It has saved your life," Socrates said to Alcibiades, "has it not?"

"It can save yours, too, if you let it," Sierra said.

Socrates smiled sadly. "I do not think so."

"But more than the two of us in this room with you have read your dialog," Sierra said. "Did you know that one of them, an inventor, has machines that can save you—"

"Heron? We have already met and conversed, more than once."

"Yes, of course," Sierra said, suddenly realizing what she had missed. "Heron must have been the source of your information about our future. About the vehicles that ply time like a sea, about the farmers who raise crops with human faces."

Socrates nodded. "She has a muse of poetry whispering in her ear," he said to Alcibiades.

"But Heron can still save you," Sierra continued. "We can still substitute a double for you. It should be arriving here soon, if it has not already. Let your double drink the hemlock!"

"No," Socrates said simply.

"Why are you so stubborn?" Sierra said.

Socrates chuckled. "You would have made a good visitor in my dialog."

"Heron may intend to kill us," Alcibiades said darkly. "Not you," he said to Socrates. "Us." He gestured to Sierra and himself.

"It is not safe for anyone here," Sierra added.

"Then you should go, both of you, if what you are telling me about Heron is true," Socrates said. "There is no need for you to die on my behalf."

"My men are watching outside, beyond the view of the guards," Alcibiades said. "They can help us."

"No," Socrates repeated. "You go. There is no—"

"Would it disturb you to know that, in the future, dialogs you composed will be attributed to Plato?" Sierra asked. She had no particular knowledge of Socrates' vanity. All Sierra knew is that she would have been bothered by someone else receiving credit for her work. Was that a modern attitude, a twenty-first-century conceit? She recalled that Benjamin Jowett had written in the nineteenth century that people cared too much about credit—was he perhaps referring to Socrates? It couldn't hurt to try this tack with him. "If you did not take the hemlock, you at least would have some time to correct that misimpression."

"Why would that misimpression be something I would care to correct? I neither own nor even created my ideas. Surely, they already existed, and my only contribution was to become aware of them, and perhaps coax them into a more public arena."

Sierra smiled sourly. "And is that also an idea that already existed? In my world, the preexistence of ideas is a theory attributed to Plato."

Socrates laughed, again. Sierra thought that might have been the most appealing part of the man. "It seems I taught my student very well."

"Is not life better than death?" Sierra tried again. "Life is hope, change, the capacity to improve. Death is unchanging, unresponsive.

You said—or Plato had you say—in one of your dialogs that writing is no good, because it gives but one unvarying answer to all questions, only that which has already been written. Can you not see that death is even worse? It is not only a scroll, it is a scroll shut tight, forever."

"If I were younger, I would be glad that a poetess such as you was alive and open—"

A sound from the outside intruded.

Alcibiades signaled Sierra to go into the room with Socrates. But she brought him into the room and joined Alcibiades in the hall.

"It does not sound like fighting," Alcibiades mouthed to her.

Two of the guards walked into the house, weapons drawn. A third man entered, with no visible weapon.

"Hold them. Do not hurt them," Heron told the guards.

Alcibiades acceded. "There is no advantage in being slaughtered here like oxen, with no weapons," he said to Sierra quietly. "We will find another moment."

Sierra nodded to Heron and the guards, one of whom put a heavy, restraining hand on her shoulder. "What do you intend to do with us?" she asked Heron.

"I take no pleasure in exercising force. It is an ugly, last resort. I employ it now, to control you, so I can complete my work with Socrates. Once I have accomplished my task, you will be free to go, to the ends of the world if you like." Heron regarded Alcibiades. "Where is Socrates?"

Alcibiades did not answer.

"Never mind. He is no doubt in one of these rooms. I do not need you to guide me." Heron gestured to the guards. "Take these two along." He looked at Alcibiades and Sierra. "Your presence could be helpful when I speak with Socrates."

"What happened to your men?" Sierra asked Alcibiades, as quietly as possible, in English, so presumably the guards would not understand. She had no idea how much more English he had been able to pick up from her device in her absence.

"Do not know," Alcibiades whispered, also in English. "Must be out there, still, somewhere. I think Heron came alone, or with few men, so my men did not see."

"The guards who let us inside must have been Heron's men," Sierra said. For some reason, knowing it was *Heron's* mercenaries looking at her naked body made her shudder.

Alcibiades nodded.

Heron and his two guards escorted Sierra and Alcibiades into the room that held Socrates.

Socrates gave a crinkly smile. "I am becoming more popular with every hour that approaches my death."

"You are not going to die here," Heron said. "Did I not make that clear to you last time we talked?"

"He wrote the dialog," Sierra said to Heron, about Socrates. "It was an experiment to see what impact his writing could have—you like being his tool in an experiment?"

"I do not care who wrote that dialog," Heron replied. "It set me on a course. I control its destiny now—I made it real."

"We were just conversing, before you came, about the parentage of ideas, and how that does not matter," Socrates observed.

Sierra muttered and shook her head.

"But though I am not in control of my ideas, and do not want to be, I am in control of whether I die, at least somewhat," Socrates continued. "I chose not to leave with Crito. And I choose not to leave with you."

"You are wrong. You have no choice." Heron looked at Alcibiades, then at Sierra. He signaled one of the guards.

The guard wheeled on Sierra. She struggled. He punched her just above her stomach, knocking the air out of her. She slumped, shaking, against his arm.

Alcibiades was moving—

But was stopped at the point of a knife—his guard's—against his neck.

"I would instruct him to use it, believe me, though it would not make me happy," Heron said to Alcibiades. "It would be easy to get your dead body into a chair, and on its way to the future. It would cause no change in history."

Socrates sighed. "What is the goal of all of this violence?"

"Are you so intent on dying that you would see these two die first, right in front of you?" Heron asked. "Whom shall I start with?" Heron looked at Sierra's guard.

Socrates grunted. "It seems the future may be more barbaric than the present, at least as far as you are concerned. Maybe those who believe the golden age is behind us are right."

"You are the golden age. Why end it this night when there is no need? Who knows what ideas you can yet bring to the world." Heron looked at Socrates.

"We, too, want precisely that," Alcibiades began—then seized the opportunity. He elbowed his guard and charged Heron. The inventor moved to avoid Alcibiades, but Socrates, with hands now clasped, smashed down hard on Heron's wrist. His weapon went flying.

Alcibiades now wheeled on the guard who was at his back and kneed him savagely in the groin. The attack met some protective covering and was not completely successful. But Alcibiades went for the long knife, and he and the guard rolled on the ground.

Sierra's captor had thrown her to the ground. It did no real damage. She was beginning to recover her breath anyway.

Her guard rushed Socrates and Heron, wriggling against the wall. The guard hesitated. He dared not hurt either man.

Alcibiades came out on top of his guard, with the knife in his hand. He drove it sharply into the guard's throat. Then he leapt to his feet, moved quickly, and plunged the knife into the other guard's neck before he knew what was happening.

Alcibiades loomed over Heron. "Unlike your guard, I have no reservation about severing your chin from your throat."

Socrates rose slowly. He looked at Alcibiades and then around the room. "What does that device do?" He gestured with his head toward Heron's little laser gun, which had skidded across the floor in the struggle.

Sierra, on her feet now, scooped up the gun. She looked at Socrates and smiled. "Seventy-year-old philosophers are apparently in better physical condition in your time than in mine."

"Alcibiades and I were hoplites—soldiers—in the wars," Socrates replied. "This is not the first time we have come to each other's aid. He saved my life at Potidaea, and I saved his at Delium."

Alcibiades searched Heron for further weapons. Finding none, he shoved him to the corner of the floor and the wall. "We want the same thing as you—we want Socrates to live. Why are we fighting?"

Heron just smiled.

Alcibiades glared at him. "Maybe I should put a knife through you, right now."

Socrates looked sadly at Alcibiades. "You take too much joy in death."

Alcibiades looked at his mentor. "Let us talk about life, then. Your life, and why—"

"I told you—"

"I know," Alcibiades said. "But if you stay here, and wait for the ship from Delos, and drink the hemlock, all of us may die, too, as a result. Heron has many men at his command. They will no doubt be here soon, with your duplicate body. Hemlock is an unkind poison. But some means of torture can be more unkind, still. You know more about me and the way I think than do most other men. If you are here when Heron's men arrive, you might provide them with information that could be our undoing. Is that what you wish?"

"No, that is not my wish," Socrates said gravely.

"Then go with her—right now. She will take you somewhere . . . I do not know where. She probably does not know where, right now. That is good."

Socrates and Sierra both protested, for different reasons.

"I will find you, you will find me, later," Alcibiades said to Sierra. "The important goal now is bringing Socrates to a safe place—"

"You can come with us," she said.

"No," Alcibiades said, looking sideways at Heron. "I cannot leave Athens and my men to him, and whichever of his plans and mercenaries are already in motion—"

Socrates breathed in sharply . . . and nodded.

Alcibiades exhaled. "Go, then. Now. Before the others arrive."

Sierra looked at Heron.

"He is still smiling," she whispered hoarsely into Alcibiades' ear. "This may be just what he wants."

Alcibiades pulled her farther away from Heron. Both kept their eyes on him. "That does not matter," he whispered into her ear, "as long as it is what we want."

Alcibiades looked at Socrates. "We may not see each other again," Alcibiades said to his mentor, voice choked. "A pity. There is so much else in the universe to discuss."

He kissed Sierra on the corner of her mouth, then spoke to her loudly enough for everyone to hear, "Do not go anywhere near Alexandria."

Tears filled Sierra's eyes.

Heron's smile widened. But at that moment, no one saw it.

"Go," Alcibiades said to Sierra and Socrates. "Please."

The two nodded, and walked out the door.

CHAPTER 10

*Athens, 399 BC*

Socrates stepped outside the little house that had been his prison. Sierra was at his side.

Socrates looked at the night. "I see no sign of Heron's men."

"That does not mean they will not be here in a few minutes," Sierra replied.

"I confess that I would very much like to see what my double looks like."

"Alcibiades is right to be concerned that all of us, not only you, could die if you stay to receive such knowledge."

"Yes," Socrates conceded. "Then let us leave now. Our destination is a port, I assume, from which we can travel afar?"

"It is a house much like the one behind us, except this one has magical chairs—such as the gods of Olympus would adopt as their own."

The walk to the house with the chairs was swift and uneventful.

"I presume we do not need to worry that Heron is lying in wait for us here," Socrates remarked.

Sierra regarded Socrates.

"Oh, yes, I see my error," Socrates said. "If one can travel through time, then an older version of the Heron we left back at the prison could come here, to this house in front of us."

"Yes, a younger version, too. Though the younger version would presumably mean us no harm."

"Because . . ."

"He would want—"

"Yes, he would want you alive, so that you could play your part in making these recent events occur," Socrates finished the sentence. "Yes. I can see that now."

"Logic hides around corners when you travel through time."

Socrates nodded. "And, of course, the only way an older version of Heron could now appear before us would be if he survives whatever will soon happen now, in the prison."

"Exactly. You know, it is extraordinary, being able to talk to you like this, seeing you grapple with difficult concepts, how you come to an understanding and formulate your thoughts. All that I otherwise know of you is from dialogs, which represent careful polishings of your thoughts, and have been passed down to my world, frozen, for thousands of years."

"This is why I dislike the written word, even though, in the interest of learning more about its impact, I have given in to its temptations, as I told you."

Sierra nodded and cautiously stopped a few feet away from the house with the chairs. She put a restraining arm on Socrates. It was difficult to see in the dark, but as far as she could tell, no one was in front of the house, or inside, either, unless asleep with all lights extinguished.

"It appears safe for us to enter," she said.


Four chairs were in the house. Sierra was beyond trying to determine their intended passengers. She knew only that she and Socrates had to use two of the chairs quickly. With any luck, Alcibiades would be arriving here soon, as well. She would set his chair to travel to the same time as she and Socrates. She had learned that programming.

For an instant, she thought that perhaps she should send Socrates on his way in one of these chairs while she ran back to the prison to help Alcibiades. No, Socrates would be clueless in any time not close to this present.

"These are our conveyances to the future? They look . . . small." Then Socrates laughed. "Of course, I have no standards for evaluating vehicles that travel through time."

*Nor do I, really,* Sierra thought. "I must examine them." She scrutinzed the controls for each of the four chairs. Socrates stared, mouth open.

"Sometimes you can set the destination in time on these chairs, so they arrive at the time you select. Not on these."

"Why not?"

"Likely because Heron set them all to arrive at the time he wanted."

"You do not want to be dropped into a nest of Heron's men, your adversaries."

Sierra considered. "We have no better choice. To wait here is to court worse danger." That was certainly true for Socrates. Everyone in Athens knew he was sentenced to die, and some would have been determined to make sure that happened . . . including, sadly, Socrates.

"Such calculations are beyond my grasp," Socrates said. "I promised to accompany you. I will sit in the chair if that is your wish."

The two sat in their chairs—perhaps the greatest philosopher of all time, from 399 BC, and a doctoral student with a half-finished dissertation, from AD 2042. The philosopher had no idea what degrees in philosophy even were, though he lived them every day of his life.

Sierra programmed Socrates' chair to leave the same time as hers. She apparently had at least that level of control.

The bubbles ascended.

*Athens, AD 2061*

A split second. The universe in a grain of sand. No, eternity in a grain of sand in an hourglass. . . .

The bubble around Sierra receded. She had a momentary, disquieting thought: If for some reason Socrates arrived a few seconds or minutes later, wouldn't that be dangerous for her, just standing in the open, in the same room or wherever as these chairs? No, people traveled together in time all the time. The chairs had to take that into account. . . . Sierra laughed, ironically. Yeah. All the time, sure.

But the bubble was gone around each chair, and there was Socrates in his chair. Unbelievable, though maybe not any more so than meeting Socrates in the first place.

She helped the philosopher out of his chair.

"The air smells strange," Socrates said.

"Yes, it does."

"Which means this is likely not your time, either."

"Yes, let us look around the room and see if we can find out when."

A bin of clothing was in the customary place. It contained coveralls, made of a thin, soft, pleasing material. "This looks like one size fits everyone," Sierra said to herself, and Socrates. "I mean, this should probably fit you," she said to Socrates, "and you probably should remove your robe and put this on your body."

"So I do not attract attention."

"Yes. Now we need to look for money . . . to purchase our means of further travel, if need be."

"I understand."

A wafer was in her coverall. She examined it. A tiny screen lit up. It had a picture of her, and a picture of Socrates. As Sierra stared at the picture of Socrates—it looked as if it had just been taken, no doubt when Socrates was in the chair—it changed to the picture of her. And then it stayed that way.

"Ah, I get it," she said to Socrates. "Look at your little . . . tablet. Looking at it triggers some sort of picture-making device, in the tablet, so that it records who is looking at it. And it freezes the image."

"Picture device?"

"An instant painting. Uh, like a reflection in a pond, but it becomes permanent."

Socrates slowly nodded. "But for what purpose?"

"It is probably proof of identity. A living parchment that tells anyone who looks at it who we are."

They left the house. "The sooner we get away from here, the safer we will be from Heron," Sierra said.

The day was bright outside. Sierra looked around. "I wonder what year this is—it seems pretty much the same as my time."

Socrates was transfixed. "It seems a deer to me," he slowly said.

"What?"

Socrates shook his head and looked confused. "I am sorry. Sometimes I choose . . . the wrong words. Not intentionally. I meant to say, it seems like a *dream*."

Sierra looked at him. "Yes, and my city will seem just as marvelous a dream to you, too. And you will have time to savor it."

Socrates shook his head no.

"We need to leave this place—and time—as speedily as we can," Sierra said. "This time and place were set by Heron on his chairs. We need to go elsewhere."

Sierra started walking. Socrates reluctantly followed.

But what year was this? Sierra wondered. It was Athens, no doubt about that. She could tell from its looks, and from the fact that the chairs traveled in time not space. And it looked like the Athens of her time, the Athens of the 2040s. Millennia of architecture densely mixed, with a light dusting of intelligent snow—telecommunicating confection, as the commercials put it—a myriad of tiny cells that could relay signals from palm phones or any other devices of communication.

She had never been in the farther future of Heron's world. Did it look like this? Or had Heron set the chairs to AD 2042?

She had to find out the date. The time traveler's eternal question.

She soon had her answer. From a floating, shimmering window, about six feet in the air above the road. It displayed the front page of the *Athenian Global Village.* The dates on the rippling mauve masthead—there were twelve of them, in twelve different languages and colors—all said 13 April 2061.

Why? Why so close to her time? Heron the engineer did nothing by accident.

Sierra summoned the window. Good, the systems still understood her New York accent. "The airport," she said slowly, clearly, in English.

"Please bring a cab here to take my companion and me to the Athens Realport." She hoped the name had not changed.

"Your means of transport will arrive in approximately nine minutes," a male compu-generated voice replied. It spoke English in a warm contralto, with an undercurrent of Greek accent, and sounded good enough to kiss.

*Athens, 399 BC*

Alcibiades looked at Heron, sitting on the floor against the wall of what had just been Socrates' prison. He tightened his grip on his knife.

One of his trusted men—Antisthenes—put his hand on Alcibiades' arm. "This is not yet over. We may need his help."

"We cannot trust him. How can he help us?"

"I know the future, remember?" Heron spoke up. "I know the fate of Socrates."

"Why should we believe what you tell us?" Alcibiades responded. "You would do better to think of your own fate." Alcibiades removed Antisthenes' hand and took a menacing step toward Heron.

The engineer smiled serenely.

Men burst into the house, shouting.

"They are Heron's," Alcibiades said to Antisthenes, "I recognize the language." Alcibiades pulled Heron to his feet and placed his knife against the inventor's neck. "You were right about letting him live," Alcibiades said to Antisthenes. Both men turned Heron around and shoved him forward. "Move," Alcibiades barked.

*Athens, AD 2061*

Socrates felt more at home in the realport than the cab, which made sense. "A chariot that pulls itself?" Socrates had gawked out of the sleek panes of the taxi the whole time. Sierra hadn't been sure how much of her explanation Socrates had understood. Now she had to try to explain as best she could the hypersonic—or, at very least, air travel.

"It travels the air the same way that boats travel the sea," Sierra said. "Except much faster."

Socrates touched his stomach. "How will it feel to me? The horseless chariot made me a little sick."

"The ride should be pretty smooth. We have had air travel for more than one hundred and fifty years. Someone once said airships were like horizontal elevators. . . . No, you would not know what an elevator was. Forgive me. Forget that analogy."

Socrates was already thinking about something else. "You are surprised that Heron's chairs brought us so close to your time, and not to his. Why do you suppose that happened?"

"It all depends on whether Heron expected us to escape. If not, then the chairs were likely set for him, and they brought us here because he had something he wanted to do here, with you. But if our escape was all part of Heron's plan, then the chairs brought us here because there was something Heron wanted *us* to do here."

"Or something he wanted done to us."

"Yes. But we lack sufficient information to decide which is the correct explanation. Aristotle—the student of your student—might have said that we do not have enough knowledge of the premises to draw logical conclusions."

"Student of my student?"

"Yes, he will be Plato's student, and for many centuries he will be considered the greatest philosopher of all time."

Socrates looked more perplexed than when he had been gazing out of the window of the computer-driven cab. "Student of my student," he said again quietly.

"In a sense, all of us, every thinking person in the Western world, are students of your students."


*Athens, 399 BC*

Two bands of armed men converged on the house that had been the prison of Socrates. One were Heron's Romans, brought back to 405 BC and trained in marital arts of the future at secret camps. The other party, numbering more than forty and four times the size of the Roman group, were Alcibiades' soldiers, loyal Athenians to the core. They were fierce fighters. But the superior techniques of the Romans equalized the contest.

Three Romans were the first to enter the house.

Alcibiades confronted them with a knife to the neck of Heron. "Drop your weapons. Tell the rest of your group to do the same."

Heron spoke in Latin.

The Romans stood their ground, weapons in hand.

Five of Alcibiades' men rushed in behind them.

The Romans turned and fought.

Alcibiades threw Heron to the ground. "Guard him," he shouted to Antisthenes, and lit into the Romans.

Antisthenes stood over Heron, the tip of his blade an inch from his neck. "Tell me about the fate of Socrates."


*Athens, AD 2061*


Finding and booking a flight to New York proved easy. The wafers took care of payment, as they had with the taxi, and with passport matters as well, as Sierra had figured.

Socrates leaned back in his seat after the hypersonic had taken off. "You have perfected comfort in your time."

"We have perfected many things," Sierra replied. "But not the soul."

Socrates looked at her. "You have been listening to—reading—my words."

Sierra regarded the gray-blue swirl beyond the window.

"Are we really in the sky?" Socrates asked.

"Yes."

"And if I were to walk outside, would I fly like a god or die?"

"Both. You would fly for a while, coast through the clouds, then fall to the earth and die."

"Like Icarus. Not a bad way to die."

"Better than hemlock?"

"Most ways of dying are better than hemlock. I never contested that."

"I know. You did not want to put yourself above the city of Athens."

Socrates smiled strangely. "And here I am, above the city of Athens now."

"We are closer to the pillars of Hercules."

Socrates pressed his face to the window.

"Are you glad you escaped?" Sierra asked.

"I am a human being, just like you. I enjoy learning, just like you. I would enjoy another lifetime, yes, contemplating these wonders you have shown me." Socrates gestured to the window. "I want to live, just like you. But—"

Sierra looked at him. "You can bring so much to the world. You must live."

"I cannot."

"You must—"

"No! You do not understand. I cannot live, however you and I may want that, and even though I have escaped the hemlock. I cannot live because whatever happens, whatever anyone does, I will die. Soon."

"I . . . you are right, I do not understand. Why will you die?"

"Because I have an illness that eats me away, inside, and it cannot be cured."

"But . . ." Sierra stopped and tried to fathom what Socrates was saying.

Socrates nodded. "Now you begin to understand. I have known, for almost a year, that I do not have much longer to live. I have seen many physicians—with different philosophies and different skills—and they all agree. I swore them to secrecy."

Sierra's eyes were wide, in the beginning of comprehension. "You provoked Anytus and the trial. I was feeling guilty about that, because I accidentally provoked him further in a conversation."

"He would have proceeded against me with or without your conversation. His anger at me runs very deep."

"And you argued your case, but in a way that antagonized the five hundred as much as possible."

"Yes." Socrates smiled, painfully, crookedly. "I almost lost that battle and won an acquittal."

Sierra shook her head. "Why?"

"I did not want my inevitable death to be meaningless," Socrates said. "If I am to die, let it make a last proposition, a final argument from me. Let it teach the world, or try to teach the world, one more thing."

"You would have been regarded as noble anyway."

"I am not so sure. And my acceptance of the death sentence was not so much about my nobility, as it is about the corruption, the failure, of the Athenian democracy—the stupid mob rule."

"But you may not need to die now."

"Oh?"

"We are in the future now. Medicine has changed. We laugh in the face of most fatal illnesses now."

"I do not think I will be able to laugh very long. Heron knows about my illness. He is sure it cannot be cured, even in your world."

"That makes no sense—why would he want you to escape, if you cannot be cured?"

"I do not know."

Sierra considered. "Even if you cannot be cured in my world, this world, we could grow another version of you, everything other than your brain, and remove the part of you that causes the illness or allows it to happen. And then put your brain into your second, healthy body. We have already done . . . procedures like that, in my world. In Heron's world, it must be commonplace."

"No. Even in Heron's most advanced world, that would not work. He discussed this possibility with me—he raised it, and looked into it. Apparently, my illness arises in the most fundamental part of me, the part that makes me who I am—"

"Your genes?" Sierra spoke the last word in English.

Socrates nodded. "That was the name he used. The part that makes my brain what it is, what I am. Heron says brains give rise to our thoughts, are the true dwellings of our souls?"

"Yes."

Socrates nodded again. "Therefore, no matter how many times my body is regrown, no matter how many times my brain is regrown, it will still give rise to this illness. The . . . bad seeds . . . that cause this cannot be removed without my becoming a different person. Heron believes my current brain is already afflicted. I feel healthy, now, but my lexicon . . . becomes jumbled sometimes, as you heard."

Sierra was unable to speak.

"It did occur to me that Heron could be lying," Socrates said. "But I could not fathom a motive. He was trying to convince me to escape—why would he say it was futile, if it was not?"

Sierra shook her head sadly. "You are right. That makes no sense, either. . . . We can confirm Heron's diagnosis with our devices, when we arrive in New York. I mean, I hope our devices do not confirm it, but . . ."

"I understand. Are you disappointed to discover that I am not such a noble soul, that I am willing to manipulate death for my ends? I believe Alcibiades was disappointed. I could see it in his face."

"Alcibiades knows this?"

"Yes, I told him in the prison right before you arrived."

Sierra sighed. "He did seem more . . . troubled than usual."

Socrates made no response. He was silent for a moment, then returned to the obvious question. "Why do you suppose Heron was still so eager for me to escape, knowing what he knows about my doom?"

"I am not sure. Perhaps for Heron, the inventor, the process is more important than the result. If the process works for you, then perhaps Heron thinks it does not matter if you die. If the process works for you, it can work for someone else in history, someone even more important to Heron. Or maybe he just wanted whatever time, however short, he could now have with you."

A cool, female computer voice announced that the plane was approaching New York.

"We had better focus on what you may need to do after this ship reaches its port," Sierra said.


*Athens, 399 BC*

Alcibiades and Antisthenes looked at two retreating groups of men—Heron and a few of his Romans pursued by a new band of Alcibiades' militia.

Antisthenes had taken his sword off Heron to help Alcibiades. They

# Paul Levinson

had succeeded in killing the Romans around them, but Heron and three of his soldiers had escaped. One of Alcibiades' men had earlier gone for reinforcements. They had arrived and were now after Heron.

Three of Alcibiades' men emerged from the house. They reported that the dead body of Socrates was in the appropriate room. Only Alcibiades and Sierra and now Antisthenes knew that the body was not really Socrates, but the body that Heron had brought with him from the future.

Alcibiades looked again at the two rapidly receding groups. He turned to face Antisthenes. "I cannot leave my men to Heron's demons. If I understand the future correctly, it can wait for as long as I need to destroy Heron here. Take two others with you. I have told you how to reach the house with the chairs. Guard it, continuously, until I return. I—" He winced and reached for his side. He smiled, but his legs buckled.

"Alcibiades!" Antisthenes reached out to support him.

"I am not seriously hurt."

Antisthenes moved his bloodied hand from Alcibiades' side. "It is not a mortal wound," Antisthenes said, examining the cut a Roman weapon had made, "but you need rest."

Alcibiades' eyes closed. He moaned.

Antisthenes summoned two of Alcibiades' men.

Alcibiades rallied, briefly. His eyes fluttered open, then closed.

"He needs rest," Antisthenes said to the men.

They nodded.

"I know where to take him," Antisthenes said.

The men nodded again. "Lead the way."

*New York City, AD 2061*

Sierra briefed Socrates on likely arrival formalities at the Greater La Guardia Airport. "Guards may want to look at our passports—these wafers—again, before they let us leave the port. I do not expect any problem, however. If the wafers worked in Athens, they should work here."

They did.

Socrates and Sierra walked out into a grim, gray New York afternoon. Socrates shivered in the down coat Sierra had bought for him in an airport shop. She had noticed the temperature on the big display: 36° F. She wished she had purchased a coat for herself, too. The best she could do now was pull up her shoulders and blow on her hands.

"It is cold in your world," Socrates said.

"It can be hot or cold in New York this time of year."

Sierra ushered Socrates into a cab. It said "neo-primitive" on the door—it had a human driver. "The Millennium Club, in Manhattan," she told him. "You know where that is?"

"You bet I do." He had wavy red hair and looked to be about thirty.

"Good." Sierra leaned back in the seat and encouraged Socrates to do the same.

"Another horseless chariot," the philosopher said quietly, "but at least this one has a charioteer."

"You and your friend come a long way?" The driver had apparently heard enough of Socrates to pick up the foreign language.

"Yeah. Greece," Sierra replied, in English.

"Greece? Good for Greece! I saw the complete replay of the Jupiter rendezvous last week! I approve! We need some Europeans out there! We can't leave the outer planets completely to the Chinese!"

Sierra didn't know how to answer. Fortunately the driver was speaking in English, so Socrates had no idea what he was saying.

"What, you don't know what I'm talking about?" the driver continued. "You been living under a rock somewhere?"

"Much deeper than that," Sierra said.

The driver laughed.

Sierra liked that a lot better than what he was saying.

There had been no Greek or European space expedition to Jupiter in 2042, though the Chinese were all over the solar system and had been for years. For a moment, Sierra worried that maybe something she had done, or would be doing, or was doing right now, would change history. She had hoped to bring Socrates back to 2042. They had arrived, instead, in 2061. What possible impact could that have on the settlement of outer space? None that she could fathom. But who could really say just what impact this rescue of Socrates might have, on anything and everything, if Socrates was wrong about his diagnosis and he lived . . . which Sierra fervently hoped would somehow happen.

But, of course, Sierra had known all along that any rescue of Socrates was playing with serious fire. She had always expected Socrates to live if rescued. What was different now was Socrates' insistence that he would soon die.

"We are in the sky again," Socrates said. "Very beautiful."

There were actually high over the East River, on the New Triborough, on which a few wet, glistening snowflakes had begun to land.

"Yes," Sierra replied.

*Athens, 399 BC*

"I have walked this path between Piraeus and Athens many times," Antisthenes told his men, as they neared their destination. "I would have walked ten times that distance to hear the words of Socrates!" His eyes glazed with emotion. "Our world will be a poorer place without him!"

They approached the house. Antisthenes looked at Alcibiades, who was being carried in a stretcher by the two men. He looked no worse. Antisthenes squeezed Alcibiades' hand. He smiled back, weakly, but his eyes remained closed.

"I must go into the house, to make sure it is safe," Antisthenes told the men. "Alcibiades should stay here, outside, with you." He entered the house.

"I wonder what is in that house?" one of the men asked the other.

Alcibiades stirred. "Chairs . . ."

Antisthenes emerged from the house. "It is empty. Just two chairs, as Alcibiades said." He turned to Alcibiades. "Can you walk?"

Alcibiades nodded and shakily stood.

Antisthenes put his arm around him for support. "Your wound needs to be treated and dressed."

"I know. Do not worry—it will be. Help me inside."

Antisthenes hesitated.

"We need to go inside now," Alcibiades said. "Trust me."

Antisthenes relented. "Stand guard here," he told the two men, "until we return."

Alcibiades and Antisthenes entered the house. "Help me sit in that chair," Alcibiades asked. "I am going someplace safe, where, according to Ampharete, they have cures that rival the gods'." Antisthenes placed him in a chair. Alcibiades examined the controls and coughed. "She showed me how to control this," he mumbled to himself. He spoke to Antisthenes. "You will need to go outside now. If you come back into the house in a few minutes, you will see that I have vanished."

Antisthenes started to object.

Alcibiades looked him in the eye. "Please. You must go now, and help our men against Heron."

"And the fate of Socrates? What Heron told me in the prison?" Antisthenes struggled, again, with his decision.

"I will see to that. I will return if I can."

Antisthenes looked doubtful.

"You must also tell no one else about this house, tell no one about the chairs in this house," Alcibiades pleaded.

"Our men outside—"

"I know. They have seen this house, of course. Tell them I showed you herbs, remedies, within. Tell them you treated me, and I am resting, and my last command was that you must pursue Heron, now, before he vanishes forever."

"Will I ever see *you* again?"

"I do not know," Alcibiades said truthfully.

Antisthenes spoke huskily, "So I may lose two mentors this one unnatural night."


*New York City, AD 2061*


The cab pulled up to the Millennium Club on Forty-ninth Street. Sierra put her wafer in the slot on the back of the driver's seat. The fare would be deducted from whatever account Heron had attached to these wafers. This transaction would therefore also tell Heron exactly where and when they were. But Heron would soon know that, anyway, if Sierra succeeded in getting upstairs with Socrates and using the chairs in the Club. Heron's chairs, Heron's wafers . . . every damn thing in this time-travel business was Heron's. Including all the advantages.

But what could Sierra do about it? She was dependent upon Heron's bugged equipment, and that meant she could keep no secrets from Heron. But who knew—maybe Heron posed no threat to them now, if he ever had. Sierra would just have to prevail, whatever the case. "Forty percent," she spoke the amount of the tip to the fare slot. A little screen lit its acknowledgment, and her wafer was ejected.

"Thank you," the redhead said, and rewarded Socrates and Sierra with a big smile. They climbed out and he sped away.

The snow had thickened and was beginning to stick on the sidewalk in front of the Club. Socrates took in the whiteness, wide-eyed. Sierra had no idea if it ever snowed in ancient Greece. She opened the big front door of the Millennium Club for Socrates. She breathed gratefully and deeply of its familiar smell.

A hallman approached. He was friendly, but not familiar.

"I'm Sierra Waters, and this is my associate, Socrates. We're not members. But I believe Thomas O'Leary or Samuel Goldshine would know us and would be happy to see us."

The hallman nodded, courteously. "It has been a while since you have been to the Club, miss?"

"Yes . . ."

"Yes, well, I'm afraid that Professor Goldshine passed, about five years ago. It was quite a loss, quite a loss."

"I . . ." Sierra fought off thinking about Goldshine, getting caught in the sadness. She had to focus on Socrates.

"But Cyril Charles said to expect you. Shall I notify him you are here?"

". . . Yes, please."

"Shouldn't be more than a few minutes," the hallman said. "If you'd have a seat . . ." He gestured to the small vestibule on the right.

*Athens, AD 2061*

Alcibiades knew only that his chair was headed for the future. He had seen that specific years were beyond navigating in this chair. If Ampharete and Socrates had taken chairs whose courses were similarly preset, Alcibiades thought there was a chance they might all meet in the future.

The bubble receded. He saw three other chairs, in addition to his. Ampharete and Socrates and . . . Heron? He hoped not.

This room around him was unrecognizable. But what was the year?

The year was less important than getting help for his wound, Alcibiades realized. Ampharete had told him, more than once, that her future had physicians who could bring the recently deceased back to life. His wound was certainly not as grevious. But how to summon those physicians?

He slowly climbed out of the chair. He clutched his knife and looked around. He saw a door. He walked toward it and pressed his free hand against his side. He knew he had lost blood. His legs felt weak.

He pushed and pulled on the door until it opened. He staggered out. This room was empty, as well. Odd-looking colored little lights glimmered on a square on the wall. . . .

A door on the far side of the room opened. The unexpected light momentarily blinded Alcibiades. He dropped his knife and sank to his knees.

A man approached and looked down at him through the haze. "My God! Alcibiades, is that you? What are you doing here?"

Alcibiades smiled weakly. "Appleton . . . help me." And he passed out on the floor.


*New York City, AD 2061*

Cyril Charles walked into the vestibule of the Millennium Club a few moments later and introduced himself.

Sierra rose to meet him, as did Socrates.

"Sierra Waters," Charles said crisply. "Good to see you."

"You know me?"

Charles nodded. "We have already met, nineteen years ago, but you of course would not recall. I'm sure you'll understand why. Coincidentally, I did just yesterday have lunch with William Henry Appleton, and he spoke quite highly of you. In fact, he asked me to give you his best regards, the next time you and I met. . . . Funny how time works—I could not be sure it would be so soon."

"Is . . . Mr. Appleton here?"

Charles smiled knowingly. "Alas, no. We had lunch both here and very far from here, yesterday, as you no doubt can appreciate."

"I can," Sierra said. "So you . . . move around."

"Indeed. I do now. The library needs considerable tending . . . over time." Charles looked at Socrates and spoke in classic Greek. "And you, sir, are Socrates. We had the honor of meeting."

"Oh, sorry," Sierra said. "I should have introduced you—"

"No, no, we have already met, as well. You see . . . never mind, no need to go into that now. You grasp what I'm saying. . . ." Charles turned from Sierra to Socrates and beamed. "And you come from somewhere very far from here, too. I hope you had a pleasant trip."

Socrates nodded.

"Good," Charles said, still in Greek. "Let us go up the stairs, then, and have a drink."

The three sat at a small, mahogany table. Charles extolled the date wine to Socrates. The philosopher's eyes lit up. "Yes," he said. The barman arrived. Charles ordered a glass of the wine for Socrates and a single-malt Scotch for himself. Sierra went for ginger tea with triple caffeine.

"We cannot stay here too long," Sierra said to Charles, in English.

"Yes, I know." Charles's eyes were fixed on Socrates, and his mouth was open. "What can I say to him? One of the greatest minds in history! I'll always be at a loss! I try to be calm about it, but it's unimaginable!" He smiled again at Socrates.

"Have you met Alcibiades?" Socrates asked.

"No . . . ," Charles said, surprised at the question.

Sierra started to explain—

"There is no need to tell me," Charles said. "We should discuss only unimportant matters now, and you should leave soon. You understand?"

"Because we will see you again in a little while, nineteen years in the past," Sierra said.

Charles nodded.

This part of the conversation had been in Greek, and Socrates had presumably understood. But he said, gravely, to Sierra, "We must warn your friend about Heron."

Sierra considered. She wasn't sure how much she could confide in Charles. He claimed to be on friendly terms with Appleton and obviously knew about the chairs and used them. But that could mean he was a friend of Heron's, too.

Still . . . "You know that the chairs were designed by Heron of Alexandria?" Sierra asked.

"Yes," Charles replied.

"Do you know him?"

"Have we met? No." Charles looked uncomfortable. "We really should not be talking about this, as I've been trying to explain."

"Yes, but I want you to know that he may be using these chairs for bad purposes. I will not say any more. But let that possibility . . . guide you."

The drinks arrived.

Charles nodded at the barman, Sierra, and Socrates and gulped his Scotch. "I am sorry to be so difficult about this, but Thomas warned me about acquiring too much information."

Sierra nodded her understanding.

"Who is Thomas?" Socrates asked.


*Athens, AD 2061*

Appleton had been in 2061 long enough to know how to summon immediate medical aid. "I saw an advertisement on a big screen in the city," he said to himself. "They apparently give free medical treatment in this era—quite humane!"

Appleton removed his jacket and placed it under Alcibiades' head. Socrates' beloved student moaned.

Appleton's face creased in thought. "Good thing I decided to take a little stroll in this future before I returned home," he said to himself and Alcibiades, who was beginning to come to. "After all, at my age, I am almost certain not to get another chance! But I didn't expect to find you here. . . . I wonder if you will need proper identification to receive medical treatment? They seem very focused on proof of identity in this twenty-first century."

Alcibiades opened his eyes and tried to stand.

"No, no," Appleton said. "You stay here. . . . I know how to summon a carriage. There is a device in the outer room."

Appleton first went to the clothing bin and retrieved two identity wafers. Then he went to a screen in the main room of the restaurant. "Let's see," he mumbled, and inserted one of the wafers. "Ah, yes, press here for English. . . . Press here for medical assistance. . . . Yes," he spoke up, "we require immediate assistance, please."

"Is this a medical emergency?" a female contralto voice inquired.

"Yes, it is. We're located at—"

"We can see your location. Is the injured party mobile?"

"Yes, I believe he is."

"A compu-cab will be in front of your location in six minutes."

Appleton and Alcibiades bundled into a cab twenty minutes later. "Estimated arrival time at Hippocrates Medical Center, eighteen minutes," the cab voice said.


*New York City, AD 2061*

Charles, Sierra, and Socrates finished their drinks and declined the barman's offer of another round.

Charles accompanied Socrates to the restroom and gave the philosopher a quick primer on the facilities.

"A fine marble palace!" Socrates cried out happily, from inside a closed stall. "If we had time, I would bathe my tired feet!"

The two rejoined Sierra outside, and all three made their way up the wide staircase to the libraries above. Charles pointed out the Greek holdings to Socrates. "Many of your words are here."

Socrates approached the bookcase. "May I see one?"

Charles looked at Sierra. "I don't suppose another few moments would make a difference," he said in English.

Sierra nodded.

Charles took a book off the shelf. He looked at it, tenderly, as if his very regard might somehow disturb or soil it. He gave it to Socrates.

Sierra and Charles watched, barely breathing.

Socrates opened the book with exceeding care, as if he were un-baiting a trap. . . . He turned the pages slowly. . . . Tears welled in his eyes.

He turned to Sierra and Charles. "The script is different. Very diffi-cult for me to read."

"Oh, I can translate," Charles began, then laughed at himself and the absurdity of translating Greek to Socrates.

"No, I can understand enough," Socrates said. "Men spend their lives reading this? It would take many more lives than one to read all of this." His hands swept around the library.

"Yes," Charles replied.

"A wrong way to spend a life!" Socrates admonished. "You might as well crawl into a grave and make love to the corpse! My words—these words—are no longer alive. They are ghosts, markers, carvings of what I once said. . . . Far better for men to spend their time talking to other men."

"But you have not been alive to talk to," Sierra said gently, "not for nearly twenty-five hundred years. Until now."

"And I will not be, much longer. . . . But there are no doubt others alive, worthy of serious conversation. Surely there are more important words spoken than the words contained in these strange, square scrolls."

"When men throughout the ages speak of important matters," Charles said, almost in a whisper, "they often speak of your words in these books."

"Come, let us proceed to the chairs," Sierra said.


*Athens, AD 2061*

A friendly young doctor in the Hippocrates Medical Center walked down the hall to see Appleton. "Mr. Cibiades will be just fine," she said, in almost perfect English. "The wound is no problem. And with a day or two rest here, the infection will be under control. The bacterium is so classic it's one for the textbooks—but he should be just fine."

"Thank you," Appleton responded.

"You're very welcome. Do you happen to know how he managed to get that wound with that infection? I guess it's not surprising, here in Mother Athens, with all of those ancient monuments. Who knows what spores they have in those cracks, right?"

Appleton nodded. In truth, he had no knowledge of how Alcibiades had received the wound, though the logical suspect was Heron. Appleton did know that he had employed those extra minutes in the restaurant— between the cab's advertised and actual arrival times—to type identities and take photographs on the screen for their identity wafers. His fingers must have slipped between the *Al* and the *cibiades*, making them look like two names.

He retired to the hospital café for a cup of tea, the universal restorative. These jaunts in time did take their toll.

*New York City, AD 2061*

Charles opened the door to the room at the top of the spiral ladder. Three chairs were within.

"These look exactly like the chairs in Athens," Socrates observed. "Could they be?"

"No," Sierra replied. "They look the same because . . . for several hundred years we have had the means of what we call mass production." She said the last two words in English and tried to explain their meaning in Greek. "It is quite easy to build many identical, interchangeable copies of the same item—including chairs."

Socrates smiled mischievously. "And people now, as well."

"Well . . . yes. It is true that before we had duplication of people— cloning—we had duplication of inanimate objects. One follows the other."

Charles was stroking one of the chairs, admiringly.

"Will you be traveling with us?" Socrates inquired.

"I think not," Charles replied. "I would like to. I would want to have the pleasure of your conversation for as long as possible, but . . . I don't want my presence to disrupt part of what I have already seen, in the past. Miss Waters understands."

She nodded.

"And I think I am beginning to understand, too," Socrates said. "We will meet again?"

"I do not know. I only know what has already happened."

"That we can converse with any certainty at all about things that have not yet happened is because of this time travel, is it not?" Socrates asked.

"I believe it is, yes," Charles said.

"But someone must have witnessed events in the future, and come to the past, in order to speak of them in the past," Socrates continued. "So, when you say you only know what already has happened, you mean you only know what you already have seen, whether in the past or the future of the world."

"Yes, that is what I mean." Charles nodded. And tears were in his eyes now. "I should be going. I hope we do meet again. But even if not . . . God bless you! You are right that you cannot be judged by your books. You can be judged by the conversations that they still and will forever inspire!"

Charles left the room and Sierra turned her attention to the chairs. "This one seems capable of being set to arrive at a time of our choosing." She examined a second chair. "This one is the same."

"But is that the way Heron intended it, or our good fortune?" Socrates asked.

"Who knows? I assume if Heron wanted us to go back to 2042, he would have made it impossible for us to go any time else—just as he did with the chairs in Athens. But you are right. There is no calculating what Heron intended."

"Why, again, are we going back to 2042?" Socrates inquired, brows furrowed. "I am not objecting to it. I only want to make sure that you are aware of your reasons."

Sierra looked at the chairs. "Mr. Charles saw us back then. A crazy, circular reason, I know, but also unavoidable, for the same reason. . . . I don't know what would happen if we tried to break the circle."

"Sometimes a circle is the best guide, especially if you want to know yourself."

Sierra smiled. "I also want to go to 2042 because there are people there that I care for."

"An entirely unparadoxical, logical reason."

"It is my time. I have lived my life in it. I have resources and people back then, to draw upon, to help you . . . for whatever time . . . you have left." She thought of Thomas and tried not to think about Max.

"Yes, I think that reasoning is sound, as well. Your time, if it produced you, would be a good time for my remaining days," Socrates said kindly. He walked to one of the chairs she had inspected. "Shall we go?"

"Yes," she said softly. She programmed all the necessary departure codes into the chair. She helped seat Socrates. "We will see each other very soon."

Sierra sat in the other chair she had examined. She looked briefly at the third chair in the room. Who would be traveling in that one? Heron, Mr. Charles, Thomas? Someone she had not yet crossed paths with in this wildcat's cradle?

She poked in her own codes and the programming that would cause both chairs to leave at the same time.

Bubbles ascended . . .

Hearts thumped . . .

Bubbles retracted . . .

Sierra got out of her chair and walked to Socrates.

The room looked exactly the same. She could easily believe they had gone nowhere, had moved not an instant in time.

But then Sierra noticed: four chairs were in the room, not three.

She helped Socrates out of his chair. The philosopher leaned heavily on her arm. The pressure felt more demanding than the last time. It had been a long day. Socrates, though still spry, was after all no youngster. Or maybe his days were getting shorter, more quickly, already.

The trapdoor to the room opened upward from the floor.


*Athens, AD 2061*

Appleton booked a room in a hotel close to the Hippocrates Center. Alcibiades was considerably better the next morning, but the physicians still wanted to "keep him under observation" for a few days. "Nothing to worry about," the young doctor assured Appleton. "Mr. Cibiades has some unusual readings—things we don't usually see in blood pressure, traces of various chemicals in his system, etc. We just want to get all of that into his file, so his regular doctor can add that to his baseline. Actually, Mr. Cibiades is a lot healthier in some ways than most people we see—where did you say he comes from?"

"Greece," Appleton answered carefully. He understood enough to realize that the "unusual readings" likely were the result of Alcibiades' coming from twenty-five hundred years ago.

"Yes. That is what his identity file says." The physician looked at Appleton conspiratorily. "Don't worry. I'm a doctor, not a cop. I checked his DNA on all of the databases. I can see he's done nothing wrong. But I can also see some . . . slight differences with the average Greek. Don't worry. I know how to respect people's privacy. You can tell me if anything more occurs to you."

Appleton spent two days in conversation, much of it cheerful, with Alcibiades. The Greek told the Victorian about life in ancient Athens, what had happened in Phrygia, what had happened in the prison with Socrates. The Victorian told the Greek about his publishing business, the great discoveries and inventions of the nineteenth century, and his house on the Hudson. Appleton found Alcibiades surprisingly easy to talk to and like. He almost felt as if they already had a longstanding bond.

But when he arrived in the hospital the third day—

"I'm sorry, Mr. Appleton," the voice from the screen informed him. "Mr. Cibiades left the Hippocrates Medical Center two hours ago."

"What? Was he taken ill and sent to another facility?"

"No. His tests at seven eighteen A.M. show Mr. Cibiades was in good health. He left of his own volition."

Appleton cursed under his breath.

"Mr. Cibiades left a message for you, Mr. Appleton. Would you like to see it here, or can I route it—"

"Here, please." A light from the screen shone briefly on Appleton's eyes. He knew it was some kind of identity confirmation.

The message appeared on the screen. "Transcription from voice," the screen spoke. The message was written in classic Greek, with accompanying English translation:

"I have decided to go back to the time of Theon in Alexandria and seek the cure for Socrates that Heron spoke of to Antisthenes. As you know, I have little regard for Heron's truthfulness. But I cannot risk disregarding his words. I am relying on you not to tell Ampharete, and not to let her follow me. I am relying on you to protect her until I finish my work in Alexandria and return. Please keep her with you. That is the way I will find her."

Appleton shook his head and cursed again. Alcibiades had told him what Heron had told Antisthenes in the prison of Socrates. Socrates had a deadly illness of the brain. But there was perhaps a cure. Theon, the last great librarian of Alexandria, had written of it. A cure lost to subsequent history. Appleton clenched his fist in white anger. . . . Theon was Hypatia's father. Was this but another trick of Heron's?

"Would you like a paper copy?" the voice on the screen inquired.

"Yes, please."

Appleton took the paper, walked out into the street, and mulled over his choices. He took his little telephone device from his pocket. It was inexpensive and he had learned how to use it. He could summon the authorities and ask them to look for Alcibiades, just in case he hadn't proceeded directly to the restaurant with the chairs. . . . No, bringing the authorities into this might well make things worse. He had gone to lengths to avoid this in the hospital.

Appleton sighed. His only sensible course of action was to wait here, near the Hippocrates Medical Center, until Sierra Waters returned by air, ship, or chair. His home on the Hudson would have to wait a bit longer.

*New York City, AD 2042*

"Thomas!" Sierra cried out, delighted. She had placed herself between the door and Socrates. Now she sagged with relief and smiled at Mr. Charles, who had also climbed into the room.

She went to Thomas, but his eyes were fixed on Socrates. "The clothes should make him less conspicuous here," Sierra said awkwardly, in English.

"Who is this man?" Socrates asked her, in Greek.

"My God!" Charles exclaimed, in English. "Is this Alcibiades? I thought he was younger."

"He was, he was," Thomas replied.

"Well, then, who—"

"Socrates," Thomas said. "This is Socrates." Thomas turned to Sierra. She flung her arms around him. He stroked her hair. "I am sorry for my part in this," he said softly. "It will be okay."


The four went downstairs to the Millennium Club's dining area. It was empty.

"We ordinarily don't serve breakfast in the Club," Charles advised, "but I'll see what I can get for you."

"He is very hungry," Sierra said, in Greek, and gestured to Socrates.

"I am very hungry," Socrates confirmed.

Charles thought for a moment. "I think I have food that you would enjoy this time of day," he said, in carefully rendered Greek. "Bread and fruit."

"Yes! Thank you!"

Charles went off to the kitchen.

"I was afraid you were Heron or his men," Sierra said to Thomas, still in Greek.

"A reasonable fear," Thomas replied in the same language. "Good for us that I was not."

"Is he still a threat?" Sierra asked, switching to English.

Thomas nodded. "Probably. He certainly has been, at some points in his life. I had a very unpleasant time with him before I returned to New York. I have no knowledge of what happened to him after you rescued Socrates, but have no reason to think he didn't live at least another few decades or more."

"What can we do to protect ourselves?"

"I doubt if Heron will come to New York City by any future means of transportation," Thomas replied. "Even if he could somehow smuggle something back to this world, in a bigger chair, or construct something from parts, it would make too much of a stir. He would likely come here by air, and there is not much we can do about that. But there is something we can do if he comes here by chair, at least in this Club."

"Oh?" Sierra asked.

"We can lock the room upstairs from the outside, so it cannot be opened from the inside."

"But Heron's an expert with this equipment. Wouldn't he—"

"With the chairs, he's an expert, of course," Thomas said. "But he has no control over the physical premises of the Club, including what we do to the outside of that room."

"How did he get his chairs into the Club, to begin with?" Sierra asked.

Socrates, who had been examining the utensils on the table, looked at her. Sierra repeated the question, in Greek.

"I do not know," Thomas replied in the same language. "He arranged it sometime in his future."

Sierra absorbed that and shook her head. "But that means—"

"Yes." Thomas caught where she was going. "Heron may well have associates in the Club—there are no guarantees about anyone."

"Who would be prevented from coming here, if the room was locked?" Socrates asked. "Who other than Heron might be locked into that room?"

"Anyone who has access to the chairs in this Club, up and down the years, future and past," Thomas replied.

"Alcibiades?" Socrates asked.

"Yes," Thomas replied.

Sierra realized that Thomas looked a little older, or younger, but different in some way from the last time she had seen him. Couldn't be younger—the Thomas across the table knew too much. "Alcibiades would have had a hard time getting across the Atlantic in Socrates' era," Sierra pointed out, "unless he was able to find a Phoenician."

"They are talented sailors," Socrates agreed. "But you do not see many Phoenicians in Athens."

Sierra nodded. "I would say Alcibiades arriving in New York directly from the ancient past is unlikely." She heard her voice quaver with emotion. "I made that voyage once, but—"

"As did Heron's student Jonah," Thomas interrupted. "But—ah, here is our traveler from the nineteenth century—Mr. Charles." Charles, back from the kitchen with a loaf of bread in one hand, a basket of fruit and cheese in the other, smiled and sat down at the table. Thomas concluded, "The Club did not exist before the nineteenth century. The chairs must have been difficult to locate before then."

Charles sliced a piece of bread for Socrates and gave him the basket of fruit and cheese. "Donovan's on duty in the kitchen, already. He'll be out soon with coffee and tea. . . . But, you know, the chairs travel back to Roman times in England. You used them, didn't you?" he asked Sierra.

"Yes," Sierra replied.

"And from what I heard, the chairs fit in pretty well back then, without a proper club," Charles observed.

Sierra turned to Socrates. "Rome was a mighty empire, after the empire of Alexander. Heron seems to recruit his soldiers from that time."

Socrates nodded with a mouthful of bread.

Thomas looked at Charles. "You are correct, of course. Still, as Sierra said, the Atlantic was not easy to navigate in those times, far more difficult than the Mediterranean or the coast of Europe. I doubt we will be seeing Alcibiades walk down the stairs anytime soon from that hatch, wide-open or bolted."

"You're thinking of bolting the door from the outside, then?" Charles asked.

"Yes—"

"Look," Sierra said more loudly than she had intended, in English. "I admit to being more concerned than the two of you about Alcibiades. Let's say he wants to come here?"

"You're worried he'll be trapped inside the room?" Thomas asked. "It won't happen. We have cameras and microphones up there—that's how we knew the two of you had arrived." He looked at Socrates, who was discovering the joys of an Anjou pear and seemed not to mind or even notice that the conversation had shifted back to English.

"And what happens if you're out of town—or out of time—or both?" Sierra demanded.

Thomas exhaled slowly and shook his head.

"You don't know anything—you can't know anything—when it comes to this," Sierra continued. "Not with any certainty. That's not possible in this world that you—Heron—whoever—created. Nothing is certain where time travel is concerned."

Thomas said nothing.

Socrates looked up. It was impossible not to feel the heat of the discussion.

Sierra was clutching the edge of the table. Her knuckles were pale. She spoke Greek. "Why did you get me involved in this, in the first place?" she asked Thomas. "Did you know Max would be killed?"

"I . . . I didn't mean for that to happen. . . . I—"

Sierra started to say something, even more angrily—

Socrates partially stood, leaned across the small table, and touched Sierra's arm. He spoke clearly, calmly. "I think you should go and look for Alcibiades. It is not too late. It is never too late. We have all proven that." He looked at Thomas.

Sierra began, "But you—"

"I will be safe here. I like this place very much. The bread and fruit are delicious. Far better than the bitter hemlock—I thank you all for that—even if I do not live much longer."

Sierra looked at Socrates.

"Go," Socrates said again. "It is not too late. Anything in the future is possible, nothing is yet written that cannot be unwritten, and, if I understand this time travel correctly, all of time is your future, the past as well as the present. Would you agree?"

"Yes, I most certainly would," Charles spoke up.

Sierra got to her feet.

"You will take one of those raindrops again across the big sea?" Socrates asked her.

Thomas looked at him, thoughtfully.

Socrates shook his head. "What did I just say? I am sorry. . . . I meant to say *airships,* airships."

Sierra winced. "Yes," she said, and walked over to Socrates. He stood as well. She hugged him, kissed him on his forehead. "Is this what they do in your Athens?"

"Anything you do is the right thing to do, because you are the one doing it. The age of the world does not matter," Socrates replied.

"I wish we had more time to talk. There is so much—"

"I know," Socrates said. "But you will find others to talk to."

She hugged Socrates again, smiled at Charles, and turned to Thomas. "I know you had no real choice. It seems none of us do. We just do the best we can."

"Your best chance of finding Alcibiades is in the Hippocrates Medical Center, Athens, June third to fifth, 2061," Thomas replied.

She started to question him, but his voice had the quiet, unimpeachable authority it had always had for her. She wheeled around and headed for the room upstairs.

No one said a word.

Charles finally spoke. "You know Alcibiades is no longer in the Golden Age?"

Thomas nodded.

"Well, then, let me at least see about that coffee and tea." Charles stood and walked off to the kitchen.

Thomas turned to Socrates, took his hand. "It has been a long time. . . ."

CHAPTER 11

*New York City, AD 2042*

Thomas O'Leary returned from the grave of Socrates. He had just been buried, in a small, private ceremony, in Woodlawn Cemetery in the Bronx. No one knew the deceased was Socrates except the mourners, who consisted of just Thomas and Mr. Charles. The tombstone said Socrates, but there were others with that name in this age. No one else would know who was really buried here, though some might pause at the inscription, which was dead-on: "He preferred speaking to writing, but the impact of his written words is immeasurable."

Charles pleaded a tiring day and went home early. Thomas went to the Club, to nurse a drink and his thoughts.

There was no way they could have saved Socrates, certainly not in the middle of the twenty-first century. The part of his brain that gave rise to his genius also gave rise to massive, inoperable tumors that riddled every part of his brain. As simply excruciating as that. You could not have one without the other. Any splice to diminish the second would inevitably have the same effect on the first. . . . Clones would be subject to the same fate. Perhaps this would be changed in some future time, but Heron had sworn it could not even in his.

And what had Heron truly wanted in all of this? Thomas had seen no sign of the inventor or his mercenaries in the months Thomas had enjoyed with Socrates. What this meant about Heron's schemes, Thomas did not know. Perhaps Heron had bowed out or died or turned his attention to something else, but Thomas doubted that. Thomas did know that access to any time in the past earlier than nine days after Socrates' last evening in the prison in Athens was now blocked, at least via the chairs in the Millennium Club. Thomas had sat in those chairs, tested the controls, discovered the limitation of access. Were the chairs in London and Athens subject to the same restriction? Thomas assumed so. He intended to go to both places and see, now that his reason for staying in New York was gone. Heron was responsible— satisfied about what had happened in the prison of Socrates, at least enough to not want anyone else from the future mucking around in that.

Thomas grieved about Sierra . . . for bringing her into this in the first place, for leading her back there. But he knew she would survive. Appleton had seen this, and Thomas could not think of a more trustworthy witness to history.

Thomas had had no choice regarding Sierra. He had needed her to lure Heron into this. To turn him from a talented inventor who had traveled back to Alexandria into maybe a madman who sought to revise more of time than just the final night of Socrates . . . But that had been necessary, too.

Thomas loved Sierra, the woman of three different names. He had been tempted to go back to Alexandria and speak to her. But he did not want to complicate her life and the world any further.

Would anyone have recognized him? Probably not. Maybe a little, unconsciously. Hard to say . . . He had taken a random assortment of distinguished genes and fashioned a new face, new eyes, new voice, and a somewhat new body. . . . And he had grown old in it . . . a real shame, in a way. He was arrogant enough to miss his original.

He pulled a piece of paper out of his pocket.

SOCRATES: What time is it?

VISITOR: The dawn broke a little while ago.

SOCRATES: I must have been sleeping. I did not see you enter—

Yes, Socrates had written that. Others had changed it over the years, either deliberately or not. Such was the way of translation and cultural inheritance. Words on the page mutated, like genes in the flesh.

Thomas wondered if maybe he should make a few additional changes. He was obliged to make one, to keep history consistent. He crossed out *Visitor*. He replaced it with *Andros*—the island in the Aegean that had saved his life.

He was tempted to make other changes. He would return to Athens someday, well after the presumed death of Socrates, and make copies of this manuscript on suitable scrolls. One of them, or a faithful copy of it, would find its way into the Millennium's library, in the 2020s. . . . He was sure of this. After all, had not the past year of his life so vividly confirmed this? Had not almost the last half of his life confirmed it even more?

He wondered if he should try revisions of other Socratic and Platonic dialogs. He could salt the past with better truths.

No. He could not think about that now. . . . He carefully folded the paper and put it back in his pocket. He had done enough today. His head was still swirling in the rapids of emotion.

Let this day be just for Socrates. He had just buried his mentor, here in an age in which neither had been born. If only they could have had more time, but he would forever be grateful for the time they had stolen. It had made everything worth it. He thought Socrates had cherished it, too. Homemade melting ice cream, the Palisades shining on a bright day, the sight of women who made your heart race . . . His vocabulary had become more jumbled, but they had hardly noticed it. The two ancient companions had even managed a little drive through the countryside, in an open convertible, from Ithaca to Syracuse. . . .

Socrates, of course, had known who he was, had recognized him, despite his new face. Socrates had smiled at him, in that way of his, the minute he had sat across the table, just a few months ago. Socrates alone had grasped the truth. It felt strange, indeed, to talk to him in that old Greek of theirs, after he had spent so much time as a nineteenth- and twenty-first-century New Yorker. That little English dictionary that Sierra had given him long ago had done its job.

Alcibiades stood, sighed, waved good-bye to the bartender, and walked slowly down the stairs. Yes, he grieved deeply about her and always would. After leaving the Hippocrates Medical Center in 2061 Athens, he had traveled back to Alexandria in Theon's time, with every intention of returning to her. He had sought out Theon. He had questioned him about a cure for what would kill Socrates, rob him of his escape from death by hemlock, but Theon knew nothing of any cure. Another trick of Heron's, is what Alcibiades thought then.

He had returned to 2061 Athens in search of Ampharete. She was gone, and the chairs were not precise enough for him to arrive on any of the specific days for which he knew her whereabouts.

So he went back to 2042 Athens and searched for her there—and he fell very ill. He nearly died.

He was sick for months, in and out of what they called hospitals. At some point, he realized that his conversation with Theon might well have been the source of Heron's information about an ancient cure for Socrates. He was furious at himself, at the whole prospect of time travel, when he realized that. But the problem was not Heron's deceit. Not that time. It rather was the inherent trickery, of heads chasing tails, of all time travel.

He learned about e-mail and left word in public places for Ampharete. Appleton, who also had mastered this writing with digital wings, eventually spotted the messages. Appleton found him and brought him back to 1890s New York. That was when Appleton told him about Sierra's rescue from Alexandria in AD 410. Jonah had helped with that, too. She had gone back to Alexandria in the time of Hypatia, after all, in search of Alcibiades.

Alcibiades' bouts with illness lasted for years. He was unable to travel. Appleton told him why. People born in the past who travel to the future acquire immunity to its diseases the hard way—by living through them, if they didn't die.

Appleton died at eighty-five years of age in 1899. If his time on the roads of the past and future was counted, he was at least a year or more older. The noblest soul in this whole enterprise. He had died content, knowing he had served as Sierra's guardian angel.

Alcibiades never stopped yearning to find her. But he knew she would be happier without him—without him as Alcibiades, her lover.

He had traveled instead to the future and acquired his new face and voice. Alcibiades became Thomas O'Leary. He was not as noble as

Appleton. Thomas set in motion his part of the events that would bring Sierra into this. What else could he do? Any other course of action would have unraveled not only his own but Sierra's life, even the last ten years of Appleton's. Thomas as Alcibiades would have been dead at forty-five in Phrygia. He might even have chosen in 2042 to take that path again, to suffer his original fate. But would Sierra have really been happier, more fulfilled, if Thomas had never approached her with the dialog? She was destined to do great things with the life he had helped make for her.

The front door of the Millennium Club opened, just as Thomas reached it.

"Mr. Charles? Did you forget something?"

"Oh, no, Thomas. I just felt lonely at home . . . on such a day. I was hoping you might still be here. Care to join me for a drink?"

Alcibiades, known to Mr. Charles as Thomas O'Leary, clapped his friend on the back. "Of course."

And the two headed back upstairs.

The following historical people appear in *The Plot to Save Socrates* (along with characters for whom there is no historical record). The details provided below are what we know of them, as of the time of this writing (January 2005).

*Alcibiades, 450–404 BC.* Reputed to be handsome, amorous, wealthy, brilliant, brave, unpredictable, egotistical, and Socrates' favorite student. The two saved each other's lives as soldiers near the beginning of the Second Peloponnesian War between Athens and Sparta. Alcibiades later became an Athenian general, with mixed results. He fell in and out of favor with various oligarchic and democratic governments in Athens. While taking temporary refuge in Phrygia, on the east side of the Aegean, he was murdered by a band of Spartans (either loyal to Sparta or hired by Alcibiades' political opponents in Athens). According to I. F. Stone and his sources (see below), Alcibiades was surprised while in bed with a woman and fought "naked, outnumbered, but brave with sword in hand" till the end.

*Antisthenes, 444?–365 BC.* Oldest disciple of Socrates, said to have walked daily from Piraeus to Athens to hear him speak. Identified in Plato's *Phaedo* as being present on the last day of Socrates' life (Plato's absence is noted). Later founded the Cynic school of philosophy and (in the words of I. F. Stone, see below) "was especially cynical about democracy." According to Diogenes Laertius, Antisthenes wondered why Athenians did not vote that "asses were horses," since they elected people as generals who had as much in common with military leaders as asses did to horses. Also according to Diogenes, Antisthenes drove Anytus from Athens in retribution for the death of Socrates, but this is historically unsupported (see Anytus, below). Antisthenes wrote a dialog about Alcibiades; just a few fragments survive.

*Anytus, dates of birth and death apparently unknown.* Smith's 1849 *Dictionary of Greek and Roman Biography and Mythology* says Anytus was Socrates' "most influential and formidable accuser" (there were two others) before and during the trial; recent sources, including Stone (see below) agree. Anytus was a wealthy middle-class merchant of hides (a tanner). Appointed an Athenian general in 409 BC, he failed to prevent the loss of Pylos (the modern Navarino); he was later brought up on charges, acquitted, but was said to have bribed the jury (in what is reputed to be the first recorded case of jury bribery). He was back in favor by 403 and moved against Socrates three years later. Most sources agree that his animus was personal as well as political: Anytus' son was attracted to Socrates' teachings, which held that philosophy was a nobler pursuit than tanning. Nothing is known of Anytus after 386 BC. Most sources agree that reports of Diogenes Laertius (third century AD) and others that Anytus was later repudiated, exiled, and even stoned are fables born of the desire to see Socrates' prosecutors punished.

*Appleton, William Henry, 1814–1899.* Became head of the publishing company D. Appleton & Co. when his father, Daniel, retired in 1844. Published Lewis Carroll, Charles Darwin, Thomas Huxley, John Stuart Mill, Herbert Spencer, and leading nineteenth-century scientists and philosophers in America. Offices in Manhattan. Owned the Wave Hill house in Riverdale, overlooking the Hudson River and the Palisades, 1866–1899. Huxley was among his guests at the house. Theodore Roosevelt's family rented Wave Hill (when he was a boy in the summers of 1870 and 1871), as did Mark Twain (1901–1903).

*Heron (or Hero) of Alexandria, 150 BC?–AD 250?* The years of his birth and death are debatable—Heron pops up throughout a four-hundred-year span of ancient history. He was a prolific inventor of devices that embodied principles and techniques that were two thousand years ahead of their mass application in the industrial age. These included a toy that ran on steam power (the aeolipile) and an automated theater that utilized "phantom mirror" and persistence-of-vision effects that are the basis of our motion pictures. Many of his treatises on other inventions, and mathematics, exist just in fragments or are known only via reference to them by later Greek, Roman, and Arabic writers. His *Metrica,* considered his most important mathematic work, was discovered in Istanbul in 1896.

*Hypatia, AD 355/370?–415.* Daughter of Theon, who was an astronomer, mathematician, and one of the last members of the museum in Alexandria. Hypatia likely assisted her father in his new edition of Euclid's *Elements* and his commentaries on Ptolemy's *Almagest,* but she was considered a brilliant philosopher and mathematician in her own right and led the Neoplatonic school in Alexandria. Renowned not only for her intellect, but her beauty and eloquence, Hypatia attracted many students and admirers. Hypatia was pagan, however, and her charm and accomplishments infuriated certain Christian fanatics, who brutally murdered and mutilated her. The death is thought to mark the end of Alexandria as an intellectual center of the ancient world; it was followed by an exodus of scholars. Charles Kingsley's 1853 novel *Hypatia* made her a heroine of the Victorian era, and she is today regarded as the first woman to have made a significant contribution in mathematics. (Kingsley is today better known for his 1863 urban fantasy, *The Water-Babies.*)

*Jowett, Benjamin, 1817–1893.* Translator of *The Dialogues of Plato,* in four volumes, with extensive analyses and introductions, first edition, 1871—still the standard English translation—as well as translations of Thucydides, and Aristotle's *Politics.* Declining health prevented him from completing a series of essays about the *Politics.* He was for twenty-eight years a tutor, and then for twenty-three years master, at Balliol College, Oxford.

*Plato, 427?–347 BC.* Socrates' student, considered by many to be the greatest philosopher in history, the father of philosophy, etc. Among his most influential ideas is that truth exists in some ideal realm, separate from humanity, and which humans can only imperfectly understand (theory of forms); and the best kind of government is an absolute dictatorship of the wisest (philosopher king). Our entire knowledge of Socrates is based on what he says in Plato's dialogs, along with lesser works by Xenophon (also Socrates' student), and his appearance as a character in contemporary plays, such as Aristophanes' *The Clouds.* Debates continue as to what parts of what Socrates says in Plato's dialogs are expressions of Socrates' original ideas and words or Plato's, whether Plato or Xenophon provides a more reliable account of the trial (they agree on the important details), etc. Most accounts agree that Plato, twenty-eight years old at the time of the trial (399 BC), left Athens before Socrates took the hemlock, traveled widely and as far away as Egypt and Sicily, and returned to Athens permanently in 387 BC. The academy that he founded in Athens continued until closed by Justinian in AD 529.

*Socrates, 470?–399 BC.* No texts written by Socrates have survived or are alluded to by ancient authors; all that we know of him is from the writings of his students, mainly Plato (see above), and a few contemporaries. Socrates taught that the pursuit of knowledge was the highest virtue, and knowledge was best obtained through continuing questioning and dialog. He was no fan of democracy—in the *Phaedrus* (where Socrates also condemns the written word as conveying only the "pretense of wisdom"), Socrates asks why, if we would not trust a man ignorant of horses to give us advice about horses, should we have confidence in a government composed of everyday people with no philosophic training in understanding good and evil—yet Socrates, condemned by the Athenian democracy on charges of corrupting the youth of the city with his ideas, accepted its death sentence. Indeed, waiting in prison for thirty days for the return of the priest of Apollo from Delos (no death sentences could be carried out in his absence), Socrates refused an offer of escape and refuge made by his old friend Crito. Socrates explains in the Platonic dialog of that name that to evade the death sentence would be to put himself above the state, which as a critic of the state he had no desire to do. I. F. Stone (see below) argues that Socrates may also have wanted his death penalty carried out as a way of permanently shaming the democracy he hated. In any case, that was certainly the result: the death of Socrates by prescribed hemlock in 399 BC redounds as one of the worst cases in history of a dissident destroyed by government, all the worse because that government was the world's first known democracy.

*Stone, I. F., 1907–1989.* American gadfly journalist, and publisher of *I. F. Stone's Weekly,* 1953–1971. In semiretirement, he taught himself to read ancient Greek, claimed that many extant translations of classical works were slightly off, and in 1988 published *The Trial of Socrates.*

# 10 QUESTIONS ARISING FROM

# The Plot to Save Socrates

## BY PAUL LEVINSON

1.  Was Socrates right to let the world think he let himself die for moral reasons, when in fact the reasons were political and personal?

2.  Wasn't there some arrogance entailed in Socrates' decision to let himself die to influence posterity? Such a decision assumes that Socrates would be important enough to be cared about by posterity.

3.  Do you believe that a man with Socrates' intelligence was critical, even disdaining, of literacy? Or was this just Plato's game?

4.  Was Heron right to want to perfect the world and human civilization through manipulation of history? Or is that too dangerous?

5.  Is it right to take an innocent life on behalf of some presumably greater good, like saving Socrates, killing Hitler as a child, or otherwise improving history?

6. Is it possible that great, pathbreaking inventors in our history—Heron, Leonardo da Vinci, Thomas Edison—are really time travelers? They all seemed to have insight into technology that went well beyond their time.

7. Was Alcibiades right to choose friendship with Socrates over love with Sierra? Do you believe he really loved Sierra?

8. Should Sierra have figured out a way to go back and rescue Max, or was that too dangerous to the rivers of time?

9. If you were Sierra, and you knew at the beginning of the novel what you learned in the end, would you have gone looking for Thomas in the first place or finished your doctoral dissertation?

10. If you were given a free membership to the Millennium Club, would you take it?